WAITING TO CRY

Travails of a Long Journey

WHIP RAWLINGS

WAITING TO CRY: TRAVAILS OF A LONG JOURNEY

This book is written to provide information and motivation to readers. Its purpose is not to render any type of psychological, legal, or professional advice of any kind. The content is the sole opinion and expression of the author, and not necessarily that of the publisher.

Printed in the United States of America.

ISBN   978-1-64552-019-1   (Paperback)
ISBN   978-1-64552-020-7   (Digital)

Lettra Press books may be ordered through booksellers or by contacting:

Lettra Press LLC
18229 E 52nd Ave.
Denver City, CO 80249
1 303 586 1431 | info@lettrapress.com
www.lettrapress.com

I t was March 1977, and the harsh winter began to give way to
forty-degree weather. We have survived another harsh winter a
winter in most eyes that was unforgiving. Most cars lay buried
deep beneath the snow, not a single indentation of a car's roof but level
ground as far as the eye could see. The snow must've been at least ten
feet deep if it wasn't foot. January's harsh weather was far from being
over; ice lined the edges of the sidewalks, turning into slush, and slid
down the sewers, cleansing the streets as its final winter act. I must
say,If I said I didn't mine the snow I would be lying are being paid to
make such a ridiculous statement. I hated going to school in the early
mornings during the winter months. I also hated going to school in
the early mornings in the spring and fall months. I guess you can say
I didn't enjoy the educational process.

I rolled over and hit the alarm clock as often as I could, giving
myself fifteen more minutes of sleep before knocking it off the table.
I didn't have time for a big breakfast, a bowl of cornflakes and maybe
a banana if I was fortunate. There were eight kids in the house, and if
you didn't hide a banana or was the first one up in the morning, dressed
and ready to go, you didn't get a banana. Most of the time, I just went
to school without breakfast but made up for it later on at lunch break,
with two pork fritter sandwiches and french fries, and I washed it all
down with a tall Pepsi. Walking to school in the wintertime wasn't so
egregious if I had someone to walk with especially a young girl, and if
it was the right girl, she could mentally distract me from ice crushing
beneath my feet and the stinging pain in my ears.

Finding someone attractive enough to distract me while I walked
through snow was a hard combination to find because the street
was only two blocks long, giving us the appearance of being a small
enclave. Most of the young girls walked in confraternity, leaving just
young boys to themselves, to disport themselves with snowball battles
all the way to the school front door. I was beginning to outgrow such
juvenile behavior; this was my last year of school, and I was scared
to death at the possibility of not graduating. I was three credits short
of graduating before I was allowed to walk with my class. Somehow

I didn't take it very seriously and continued to cut class at least two days a week. I tried desperately to escape the harsh winter by spending some scrupulous amounts of time seeking female companionship with young girls who lived walking distance from the school.

Walking to school was like working a part-time job trudging through the snow and ice and arriving at school as wet as the troops landing on the beaches of Normandy. It wasn't a total lost cause. My close friend that lived next door was often overly indulged by his auntie and grandmother. He often had more money and newer clothes than the rest of us, so for them to requisition him a car wasn't overly surprising. However, it was surprising he didn't earn it through merit, not for any special achievement or special occasion. She just gave it to him. I would've liked to have gotten a ride to school, but he was growing up; and like the rest of us, he discovered a new social interest in different parts of the city. All the young men in the neighborhood were growing in different directions. I spent most of my time at Riverside Park in the boxing gym, some of the time boxing and the other percentage of the time chasing young girls around the park. My two childhood friends joined the Army National Guard together; and the other young men were on their way to prison, or because of their refusal to change their lifestyle, they found death at an early age. Every month I moved closer to graduation, I grew increasingly scared and uncertain about the next coming year. I often awakened early in the morning with my senses disturbed by my future life plans. *Where are we going to go? What was I going to do? Will I be successful?* The sun hadn't even risen as I stood in the window at four in the morning, gazing at the Fantasy Hotel two blocks away. I often wondered where the people came from and where they were going. I was fascinated with the ideal of travel and wanted to experience it for myself. I no longer wanted to live vicariously through other people's lives. I wanted to taste the wines of other countries, feel the breeze of the ocean on my face, and live among the common people. Before I knew it, the sun was peeking above the hotel, telling me it's time to go to school.

I love the early mornings; 4:00 a.m. was my favorite time of the day, staring out the window before taking the plunge onto the icy, slush-covered streets. Somehow it made it easier for me to accept the fact that it was my choice in the next seven months whether I stayed in a snow-impact city or relocate to the places I discovered in a *Right On* magazine.

I abhorred the snow. It invaded every unoccupied space imaginable: sidewalks, trees, rooftops, and windowsills. Snow even crept its way into my Chuck Taylor tennis shoes. Having soaking-wet socks made the journey to school more treacherous—three times as miserable than it already was. I detested having wet feet. Through my whole day off, I couldn't focus on what the teacher was saying, and I definitely couldn't focus on the young girls who so desperately deserved my attention. Every morning I put an extra pair of socks in my pocket just in case to snow didn't feel merciful the day. Once I got to school, I took my socks and shoes off, wrung the water out of my socks in the bathroom, and placed them under the radiator in the classroom. I wasn't surprised that I wasn't the only person with this ritual. The locker room was jam packed with young men trying desperately to dry their feet before making it to class.

The unfortunate of the unfortunate students had it worse than I; they didn't have the finances to acquire a winter coat or have money to purchase lunch. They were just sitting and watching everyone eat while pretending to do homework. One student, a girl I recognized from the ROTC program, waited for another student to leave the lunch table. She finagled the unfinished plate of food in front of her by placing her book in front of the plate, pulling the plate toward her as though the plate was there the entire time all. I felt sorry for her because the plate was eaten down to scraps. There wasn't enough food left on to feed a small mouse, certainly not a full-grown starving female. I didn't want to embarrass her, so I ordered large french fries, then cruised over to her, and introduced myself as one of the ROTC commanders. I sat for a couple of minutes, nibbling on my fries, striking up idle conversation. Three fries into the conversation, I said, "I have to go.

You can have the rest of the fries if you want them." I made my way to the cafeteria door, stopping in the hallway and peeking back through the window. I watched her dip dill french fries and ketchup, vigorously devouring the french fries two at a time. It made me feel good to know that I can help another person without any reciprocity or quid pro quo.

It's a sad commentary but high school was my only social function outside of going to work, communicating with customers and brain-dead coworkers. Shortridge High School provided the social outlet I needed. It helped me escape my routine and boring day-to-day life. It wasn't enough that I led a boring life, to add insult to injury, I worked part-time as a dishwasher and busboy, making a minimum wage of $2.32 an hour. I couldn't afford rubber booties to protect my shoes from the snow or money to buy the other things I desperately needed such as prophylactics and breath mints.

Being poor wasn't a big deal to me because everyone in my neighborhood suffered the same fate as I; some families had a little more money than others, but it wasn't enough to escape the hood. The vicissitude of fortune was common throughout the neighborhood. Although some kids at my school had more materialistic possessions than others, it was obvious by the shoes and clothes they wore their parents overly indulged them; seemingly they were always in fashion and in touch with the times. It was a year of maxi coats, platform shoes, granny dresses, bell bottoms, and hot pants.

Those fortunate kids appeared comely as they strutted to school dressed from head to toe in their new attire. The stench of new blue jeans and patent leather shoes was overwhelming. I'm sure their parents weren't rewarding them for good grades because most of their grades were as bad or worse than mine. I wasn't so fortunate to have parents that would spend endless amounts of money on my wardrobe. I worked like a dog for every stitch of clothes I wore, not having time to study or complete any homework I was often bemused once class started. It didn't take long before teachers challenged me day in and day out about my homework and why they weren't completed. Next came the request to stay after school to complete assignments. I wasn't a dumb kid. I lacked structure, I was functionally illiterate, and I just needed a mentor to help me tap into the potential that lay tucked away deep in my untapped subconscious and awake the sleeping genius the lay within; but I had no such person living in my neighborhood, only would-be gangsters and fake NBA prospects.

In 1968 I lived within a small sector of the city, moving between Delaware Street, Park Avenue, and our final destination Twenty-Ninth and Talbott Street in 1970. The first school I went to was School 38 Audubon, the same school the notorious gangster John Dillinger attended years before. I spent the fourth grade at school 76 on Thirtieth and college, and by the fifth grade, I moved to Twenty-Ninth and Talbott where I attended school 60. I was in the fifth grade and would discover my first girlfriend, Cheryl. She was a bully. I just didn't know it yet. Out of the clear blue sky, she walked into my life unannounced. Cheryl and her girlfriends forced us into a relationship, shoveling us together in the hallway, trying to provide themselves with a form of entertainment by making us kiss. I was so goofy and inexperienced I accidentally ended up hitting her in the mouth with my forehead. As part of our relationship, she made me walk her home from school every day, which was five blocks out of my way in the other direction, taking me at least a half mile farther away for my home. Her brother resembled a threatening presence; he would kill anybody he saw with his little sister. She wanted to keep walking closer and closer to the house. I wanted to stop five blocks away to ensure that I wouldn't get pummeled into the ground. So I stopped two blocks before we reached her house then kissed her on the cheek good-bye. The relationship was a total disaster and ended within two weeks. She called me on the phone one night and said, "Whip, you're through booking." I didn't know what in the world she was talking about, so I said, "Huh?" She said, "You're through booking." She totally misused the street slang known as BEV (black English vernacular). The term *you're through booking* means *I'm going to beat you up*. She thought it meant *I want to break up with you*. She should have used the term *you're fired,* which means *I'm breaking up with you,* and there would have been less confusion. I didn't know what I was doing anyway. I never had a girlfriend before, and if it was going to continue to be this awkward, I didn't want to have another one.

Just as I was getting used to not having a girl in my life, she came back three weeks late, wanting to rekindle our relationship. She made me work too hard in our last relationship, and I was reluctant to give her another chance. I wasn't ready to kiss girls. It was more than I was willing to bargained for; besides, I was still playing with hot wheel cars and riding bicycles. I was barely the age of Peter Pan, and surely, I wasn't ready to grow up. My brother and cousin stood close by, listening to every word. They even egged her on until she relented to have sex with me. My brother offered to park his car in a secluded place down the alley so we could have our privacy, but I wasn't ready for sex just yet. I was only twelve years old, still playing with Hot Wheels and Johnny Lightning cars; so I got on my bike and rode off, leaving her standing in the front yard. I rode up Pennsylvania Street toward school 60 and sat on the steps of the flag pole for a moment of peace.

I didn't know it at the time the short walk up Pennsylvania would be my destiny for the next ten years. I would spend ten years of my young life walking back and forth between three different schools. Mapleton Fall Creek and school 60 were on the same block. Shortridge High school was across the street on Thirty-Fourth and Pennsylvania Street. I hated our school system. I felt closed in, seeing the same faces year after year. I wanted exposure to different cultural groups and different ways of thinking. I was a maverick. I wanted to live my young life outside of the neighborhood I grew up in. I wanted to explore other cultures and experience how they live. Most people wanted to avoid being bused to another school, but I'd prayed for and relished the day to come.

I wasn't like my siblings who were content with being idle and staying in one place, going through the same routine day after day. That seemed to me insipid. I had a fire burning in me that I couldn't extinguish, and I was bored out of my mind. Our community was very close-knit. Anyone living within a five-mile radius in any direction was mandated to attend the three schools and suffer the same mundane faith as I. Some children found refuge when their families moved to bourgeois sections of Indianapolis, providing them with educational advantage and a different economical prospective.

Just being around affluent people allowed them to increase their knowledge through osmosis, by seeing what was possible and the opportunity for a real chance to go to college rather than being stuck around a bunch of people that had no idea they could ever afford or qualify to attend college. I scarcely recall having conversations about college or the possibility of going to college in school or at home; it was a conversation that just didn't happen. Sometimes my mother would talk about signing me up for trade school, but somehow I wasn't feeling it. I did not adhere to anyone's opinion about my life beyond high school. I wasn't willing to be subjugated by anyone's plan for my future other than my own.

I could understand my mother's reasoning. She spent two years at a junior college in a nursing program and received an associate degree and did quite well for herself, raising eight children along and never having to worry about any of her kids going to jail. I believe I wasn't the only one of her children that noticed the difference her education made in our lives, but I was the only one to follow her example and change the hand I was dealt in life. We went from eating air sandwiches to eating a full three-course meal on a regular basis. No one noticed change in our diet except me,. My other siblings were too busy hanging out with their friends; my oldest brother was too busy chasing women and working at Saul Subway, making corned beef sandwiches, and having visions of grandeur anytime a woman looked in his direction for more than three seconds.

My rumination after going to bed was a great contributor to my fantasizing about living in California. I spent a fair amount of my time looking through *Right On* magazines, daydreaming about the day I'd move to sunny Los Angeles, California. I envisioned myself sitting under palm trees and hanging out with the Jackson Five. (Little did I know it would be faith come calling several years later.)

I wanted to travel to faraway lands, the places I read about in *National Geographic* magazines. I no longer wanted to be a myopic-minded individual; I wanted to expand my horizons. I detested walking to school day after day, year after year, knee deep in snow. Although Shortridge High School was only four short blocks from my home, snow still found its way inside my shoes, dampening a good pair of Converse and tube socks. I thought to myself, *I had it with this one horse town;* however, Indianapolis wasn't much different than any other city I've read about. It had its rich and poor and suffered the same racial inequalities as any other large city. My neighborhood was slightly different; it was gentrification in reverse, two blocks of lower middle-class people were squeezed into a small section of the once-bourgeois neighborhood. Less than two blocks away were mansions sitting on top of a hill in their utopian world, looking down on the poor peasants that lived below their feet. They had their ideas about us, and based on history, we had our facts about them.

The people in my neighborhood were very closely woven. Because of our closeness, we were able to refrain from any gang violence or anyone being killed within our two-block radius. Although young adults and kids came from other neighborhoods to enjoy the park and basketball courts, they never brought chaos and destruction with them. I was often discontented with the lifestyle. A deep desire was burning within me like a hot fire on ice. Something was pushing me to see the world—pushing me to go out of my comfort zone. I wanted to fly a way someplace I hadn't been before. I did not understand it, but I knew I had to leave.

I needed a way out, but I had nowhere to go; and more importantly, I didn't have the finances to support any decision to move to a different place. My paltry $2.32 an hour income barely paid for my daily living expenses, such as eating lunch at school and having extracurricular activities with my girlfriend. To add insult to injury, there was a rumor that my job was going out of business. Saul Subway was a popular restaurant with three dining sections: Cellar, Attic, and Bedroom. The restaurant was a stone's throw from my front door, which made it very a convenient place to work.

Since I often went directly to work after school, I began my day at Saul Subway at 3:00 p.m. and worked until midnight. By the time I got home, my clothes had the stench of corned beef and my shoes looked like they'd been chewed on by a rottweiler. I was so tired I bypassed the bathtub and headed straight for the bed. To my dismay, the bedroom door was locked. My older brother had invited some young girl into our room. He didn't excogitate his decision before lying down with the young lady. He just purchased a box containing three prophylactics. Three dollars was wedged in the crack of the door. This was payment to sleep downstairs, so he could have his sexual escapade. I thought, *Why not? It's the cheapest motel rate in town.*

I reluctantly made my way downstairs to an unrestful night on the couch, vowing to never sleep downstairs again no matter how much he paid me. Passionate screams echoed down the hallway as he pounded against her flesh. I fell asleep to the tune of "Yes, baby. Yes, baby." I was awakened several hours later by footsteps creeping down the stairs at 5:45 a.m. My brother was cleaning up the evidence before my mother finished her graveyard shift at the hospital. It really didn't matter whether or not he cleaned up the evidence. My sisters couldn't wait to tell my mother his little secret and how disrespectful he was, having sex with a strange girl while they were trying to sleep. I didn't care. Either way, I was being paid $3 a night to sleep downstairs; and on a good night, he'd give me $4 and a bag of leftover White Castle hamburgers.

I slept for thirty more minutes then went into the tub, and quickly I ran up the street four miles to my girlfriend's house to walk her to school. Up Pennsylvania Street I ran, hands sank deep in my pockets, my nose pressed down into the top of my coat, trying to keep the icy air off my chin.

Weak for the Flesh

May lived in a brick double in the middle of the block on Park Avenue. The house looked as though it was built in the forties and was in need of slight remodeling. Once I arrived at her house, I knocked on the door, then noticed the door was slightly ajar. I knocked again and yelled out her name, "May, May!" There was no answer, so I moved to the bottom of the staircase and yelled out her name once more— still no answer. I slowly made my way up the stairs. With each step I took, the wooden stairs creaked beneath my feet. I reached the top of the steps and stopped to look in both directions. I didn't see anyone in the hallway. As I turned the corner, there she was squatting down looking through her dresser. She was wearing a see-through waist-length negligée.

Her minuscule frame looked nibile for her age. May did nothing to accentuate her figure, but she still incurred the wrath of many women within her age group who I considered to be naturally sultry. Her beautiful tan skin accentuated her perfect 36DD breasts. Her huge breasts were like kryptonite. I stood there in awe, feeling lightheaded as the blood left my brain then my feet centralizing in the nonthinking part of my body. I briefly lost consciousness and fell back against the door from the unexpected eye-popping surprise. I asked her, "When are you going, May, to school?" She replied, "Not today." I quickly guided her toward the bed. She flopped down on the bed like a wet fish. I was so overwhelmed I went straight for the prize but got a surprise instead.

She was so tight I couldn't get a finger in her if I wanted to. I gave up and sprang to my feet, pulled my jeans up, then flopped back on the bed in utter disappointment. She lay there like a mannequin for several minutes before we headed off to school. The sidewalks were piled high with snow, so it forced us to walk down the middle of the street, staying clear of the snow- and slush-covered sidewalks. As we reached he corner of Park and Thirty-Eighth Street, I noticed that she was staring at the Roslyn Bakery sign. Then it hit me: she loves donuts.

All of a sudden, I was back in the game. I was not going to pass up a close encounter for the second time. I dropped May off at school, then ran four blocks home, and broke into my stash hidden in a pickle jar in a draw at the top of the closet.

I made it back to school just in time to get scratched up by Mr. Carter, the dean of boys, a six-foot-tall, three-hundred-pound black cowboy that loved to place late students on yard bird detail, cleaning up the football field and picking up paper around the building. But I was rescued by First Sergeant Woods, the ROTC instructor. He ordered me to go straight to class, but I was on a mission. Visions of 36DD sugar plums danced in my head. I patrolled the hallways, looking in each class, until I captured a glimpse of May sitting in the third row of the journalism class. So I did what any young man in my situation would do in a concupiscent moment: I posted up outside the door until the bell rang.

I was on a lascivious mission. I had donut money and an erection that would cripple the average man. The bell rang, and I escorted her toward the school exit. May said, "I have another class." Then she looked down at my pants. She laughed to herself. She could see I was still fuming from early in the day. I put my arm around her as we walked home in our horny splendor. I purposely walked past Roslyn Bakery to whet her appetite with two jelly donuts and possibly an orange juice. She couldn't have been more elated. She peeked in the donut bag every two minutes, brandishing a smile from ear to ear.

Once in the house, I stopped by the staircase and, using a suggestive body language, pointed toward the steps; but she kept walking to the kitchen. Reaching into the cabinet, she removed a saucer, unraveled the pink Roslyn Bakery bag, placed one donut on the saucer, then began to meticulously cut the donut into small sections. She slowly ate each piece as though she was purposely messing with my head. I sat at the table, watching her eat piece by piece. She tried to hold a conversation with me, but my brain was between my legs at the time. My only thoughts were *I wish she would hurry and finish eating. Why was she taking so long in eating a donut'? Just shovel it in your mouth, chew, and swallow.*

Finally, my wish was granted. She finished eating then grabbed the donut bag. My heart stopped. I thought for sure I was going to have to relive fifteen more minutes of pure hell in my pants while she ate another donut. I was so erect my eyes were beginning to roll in the back of my head. I can hear bells ringing as though I were in a heavyweight championship bout. I reached around the table, grabbed her hand, and said, "You had your donut. Now it's time for me to get mine." Upstairs we went. She disrobed down to her polka-dot panties, and once again, her perfectly round 36DDs were staring me in the face. Drool fell from my mouth like a glue gun. I ripped her polka-dot panties open like a bag of Chesty potato chips. My adrenaline was running at an exaggerated pace as though I were lapping the track at the Indianapolis 500. It was the best 5 minutes of sexual pleasure I had all year, in and out with little clean-up. I pulled up my pants, kissed May good-bye, then peregrinated three miles to the entrance of Saul Subway.

Olive Oyl

I stood outside for a brief second, trying to compose myself and catch my breath. I can smell her sexual scent, still strong on my fingers, so I was totally at ease and ready to get to work. I shot upstairs into the attic to fire up the dishwasher. I grabbed a slice of chocolate mousse pie from the freezer and slouched back comfortably against the dishwasher and began forking the pie down my throat. Once I had my shot of sugar, I began to prepare julienne salads until the salad prep girl arrived. The salad prep girl's name was Eileen. She was six feet tall—slim white girl. She wasn't very attractive. I thought she resembled the character from the *Popeye* cartoons Olive Oyl. Her body was as flat as a surfboard. She had an unassuming nature, with a nondescript personality. She only spoke when she was spoken to. I believe she had a borderline developmentally delayed personality or she's a dull normal. But there was something about her looks that was unescapable. She was soft-spoken and had a delicate touch. She moved very slowly but was very meticulous in the way she wheeled her knife, slicing every bit of the cucumber as if there was an intentionally diabolical purpose to the way she made each cut.

She applied excessive pressure on the knife, and with every cut, she grinded her teeth. Somehow she was able to reveal the softer side of her enigmatic personality. She piled salad on the plate, undulate in her movement placing freshly cut cucumbers and boiled pickled eggs and generous strips of ham on top of the lettuce. Yellow onions were used to intensify the flavor. Croutons covered the rest of the plate to enhance its size, making a common salad into a thing of artistic work. It wasn't long before I was summoned to go downstairs and prepare four trays of rosin potatoes. I wrapped each potato in aluminum foil, placing twenty-five to thirty potatoes on four metal cooking sheets, then set the ovens at 350 degrees. I slid the sheets into the oven. It took me about thirty minutes—thirty of the longest most uncomfortable minutes of my life. I was totally creeped out by the stories of other employees being bitten by rats as large as my foot. I've even witnessed large ghetto rodents running freely under the tables, eating the droppings of food left by the rich patriot pigs.

To put it another way, customers were mostly upper-middle-class professionals and appeared that they didn't care about the condition, which they left on the tables and floors or the clean-up that will follow. All they wanted to do was gorge themselves with succulent steaks prepared by uneducated would-be chefs from the ghetto one block over from the restaurant. They forked out on the rosin baked potatoes topped with whipped cream and chives, unknown to themselves prepared by a dishwasher. The restaurant was famous for its food, often patronized by doctors, lawyers, and anyone else of prominence in the city.

I made it my business to cruise around the restaurant in between picking up dish tubs from various stations. I watched the customers and secretly listened to their conversations. I mostly enjoyed talking with Olive Oyl. After six hours of working together, she began to open up and allowed me to enter her cucumber-cutting developmentally delayed world. I couldn't help but to listen closely as she laid her life story at my feet. She said she had been raped two years ago by an African American male, and since that time, she had been trying to find him to force him to be a father to their two-year-old daughter. She talked nonstop for an hour. I passively listened as she pontificated on and on. The longer she talked, the more twisted and perverted her story got. She loathed the idea of searching for her rapists, but she felt it was necessary to let him know that he fathered a child.

During her time off, she would cruise up and down Indiana Avenue, the last place she saw her assailant. After three hours of walking there, she saw him mindlessly leaning against a concrete building without a care in the world. She confronted him without an accusation, only with a handful of baby pictures. She beseeched him to come see his daughter, but he chuckled to himself with the condescending smile then escorted her to what she thought was his apartment. Instead, it was just another vacant building, with not as much as a mattress on the floor. He proceeded to rape her once again. I couldn't help but feel pity for Olive Oyl because even after telling me this sad story, she punctuated it with "I'm going to keep looking for him until he accepts his role as the father of my child." I began to develop a bad taste and disliking in my mouth for Olive Oyl. She finally stopped talking. I can see the lightbulb turned on in her head. At that moment, she invited me over to her house, but I demurred because of the possibility of our spending the night together. I didn't want her to divulge any more depressing stories of her life.

I tried to stay out of the kitchen and made it a point to hang out around the bus-tub stations. I only went into the kitchen when it was absolutely necessary because I didn't want this woman to soliloquize herself around me anymore. By this time, I was tired and pretty much done for the day. My shoes we're soaking wet, and my fingers looked as though I had been in water for twelve hours. My clothes smelled of corned beef, and my pockets occupied empty spaces where tips would normally fill those gaps. I didn't vociferated about the tips that were promised to me by the waitress hours earlier. I was a dishwasher and a busboy; therefore, I only bused tables at the waitress's request, but the request came with tips at the end of the shift. One waitress stepped forward and gave me $3 for busing ten tables there were shoved together for a birthday party.

I was young, but I wasn't that young. I wasn't going to put up with the BS; therefore, I was forced to create my own rules about tipping and the percentage I deserved. If the customer left $10, I took $2. I didn't enjoy taking tips, but they forced my hand. After cleaning several tables and not being tipped by the waitress, I no longer felt guilty about forcing my own trip. Sunday morning I was at work for the evening shift, which began at 3:00 p.m. The deli and the dining room section of the restaurant were closed for the day because prohibition laws still applied in Indiana on Sundays. No one was allowed to sell liquor anywhere in the city, but somehow the alcoholics and the obsessive drinkers would find adventure in seeking out club owners that would risk their license and their business to sell a six-pack of beer at twice the price out of the back door of the bar. I can't believe people will go through this much trouble just to have a beer because the law says you can't have one on Sunday.

No one ever thought it will be just as easy to buy the liquor on Saturday and put it away to drink on Sunday. Maybe people do that because it would take all the fun and suspense out of the game. In the meantime, I was stuck at work on Sunday, baking potatoes in the rat-infested restaurant, looking at my feet and around the machines to ensure that no rats were biting at my shoes. I wrapped those potatoes quickly as if I were in a potato recipe contest. I was totally creeped out; the kitchen was dark and spooky. I took every shortcut possible to get out of the kitchen as quickly as I could. Once the ovens were set and the potatoes were baking, I sneaked around the bar in search of an open liquor or beer tap. Instead, I found a bag of Lay's potato chips and an open soda can.

I placed my mouth under the Coke tap and drank soda like a horse drinking from a water trough. I was in hog heaven until I felt something squirm over the top of my foot. I threw the chips in the air, jumped over the bar, and, scared, ran outside to the sidewalk. Just as my feet hit the sidewalk, two young women were strolling by. I wasn't really interested in them. I just didn't have anything to do at the time, so I convinced them to come back and talk to me. They kept walking when I called them. I didn't give up. I yelled at them two more times before they turned and began walking in my direction.

One was tall and fair skin with an awesome figure. The other one was small, quiet, and reserved; her face was covered partially with a bonnet hat, and I could barely get a glimpse of what she looked like. The tall light-skinned girl was more of my type. I threw out my best lines, but after two minutes of talking, she mentioned she was dating one of my friends. I didn't want to come up empty-handed; therefore, I shifted my conversation to the quiet and reserved one. I didn't care for her at first, but she slowly grew on me. I was partially attracted to her because she was soft-spoken and appeared to be a very gentle person.

I was loath to give her my phone number because of the crazy cucumber-cutting bitch upstairs who was also quiet and unassuming but was prated underneath it all. Cindy and I talked over the phone for the next couple of weeks although I was still technically involved with May. May and I began to drift apart, spending less and less time together. Every time I saw her, she spoke of moving to Arizona to go to college; therefore, we ended our relationship on that note the day after our high school graduation. Cindy and May were two extremely different personalities.

Cindy was good at math and was very focused on doing well in school. She wanted things in life and was willing to work hard to achieve her goals.

I would sit with her and write out math problems just for the fun of it, but there was something mysterious about her that I just couldn't put my finger on. In the meantime, her ignorant jackass of a brother would interrupt my thoughts by trying to show how tough he was by punking his friend Jeff, yelling absurdly close in his face, and making threatening comments about hurting him physically. I just ignored his dumb antics as well as his dumb comments. He even tried to cajole Jeff to start a fight with me to entertain his sick, twisted mind. He was a true pain in my butt, and I was sure we would lock horns in the foreseeable future. Cindy had four brothers and two younger sisters. They lived in a large wooden double with three bedrooms on each side. The couch was fitted with the traditional plastic covering that no one would dare sit on in fear of falling asleep and hydrating to death. Cindy's mother was a very light-skinned woman closely resembling someone of the white persuasion. She was a country girl from Mississippi with telltale signs over Mississippi culture in her behavior.

She wore a gold tooth in the middle of her mouth that was hard to miss because of her infectious smile. She had a way of luring men into her sinister web, destroying marriages along the way. She even had a theme song ("Clean Up, Woman") sung by Betty Wright. She would repetitiously play the same song twenty-four hours a day until the needle on the record player was worn down and no longer usable. I sat quietly in the living room and watched her dance around in a circle with a glass of liquor in one hand and a half-smoked cigarette in the other. I tried not to attract attention to myself, but Cindy's sister sat atop the staircase and shot paper spit balls through a straw onto my Afro.

I alerted Cindy to the situation. Before I knew it, Cindy ran to the top of the steps and dragged her sister down the steps by the hair. "Say you're sorry." Cindy placed her foot on my her sister's neck and pulled her with her right hand, making her apologize before striking her in the back with her fist, then shoving her toward the staircase, whining. This was a side of Cindy that I had not yet seen since it was early in a relationship, but I did notice she could go from zero to eighty in less than ten seconds flat then back to zero as if nothing ever happened. It seems as though the house was always packed with people or people constantly ran in or out, taking bites of food here and there before running then back into the streets. This was a very unpredictable place. I never knew when we would get a moment's peace to ourselves. By the time I was seventeen, I had acquired my driver's license.

I had been driving around for six months, mostly running errands for my mother to the grocery store on Capitol Avenue or to the 7-Eleven on Fairfield. Either way, I didn't care. I just wanted to drive and be seen cruising around by all my friends who weren't driving yet. Friends of the family began to take advantage of my mother, asking her for rides to and from the store on a daily basis. My mother didn't have the heart to tell them no, so she shifted the responsibility to me. She knew that I had just got my license and I love to drive. All of a sudden, it was my responsibility to take all her friends and friends of the family to shopping and other places they wanted to go. I love driving. I just didn't want to be trapped into sitting on the grocery store parking lot once again, waiting for two hours. I had to find a way out. After two hours of waiting, the two women emerged from the grocery store, smiling from ear to ear after a successful Thanksgiving shopping trip, food almost spilling over the top of the cart.

I couldn't believe it. They just left the bags in the cart and sat comfortably in the backseat while I begrudgingly unloaded the cart into the trunk. I started the car, threw it in gear, and slammed on the gas. The back of the car almost did a hundred-and-eighty-degree span before I could straighten out the wheel. I must've been going eighty miles an hour before I reached the first corner. I didn't even step on the brakes. I turned the corner, making the back of the car fishtail around the curve. I looked in my rearview mirror; both women were pinned to the backseat with their eyes bulging out of the head. They thought for sure they were going to die in that moment.

I thought I heard a prayer coming from someone's mouth, but I didn't let up. As soon as I reached the street, I slammed on the gas as I turned the corner. Before I knew it, a police car was behind me, flashing his lights. Now I was scared. Slowly pulling over to the curve, I took out my driver's license and rolled down the window. Very timidly, I asked, "Is there a problem, Officer?" The officer shined his flashlight in my face then asked for my registration. I opened up the glove box and felt around the loose papers for my registration; to my dismay, my mother's 22-caliber pistol fell out of the glove box onto the floor. I froze in position, waiting for further instructions from the officer. Hoping he didn't see the gun lying at the tip of my fingers on the floor, I positioned my body, trying to block the flashlight from shining on the gun; then I removed the registration from the glove box and handed it to the officer. He walked around to the back of the car and asked that I step on my brake pedal. The officer said, "I didn't see your brake lights when you turned the corner. I want to make sure they were operating properly." He handed me back my license and registration then pulled off.

I sat in the car with my head pressed against the steering wheel while the two women expediently unloaded their bags then ran into the house without saying a word. I was mentally exhausted from the exchange. All I wanted to do was take the car back home and hand my mother her keys. It wouldn't be long before I got over that night and was back in the saddle. I turned my attention to my new girlfriend. I had to find a way to get her away from her family so we could be by ourselves. The first place I took her was Riverside Park where most young lovers seemed to go for a moment of peace or possible sexual experience. Our relationship was still new, and I had to find a way to loosen her up so that I could take it to next phase. She wasn't a drinker, and I wasn't old enough to buy alcohol and didn't have the courage to ask an older person to buy it for me even though I knew many boys that were twenty-one years old in my neighborhood. I was embarrassed at the prospect of anyone knowing my true intentions. Cindy was younger than I and was inexperienced in the art of manipulation.

In the month of April, we were sitting idly on the couch. Cindy's legs were stretched across my lap, her back resting comfortably against the arm of the couch. We sat around talking while I massaged her feet, purposely hitting the points that would sexually arouse her. I could see she was softening up, so I began to pick her brain. I made a $5 bet with her that she would not have sex with me on the couch. She was so preoccupied with winning the bet I don't think she realized what she was doing until it was done. She sat on top of me, and I hastily unzipped my pants and slowly slid them partially down just past my knees. Before she knew it, I was deep inside of her cavity. Three minutes into me losing my bet, her pasty older brother was standing outside on the front door, finishing a cigarette. I tried to get her off me, but she wouldn't budge. She looked at me and laughed, refusing to move. She sat very still on top of me while her brother walked from the front door to the kitchen, gazing at us with a stupid smirk on his face.

I could hear the squeaking hinges of the refrigerator door. I quickly lifted Cindy off me and wiped away the evidence of our sexual climax with the sheets covering the couch. Her brother came back in the room and said, "What the hell is going on here?" He reached down and grabbed Cindy by the arm, snatching her off my lap, but to his surprise, my pants were zipped up and securely fastened. There wasn't any sign of fornication. He looked at both of us with an evil eye, made a moaning sound, then walked back out the front door, eating his baloney sandwich. Cindy sat next to me smiling. She laid her head on my shoulder, stuck her hand out, and asked for her $5. I whispered in her ear, "I'm still erect." She laughed, jumped up, and sashayed toward the front porch as her brother Rayford walked back and forth, peeking in the window.

I cleaned myself up the best I could and reluctantly walked outside on the porch and sat ten feet away. We smiled and laughed to ourselves as if we had got away with the perfect crime. Rayford leaned heavily against the frame of the front door, cutting his eyes back and forth at both of us while he devoured his dried-up baloney sandwich. I was done dealing with this asshole. I had a pressing business elsewhere. So I leaped from the pouch, waved to Cindy farewell, then made my way back across the bridge toward my mother's house. I couldn't help but to pass by Sabrina's house. She was the prettiest girl in school, but there was one small problem: she didn't brush her teeth. I had never seen that much food caked up on someone's teeth. I didn't understand how a girl so pretty could miss the most vital part of her conversation piece: her mouth. I thought it was a fluk the first time I saw her, but she was this way every time we talked. Teeth caked over as if she had not brushed for months. I had no time for a yucky mouth, so I made my way down two blocks to the park on Twenty-Ninth and Talbott.

I was in luck. There were two boys playing a game of 21. After playing for ten minutes, we changed the game to booths. Whoever had the lowest score at the end of the game gets kicked in the butt by all the other players. The rules where we could only kick the person with the side of our foot. The game got under way. I played harder than I ever had played before. Ben was the best player and a natural shooter, so I tried to keep up with him, making basket for basket. The other guy fell far behind on points. I smiled and stepped out of the way as Ben easily ran by me and laid the ball in the hoop, making the final point of the game. Ben told the other kid, "Well, you lost. Lean on the fence." The kid did what Ben said, placing both hands on the fence. I went first and did just as the rule said. I kicked him with the side of my foot. Ben got a running start from fifty feet, ran as fast as he could, and kicked the boy with the point of his foot as though he were trying to kick him to the moon.

The boy must've jumped fifty feet in the air, clutching his butt on the way up and falling to the ground in agonizing pain. Ben laughed and ran through the sandbox, climbing over the concrete castle and the other obstacles on the playground, trying to escape the screaming young boy chasing him around the park clutching his butt with one hand, seemingly in utter pain. I couldn't help but to laugh at the spectacle before me although I did feel sorry for the young boy, but he knew the situation before getting involved in the game.

He knew Ben was not going to honor the terms of the game and use the side of his foot. This wasn't his first time the young naïve boy was tricked by Ben. Once, we were playing football in the big field across the street from my house. Ben kicked the ball to the young boy then pretended he was going to let him run by him and score a touchdown. Once the boy got side by side with Ben, Ben stuck his arm out and clotheslined the young boy, making him flip in a complete

360-degree circle, then took off running down the street, laughing. Everyone on the block knew Vin and the type of stunts he pulled. I didn't have much time anymore for tomfoolery. I had an appointment to meet with a marine recruiter that evening.

I felt my life was at a stalemate, and graduation from high school was just around the corner. I knew there will come a time I would have to leave my mother's house and make it on my own. I was so excited I could smell my emancipation in the air. I was mentally exhausted thinking about paying my own rent, utility bills, car payment, and other life-changing chores adults were supposed to do to survive. I was scared out of my mind at the possibility of failing the military entrance exam for the second time. I knew I had to change my methods of study if this was going to become a reality, so I acquired four pages of word knowledge, covering front and back page.

I sat in my room for three days, not going down the street to play basketball, not hanging out with any girls, or spending time with my friends. All I did was study and pray until I knew the list back and forth. In between study times, I would stand in the mirror and imagine myself wearing a set of dress blues; a white hat with a black brim flanked by gold buttons on both sides, placed squarely on my head; and a high collar with two gold Marine Corps emblems. Then all of a sudden, my chin was squared, and I was a marine.

My only focus at that time was becoming a United States Marine. Nothing else mattered, not even my high school diploma or the fact that I was leaving my hometown and people that I loved behind. I wanted to challenge myself. I wanted to see if I can stand on my own two feet and take whatever they can dish out. Growing up without a father created a huge gap of uncertainty in my mind. I questioned everything I did, right down to the smallest detail. I was never sure if I was making the right decision about anything because I wasn't talking or thinking on my feet. Everything I learned I learned from the streets and the people I associated myself with. However, my mother did teach me how to respect others and things that belonged to other people. My mother never overindulged me. I received the basic needs:

shoes, clothing, food, and roof over my head. Learning how to become a man, I had to learn from examples in front of me.

All the men in my life spent their time chasing women. If they weren't chasing women, they were getting drunk at a local bar on Indiana Avenue or planning some scheme to get some sort of ill-gotten gain. I never saw an example of a man going to college, raising a family. The closest I came two seeing a man working at a steady job was my stepfather. He would get up at four in the morning, go to work, then come home sloppy drunk at 10:00 p.m., sit at the table, eat dinner, then stagger upstairs, walking right past me, not saying a word. He would flop down on the bed and pass out. He was the most direct example in my life that I had on what a man did on a daily basis. I did not know any better because I didn't have any better examples. I did have an uncle named George. He worked at a bakery, and I'm pretty sure he went to work every day on time for thirty years. He and his wife, Dorothy, my mother's sister, always had the newest cars in the family. They had a small dainty two-bedroom house with plastic covering the couch and chairs. I found it odd that my auntie was a schoolteacher, yet her husband cannot read a word, but he was good with his hands and can build almost anything. He was also an excellent mechanic. I do believe he would've been a good role model, but I only saw him once every five or six months when he came by the house with a box of stale donuts, trying to put a smile on our face. But I was no longer a little kid. I was eighteen years old, and a box of stale glazed donuts wasn't going to change the dynamics of my life in the next two months.

My life was changing for sure. I was growing as a person, and this path that I had chosen I must walk along. Later that day, I made my way downtown to the recruiting station where more than fifty other individuals of different ethnic backgrounds and genders were all taking the same test but for different branches of service. I was very proud to be one of the few in the room taking the Marine Corps exam, but in hindsight, I was one of the few idiots taking the Marine Corps exam. I finished the exam and was escorted into the other room. Anyone that failed the exam was shown the door.

I was so excited I couldn't hold it inside. I told everyone, even the people on the bus. I ran down Twenty-Ninth and Talbott as though I won the lottery. Once I approached the front door, I stopped. I walked in as cool as a glass of water in the summertime. I sat at the kitchen table, crossed my legs, and grabbed a section of the newspaper. My mother stared at me as she stirred her Folgers coffee. "Where have you been all day?" she asked. "I was at the recruiting station. I took the Marine Corps exam and passed it. My departure date is July 18."

My mother's eyes got big, and suddenly she stopped sipping her coffee and began haranguing me about the corps. "Why in the hell did you join the marines? Are you crazy?" "I wanted to be tested. I want to know who I am and if I can stand on my own two feet. This is something that I must do alone." "I hope you know what the hell you're doing," she said. "Well, if I don't, we're going to find out on July 18." So back upstairs I went. I couldn't sleep a wink. I swear I must have been awake for five days straight. I pretty much kept to myself other than occasional visits to Cindy's house and our well-planned 7:00 p.m. trips to Riverside Park where I would park, turn out the lights, turn on the radio, then climb in the backseat where the seduction began. I was no stranger to the Riverside Park area. I was on the Riverside boxing team, and I dated two young girls in the area the year before. I think Cindy liked all the personal attention I was giving her. We stopped at White Castle and picked up a 10 sack and two chocolate shakes. We threw our feet up on the armrest of the front seat and choked down our White Castle hamburgers until one of us let out a raunchy fart and belch.

We had gotten very comfortable after stuffing ourselves with hamburgers, so we took off our shoes and unbuttoned our pants at the waist to let our stomachs stretch freely. I massaged her feet as she sank deep into relaxation, moaning as my hand found its way up her thighs and under her buttocks. I squeezed and kissed and took her breasts in my mouth. Before I knew it, I had her yellow pants off and tossed them on the front seat; and once again, we were deep into sexual ecstasy. Once I was able to catch my breath, I realized we had forgotten about the time. Three hours had passed, and my mother had to be at work within an hour, so we began scrambling around on the back floor, trying to find our underwear and cleaning up any evidence. All of a sudden, it hit me. She didn't know I was moving 2,500 miles away. I might as well move to the moon because the corps doesn't allow phone calls until the tenth week of boot camp training. I dropped Cindy at her door then went off to the gas station to replenish the tank, arriving home just in time to hand the car off to my mother. I stood on the side wall, watching her turn the corner on Thirtieth Street. I went one house down the street and plopped down on the steps with my friends, where we sat outside until midnight when the street lights began flashing. Off we all went to our separate homes.

I stayed up late that night, wide awake, staring out the bedroom window. My mind was going one hundred miles an hour, searching for an answer about my future in the military and where I would be five years from today. I couldn't help but wonder how my mother sustained herself and eight children all these years. I could barely stomach the fact that I would be expected to support myself from this day forth. It scared me to death because I had always been under my mother's roof, eating my mother's food, wearing the clothing she brought. All this would come to an end in forty-five days. I'd be reluctantly cut free of the apron strings.

It had been a month since I enlisted in the marines, and still I could not muster the courage to tell Cindy. So I just let it ride until that one fateful day. Tiana, Melody, Herb, and I were playing cards in the front room. The rules were if you lost a hand, you had to drink a glass of water.

Everyone was willing to comply with the rules except Tiana. Tiana lost a hand and refused to drink the water I obliged her by pouring a tall glass of water and placed it in front over. Tiana said, "I'm not drinking the damn water." I told her, "But you lost. It's the rules. Everyone drinks water when they lost, and you know you better drink the water like everyone else." She still refused, so I grabbed the pitcher of water sitting at the opposite end of the table and tossed it in her face, then jetted up the steps to my room, and locked the door.

Melody and Herb laughed uncontrollably, which enraged Tiana even more; so she ran up the steps behind me, screaming my name and cursing like a drunken sailor. I was quick to slam the door in her face while laughing on the other side of the door, which infuriated her more. She began kicking and hitting my door profusely with her fist. She stood there soaked as though she accidentally fell in a swimming pool. She pounded, screamed, and kicked on the door until she realized it was of no resolve; so she grabbed my brand-new pair of white Converse and flung them outside in the mud, giving my German shepherd something to chew on. I was so pissed off I ran into her bedroom, grabbed her favorite nightgown, tied it in a knot, dipped it in the toilet, then flunk it on the roof next door. Tianna ranted and whined until my mother forced me to get a stick and get the nightgown down from the roof, and Tiana was forced to retrieve my shoes from the backyard and clean them off. I ran off down the street to the park while Tiana stood outside, fuming over the incident and cursing my name as I ran to the basketball court for a brief game of 21. I soon was crossing the bridge on Twentieth and Central to Cindy's house.

As I approached, there was a crowd standing on the front porch: her brothers, sisters, mother, and stepfather. I could see something was amiss, and it made me very uncomfortable as I approached the porch. Cindy turned her back toward me as I stepped on the porch, then ran into the kitchen, and pretended as though she were cooking. At that moment, I knew Tiana had called and informed Cindy about my enlistment in the marines. Cindy wanted nothing more to do with our relationship and wanted to move her life in a different direction than the path I had chosen, so I walked away with an eerie feeling in my stomach as if someone had kicked me. A month and a half later, I was being picked up by my marine recruiter at nine in the morning to be transported to the recruiting station for final processing and a flight to San Diego. My mother and I stood outside that morning, waiting for the recruiter to arrive; as usual, he pulled up in a little Ford Escort with the Marine Corps emblem on the side.

I began dragging the seabag toward the car. The recruiter said, "Where are you going with that?" I said, "To boot camp." The recruiter said, "I don't need that. I just need you." So I gave the bag back to my mother and hopped in the front seat of the recruiter's car. As the car drove away, my mother stood in the front yard, watching me drive off. She was teary-eyed with a slight lump in her throat; however, she did summon enough strength to wave a final good-bye. I stared at her out the window until the car turned the corner on Thirtieth Street. I barely caught a glimpse of her struggling to drag the seabag back up the steps into the house. I scanned the neighborhood with my eyes, hoping to catch a glimpse of someone I knew so I could wave good-bye to them, but no one was around. It was as if the streets were purposely empty. No one saw me leave. There was no one there to say good luck or "I'll see you when you get back." It made me feel empty, unloved, and alone. For the first time in my life, Twenty-Ninth and Talbott was empty. There wasn't a soul to be found. Everyone had disappeared into their own lives, and I was on my way to a new life. There were a lot of firsts for me that day: the first time I'd flown on the plane, the first time I would visit California, the first time I would feel what it was like to miss my mother, and first time I would miss someone that I cared deeply about.

The most significant thing of all, I was leaving as Mikey but I would return a marine. My plane touched down in San Diego at seven that evening. The night was crazy. Everything was moving at a crazy pace. We got our heads shaved, and we're stripped naked. We were issued and inventoried all our clothing and took showers. I was in the bed by 1:00 a.m. I was thoroughly shaken up. I didn't know what had just happened or if I could keep up with this fanatic pace for long. The receiving barracks were located right next to the San Diego airport. I could see the planes land and take off behind the twelve-foot-high wooden fence.

The airplanes seemed so close it was as if I could reach them out of my window and touch the wings. Glover, the kid I flew from Indianapolis to San Diego with, wanted to go AWOL. We decided once everyone was sleep, we were going to jump the fence and crawl into the landing gear of the airplane. I closed my eyes for a brief second, waiting for everyone around me to go to sleep; before I knew it, it was 4:00 a.m. The lights flickered on, and trash cans were being thrown about the squad bay. Drill instructors were running and screaming and getting in our faces. We were walking down the street in a big mob, flashlights in our hands, our knowledge and toothpaste in our cargo pockets, our shirt's button all the way to the top. Drill instructors were yelling at the top of their lungs, calling cadence in an untraditional fashion as we tried to get in step while marching down the streets toward the chow hall.

I was starving, but I was confused. It was dark and cold. I could barely see three feet in front of me. We were rushed through the chow hall like cows, given two minutes to swallow whatever food we could get in us, then pushed out the back door, and forced to march back to the barracks at an insane pace. We scrubbed and cleaned the showers and bathroom floors with toothbrushes. Everything was at an extremely fast pace with the exception of getting out of receiving barracks or being picked up by our drill instructors. It had been two weeks, and we were still hanging around the receiving barracks, waiting for eighty-two training days to begin. We practiced cleaning the barracks and freeing our uniforms of any iris pendants.

Then all of a sudden, there were three drill instructors kicking seabags down the steps and tossing our uniforms and boots over the balcony rail. Everyone got treated the same because we looked the same in the eyes of the drill instructors. We were all equal idiots. The torture continued on a twenty-minute walk to our new barracks—twenty minutes that seemingly took an hour before we were able to reach the barracks. The drill instructors couldn't resist playing head games, kicking our cover blocks ahead of us as we walked in a disorganized fashion to our new barracks. As we walked right in front of the other, asshole to belly button, they yelled, screaming and spitting in our faces.

The pace was excruciatingly fast. I was beginning to feel the effects of hunger from the corner piece of bread and one spoon of eggs I was able to shove in my mouth before we were dragged from the chow hall and tossed in a half-baked formation. Rush, rush, rush, rush. Before I knew it, night had fallen upon us. By nine o'clock, we're all in the bed, lying at attention on the top of our olive drab wool blankets, listening to the bugle play taps. I tried to stay awake by listening to the comforting sound of the crickets, but there were none. All I could hear were the planes taking off and landing at the airport next door.

I couldn't help but ask myself, *How did I let myself get into this?* We plotted to escape and jump over the fence that separated the marine base from the airport. Once everyone was asleep, we were going to crawl into the wheel landing gear and successfully make our escape. But unfortunately, for both of us, the day was so grueling we slowly dozed off. It seemed like I was asleep just for a second when the lights popped on, trash cans were being thrown down the center of the squad bay, and we hopped right out of bed and stood at attention in the front of our racks. Drill instructors were yelling and screaming, "Don't blink. Don't you fucking blink. You're not allowed to blink or speak. Breathing is your only luxury you will have while at MCRD."

These were eighty-two of the most intense days of my life, but I was made the better man for it. During those eighty-two days, Cindy and I touched bases once again, and I had to say her letters did help get me through boot camp. Cindy couldn't help expressing the way she felt about me. She planted kisses on the envelope of every letter. Each time I got a letter with the imprint of lips, the smell of perfume, or salutations written on the outside of the envelope, I got thrashed by my drill instructors. I was removed from squad bay and made to roll around in the dirt and perform mountain climbers, jumping jacks, and bends and thrusts for every salutation or print on the envelope.

I became friends with the young marine named Sampson. I thought it was really cool that he was from Chicago and I was from the neighboring city. One day the drill instructors had the bright idea to place Sampson in charge of the rifle rack and wear more than eighty

M16s that were locked away. He was also given the responsibility of being the platoon guide on Baron until one day he lost the keys to the rifle rack. The drill instructors became infuriated and thrashed Sampson up and down the squad bay, doing push-ups, sit-ups, and mountain climbers until he sweated out a pool of blood. The drill instructor then grabbed Sampson's foot locker and tossed it against the wall. Out came the keys sliding down. The squad bay stopped at the front of my feet as I stood at attention, watching the incident unfold.

Sampson was pulled into the drill instructor's office. They slammed him against the wall lockers and bulkhead then tossed him out into the squad bay where he landed on his face, sliding almost through the double exit doors. I was glad he was okay. I smiled and chuckled to myself as he ran back and stood at attention in front of his rack. Every morning was the same for the next eighty-two days: fast paced with a lot of pushing, shoving, and yelling. Each day started with a shit, shower, and shave. We played mind games, ripping our beds apart and putting them back together as fast as we could. This was our usual 4:30 a.m. ritual before we went to breakfast. We were marched to breakfast as though we were running the fifty-yard dash. We were new to the corps and not yet disciplined.

Everything we did, we did together in close proximity of one another. They called it asshole to belly button. Even in the chow line, we were not allowed to look anywhere other than the man's head in front of us. Once we reached the serving line, we locked eyes on the wall in front of us and side stepped our way through the chow line. I locked eyes with an authoritative-looking major. Because I had a good nature and wasn't fully aware of Marine Corps policy, as a kind gesture, I smiled at the major.

The major pounced on me like a lion on a hyena, right up to me asshole-to-belly-button style, and pressed his nose against mine. "Do you want to go to jail?" he asked in a very convincing voice. "Sir, no, sir," I said with a nervous expression. "Then wipe that fucking smell off your face." My drill instructor stood at the back of the chow hall, observing what had just taken place. I could feel the telepathic waves of anger being getting off the side of my face as my drill instructor ran toward me seemingly at one hundred miles an hour then pressing his campaign cover to the side of my face. The pressure was so great I was slightly knocked off balance. He leaned over and whispered in my ear, "You fucking owe me, bitch." I was so traumatized I could barely eat my breakfast with that thought of going to jail or being thrashed by my drill instructor. Either way, it wouldn't have a good outcome.

Right after we had our limited portions of food, we returned to the barracks and changed into our PT gear. We then headed to the obstacle course and for three miles ran alongside the wooden fence line separating the Marine Corps base from the airport. I couldn't help but be envious every time I saw the naval sailors standing outside smoking a cigarette and laughing at us while we ran for three miles in the one-hundred-degree weather.

The navy boot camp was next door to MCRD. There was one small difference: they were on a six-week vacation, and we were going through sixteen weeks of hell. The naval boot camp program was very different. They ate chow whenever they wanted to and weren't forced to eat vegetables like I was. My drill instructor would stand behind in the chow line at breakfast, lunch, and dinner and order the line personnel to put stacks of broccoli, cauliflower, and carrots on my plate. I would take the vegetables and give them to the marine next to me or hide them in my ice cream cup and cover the vegetables with napkins. Sometimes my drill instructor would stand by the exit and inspect my tray if I still had vegetables on my plate. He would stand over me until I ate them, but most of the time, I was able to get away with throwing them in the trash. The drill instructor said I would need the vegetables to get up mount motherfucker. I didn't understand what he meant at the time because it was too early in my training, and I was still adjusting to all the yelling and screaming at 4:00 a.m.

The sailors stood outside on their balconies, smoking cigarettes, laughing, while pointing at us as we ran along the fence line in the sweltering heat. Sampson and I were running neck to neck, and all of a sudden, he disappeared. Someone shoved him into a fire hydrant, breaking his right leg. I finished my run around twenty-one minutes. Then down the strip came Sampson. He completed the three-mile run in twenty-four minutes with a broken leg. The drill instructor didn't seem to care that Sampson had just broken his leg. He ordered Sampson to continue running until he reached the ambulance, so Sampson limped his way over to the ambulance and disappeared for three days.

The drill instructors could have dropped him from the platoon at this point, but he demonstrated courage and heart when he finished the three-mile run in twenty-four minutes with a broken leg. Having a broken leg aided Sampson with skating out of a lot of duties. He didn't have to march to church; he was allowed to stay in the barracks and watch all the gear. Everyone went to church. It didn't matter what religion you were; you were forced to attend. After church, we spent Sunday afternoon washing our clothes on a concrete slab then hanging our clothes up on a clothesline. We finished the weekend off with polishing our boots and reading on knowledge while the drill instructor paced up and down the squad bay.

After the second month, my sleep had a new definition: the definition of military time. I no longer slept until eight in the morning. My mind was now preset to 4:00 a.m. We packed our gear and lined up in formation on the parade grinder. We're on our way to Camp Pendleton for marksmanship training. I was feeling pretty cocky at this point. I even felt like I could complete the entire sixteen weeks of training. We were allowed to unbutton our collars and roll up our sleeves and blouse or trousers. I had a smile hidden inside that I dare not reveal in front of my drill instructors, but I must admit I was feeling pretty good—so good that I leaned over and spit on the parade deck.

The drill instructor saw me out of the corner of his eye. He yelled, "Get your ass over here, Private." I ran over to the drill instructor and locked my body at attention. He leaned forward, pressing his campaign hat against my forehead. He said, "Lick it up!" He stared deep into my eyes as I took a deep breath. I squatted down and wiped to spit up with my right hand. I locked my body at attention, assuming the worst. I thought for sure I was going to jail, but he gave me a stern look and said, "Get on the bus, crazy one."

The bus ride from San Diego to Camp Pendleton took about forty-five minutes. We sat at attention the whole time with our eyes on the back of the head of the man in front of us. My drill instructor sat at the front of the bus and began to doze off. I took the opportunity to enjoy the scenic view. I relaxed my shoulders and shifted my eyes outside of the window, getting a quick view of the red rooftops that we stayed at from our barracks for the last two months. It looked just like the pictures in the *Right On* magazine—beaches stretching along the coast of the highways and palm trees as far as the eye could see. My daydreaming came to an abrupt end once the bus came to a screeching stop. All hell broke loose once again. The harassment continued even while we sat on bleachers in the marksmanship class. Our drill instructor would tap ten of us on the shoulder, then take us behind the bleachers, and thrash us for fifteen minutes, making us roll around in the sand until our bodies were totally covered from head to toe. "Make it rain," he yelled as we threw sand in the air.

Once we were filthy from head to toe, he would get ten more recruits until he went through the entire platoon. I couldn't focus and learn a damn thing. Every time they tried to teach us something, the drill instructor would find a way to harass us in the midst of our military education. I was qualifying at the marksman skill level, but I was losing confidence fast. A young recruit next to me had been recycled back two weeks because he failed marksmanship training. I wasn't about to repeat any cycle, so I pretended as though I couldn't see the target and needed glasses. I was pulled from the firing line and told to guard all our file cabinets and seabags on the parade grinder. The shooting finally stopped as the young recruits completed marksmanship qualification. Everyone lined up to turn in their empty shell casing and wooden ammo blocks. All of a sudden, there was a single shot fired; and within seconds, one of the drill instructors came running toward me, asking for a file on the private that shot himself, then ran back to administer first aid.

The young marine recruit that stood next to me killed himself rather than repeat another two weeks of hell. We returned to San Diego for our last month of boot camp. Part of our training included working in the chow hall or working on the lawn maintenance detail. Two weeks after that, we packed up once again to return to Camp Pendleton for infantry training school. We were still at an incredible pace, and that pace would intensify once we went through the infiltration course with machine guns firing over our heads as we crawled on our stomachs under barbed wire, trying not to trip the wires and set off the night flares. I thought it was easy and fun, but other recruits thought it was a horrible ordeal to go through. We slept outside the infiltration course that night and awoke to a mountain towering ten miles up into the air.

We wore full combat gear including a backpack, helmet, and a long wooden shovel that beat the crap out of our leg as we climbed steadily up the mountain at an insanely fast pace. My drill instructor was right. I did need the vegetables, and I was paying the price for dumping them in the trash. The mountain was steep— so steep that my face nearly scraped the ground as I went up. I watched the first platoon flag as it turned the corner and disappeared. I thought for sure we're at the top, but as I turned the corner, the flag was still going up and up. I had no thoughts of home in my head. I didn't even think about finger banging Cindy through her pretty pink panties.

I was in excruciating pain from head to toe. The marine that I gave my vegetables to asked if I wanted to grab onto his backpack, but I was too proud, so I sucked it up and picked a focal point. Up the mountain, I went. As soon as we got to the top of the mountain, our drill instructors begin to bin and thrash us. "Make it rain," they yelled as we rolled around in the dirt. The dirt clung to our body because our camouflage utilities were saturated with sweat. Our face was covered with dirt and sweat, slowly turning into mud with small thorns from the brush lying on the ground sticking out of our trousers. We stood at attention with our eyes locked on the back of the head of the man in front of us. We couldn't blink, speak, or wipe the sweat and mud off our face. All I could think about was I had three weeks left and I would be done with this nightmare. We returned to MCRD (Marine Corps Recruit Depot) two weeks after arriving at infantry training school. All we had left was guard duty. Then we turned our rifles in and prepare for graduation. The Marine Corps boot camp definitely changed me. My good nature had been soured, and my infectious smile had all but disappeared.

I had been beaten on and beaten up for eighty-two training days in a life I wouldn't recommend for my children or grandchildren; in fact, I wouldn't recommend it for anyone. Three weeks later, I was back in Indianapolis as a different man with different perspectives but one agenda. After two weeks of leave, I was on my way to Camp Pendleton where my tour of duty would begin. Our routine wasn't much different than boot camp. The only difference was I didn't have drill instructors yelling in my face, and the pace was slightly slower. Other than that, it still sucked. Cindy and I wrote to each other every day. I'd go home to visit twice a year except for the summer 1979. I was still just a nineteen-year-old kid running around the barracks, pulling pranks on the older marines. I always believed it's not where you live but how you live.

Living in marine barracks was very boring at times especially if you didn't have money. I spent most my time at the recreation center on base, playing pool or watching one of the two TV stations. Sometimes I became very mischievous. One Sunday I had absolutely nothing to do, so I began organizing my room. I was cleaning out the old wall lockers. While shuffling through the wall lockers, I found a mask of a scary monster stuffed away at the bottom of the empty locker. I put the mask on and walked around the barracks, knocking on doors unexpectedly, scaring everyone that answered the door. The biggest toughest guys in unit would slam the door in my face until they realized it was just a mask. I went from door to door, scaring everyone I could until it's my time to return to duty desk.

It was my turn to stand duty that night, but I wasn't sleepy, so I sat outside on the steps of the barracks and listened to the quietness of the night. I often thought about Cindy and how much I missed her. I enviously watched the buses leave the base loaded down with marines trying to escape for the weekend in Oceanside. Later that evening, I was summoned to put on my cartridge belt and sit at the NCO desk; occasionally, I would patrol the hallways of the barracks, ensuring that no rooms were broken into and there were no fights. Anything that happened out of the ordinary, I'd record it in my duty log and call the duty NCO or officer of the day.

Having duty on the weekends was a much-disliked responsibility each marine performed monthly. Most of the marines would offer to pay someone $30 to stand their post on the weekend. I obliged them as long as they paid me $30 upfront cash. I wasn't familiar with Oceanside or the people that inhabited the city, so I spent most of my time hanging out on the base. I thought to myself, *Since I'm going to be here anyway, I may as well get paid for it.* So I sat at the duty NCO desk, reading my magazines and counting my newfound wealth.

One night, while patrolling the barracks, I began to smell smoke. I alerted the duty NCO and showed him the location of fire. We banged on the door, trying to wake the sleeping marine, but to no avail. I was ordered by the duty NCO to climb through the window and open the door. I did as I was ordered. I climbed through the window and discovered a marine sleeping on a burning mattress. I opened the door, then went back, and grabbed the marine under the armpits and dragged him in the hallway to safety, dousing the mattress with several buckets of water.

The next week I was hailed as a hero and given a meritorious mast certificate. Nothing changed for me at that point. I was still an E-3 and performing every shit detail the other seasoned marines didn't want to do. If the cannon base plates needed to be greased, I was sent up the hill to the gun park to grease all six base plates for the cannons. No liberty was granted until all the rust was removed from all six cannons and the base plates were greased for the weekend. So I ran up the hill in the rain, slipping and sliding in the mud. As I dug the toe of my boots into the mud, the marines stood down the hill, sarcastically cheering me on, "Hurry up, you boot. Come on, get a move on, boot!" *Boot* was a derogatory term used for marines fresh out of boot camp, and I was as green as they came. So I climbed the hill and greased all six cannons base plates then I ran back down the hill, demonstrating sure-footed accuracy as if I was a goat scaling the Rocky Mountains, back down through the brush cover trench, and up the slight incline to the paved parking lot where formation was being held.

My unit was still screaming, "Boot, boot, boot, boot!" I stood there soaking wet listening to the chants. My highly spit-shined boots were covered with a clay-like mud; my camouflage utilities were soaked from head to toe. It was pouring down at this point. We were standing at attention, silently looking and listening to the first sergeant pontificate the rules of how we should conduct ourselves while on weekend liberty; and finally, he yelled, "Dismissed!" I ran from the formation back to the barracks and began stripping my uniform off as my foot hit the door. I quickly threw my clothes in the washer and jumped in the shower to wash off the reminisce of grease deep in the pores of my skin.

I could see a person's head poking back and forth on the other side of the shower wall and occasionally peeking around the corner into the shower. I paid no attention because there were no females on base, so I ignored it and finished taking my shower. Wrapping my towel around my waist, I slipped and slid my way back to my room, my shower shoes sticking to the floor, eventually breaking apart, leaving one shower shoe in the hallway as I hobbled back to my room on one leg.

I was starving. The aroma coming from the chow hall was fiercely whetting my appetite. I quickly got dressed in my civilian clothes, pausing for a brief second to stare out the window at the line of marines that stretched around the chow hall. Marines stood in the pouring rain, waiting to enter the building. I was very fortunate I could sit in the warmth of my room and watch the line shrink. It was an off payday. Everyone was broke. This was very typical for young marines. If you were an E-1 to E-3, you only got paid $600 a month. Half our money was spent on the roach coach, a lunch wagon that came around the barracks blowing its horn at night, soliciting snacks and getting marines to spend the last bit of their pay. The other half of our money was spent on bars in town, on movies, and on women at the possibility of having a one-night stand. I wasn't broke. I was one of the few young marines in the camp that had money. I had a pocket full of money and nowhere to go.

I spent most of my time at the gym on base, hitting the punching bag, jump-roping, or just reading a book in my room. I wasn't familiar with my new surroundings; therefore, I only went to town when I was with a group of trusted friends. Most of the guys I hung around with were young and inexperienced like me. We didn't hang out in bars as the mature guys did. Sampson and I would go to the beach, mall, movies, or Burger King.

He hobbled along beside me casket and all. I wasn't a party type of guy, but if I wanted to, I could go in a bar and drink even though I was underage. The barkeeper didn't care about age. He only cared about how much money they could get us to spend. Every night was the same once we left town. Everyone would crowd around the bus stop and rush the door before the bus door opened or came to a complete stop. The bus driver would just take off and go to the next stop, making us chase the bus to the next block. Once we got on the bus there was standing-room only. When the bus entered the gate to the base, the military police (MPs) made everyone get off the bus and conducted an informal search of the bus and all the marines riding on it.

Within twenty minutes, we were back on our way. The marines thought the bus was moving too slow, so we rocked the bus bac and forth, demanding that the bus driver go faster. The driver pulled to the side of the road and demanded that we stop rocking the bus. The more he demanded, the more we rocked the bus, almost turning it on its side. The bus driver became so scared he jumped in his driver's seat and raced down los pocus road, breaking the speed limit by at least fifteen miles per hour. Every night it was the same thing, and every night I just sat back in my seat and laughed. We worked hard, and we played hard as well.

Most of my free time I spent in the barracks writing letters to Cindy and thinking about my old friends in my neighborhood—what they were doing and who was at the basketball court. I thought about my mom and how I've missed living in her house. I thought about my oldest brother and his sexual escapades. I thought about my brother Reggie joined the army and my sister Sherry in the air force. I thought about how nice it would've been if I had stayed home and got a regular job and had a regular life. But that wasn't reality, and this was my new reality. Something inside of me was changing, but I didn't know what it was. Maybe I was becoming a man, or maybe I was becoming a professional killer. Whatever it was changing inside of me would alter the way I think forever. I love the beach and the palm trees and the entire California atmosphere. It was far different from Indiana.

California seemed very fast paced. Women would roller-skate along the beach, wearing bikinis. You would've never seen anything like that Indiana. She would have been arrested and put in jail for indecent exposure. California even had nude beaches that I spent most my time trying to find, but I was told they were forty-five minutes away by bus ride. There were orgy houses, where a person could pay $25 to get in and have sex with anyone they saw including someone's wife. California was wild and out of control; therefore, I stayed to my boring Indiana ways: watching TV, playing an occasional game of basketball, or spending time in the gym. I stayed in the barracks so long I was beginning to get cabin fever. I just couldn't eat one more burrito from the roach coach or watch one more episode of Gomer Pyle. I had to get out of the barracks and out into life.

A Day of Normalcy

Saturday morning I decided to venture out in town early. I put twenty bucks in my pocket, just enough for a round-trip bus ride to and from base and possibly some lunch. I tucked the rest of my money inside of a book hidden on the top of my wall locker. I had a safe-proof lock, so I thought. I watched the commercials of a lock being shot with a rifle and still didn't open until one marine demonstrated how quickly he could get through my lock with one slap of his hammer, so I relocated my money to another spot. I lifted my bed up and removed the stopper at the base of the bed post. Then I shoved my money up the pole of my bed, and off to Oceanside I went. I walked around the town, endlessly looking in the store windows, hanging out on the beach, or just watching people as part of my weekend fun; finally, I went into the barbershop to get my weekly haircut.

This was something new for me. I had never been to a barbershop what all the barber were white males. I was unsure about the outcome, but I thought, *Marines only wear regulation high and tight haircuts, so it really doesn't matter how the haircut turns out.* When he was done, he handed me the mirror to check out the back of my head. I noticed a ball spot beginning to form in the center of my scalp, indicating the first signs of alopecia. I was horrified at the possibility of going bald. I must have sat in the chair for two minutes, looking in the mirror while rubbing the small circle spot on the back of my head.

I couldn't stay there all day; so I jumped out of the chair, gave the barber $5, and out to the sunny streets of Oceanside I went. The streets were jam-packed with young marines and young prostitutes relieving them of their hard-earned pay. It was a total culture shock, not like Indianapolis, which was restricted by color. In California, more than just blacks and whites populated the city; the population of California was well mixed. Women from different cultures with long beautiful black hair stretching down their back lay openly on the beaches in their skimpy bathing suits. I thought I had found a part of heaven, walking along the beach with my tongue dragging in the sand, looking at all the beautiful exposed bodies as far as the eye could see.

I couldn't stand it anymore, so I jumped on the bus and headed to May Company Mall. There was a young girl on the bus sitting directly across from me. Her long athletic legs were covered with stockings that had runs in them. I didn't care. I worked all day five days a week, so this was a sight to behold. She wore a black miniskirt with a tight white T-shirt displaying her well-proportioned torso. She stared at me for a while then struck up a conversation; before I knew it, we were walking around the mall together, shopping. She couldn't have been more than eighteen years old or the same age as I. We walked and talked for hours, browsing through several stores. I was becoming quite comfortable with her, stepping close behind her while she looked at his shirts and pants. I seductively assisted her by holding some pants to her waistline while she looked over her shoulder into the mirror. I was in hog heaven. I hadn't been this close to a woman in months, and I had to say it did feel good. I stayed with her that day for about five hours, looking at stockings, jewelry, and miscellaneous items of furniture. I walked closely behind her, heading toward the register so she could purchase a new pair of black stockings.

She led me into a part of the mall I had never been; then she walked into a secluded corner of the mall, placing one hand on my shoulder to bounce her weight. She reached up her skirt and pulled off her stockings. "Hold on to these," she said, laying the stockings on my shoulder. She removed her new stockings from the packet and began putting one leg at a time in each stocking then pulling the pantyhose up slightly to display her naked pelvic region.

She wasn't wearing a stitch of underwear. Her skin was as smooth and soft as cotton. Her unshaved vagina looked like a beaver pelt. I felt faint as the blood left my feet, and my head centralized once again in my pelvic region to form a massive erection. I felt lightheaded and unresponsive. I was just beginning to go into starvation mode when she suggested going to lunch. I stood there in a daze, staring at her. I could see her mouth moving, but I wasn't hearing anything. She snapped her fingers and patted me on the side of my face, saying, "Come on, let's go eat. I know the perfect place." She grabbed my hand. Her female touch almost made me drool from the mouth, but I stayed in control. Off we went back into the mall. She walked slightly in front of me, pulling me down the hallways of the mall as if I were her boyfriend or husband. I purposely lingered behind her, trying to catch a glimpse of those long beautiful legs covered with $1.98 stockings.

The restaurant was beautiful. White tablecloths covered every table with fancy napkins made into the shape of animals, with a candle burning brightly in the center of each table. *What was I doing in a place like this?* I thought to myself. I began to feel awkward or out of place because I barely had enough money to pay for myself, and I always felt it was the man's job to pay for the meal. I told her to give me a second; then I ditched around the corner. I began counting my money. I had $11 to my name. I was so embarrassed I could only afford to pay for my meal and definitely knew I couldn't pay for hers. We sat down to lunch. I scooted her chair under her, trying to be a total gentleman. It was my first time using an actual menu. I knew I was in trouble.

I scoured the menu quickly with my eyes. The cheapest thing on the menu was a tuna melt sandwich, and it cost $7 without fries. Even the water was a dollar a glass. I frantically calculated the taxes in my head. My meal cost slightly less then I had in my pocket. I had another $1.50 stuffed in my socks, but I wouldn't dare use it because it was my means of transportation back to the base.

She could see the trepidation on my face. She reached across the table and delicately touched my hand. "We can go Dutch," she said. I squinted my eyes, indicating I was confused. "We can each pay for our own meal," she said. I internally let go a sigh of relief. My vertebrae were no longer locked into position, and I was finally able to swallow the lump in my throat. She ordered a huge meal costing somewhere around $15. I felt naked, sitting there with my paltry little tuna melt sandwich with garnishment decorating the plate. I pretended as though I hated fries to save myself the embarrassment when the check came. I played smart and just ordered tuna fish sandwich, and $0.10 more, I added a slice of cheese so as not to show that I was too broke. She sat in front of me with a huge platter of food, forking it down, not even catching her breath between bites. She ate fast like she was in boot camp. I nibbled around the edges of my tuna fish sandwich, taking my time and trying to make it last. I stared across the table at her slim perfectly built frame, fantasizing about the possibility of a sexual encounter.

We talked for an hour and seemingly grew comfortable enough with each other to talk about our heritage and where we were from. She said she was from East LA. She was Hispanic. She grew up in a dysfunctional family plagued by gangs and violence. She needed to get away from the violence of her everyday life. That's why she moved to Oceanside, California. I began to feel a sense of friendship developing between us. The thought of pulling slick moves to get close to her dissipated from my mind. I gave her space, not even trying to slip my hand around her beautiful thin waist. Eventually, we caught another bus back to Oceanside Boulevard where she led me into a pool hall filled with young marines smoking cigarettes and drinking beer. The last place I wanted to be was around a bunch of jarheads. She seemed very popular and right at home as she made her rounds greeting everyone she saw. Everyone in the pool hall knew her. A few men walked up to her, picked her up, and kissed her on the jaw.

Several men propositioned her for dates later in the evening; before accepting, she looked over her shoulder at me then back to business as usual. I observed her for few more minutes, and all of a sudden, it hit me: she was a prostitute. I quietly slipped out of pool hall and walked down to a hoagie's corner and purchased a $0.50 piece of beef jerky to snack on for the bus ride back to the base. I climbed onto the first bus and stared out the window, thinking about my day as the bus twisted and turned down Los pogus's dark winding road. It was a long quiet ride; only two other marines occupied the bus because it was still early in the day. Most marines didn't return to the base until the last bus left Oceanside at twelve thirty early in the morning. I sat in the back of the bus, trying to get clarity about what just happened. I came to the understanding that this young girl just wanted to feel normal for one day. Maybe she wanted to experience what it was like for other girls her same age who weren't dating for money or being offered money for sex. I believe this was the closest she would come to feeling normal. This was the first time in months that I had an intimate relationship with a female. The woman's soft touch and the smell of her perfume was a welcoming fragrance.

It had been seven months since I'd visited Indianapolis as well as several months since I had sex. I was nineteen years old and horny as hell. I had trouble sleeping at night and often lay on my back due to the massive and out-of-control erections I was having during sleeping hours. I was so young and inexperienced I didn't even know how to masturbate. At that time, I had only seen one porno magazine in my life when I was twelve years old, sitting on the front porch of the Kemps house. I was fine doing daylight hours because I was preoccupied with my job as a cannoneer. But when the night fell, I was alone and didn't have anything to deter me from thinking about the 36DDs I saw during my high school days and the last time Cindy and I had sex .

I stayed up most nights with an erection that would cripple the average man. *I can't take it anymore!* I screamed in my head. I was determined to get laid. After several months of abstinence, it became mental sexual torment. Five in the evening on Friday, we were released to go to chow then return to begin cleaning the barracks. We scrubbed and polished the bathroom floors for three hours before the first inspection. The tall squared-away brass lieutenant walked in as though he was inspecting the barracks at the eighth and I duty station in Washington DC. He rubbed his hand across the wall and under the bathroom sinks, pulling one finger out with less than a microfiber of dust. He said, "It's not clean. Continue to field day and call me when it's ready."

Everyone was thoroughly pissed off. The lieutenant want to play mind-fuck games and keep us cleaning the bathrooms all night. After two more hours of thoroughly cleaning the barracks, scrubbing walls, scrubbing in and behind the toilet, we felt we were ready for another inspection. We sent the runner to summon the lieutenant. He strutted down the hallway of the barracks, belching from the tuna fish sandwich he just finished. He walked in the bathroom and looked at the rolled toilet paper. "It's too thin," he said. "Replace to roll and call me when you're done." He strutted toward the door as though he owned world. After replacing all the rolls of toilet paper in the stall, we sprayed Windex on the toilets to give them a nice shine and the appearance of being brand-new.

We used our toothbrushes and scrubbed around the edges of the toilets, spotting any visible seam. We sent a runner into town to purchase civilian bathroom cleaning products. After three more hours of cleaning and scrubbing, we sent for the lieutenant. By this time, it was one in the morning. The lieutenant strutted down the hallway as fresh as he was at 5:00 p.m., not a hair out of place. I sat back and observed as he bent down on one knee and wiped his finger around the edge of the toilet. Lifting the seat of the toilet, he turned and said, "This toilet is not clean." A sergeant said, "Pardon me, sir. The toilet is clean." "Well, Sergeant, this toilet is not clean, and you just failed another inspection. I'll come back at 4:00 a.m.," the lieutenant said. The sergeant said, "Sir, if I can prove the toilet is clean, would you release us for the night?" "How are you going to prove that?" said the lieutenant. The sergeant got down on one knee. Reaching into the bowl with both hands, he scooped out water from the toilet and drank from his hands. The lieutenant looked at the sergeant and said, "You're secure for the night." It was almost two o'clock in the morning. The bus was no longer running on the base at that hour, and I think everyone was too tired to chase women or go bar hopping.

Saturday mornings were the best of all. It was one of few days the Marine Corps didn't bother us. So I moseyed over to the chow hall before catching the bus to San Diego to see a movie. I thought a movie would help distract my thoughts from any sexual desires, but the movie had two sexual scenes that had me reeling from the theater in search of a drug store where I could purchase some type of prophylactic for a possible night of sexual ecstasy. Right after the movie, I decided to cruise the San Diego strip. I was one block away from the theater before being quickly approached by a young white girl. She was around twenty-five years old with dirty-blonde hair. She was a BWG (basic white girl) with a nondescript body. She looked and smelled different from the girls I grew up with. The girls at my high school smelled like pickles and Kool-Aid, a popular snack in the seventies. The girls carried pickles and Kool-Aid straws in their purses, providing themselves with a snack in a moment's notice.

The pickles looked as though they were on steroids. They were large and sealed in a plastic bag with juice. The Kool-Aid straws were long, at least twenty-four inches, hosting several different flavors. This girl was different: not only was she from a different ethnic group, her blonde hair was straight and lifeless, not possessing any body, curl, or style. She reeked of cigarette smoke and seemed very overt and aggressive as she walked upon me fast as if she was trying to beat someone else to the punch. She said, "I am the best." I looked at her with a confused look on my face and said, "You're the best at what?" She paused for a second looked at me, squinting her eyes while taking a long drag from her cigarette. If I didn't know better, I would think she was rehearsing for a Humphrey Bogart movie. "I'm the best at giving head," she said. "You're a cop," I implied, "and I don't have any time to sit in jail." She looked at me with astonishment and said, "I'm not a cop! Just ask the other women around," so I made my way up and down the street, checking her credentials. After ten minutes of asking questions while observing her from a distance, I discovered she was telling the truth that she wasn't a cop.

I slowly made my way back toward her within an out-of-control erection. I leaned over and whispered in her ear, "How much?" She said, "It'll cost you $20." " I don't have $20," I said while searching through my wallet. "How much do you have?" "I have $14." She looked at me disappointedly, rolling her eyes. "That's okay. It's enough to buy me a pack of cigarettes. Let's go," she said. We jumped into a yellow taxi heading around the corner just a little more than a mile to her house. I was creeped out by the entire scene, but I was being led blindly by my massive erection.

I didn't have a clear thought in my head. I was being controlled by my little head, not my big head, which made me forget about any possible dangers that might have been lurking inside her house. Her room was a very basic setup—just for business—with a full-size bed shoved in the corner, a cheap night table, and a lamp without a shade using a low-wattage bulb. She sat on the bed next to me and went right to work. She unzipped my pants and pulled them down to my knees. My penis popped out like a jackknife slightly grazing her nose. "Oh my, you're ready," she said. She reached into the drawer and pulled out a box of Magnum condoms, but condom after condom kept breaking repeatedly as she tried to place it on my massive erection; finally, she gave up and went down on me to provide a form of lubrication. This was another difference between her and the girls I knew in high school. It was a new experience all around, and I instantly loved it.

Finally, she succeeded slipping the rubber on after ten minutes of oral lubrication. Once she was done performing oral sex on me, she propped herself up against the wall in an upright position, indicating I should return the favor of going down on her, but I gave her a look as though "You got me fucked up. I'm not your boyfriend and I'm definitely not going to perform oral sex on you." So I climbed aboard, and I rode her for fifteen minutes. To my surprise, she wasn't stretched out beyond belief. Her vagina was as normal as any high school girl I slept with in the past. I exploded inside of her like a fire hose. Her legs shook like spaghetti in boiling water, and she slightly dug her nails into my shoulders. She couldn't believe the amount of semen I unloaded in her. She screamed as I filled her vaginal walls with my semen. I was so exhausted afterward I thought I lost at least one pound. She didn't even give me time to recover. She Hurried me out of her room, keeping on schedule for the next John, so I got dressed quickly and started jogging back to the bus station before the last bus departed to Oceanside. I felt slightly better, but I was still horny as hell and could hardly wait until next month to go home on leave.

Two Thousand Five Hundred Miles Away from Home

After weeks and weeks of dreaming about going home, July arrived; and before I knew it, I was thirty-five thousand feet in the air, catching jet lag. Over the course of seven months, our relationship thrived only on letters and postcards, continuously building on a relationship of infatuation rather than love. I hung out at her house day and night. Her mother never requested that I leave, but she listened throughout the night to ensure that Cindy did not creep back down stairs; but unfortunately for her, we were young, so we did what people do. We fell into the age-old trap of lust and desire. At two in the morning, Cindy found her way downstairs, and I found my way inside her nightgown.

We fed our starving sexual desires at the Quality Inn Hotel across from the state fairgrounds or at Riverside Park where we quenched our sexual appetite three or four times throughout the week. Cindy was just as excited as I. We made love for hours, playing catch-up, after a seven-month dry spell. We spent the next fifteen days hanging out at the park, having sex where time and space permitted. Cindy loved material possessions and felt since I was her boyfriend, I was supposed to buy her a $400 stereo system. I had just under $300 to my name, but I reluctantly gave it to her in hopes it would make her happy. But she was thoroughly pissed off because I was $100 short, so she tossed the money back to me and went home. I felt kind of bad about the whole thing, about her not being able to buy her stereo, but I didn't feel bad enough to give her the money again. I purchased a ten sack of White Castles and a large chocolate shake and sat on my mother's patio and wished I didn't have to return to the base; before I knew it, I had to return to camp Pendleton.

My fifteen days of leave came to a bitter end. I grabbed and hugged Cindy before reluctantly boarding the airplane. I walked down the lonely thirty-foot ramp and took my seat in the coach section of the plane. I raised and lowered the window shade on the plane several times, signaling good-bye. Everyone else walked away, hurrying to the car to claim the shotgun-seat ride back home. My mother stayed until the plane flew out of the tarmac. Once the plane was in the air, she went to her car. I sat on the plane, looking forlorn with my face pressed against the window, staring at the open sky. The stewardess noticed my uniform and the lone look on my face, so she walked over and asked if I wanted to sit in first class. I looked up at her, holding back my tears. I could barely speak, but I was able to say, "No, thank you." I knew I had made a mistake enlisting in the corps for four years. I missed my family and my friends. It was a part of my life that I could never get back, watching my siblings grow up and my mother gracefully age to the person she came to today. I could feel the distance widening between us as the plane climbed to thirty thousand feet. I had four years of family memories that would never be realized, only memories of myself and the man I served with in the corps.

Chocolate Mountains

I reported back to my unit and was told to pack my gear as we're heading out to Chocolate Mountains, Arizona. We loaded our trucks with axes, picks, shovels, a huge camouflage net, and personal weapons including an M-60 caliber machine gun and a 50-caliber antiaircraft weapon. We hitched our cannons to the back of the five-ton trucks and staged them at the gun park. We stood in formation to listen to a one-hour lecture on safety: Don't play with the rattlesnakes. Don't mess with unexploded ordnance. They told us not to do all the things they knew marines would do.

The next morning we were off rolling down the highway at sixty miles an hour, dragging 15,500-pound cannons behind us, trucks stretching two miles long down the highway. The ride was long. Sweltering heat and hard wooden benches made it very difficult to enjoy the scenic view. Seabags were stacked ceiling high in the back of the truck. The locker meant for storing tools was jam-packed with pogey bait, extra food marines bring to the field to keep from eating sea rations. We became very creative in our boredom. We ripped apart cardboard boxes and wrote messages, asking women to pull their shirts up displaying their breasts. Screams could be heard from the last truck all the way to the leading truck as the civilian women passed by exposing their breasts.

Two guys in the back of my truck began to argue about nothing. The white guy repeatedly called the Cuban guy Fidel. They were almost at blows, so I positioned myself between them to keep them from fighting. It was all I could do prevent them from destroying the back of the truck. Later that evening, we arrived at Chocolate Mountains, Arizona. In the distance, I could see heatwaves streaming across the desert. It was as if the devil had turned on the oven to boil and walked away. It was seven at night and still one hundred degrees in the shade. No one was allowed to bunk down until all the vehicles and equipment were prepared for a training exercise: setting up our nets on top of the trucks, reorganizing the back of the trucks, making room for loading one hundred live artillery shells, and stacking case after case of sea rations, as well as four five-gallon cans of water.

The next morning I was awakened by the sound of diesel fuel coming from trucks, revving their engines. Thick gray smoke poured from their stacks. Amtrak's amphibious assault vehicles and tanks were the first to pull out. Artillery followed close behind. The infantry hit the ground, running the same day we arrived. They never stopped humping until they marched ten miles beyond the artillery and tank units. After hours of driving, we took position in a desolate place in the middle of nowhere. I was given a five-gallon can of water, a case of C rations, and a prick radio. I was told to guard the road and not allow anyone to come within five miles of the live fire zone. I was left in that desolate part of the desert by myself for four days without seeing another human being. I spent my nights staring at the sky full of stars thinking about Cindy and what she was doing. I spent my days trying to stay out of the sun and the sweltering heat. I found myself doing all the things they told us not to do in the briefing before coming to the desert.

In my fourth day guarding the road, I became extremely bored, so I began to do all the things the Marine Corps told us not to do. I looked for snakes, poking and prodding in the holes, hoping to force him out the backside. While walking, I nearly tripped over a five-hundred-pound unexploded bomb dropped by one of our navy jets. I backed up very slowly, placing one foot behind the other delicately on the ground until I was nearly one hundred paces away. I grabbed my prick radio and reported the unexploded shell. Jeeps filled with ordnance personnel appeared out of nowhere as though they rolled right out of the sand. I was transported to the top of a hill and watched as the ordinance crew placed C-4 and Primacord wrapped around the unexploded shell, destroying the shell and everything within fifty meters of it. An hour later, I was returned to my unit three shades darker than when I left. I couldn't help but smile from ear to ear as I tossed my gear into the back of the truck and squatted down next to the tire to prepare a stove to heat my C rations. Just as my food was warming up, I heard a loud explosion. Everyone stood up at once, trying to get a fix on what direction the explosion came from. We could see smoke coming from 150 yards away; then all of a sudden, a navy jet broke through the clouds, swooping down on top of us, dropping another shell a little closer this time within 125 yards of our position.

Scrap metal sprayed the area, ripping through the truck tarps and piercing the metal on the truck doors. Captain Moore grabbed the prick radio and tried to call for ceasefire as the third navy jet was turning the corner. Everyone was running for their life, but there was nothing to hide behind because the shells were falling to close to the trucks to take cover. We ran as far and as fast as we could from the drop zone before the third shell hit the ground. Three marines were hit with strap metal, and one marine jumped on a cactus bush. I lay behind a telephone pole that somehow ended up in the middle of the desert. I buried my face deep in the sand. I could hear the scrap metal hitting the pole and grazing the top of my helmet. Just as we thought it was safe, another jet turned the corner with its engine roaring. The jet was ahead of its sound, but this time, I looked straight at the jet coming down right on top of us, preparing to drop another five-hundred-pound shell. My commanding officer grabbed a smoke grenade and tossed it as far as he could into the drop zone. The jets saw the smoke and pulled away from our position.

The scrap metal from the boom disabled two of the cannons, flatting their tires and shattering the windshields of several trucks;

therefore, a marine and I were put on a truck and sent to the rear to guard the ammo dump. I reluctantly grabbed my gear and dragged it over to the ammo dump. I sat at the dump for two days with the sun beating directly down on my head. There was no cover. We weren't allowed to put up a tent because the helicopters would come in and kick up so much sand and wind it and pull the tents out of the ground and rip them into shred. So we sat there in the sweltering and blistering sun reluctantly getting a complete body tan that we didn't need.

We had only been in the desert a week, and already, my skin was looking dry and brittle. My lips were chapped, and the lip balm and Vaseline provided little relief. The winds were picking up, making little sand twisters less than a foot from the stacks of ammunition. There was news of a possible sandstorm heading our way. Only, the news had arrived two minutes too late. I couldn't see one foot in front of me, and within minutes, our cannons were practically buried up to the top of the tires. All the low-ranking personnel were forced to walk guard duty, standing outside in the middle of the storm, protecting equipment that no civilian knew was even there. We rotated shifts: three hours on and three off. No one really stayed awake during the twilight hours. They would just pass the fire watch list, watch and flashlight on to the next fire watch. I had the 2:00 a.m. to 4:00 a.m. shift. I loved being away doing the twilight hours when everyone else was asleep, but this was different.

I was totally exhausted from the day's activities and quickly fell into a deep sleep. Someone tapped me on the shoulder then handed me the flashlight and watch. I shined the flashlight on the watch to check the time. I rolled over and just stayed in my sleeping bag until my shift ended, wearing nothing but boots, a T-shirt and camouflage utilities. I walked twenty-five meters to the other cannon and handed the watch and flashlight to the next person on patrol. I turned around and took ten paces and realized I couldn't see one foot in front of me. I waved my hand back and forth less than an inch in front of my face. I couldn't see it because it was pitch black. I yelled out to the marines sleeping around my cannon, but there was no response, so I walked in the direction from which I came. Still, I couldn't see anyone; so I squatted down, trying to see an outline of a truck or tent, but there was nothing there. So I yelled out once again, and once again, no one responded. I began walking in the direction I thought it came from. I must have walked around for more than an hour, believing I was walking around my unit's location but I was at least five or six miles down the road where the amphibious assault vehicle division was located. I kept walking in the freezing cold from the bitter night air. My leather boots felt hard as rocks because of the cold weather and the absence of wearing socks. The farther I walked, the farther I was moving away from my unit. I looked down and saw grunts lying in their two-man fighting positions. I knew I had gone too far, so I did a 180 and went back in the other direction. More than an hour and a half passed, and I was finally back to my unit. I located some communication wire in the middle of our camp clearly marked and leading to each cannon. I figured out which wire led to my cannon, so I traced the wire all the way back to my canon then lifelessly lay down on my cot and closed my eyes for ten minutes before reveille was sounded. I was exhausted, and my misfortune was we just began a three-day no-sleep training exercise that morning. We moved nonstop all day and silently into the night, dragging our cannons behind us kicking up nose-clogging dust only, stopping temporarily to jump from the trucks when the navy jets flew overhead, spraying us with CS gas.

The marines moved hard and fast, stopping occasionally to perform hip shoots then back on the trucks. The other days we spent performing helicopter raids, pushing the small 105 cannons into the back of helicopters then landing for approximately five minutes, firing off two artillery shells, then back in the helicopter to repeat the same raids over and over until it was time for night fire. The roads were long and hot. I could see heatwaves in the distance covering the vast empty desert. As miserable as I was, I couldn't help to have an occasional thought of Cindy and what she was doing at the moment.

My euphoric thoughts were interrupted by more CS gas and the hundred-and-twenty-degree temperature inside my mop suit. The water drinking device on my gas mask didn't work, so I had to go for hours without water because they didn't allow us to remove the gas mask until all that was given. It was like a scene out of a war movie. As far as the eye could see, trucks were lined up along the desert road, and the navy pilots couldn't help but to spray us with the gas one last time as we headed to base camp. We jumped off the trucks and scattered in all directions, pointing our weapons in the air and firing blanks at the jets while trying to don our gas mask and cover ourselves with ponchos to protect us from the CS gas. Immediately, after all clear was given, two marines ran from the road down into a huge crater and began hitting each other with shovels and tent poles and whatever else that was in reach. The marines stood around the top of the crater, taking bets as the two marines bludgeoned themselves half to death until one marine corporal stepped in and ended the fight. It was the two marines I prevented from fighting in the back of the truck on the way to the desert. They finally had enough of one another and decided to settle the difference Marine Corps style.

The fight was soon forgotten, and before we knew it, we're on our way back to Camp Pendleton. The ride home wasn't as fun because dirt soaked deep into the pores of our skin. We choked and threw up in the back of the trucks. Remnants of sand caught in our throats, particles of sand were trapped in the corner folds of our eyes. We had not bathed for eight weeks, and the C rations gave off an awful smell while Marines tried to cleanse their bowels, grunting while clutching the bathroom stall because they were constipated from the military diet of C rations. In the marines, we were supposedly guaranteed one hot meal and one hour of sleep per day during combat conditions, but we never saw the hot meal and scarcely saw one hour of sleep during training. I often thought of Cindy and what she's doing and whether or not she thought of me as often as I thought of her. We were young and in the midst of puppy love. I often thought about the way we were and wished I were more mature and prepared for what was about to take place in my life. I hadn't experienced anything compelling or jolting to my character. I had yet to be tested, but I rest assured the test was coming.

A Fall from Grace

I was back in the barracks now and could easily find time during the quiet hours of the night to write Cindy letters, but to my surprise, I was selected for (NCO) noncommissioned officer school where corporals and sergeants went to improve up on their leadership skills. I was not yet an NCO. I was just in E3 with less than a year in the corps. The leadership school was eight weeks and a modified version of boot camp: fast paced with a lot of physical activity. There were more than fifty marines in the leadership school, and I was the only E3 in the entire class. I felt so out of place and so overwhelmed. It wasn't long before the corporals and sergeants tried to place me on every shit detail they could create, but they were easily reminded that pulling rank wasn't an option at the school; but they plotted and threw obstacles in my way, trying to find ways to drop me from the program.

From the very first inspection, I would receive unwarranted demerits that other marines received a pass on. We were separated into nine-man squads. No one wanted to be in the squad with an E3. They had no choice but to allow me to participate, but they didn't make it easy. I was placed with eight other marines that could run three miles in seventeen minutes. I wasn't the slowest runner at the time. My best three-mile run was twenty-one minutes. During the final three weeks of NCO school, we had a squad run competition. We were the last squad to start the six-mile course. By the time we reached three miles, we passed all the other squads and were ahead of them by at least three minutes.

Four miles into the run, one of our corporals fell behind. The pace was very intensive. We were running a six-minute-a-mile pace. My knees began to feel pressure from the uphill-downhill interchange, causing me to fall back five feet from my squad. The other marine fell back more than fifty yards, causing the squad to slow down so that he could catch up. Finally, we made it back to the barracks after a grueling fast-paced six-mile run. Everyone blamed me for the other marine's inability to keep up with the squad. They said, "If you hadn't dropped back, he would've run harder to keep up." Only one marine came to my defense, saying that it was bullshit and that it wasn't my fault that the other marine fell behind. I knew I was being targeted for blame, and it wouldn't be long before I was dropped from NCO school.

It had been six weeks, and I could see the finish line; but later that evening, I received my mail from Cindy. She reluctantly informed me she was pregnant, and her mother was very upset, threatening to call my commanding officer if I didn't marry her. Personally, I could give a flying bat butt about her mother being upset. I was more concerned about becoming a father. That night I rode the city bus down to Oceanside Boulevard and walked into one of their sleazy bars. They could tell by my high and tight haircut that I was a jarhead. Even though I was only nineteen, they allowed me to drink my problems away.

I was so distraught by the information of becoming a father I lost my focus and could no longer study; therefore, I was put out of the (NCO) noncommissioned officer program doing the final two weeks before graduation. I was embarrassed to return to my unit because I was a failure, but I had bigger fish to fry. I had a child on the way and soon a wife. There wasn't any way I was going to let Cindy have my baby unwedded because I believe my infatuation for her slowly turned into a love. The month of October, I received orders to go overseas to Okinawa, Japan, the following year, January 5, 1980; and I was given thirty days' leave before shipping out. December 1, I landed in Indianapolis. My first stop was my mother's house; then across the bridge, I walked to Cindy's house. Her mother answered the door and said, "Cindy is in the kitchen." I walked toward the kitchen, and in a flash, she ran down into the basement then out the side door. She was reluctant to let me see her stomach protruding past her unfastened blue jeans. So I sat on the living room couch. The couch was covered with plastic. If it were hot outside, I surely would have been on my way to dehydration. I waited patiently for Cindy to collect herself. She was being obnoxiously shy, but I understood, so I sat on the couch until she walked into the room and sat down beside me. I reached over, opened her coat, and rubbed her stomach. At that exact time, I knew I loved her, and I couldn't allow her to be an unwed mother. I stared deep into her eyes while running my fingers through her hair, and once again, she became soft and melted into my arms. She cried, and I whispered softly in her ear, "Would you be my wife?"

She said yes. We set a date for December 29, 1979, at Stouffer's Inn, a very prestigious hotel less than a mile from my mother's house. I took my last $900 and paid for the ballroom and catering. Cindy and her close friend were in charge of the decorations. The room appeared very idyllic. Many of the wedding invitees were not particularly interested about the wedding themselves but attended the wedding to observe firsthand the pulchritudinous view of the ballroom. Around fifty people were in attendance for the wedding including my grandmother. Seeing her attend my wedding pleased me. Cindy and I were both so young—barely out of high school—naive and very uncertain about raising a child. I stood on the left when I should've been on the right, which caused me to place the ring on the wrong finger. I just wanted this process over with and get on with life.

The thoughts of living in Japan settled quietly into my murky subconscious. We ate cake and slow danced to songs by Earth Wind and Fire. Everyone seemed to be having a good time until Cindy's stepfather began complaining about the food and how little he was able to get. As quiet as it was kept, I spent my last $900 to have the food catered, but Cindy's mother took credit for paying for the food and the ballroom. By the time the rumor made it back to me about who paid for the food and ballroom, I didn't care. I just wanted tonight to come to an end. Cindy and I were whisked away to my brother's small two-bedroom house where we would spend the first twenty-four hours of our marriage. We were reluctant to stay, but unfortunately, we were short on funds and with not many other options; therefore, we agreed to stay the night. But within an hour, we were bifurcate into disagreeable factions. Here we were one hour into the marriage and already had our first fight. Cindy sat in the bedroom, trying to codify our life, while I stared aimlessly out the front window, trying to get a grasp at the fact that I will be more than twelve thousand miles away within five days.

I believe that's truly what the fight was about. Before I knew it, I was sitting on the plane, face pressed against the airplane window, trying to get a glimpse of my pregnant wife as the plane backed out onto the tarmac. The flight was overcrowded, and it was just my luck to sit next to an obese women reeking of cheap perfume. I was being mentally tormented, covering my nose with a wet handkerchief. The smell was worse than CS gas because we were in a closed-off area. The twenty-two-hour flight laid over in Anchorage, Alaska, for one and a half hours, then on to Guam airport, a small building less than a two thousand square feet. A barracuda hung lifelessly on the wall, displaying all its teeth, trying to provide some sense of art and style in the dainty little airport. Pictures of the island hung freely on the walls, telling the history of the battle it took to keep the island. Two hours into my layover, we boarded the plane for our final destination: Okinawa, Japan. I was fortunate to arrive while the sun was still high in the sky. I sat pensively, internally feeling the distance from home with every screeching sound of the airplane wheels touching down on the runway. I wasn't comfortable being in another country, so I stuck close to the base the first two months. Occasionally, I walked around the perimeter of the fence, getting a feel for what it was like to be in a Japanese neighborhood. The houses were close together, one right on top of the other. Vendors stood on every corner, selling sushi and other types of exotic seafood. I thought the people were very pleasant, more so than the foreigners that moved to the United States. I ran around the island like an idiot with a Japanese translation book, yelling moshi, moshi, meaning hello, hello. Once a person stopped to talk to me, I thumbed through the book for something else to say, but they always walked off before I could find the next phrase.

I stayed very close to the barracks, bored out of my mind. I watched the Japanese cartoons *Transformers* in their language. I didn't understand a thing. All the street signs were in Japanese, and the streets ran in the opposite direction of those of the United States. I searched the newspaper for criminal activity, picking up the word here and there. I was totally frustrated and felt out of place. Culture shock began to creep in; and before I knew it, I was shipped to Korea for cold-weather training (Jack Frost), a training exercise conducted yearly throughout the entire fleet marine force (FMF pack). I was tired and wanted to sleep, but I was thrown into a group of marines and marched to the nearest supply room and began withdrawing my substandard cold-weather training gear. I arrived in Korea five days later and was immediately escorted to a government personnel tent (GP) where eighty other marines were suffering the same fate as I. We were living in the chosen frozen, a name that was given to South Korea during the Korean War. Usually called the demilitarized zone. Fortunately for us, it was the cold war era. South Korea was at peace, but North Korea maintained a threatening presence just on the other side of the fence line. Marines were stretched out along the demilitarized zone (DMZ) to prevent the occupying North Korea forces from crossing into the forbidden zone.

Most nights the temperatures plummeted into negative thirty degrees. All I could do to stay warm was put two rocks on the pub stoves to get them hot then place the rocks in the foot of my sleeping bag to prevent my feet from turning into walking ice planks. The ceiling of the tent was covered with twelve-inch icicles that hung desperately close to our face as we lay sleeping in our ill-equipped cold-weather sleeping bags. I woke at 4:00 a.m. and made my way outside to the tent-covered bathroom just fifteen meters away. I was thoroughly disgusted by the bathroom facility. The toilets were knee high, making it difficult to mount and have a seat. We had to remove three layers of clothes including a parka and snow boots before we could take a dump. Frozen feces covered the top of all the toilets from one end to the other. There were at least ten toilets with two rows, five toilets on each side. The toilets were wooden with no supporting back structure, resting on top of ice-covered rice fields. We had to lean against the person behind us or squat on top of the toilet, which was what most marines did according to the evidence they left sitting on top of the toilet. Every morning a maintenance crew with high-pressure steam sprayers tried to clean the bathroom using a water hose and scrub brushes. The feces would just liquefy then freeze on top of the toilet, leaving a brown slippery residue.

Most marines got fully undressed so they could balance themselves while taking a dump. There was no place to hang your clothes, so we had to be very creative each time we visit the latrine, holding our clothes in our hand while slipping and sliding on the ice-covered rice patties. The marines believed in teamwork, and this was teamwork at its best. Two men had to travel to the latrine together to assist each other with completing their morning ritual of pinching a loaf. I became so frustrated with the process I grabbed a shovel and began searching for a secluded place bordering the camp. About one hundred meters from my tent was the air force campsite. I wanted to see for myself how nice they lived. Up to this point, I only heard rumors about how they were living like civilians. So I crept over to the nearest air force building then peeked inside. I couldn't believe how nice their bathrooms were. There were mirrors on the wall, clean porcelain toilets, and wooden floors. Not to mention the bathroom was fully heated. I couldn't believe it. It was paradise in the wilderness.

At last, I could drop my pants, lie back against the porcelain toilet seat, and pinch a loaf as though I was in the civilian world. Although I was in the air force's plush bathroom, the twelve weeks of C rations had worked its magic. It did exactly what it was designed to do: it made me constipate, preventing me from pinching a loaf at will. I hated going to the bathroom. It was a very painful and unpleasant experience, although I only had to go to the bathroom once every three weeks. I hated stripping down totally naked just to cleanse my colon. Once I discovered the dietary purpose of C rations, I stopped eating what the military gave me in exchange for carrying my own pogey bait—food that we purchased from the PX, such as tuna, ramen noodle, cookies, crackers, and other canned foods. I went hungry for my first three weeks in Korea because Lance Corporal Bird was assigned to mess duty. He would get up at 2:00 a.m. and crack eggs all morning long.

He was so agitated by the process and pissed off at the world he mixed the eggshells in with the eggs, ruining everyone's breakfast.

The bacon was frozen solid, smothered with frozen grease. The grease had to be wiped away with napkins before we could eat it. The coffee was the safest bet—pure black and steaming hot. No one in the unit liked Bird, so they sent him as far away from our unit as they could. They assigned him to work on shit details just to keep them away from us. Bird was a compulsive liar. He would tell grandiose lies about owning a home on a rotating mountain. People were sick of listening to his lies. Every time he came around, we just walked away.

All the training and living conditions were very harsh in the Marine Corps. Even the showers were run by generators. There was no way for the operators to control the temperature. Scalding hot water was piped through the tubes attached to a rod coming from the generator. It was as if we were lobsters being boiled in a pot. Wooden shipping pallets were used for floors. The floors were so cold the hundred-degree hot steaming water couldn't prevent the wooden pallets from being covered with ice. Even the dressing area entrance to the shower was rice patties covered with ice. Everywhere we stepped, there was ice under our feet. It didn't matter how hot the shower water would get. The ice just wouldn't melt. Every morning for twelve weeks, everyone crowded around the small pot stove, sucking up all the heat before it could reach anyone else. I couldn't believe how stupid I was getting myself in this type of situation. It should be a crime to be so stupid. The air force camp was just two hundred yards across the grinder, living a life of luxury in plush two-man tents with real wooden floors, not shipping pallets.

They had dressers with the mirrors attached to put their clothes in and a civilian-made quilt covering their beds. I envied and I hated them at the same time. Our lifestyles were totally different, but our mission was the same: keep the North Koreans in the north. I spent twelve weeks sleeping on ice-covered rice patties, pulling icicles from the ceiling of our tent, using them for water to make coffee. I never drank pure black coffee before this experience, but it was so cold milk and creamer weren't even a secondary thought. I just wanted something hot to drink. I didn't care what it tasted like. I couldn't imagine fighting a war in these types of conditions as the marines did who came before us. It didn't matter how cold it was. There was always something to do outside in that horrid weather. We parked our cannons in rice fields of some poor farmer. His home was less than one hundred meters away from our firing positions. We didn't care whether it kept him up all night, so we shot our live artillery shells over the city highway onto desolate land designated as the live fire zone.

We stood on the firing line for hours in thirty-degree-below weather with a wind chill factor of twenty-five miles per hour, waiting for a fire mission. The fire missions came few and far between, and by three o'clock that evening, someone got the bright idea to swap off gun sections every couple hours. We stood out on the firing line until 10:00 p.m. at night. My eye sockets were just about frozen in place. My mouth had frozen stiff. I could barely pronounce words or talk. As it got later in the evening, bush bunnies made their presence known, whispering from the bush, "GI, GI, fucking sucky $10." I just kept walking my post, pretending not to notice them, but some marines couldn't resist the temptation of having sex with the young girls. They gladly jumped into the bushes for a cheap thrill that turned out to be a very painful visit to the dispensary. Bush girls weren't tested by the military for sexually transmitted diseases. Prostitution was legal in the bars of Soul Korea; therefore, the military ensured that the women occupying the bars got routine physicals or vaccinated against the venereal diseases. If the girls refused to be tested by the military, the business owner would have to place a pile of salt on either side of the door, alerting young soldiers, sailors, and marines to the presence of sexually transmitted diseases within that establishment. I was married. I didn't want take any chances on the possibility of spreading any diseases to my wife, so I stayed away from the bush bunnies and the bars for the time being. Most of the time I didn't think about sex because it was so cold in South Korea. I couldn't occupy another thought in my head other than how to get warm.

Once we returned back to our base camp for a weekend of R&R, I found solace just lying on my cot. My toes were just about frostbitten—frozen with a painful, tingling, and needle-pricking sensation as though I were a sickle-cell patient. The doctors were busy treating high-ranking officers; therefore, I was requisite to be examined by a Navy corpsman with no formal education and just a quick eight-week training course in the medical field. Several hundred of us suffered the same predicament, overwhelming the two corpsmen in their small CP tent. I still had feeling in my feet and the ability to work, so I returned to my unit to help tear down and pack away our tents and load equipment onto the deuce-and-a-half trucks. Most tents were frozen solid a foot or more into the ground. Marines became frustrated breaking picks and axe handles while trying to free the tents from the ice. We worked on the tents for hours, barely making a dent in the ice. It was taking far longer to remove the tents from the ice than anyone expected. To free the tents, we began chopping off the bottom flaps using picks, axes, and diesel fuel to free the edge of the tents from the ice-covered rice patties. I was sick of this outdoor icebox and was ready to return to Okinawa where the weather was normal or at least felt normal.

After twelve weeks of taking only one scalding-hot shower and sleeping on ice, I fantasized at the possibility of sleeping on a mattress and eating something else besides C rations. Several days later, we boarded a C-130 with our 105 cannons and half-ton trucks shoved right in the middle. We rode the entire trip with our knees shoved in our chest while holding our seabags on our lap. As uncomfortable as the ride was, I was glad to be out of Korea and on my way back to Okinawa to a warmer climate. I couldn't help but to get lost in thoughts of Cindy and my new daughter. How fun it would be to be a father and the possibility of spoiling my daughter rotten. I removed her picture from my pocket and occasionally stared at it, creating subliminal thoughts of spending time at the beach and park and celebrating her birthday. Thinking about my family make time pass quickly, and before I knew it, I was circling Okinawa, looking across the vast wingspan of the

C-130 airplane. We touched down several hours later. Shortly after landing, we secured our gear then were released for the day.

Most of the marines ran down to the USO and stood in the long lines, yelling for a honcho (cab) to whisk them two BC Street or Gate, two known places for legal prostitution and seductive nightclubs. I didn't have interest in such things; so I stayed to myself, sat on my bed, and envisaged being with my wife and my new baby girl. A month had passed, and I still found myself hanging around the base, playing bingo and Space Invaders at the USO. I learned to eat with chopsticks; however, the food was still foreign to me, so I stuck with the simple dishes: large bowls of ramen noodles or shrimp fried rice. That's how I envisioned myself for the next nine months: spending all my time on base playing bingo, eating ramen noodle, and watching *Transformers* in Japanese.

A week later, I was approached by my bodybuilding roommate,. He suggested showing me the layout and inner workings of the city. I was reluctant and callow. He was very bumptious and churlish, refusing to take no for an answer. I got dressed, and off we went to BC Street in the back of the honcho (Cab). Jackson yelled, "Coco cing" that means Play Black music. The ride lasted less than five minutes. We walked at an infantry pace down the crowded military-occupied streets of Okinawa, Japan. Bars and clothing stores lined both sides of the street. A paragon Asian woman strutted back and forth in front of the bars, touching, groping, and caressing each soldier, sailor, airman, or marine that happened to pass. We walked from bar to bar until we struck gold. A female stripper was about to perform a banana show. I was naive to the night culture, but I was eager to watch and learn of this new culture. I soon discovered this new culture would cost me at least two drinks. A pleasingly six-foot-tall demimonde Japanese stripper strutted out onto the ankle-high stage. She concealed nothing. Her breasts and vagina were on display for all to see as she frolicked on the floor, making love to a giant pillow, spreading her legs so I could visually conduct a pelvic exam.

I was unimpressed. Although I had never been in a strip bar, I thought it was bromidic and mundane. The marines began to pound the tables, yelling, "Banana show, banana show, banana show, banana show" until the stripper agreed to perform the banana show if everyone purchased another drink. We were all too happy to accommodate her. I tried to get away with purchasing a Coke, but I was forced to buy hard liquor if I wanted to stay for the show. I ripped out a few dollars from my pocket and slapped it on the table, ordering a rum and Coke. Most marines in the club were only twenty years old and were therefore younger than most patrons, but it never bothered the club owners. They only wanted our U.S. currency and didn't care about U.S. policies regarding age limits placed on drinking. Most of the merchants didn't want their own yen. They would rather have U.S. dollars, so I didn't bother to exchange my money for yen. I found the money system in Japan to be very strange; 1,000 yen equaled to $5 in 1980.

The strippers sashayed back and forth on the stage, reminding me that I had been without a woman for three and a half months, so I sat anxiously waiting for the banana show to commence. Slight drool leaked uncontrollably down the side of my mouth in a fountain of concupiscence. Suddenly, she seductively pulled her see-through gown over her head, tossing it on the floor for everyone to pass around the room and smell. She appeared lascivious, at least we thought so, because she spread her legs wide open and rubbed her breasts and thighs with coconut oil. She grabbed a banana and began eroticizing it while slowly peeling away the skin. She licked the tip of the banana in a circular motion then began feeding the entire banana down her throat. We were all in a moment of prurient. Moans and groans filtered the room as young marines creamed in their pants.

I clutched my glass of rum and Coke, nearly shattering the glass from the sultry sex act I just witnessed, but there was more to come. She laid her head back and slowly and slid the banana inch by inch into her well-stretched-out bottomless pit of a vagina. You could have heard a pin drop as she slowly made the banana disappear into her deeply-gorged-out vagina. Then all of a sudden, bananas fell piece by piece—perfectly sliced into perfect half-inch pieces—on a newspaper placed on the floor at her feet.

The slices were passed throughout the club and served on toothpicks as free appetizers for anyone who wanted more flavor in their drink. I liked to get my freak on, but I found this utterly disgusting, so I took the party elsewhere. Jackson and I cruised the strip, sticking our heads into different hotels and philandering the prostitutes behind the windows until we happened upon a hotel that had women that resembled models. Jackson quickly pulled out a wad of cash, tossing $15 to a *mama-san* and said, "Take your pick. I'm paying." I said, "No, man, I'm married." Jackson looked at me and said, "It's already paid for. Don't waste my money." Then he walked away, leaving me standing there, staring at ten Asian beauties in the face. I couldn't resist. I asked mama-san if she could have them all stand up. Then I chose the tallest one. Mama-san said, "Go upstairs to the last room on the right side at the end of the hall." Full of apprehension, I slowly made my way down the poorly lit hallway. I slid open the door. There was one twin-size bed shoveled against the wall. The shower was two feet away with a water hoses connected to the nozzle. I was totally naive. I sat on the bed fully clothed, burning up part of my fifteen minutes. A minute later, a slender graceful Asian female walked into the room and immediately began stripping. Her perky little nipples sprang out like flowers in the springtime.

I couldn't believe my eyes. Her skin was as smooth as a mannequin, and her hair stretched down her back between the cracks in her butt. She appeared very at ease as she laid her slender beautiful body across the bed. I froze like a deer in the headlights, but she was unwilling to put up with my puerile behavior. She unzipped my pants and put them down below my ankles. She reached up, grabbed the collar of my shirt, and pulled me, crashing down on top of her small frame. Then she slipped my throbbing manhood deep inside the gored-out wound.

She began thrashing her hips back and forth in a circular motion. Her moans and groans were euphonious to my ear, but it didn't help remove the guilty pleasure I was feeling at the time.

I couldn't believe it. I was down and out in less than five minutes. She jumped up, stepped into the shower, and began washing her vagina with ice-cold water from a water hose. I lay motionless on the bed, smoking my mental cigarette, thinking about how good it was but how bad I felt inside. Before I could process thoughts, she motioned me into the shower where she rinsed me off with ice-cold water from the hose. I stood there, silently looking at her beautiful smooth skin and long dark soft hair scratching the bathroom floor because it hung freely down her back.

I thought for second that I could go again, but she departed the room as quickly as she had entered. I didn't know what to think. This was definitely a vagary in my life. I didn't know whether to be happy or sad. Knowing it was a common practice on the island to pay for sexual pleasure didn't make me feel any better because I had broken my sacred marital vows. I resorted back to spending a majority of my time at the USO club, playing Space Invaders, watching TV, and participating in occasional bingo games. Fortunately for me, our next training exercise was less than a month away; and before I knew it, we packed up and shipped out to Mount Fuji, This time on the U.S. naval ship call the USS debuket. The berthing spaces were small and cramped. The metal bunkbeds were stacked five high with a rope supporting a piece of canvas used as the bed padding. The one-man shower stall was very small. The toilets continually overran, spilling all over the bathroom floor because of the rocking of the ship.

This was my first time on a transporter ship and my first time feeling what it was like to be seasick. I lay on my cot for five days, eating only what the more experienced marines brought me from the chow hall. I ate applesauce and drank water for the next five days. A couple more days had passed, and I'd grown less weary to the swaying and rocking of the ship. I was summoned by one marine to follow him into the weld deck of the ship. I stuck my head out of the port, and I couldn't believe my eyes. Waves as tall as the buildings in downtown Indianapolis slammed unsympathetically against the bulkhead of the ship. It was as if we were being swallowed up by the ocean, never be seen or heard from again. I'd never seen something so powerful and overwhelming. It made me realize how small and insignificant my life was and how powerful and forceful the earth is.

I lay in bed that night, praying that we would arrive safely on the shores of Mount Fuji. I lay on my cot with my eyes wide open, listening to the ship engine and propellers slowly whine and the powerful waves slam continuously against the side of the ship. I couldn't help but think about Cindy in that moment—her meek but violent nature. Just like the ocean, she was calm until the plate tectonics in her mind changed its course, creating friction and causing her to erupt. I didn't know where I was going in this marriage, but my first order of concern was surviving while on this ocean.

The waves simmered, so I made my way to the top deck. All I could see was endless waves of ocean. I never felt so small and insignificant and so out of place in the universe. I watched the ocean until I fell asleep with my back resting comfortably against a tire on a 105 Howitzer. I was awakened four hours later by the coolness of the ocean mist on my face; and there she was: Mount Fuji, her summit peeking up toward the heavens and crested by the clouds more than twenty miles away. I spent most of my life watching the tip of this mountain on TV and postcards. Now it was right within my reach, up close and personal. I couldn't believe it's something I had fantasized about since I was eight years old while I watch Dean Martin and Jerry Lewis scary around Japan having fun. The moment of truth had arrived, and I would be getting to know myself better than I had never known myself before. Here we were arrogantly occupying another man's country, with rifles, cannons, helicopters, planes, and occupying force of ten thousand men.

We made an amphibious beach landing on the beaches, smoke billowing from the top of the tanks and amtracs as they plowed past the rugged shoreline. Landing crafts were the main source used to land the infantry on the beach. Others went to shore by helicopters and trucks. It was the most impressive sight. I'd never seen so much armor and ships in my entire life. Ships lined up all the way out toward the break of the ocean and slowly disappeared into the fog.

Later that day, we convoyed our way up the mountain to base camp, tanks, amtracs, and trucks stretching from the shore of the beach to ten miles inland. The base camp looked like something straight out of 1950s Marine Corps movie. Metal Quonset huts in badly need of repair began at the edges of the nearest town, angling up toward Mount Fuji, ending at the motor pool. We spent four months in mountain warfare training with Japanese soldiers who were located across the street. Unfortunately, we didn't have any women at our base. Neither did the Japanese. I don't think the Japanese soldiers mind not having women as much as the Americans did. Any spare time the Americans had, we ventured out to nightclubs located downtown in the Tokyo skyscrapers. The buildings contained nightclubs on each of the twenty-five floors. There was a $25 admission that allowed us to go from floor to floor, stopping at each nightclub along the way.

The native Asian girls were restless. They fell in line just to dance with us, leaving their Japanese counterparts standing alone, holding up the walls in envy. The young Japanese men appeared to be afraid to express themselves freely because of their totalitarian society.

The Japanese army base was right where it was supposed to be far out in the middle of nowhere. The United States Marine Corps base was right across street within rock-throwing distance from the Japanese base. I couldn't imagine having a Japanese base across the street from the Marine Corps base in the United States. No other country will be able to set up shop and patrol neighborhoods throughout the United States without being attacked by its citizens. I thought it was very arrogant of the United States, and I knew deep down inside, Japan hated having the United States monitor every activity with their foreign occupying forces. In retrospect, the base was very small and was situated right next to the well-known Fuji volcano. Every morning for four months, I started up at the snowcapped mountain, wondering when we were going to make our way to the top.

All the marines knew the Marine Corps could not resist climbing a volcano. It was a small challenge but one we would have to face before leaving the island. The ground was covered with broken-up pieces of lava on a concave slope. The motor pool and gun park were placed at the highest point on the base directly in front of the volcano. The base looked very barren, old, and run-down. There wasn't a woman within miles of the base. Takahara was the closest town to the base approximately two miles away, the perfect walking distance for a fit marine.

There was nothing on his base except for marines. The recreation department tried to entertain us by showing us old movies in an empty shack and giving us discounted blue ribbon beer. What they couldn't sell they gave away for free. Old cable sprools were used for tables, which turned out to be a good choice because marines fought every night over things that wouldn't make sense to the average civilian. After having a few beers, someone would we get motivated, stand up, and yell out, "Artillery!" Another marine would yell out, "Amtracs!" And another would yell out, "Infantry!" Before I knew it, there was a full-fledged fight taking place. I punched my way to the door and out the back exit before the MPs arrived.

The next morning, the marines were lined up at the chow hall bandaged from head to toe. The commanding officers didn't seem to mind. They were raking plenty of money; therefore, they decided to let the club continue to operate for the next several months. Every night for four months, there was a fight. I stayed in the club long enough for the first bowl of peanuts to be thrown. Then I left before the full fight involving more than thirty young marines could escalate.

We had nothing to do but drink liquor, eat ramen noodle, and beat one another senseless. I spent my weekends with two other friends, trying to learn the city and figure out how to catch the train to Tokyo.

We got fed up with hanging around the base and fighting in the nightclubs, so we got dressed one night and ventured out to the train station in Takahara. We couldn't read the signs. Everything was in Japanese, not a single word in English. Unlike the United States, Japan was culture friendly. The only concern was with their native people and language. No other language could be found anywhere in the city, but we were desperate; so we paid our money and boarded the train, hoping to land somewhere near Tokyo. Four hours passed by, and we were still in the middle of nowhere. All we could see from the train window was farmland and rice paddies as far as the eye could see. We rode from sunup to sundown and never reached anything that resembled a city. We got off the train at several stops at different stations, wondering around like tourists from another country lost in the United States. By this time, we came to realize the only way we're going to find Tokyo was if Godzilla were to appear and start chasing Japanese all over the place, leading us to downtown Tokyo.

At least seven hours had passed, and I was no longer interested in going to Tokyo. I just wanted to return to the base because I was starving at this point. Even a box of C rations sounded edible. One Japanese citizen couldn't help but notice how confused and lost we were. He offered to help us find our way back on the right course to Takahara if he could practice using his English on us. We were more than glad to oblige him. He spoke English, and we complimented his language skills and praised him on everything he said. Although we could barely understand anything he said, we wanted to make him feel comfortable enough to ride four hours back to Mount Fuji with us. He was a very nice and pleasant man. It appeared that he had just gotten off work and was heading home with a newspaper tucked under his arms when he decided to help a fellow man in need. I thought it was the most thoughtful gesture I had ever witnessed.

The other two marines were flabbergasted by his annoying nonstop talking and the way he pronounced his words, abusing the English language, so they called it a night and passed out on the benches of the train. I tried to be grateful and listen as he talked, nodding my head occasionally as if I was actively listening. I was so focused on getting back to the base I hardly noticed the beautiful Japanese women standing shoulder to shoulder less than a foot away. The train slowly pulled into the Takahara station. We shook his hand and waved good-bye and began to our tomorrow's journey back to the base. It was pitch black. We could only see three feet in front of us. Fortunately, a Japanese soldier happened to pass by. "Where are you going?" he asked. "We're on our way back to the Marine Corps base." "This way," he said. I was shocked by the continued kindness. Everyone I encountered at Mount Fuji went out of their way to ensure that we were okay. I was confused. I thought they would have hated us for occupying their land and forcing our will and the American way upon them, but they were kind and very humble. Train station was only a twenty-minute walk from the base. The Japanese soldier walked beside us and began asking us if we would like to sell our high school ring or if he could buy porn magazine from us.

He reached into his cargo pockets and pulled out a Japanese porn magazine. I flipped through the pages. All the women were stretched out with their legs wide open, but there was one small problem: they were wearing panties only, exposing their breast. I immediately understood why he wanted American pornographic magazines. Our women weren't so modest; you could see right into their birth canal if you looked in the right magazine. We didn't sell any high school rings that night or give away any American porn magazines. We waved good-bye as we turned left, and he turned right back into our military commands. I couldn't help but to make my way back out to town once more but not before stopping and getting a $1 succulent, juicy burrito loaded with on identifiable meat.

I heartedly chowed down on the burrito while walking toward the front gate. Halfway into the burrito, I bit something hard. I reached in my mouth and pulled out a huge canine tooth. I thought nothing of it and tossed it to the side and continued chowing down. I didn't venture far from the front gate—just far enough to browse through a few stores, meet a few of the townspeople, then go back into the gate. Later that day, I was informed I would be standing guard duty for the next fifteen to twenty days. I didn't mind because my unit was starting to go on fifteen- to thirty-mile hikes with the infantry division every Friday before securing for the day.

I stood at the armory and watched my unit leave every Friday morning at five with full gear including backpacks, helmets, rifles, flak jackets, and 60-caliber and 50-caliber machine guns. I wanted no part of it. They were gone all day until five in the evening, returning with blisters on their feet and barely able to walk. Somehow I believe the Marine Corps use this as a device to slow the marines down and tire them out before letting them go on weekend leave. Although the guard shifts were four hours on four hours off, I didn't mind even when it rained. I would just walk to the back of the armory and stand beneath the shelter we had jerry-rigged just for that purpose. At two in the morning hunger would set in. There was no shortage of food because C Rations for the entire battalion was stored at the armory. All I had to do was pull a case of C rations from the stack and take what I wanted out of the box. This was called rat fucking the C rations. The rain poured down unforgivingly as I stood under the tarp, cutting holes in the bottom of a C rations can to make a stove. I shivered uncontrollably from my soaked camouflage utilities and my saturated leather boots. I couldn't believe how cold it was turning. I was hoping we would return to Okinawa before winter weather hit.

I had just come from Korea, and I wasn't mentally or physically ready to freeze to death anytime soon. The top of the volcano already had a snowcap, and it was rumored that we would be climbing the volcano within a week. Just as I was feeling sorry for myself, I heard a banging sound coming from one of the canisters. I reached down into my ammo pouch and removed three 12-gauge shells. I loaded my pump shotgun, cocking it, placing one shell in the chamber. I crept toward the banging noise, slowly squatted down, and peeked around the corner. A hooded man was pounding away, trying to break the lock on the canister that housed more than three hundred weapons. "Halt," I yelled as I stood up. The would-be thief threw the crowbar at me, hitting the cocking mechanism of my shotgun. Defensively, I let go of a burst, barely catching the would-be thief on the side of his face, knocking him to the ground. The pumping action on my shotgun had been damaged just enough to prevent me from housing another shell, so I rushed toward the thief and smashed him in the face with the butt of my weapon. "Halt," I said once again while pressing in the burrow of my disabled shotgun into the side of his face. Within seconds, the reactionary team surrounded us and took the thief into custody.

I was loving guard duty. It got me out of shit details throughout the day. I was no longer the guy to call when the head needed to be scrubbed down or when the shitters needed to be burnt. I spent my mornings hanging around the barracks, cleaning my cameras and writing letters home. Cindy often occupied the blank faults in my mind during idle moments. I couldn't help but think of her and the mistake I had made joining the military. She was always on my mind even at night as I cried in my sleep, thinking about her and my daughter. I didn't know this would be a common theme of my life every time we're apart.

The nights were cold and silent with the exception of the enlisted men's club where fights broke out every two minutes. One night I was lying soundly asleep in my rack. The lights flickered on; then, the reactionary alarm sounded. My guard unit was summoned to the club to break up a fight. We surrounded the building with nightsticks in hand. One white man ran out of the club, yelling and screaming, pointing in my direction. He yelled nigger at the top of his lungs. All of a sudden, there I was staring into the twisted face of hate. I live my entire young life in Indianapolis, and only in America do I have to travel five thousand miles across the ocean, to Japan, to be called a nigger by an American marine.

I wasn't fazed at all by his uneducated remark. I simply tossed him on the ground and cuffed his hands behind his back, making sure he didn't break free. I squeezed the handcuffs extra tight; then, I locked them in place with my handcuff key. I stood guard for another ten days before returning to my unit just in time to go on a 24.3-mile hike with full gear. We were packed up and ready to move out at four in the morning. The torrential rain was coming down hard in golf-ball-size droplets that morning. The base was flooded within two minutes of the first rainfall, letting up for two minutes at the most. We held off the march as long as we could, but there was no signs of the rain letting up, so we headed out with our fifty pounds of gear, 50-caliber machine guns, 60-caliber machine guns, mortars and mortar plates, and tubes. We slipped and slid up and down the mountains and slippery roads. One marine took the time to turn around and snap my picture as we came to the end of our hike.

We ran up and down around the mountains in infantry pace. If I didn't know better, I thought this hike wasn't going to end. Five hours into the hike, I began to feel blisters forming on my soaking wet feet. Temperatures began to drop as we approached the end of the fall moving toward the winter. The ground became a little harder and colder, and the rain fell like ice water hitting our bodies. I didn't know what hurt most: my feet or the edges of my ears. My camouflage utilities and flak jacket were so saturated they felt like fifty pounds of wet sand. And then there was a signal for my battery to move to the head of formation. That meant we had to run two miles past the platoons while they stood on the side of the road, cheering us on as we ran in formation through the battalion, water slashing beneath our boots while dragging the machine guns to the top of mountain. Finally, the end was in sight. I could see the antiquated barracks as we toppled the rise of the mountain, but the birds were still at least three miles away. One of the commanders got motivated and decided we're going to jog the last three miles, and off we went, machine guns and all. We came to a halt in the front of the barracks. I was so exhausted and dehydrated my eyelids felt as if there were glued to the top of my head. After we put away our gear, we were dismissed for the evening, although our feet were blistered and we were exhausted, the entire battalion headed for the showers all at once. Everyone scurried into the shower, trying to wash up before going to town. One man jumped in the shower and got wet then jumped out and soaped down while the other man was getting wet. Then the man jumped in the shower, rinsed off the soap, while the other man soaped down. It was very systematic universal method of expedience while in boot camp.

The showers ran constantly until everyone was done. The water on the floor was at least ankle high if not higher. Everyone was required to wear shower shoes, but scum floated, and razor blades left by marines floated freely in the water for the cleanup crew that was formed out of anyone who dropped back out of the hike. I was glad I was in top physical condition, but because of the scum floating above the water, it would be the first time in my life I would contract athlete's foot. My feet were blistered from front to back, and there were still rumors that we would be climbing Mount Fuji the next coming week.

Most of the marines got dressed and headed to Tokyo. I stayed around the base, writing letters to my wife and playing basketball with two of my good friends. Before I knew it, we were boarding ship and on our way back to Okinawa. Two days into the trip, a typhoon hit, and we were forced to pull into the naval port in Yokohama, Japan. We stopped in Yokohama, Japan, for three days until the typhoon passed by. Most marines took advantage of the military base and PX. I spent my time running back and forth to 31 ice cream and Japanese barbecue restaurants. Unfortunately for myself, my system was backed up. I hadn't taken a dump in fourteen days. Because of the lack of proper dietary meals provided by the Marine Corps, I was destined to report a sick day.

The C rations did exactly as they were designed to do. I sat on the toilet for hours while the boat rocked back and forth, splashing the toilet water all over my butt, forcing me to call it quits and visit sick bay. The corpsman said I was constipated and he needed to give me an enema. I thought it was something to eat like chocolate. Smiling from ear to ear, I stuck my hand out and said, "Given here." He said, "No, you have to get undressed." "Just to eat a piece of chocolate?" I said. He went to his medicine cabinet and removed a plastic bottle with a long stem. "I will have to fill this with a solution. Then you'll lie on your side while I put this tube in your anus and squeeze the liquid from the bottle into your rectum." While pulling my pants up, I said, "I'm feeling a little better now. I think I can use the bathroom without your help. Thanks anyway." All of a sudden, the navy sailor blocked the door.

"We can't let you leave. We must perform the procedure," he said. "But I'm feeling okay. I don't need a procedure," I said while backing up toward the door. Two gay navy corpsmen stood in the room watching, smiling, and giggling to themselves. I thought to myself, *When I get a chance, I'm going to throw both of these assholes overboard.* However, I had no choice, so I lay on the table and turned on my side, allowing the corpsmen to perform this procedure. It was a valuable lesson learned. The next time I have this problem, I would keep my mouth shut and wait it out.

By the time I returned to the Okinawa, I only had one month left. I spent most of my time hanging around the base and trying not to get myself into any more quagmires or promiscuous situations. I couldn't believe it January 5, 1981. I was on my way back to Indianapolis. I could barely sit still on the plane. I tried to fall asleep to hurry time. I fell asleep for four hours. When I woke up, I still had fifteen hours to go before I even reached Alaska. I counted every second, every hour, and every minute until I touched down in Indianapolis. I walked in the door of Cindy's mother's house, and there she was in the middle of the room, trying to peek over the top of her playpen. She was so pretty with her hair resting on top of her head and a pretty little face any dad would love.

I scooped her up into my arms, and it was as if she knew who I was the whole time. We immediately bonded. Wherever I went, she went with me; and for a brief second, I forgot all about Okinawa, Japan, and the shame I brought to my marriage. Later that evening, Cindy and I lay in bed, staring at each other while our daughter sat between us, sucking up all the attention. At one moment, our eyes locked, and I could see the wheels spinning in Cindy's mind. She looked at me with a question mark on her face, and I looked back at her as though I knew the answer to whatever questions she wanted to ask. She never asked the fatal question of whether I had been faithful to her while overseas. She just rolled over onto her side and rubbed Michaela's back, trying to get her to fall asleep.

The sun flickered one last time then closed its eyes as it set down for the night behind the skyscrapers. Cindy lay on her side, wearing an inviting pink nightgown. I stared at her back, inching closer and closer until we were locked in the human pretzel position. I slid her panties down to her knees and pulled them off with my foot. I ran my hand up and down her thigh and in between her legs until she submitted and turned over on her back. I slowly mounted her and began thrusting her spacious wound. I noticed she wasn't tight at all. I became immediately suspect about her loyalty during my twelve months in Japan. No, I had questions of my own. Who was she with, and how often was she with him?

I quickly forgot about her possible disloyalty and remembered my own disgruntled behavior. To balance the scales, I was going to fuck her brains out. Either she was going to confess to her infidelity or she would have to beg me to get off her. Therefore, I pounded her for six hours straight. Her body went limped, her legs flopped around like a fish dying on the shores of a fisherman's wharf, her arms lay loosely above her head, and her thighs were swollen like two ham hocks. She begged me to stop, grabbing my head with both hands. She said, "That's the answer to my question. You never performed sexually like this before you went overseas." I lifted myself off her, dripping with sweat from head to toe as if I had just worked out of a sauna. I couldn't say anything. I couldn't deny it, and I didn't want to admit it, so I just lay there as if I never heard a word. My mind ran wild, thinking about her intimately making love with another man; and before she knew it, I mounted her again, this time hitting every possible corner in her vaginal wound. She dug her nails deep into my back, breaking her freshly manicured nails off into my flesh. I wanted to make her pay for her infidelity by riding her into a new reality. I knew she was young and had been seriously mounted, so I wanted to make it clear that I would be the only one mounting her from this time on.

The next twenty-nine days would be more of the same. I felt the boundaries of our marriage had been breached at both ends of the spectrum, and no one was innocent. I worked her like a job clocking in and only taking two fifteen-minute breaks during an eight-hour lovemaking session. She was glad to be the receiver of my new sexual prowess, but she didn't want to experience it all in one night. Three weeks later, I was on my way to Camp Pendleton to report for duty. My family would come to the base within the matter of two months, so my first order of business was to buy a car because the base was more than fourteen miles one way from base housing. Although the city bus was walking distance from my front door, I wanted the luxury of leaving the house at the last minute and not having to leave two hours early just to catch two city buses and one military bus before reaching my barracks.

I purchase a 1972 lavender-blue Cadillac El Dorado. It was a piece of junk. The car had no problem leaving me stranded. The first week the engine caught fire; then the transmission went out, the horn didn't work, and the gas-guzzling piece of junk only got twelve miles a gallon. I couldn't have picked a worse car if I try. People seemed to be impressed that I was driving a Cadillac and often questioned whether the car was mine. Cindy arrived right on schedule two months later. I wasted no time preparing the house, making it livable and comfortable. We didn't have many friends; therefore, we just occasionally walked to the beach or took trips to the mall. I was excited for Cindy to experience California. It would be her first time traveling that distance from home. I knew I had to make personal adjustments, making sure she was comfortable, but those adjustments wouldn't last long.

Sometimes during the quiet hours of the night, when Michaela was in bed asleep, Cindy would lie on the front-room floor and talk about missing her brother as tears streamed down her face. I didn't know what to do in this type of situation, so I just listened. Once in a while, I would try to redirect her thinking toward other things. Later that month came the news that she was pregnant again. I wasn't surprised since we just came off a thirty-day sex binge, but I would have to start making plans for the near future because I would be getting discharged within fifteen months. Cindy didn't care for the military life. She never got used to me being gone for extended periods of time. I did understand her reasoning, so I offered to send her back to Indianapolis for twelve weeks or until she was ready to return. In two months, she was on a plane back to Indianapolis, and I was on a five-ton truck heading to Twentynine Palms, California, for twelve weeks of desert training.

The training was gruesome and dirty. The sand stung my skin like bits of broken glass. There weren't many places to take cover, and the sun beat down on us mercilessly, not giving us much of a break during the waking hours. During night training, the sky was lit up for miles covered with illumination shells floating in the sky long enough to light a target area more than a mile long or at least several grid squares. Before the illumination flickered out, we unleashed over one-thousand-artillery tank, mortars and aircraft shells across a mile-long stretch of desert. Tanks sat one hundred meters in front of our cannons dug deep into ditches. They would roll up on top of the ditch long enough to pump out one shell. Then back down in the ditch they would go. Helicopters were next. They would fly and shoot up the area with one thousand rounds then spin off just in time for the low-flying jets to drop a quick five-hundred-pound white phosphorus bomb in the target area. Next the artillery pumped out five shells from each cannon, simultaneously firing a 50-caliber machine gun from the top of the truck.

We repeated this operation over and over until we had it perfect. We call this the iron curtain. This was a last-ditch effort when all else had failed and the enemy seemed unstoppable. The constant firing drove the cannon spades deep into the ground. I knew we were set in for the night, not making another long-dreaded road trip to the next position—or so I thought—until someone yelled out the word "CSM0" that meant to pack your gear and move out quickly. Everyone began slinging artillery shells, shovels, picks, and axes onto the half-ton truck. Tanks came out of nowhere as though there were hidden in the ground, smoke billowing from their stack, helicopters hovering above us, escorting us to our next position. While jet buzzed the ground, leaving trails of CS gas, the young marines scrambled to don their gas masks and cover themselves with their ponchos.

The CS gas burned our eyes, causing us to choke and vomit as we hurried to displace our weapons. The sun flickered one last time before it hid its fiery face behind the slopes of the mountains. Everyone was lined up on the road, ready to move onto the next position, everything was on the truck, but the spades of my cannon were stuck deep in the sand. This was quite the conundrum. All the other trucks were lined up and slowly pulling off. We had to dig out a spot beneath the trail of the cannon and place a jack under the trail of the cannon and deracinate the spade far enough out of the ground to allow us to move it slightly toward a closing position. After twenty minutes of furiously digging out the space of my cannon, we got the cannon hooked up to the truck. I looked up, and my unit was gone as well as the sun. I brought out my night-vision goggles, map, compass, and combat flashlight and navigated my way to our new firing position.

At one point during the drive, I thought for sure we were lost. It seemed as if we had been driving all night into the morning. I didn't see my unit for hours, but I knew how to effectively read a map and use a compass. Finally, when we arrived at the new position only minutes behind my unit, everyone was so exhausted from the long drive and the late hours. No one seemed to notice that I was not in the proper truck line order.

We repetitiously placed and displaced the cannon several times throughout the night. By the time I had a chance to look at my watch, it was close to two in the morning. Everyone was just concerned with getting their cannons in position for the next artillery barrage. The entire firing line was quiet and pitch black. All of a sudden, at in the morning some young private got the urge to make coffee. The inexperienced marine lit a heat tap, which illuminated the entire gun line. You could see the man walking around the cannons from a mile away.

A dust storm with feet scurried across the desert, yelling and screaming while walking at infantry pace. Gunnery Sergeant Jeffords came yelling down the gun line, "Who the hell lit that fire? Put it out, goddammit, put it out." He said while walking at an infantry pace with his hands shoved deep in his pocket and the light of the moon refracting brilliantly off his bald head. It was freezing in the desert, and at this time, we were on our third day of training with no sleep. Everyone was on edge. We were a bunch of walking time bombs waiting to explode. Our physical condition and stamina were being tested in every sense, heat exhaustion in the afternoon and freezing half to death at night. I just about had enough of the desert and the military training. The wind was beginning to kick up again. My goggles couldn't prevent the sand from edging its way into my eyes. By the time reveille was sounded, my eyes were woefully swollen shut. I made my way to sick bay located in the back of a supplies truck, not before emptying two canteens of water on my face, loosening the sand that scratched the cornea of my eye.

The navy corpsman only cared about getting to the charter early in the morning, so he just poured water on my eyelids and told me to report back to my unit. I pried my eyes lids open with my finger. Once I cleaned the sand from the corner of my eyes, I was able to see well enough to set the deflection and quadrant on the cannon sight for the next fire mission.

Once again, the sand kicked up like a small tornado; but this time, it was due to the helicopters that came out of nowhere and landed fifty feet from my firing position. I was ordered to push the cannon into the back of the helicopter and carry one case of artillery shells. Off we went flying to another desolate place in the desert to conduct what we call hip shoot. Once the helicopter landed, we pushed the cannon out of the rear of the helicopter at an exaggerated pace. I shot a quick asthma with my compass, pointed the cannon in the designated direction, and then we pumped out two artillery shells. Then we went back to the helicopter as quickly as we landed.

This was called internal raids because the cannon was placed inside the helicopter rather than being towed from the bottom of the helicopter. We landed back in our staging area, connected the cannon back onto the truck, and off we went down the road to our next firing position. I was starving, so I dug into my cargo pocket and pulled out a piece of pogey bait. I ripped a big jerky upon with my teeth and chewed on it to get some type of nutrition. I could hardly eat while the truck raced down the desert road at fifty miles an hour, tossing artillery shells around in the back of the truck while the man got swallowed up by the desert sand.

It was tremendously fast paced and very early in the morning. It was hardly 4:00 a.m., and I hadn't had breakfast. I hadn't got a shave or a dump. We continued at this pace for the next twelve weeks. I was truly physically and mentally beaten up and drained. At the time, I didn't believe anything in my life could have matched what I was going through at this time. The more training I had, the further removed I was from society. I didn't think I could ever be a civilian again. I could only exist in the civilian world in a physical state, but my true heart and experiences and life lessons would come from what I experienced in the corps.

After twelve weeks of eating nothing but C rations, my digestive system was permanently damaged. I hadn't taken a dump in eight days. Subliminal thoughts flashed before my eyes. There I was in the middle of the desert, visiting an oasis of regular food. Even the food from the chow hall seemed appetizing to me at this point. If we were fortunate, they would give us one hot meal from the main side base. But that was wishful thinking. C rations were the only meal we would see until the end of this training because C rations were designed to clog our system, making us constipated so that we couldn't interrupt our work by running to the bathroom once a day.

This gave us more time to focus on our job. It took most of us twelve minutes to take a dump, so the order of the day was too carry a stack of newspapers or magazines to provide a distraction so we would focus on something other than the pain while cleansing our colon. The portable toilet was crafted out of an ammunition box with layers of duct tape used for padding the seat. It was a hard way to live, and I promised I would encourage any young person to go elsewhere. The marines weren't the place to be. Living in dirt and squalor, sleeping one hour a day, and working eighteen hours a day were the norm during training.

This life was certainly not for the weak at heart, and for the moment, I didn't think it was me. I had approximately thirteen months left in the corps, and I lost plenty of sleep thinking about the possibility of becoming a civilian. Working a nine to five, no NCO duty, no field ops, and no unit rotations or overseas deployments. I was ready for the real world and for the civilian-minded attitude that would come with it. The marines have made me into a very punctual and dependable person. It would be a hard adjustment to be around people who just cruised through the day. The marines function on high energy and fast pace. Slowing down to a civilian pace would be mental torture. I didn't have any idea on how to be a civilian again, but I was willing to give it a try even if it meant I would lose some of my military bearing. I was ready to try something different, something that didn't require me to polish my shoes or press my uniform. I was thoroughly tired of the bullshit. I was ready to resume my life as a civilian, with civilian job and civilian ideas.

The Me Nobody Knows

After twelve rugged weeks of dragging our cannons behind half-ton trucks in the desert, we packed up and headed back to Camp Pendleton, or so we thought. Right before our convoy was rerouted to the San Diego Pier, we received two new privates fresh out of boot camp. We boarded a troop transporter ship headed overseas, and Private Dunbar, one of the new privates, was assigned to my section. He was kind of a goofy kid, and if a strong wind came, it would blow his 110-pound body right over. I didn't think much of him, and my presumptions were right. He immediately began to get into mischief, and I found myself standing in front of the captain's door, explaining why I did not have control of him. I had to manually resolve this issue; therefore, I placed them on every shit detail that came down the pike. It was time to depart, and as the ship slowly backed away from the port, the entire battalion stood on the deck of the ship while being dragged out of ocean by two tow boats. Dunbar stood next to me, practically leaning against me as the wind blew violently across the deck of the ship, losing some of our cargo from their straps.

I didn't know where we were going, and I did not bother to ask. Once aboard the ship, I settled into my berthing area and sacked down for the night. I stayed in the bed during most of our two-week trip except during the times we held formation or when I had to stand guard duty. I found the ship to be very peaceful. The quietness in the night gave me a chance to think clearly about what I would do after I left the Marine Corps. Sometimes I would sit on the top deck from sunrise to sunset, watching the ocean and the dolphins swimming alongside the ship. After about a month of floating around aimlessly on the ocean, a small rise of land appeared out of nowhere. I could hear the captain of the ship talking to my company commander. "That's our next objective," he said about the barren land.

I started preparing my section by taking an ammo count and ensuring that we had night-vision goggles and binoculars. I sent Private Dunbar to the armory to two secure two pairs of night-vision goggles. He took the liberty to tell the armory sergeant he was promoted to squad leader and was to be issued a 45-caliber pistol with four magazines along with several pouches of ammunition. Dunbar returned to the squad equipped with two pairs of night-vision goggles, smiling from area ear to ear as though he had just won the lottery. With his 45-caliber pistol tucked safely out of view, he became mysteriously quiet and off to himself. I was rather pleased and thought I had broken him from his bad habits and childlike behavior, so I left him alone until it was time to board the landing craft.

Three hours later, we were shoved into a landing craft. Once again, the onslaught of ocean water spilled uncontrollably inside the craft. I was hoping it wasn't another training exercise where they made us jump out of the landing craft and swim ashore. I thought for a second. *This couldn't be a training exercise because we were carrying full clips of ammo.* After wandering aimlessly around the ocean for several hours, we began our journey toward the shore. The landing craft went up and down the shore, trying to bypass the coral reef, but we had no such fortune. They had to let us out about one hundred yards from the beach. The door fell, and the ocean water rushed right inside the landing craft, soaking us up to our knees. From the back of the landing craft, I got a running start and jumped three feet out into the ocean. I kicked my way ashore, pulling Private Dunbar and one other marine right along with me, who were struggling to stay afloat because of the heaviness of their camouflage utilities and flak jacket. After reaching the staging area, we quickly divided our sections to two squads. This time, we didn't have our cannons. We became instant infantrymen gearing up to head out on a recon mission. We were divided into two small nine-man squads. We quickly wiped the salty ocean water off our M16s. Just as my M -16 was wiped down with oil, it was snatched from my hands and replaced with a 12-gauge pump shotgun. "Rawlings, take this compass and map. You're on point," the staff sergeant said. I only had thirteen months left in the sack, and I wasn't trying to get killed with a little more than a year left in the corps. I couldn't help but to ask, "Why am I on point? This job is reserved for a private, not an NCO!" "We need someone that knows how to competently use a compass and read a map," the staff sergeant said. I loaded six shells in my shotgun, orientated my map, and shot an asthma toward the designation.

We formed a line on each side of the road. I thought for sure we would ride a portion of the way, but instead, we humped on foot like the infantry. The American arrogance was upfront and in your face. We're in country less than three hours, and we walked around like we owned the place. The sun fell down behind the landscape. Before we could walk fifteen miles, it was instantly dark. I couldn't see two feet in front of my face. The marines behind me watched the reflectors on the back of my helmet. Every time I stopped, both squads would stop then move to the side of the road until I started moving again. We must've walked for hours. My mouth was dry like cotton, but we were forbidden to drink for our canteens to prevent water from splashing around. We stopped for a minute and set up on the side of the road. They said there was movement coming our way, a small group of about fifteen soldiers, so we positioned ourselves to set an ambush.

Two hours went by, and still, there were no soldiers. In the meanwhile, Dunbar lay at the rear of the squad off to the side of the road in his own world, playing with and polishing his new 45-caliber pistol, loading and unloading it unbeknownst to the rest of the squad. Suddenly, a group of undisciplined Lebanese soldiers we're patrolling directly for us. I signaled for both squads to stand by. The moment intensified with each step. I was so nervous. Every step they took echoed like big drums pounding my ear. I could hear myself breathing heavily the closer they got. I slowly began to get into a kneeling position, rotating the butt of the weapon into my shoulder and positioning my finger to squeeze off the first shut. Just as I was applying pressure to the trigger, an unauthorized shot was fired from nowhere, making the soldiers turn and run the other way. Dunbar had accidentally discharged his unauthorized 45-caliber weapon. My first response was to send to the rear and place him on a shit detail until we return to the rear and processing for NJP. But that didn't happen because we went too far out into the sticks—enough far from the first town—and there was no turning back at this point, so we were forced to allow him to continue on with us. We walked for more hours before the rock in my boot began bruising my foot. I was just about growing tired and weary of playing marine when all of a sudden, I bumped into someone coming from the opposite direction. We stood there facing each other for what seemed like an hour, but it was less than fifteen seconds. I didn't know how he felt, but I didn't want to die or kill another person. I couldn't see him, and he couldn't see me. I know all the friendlies were behind me, not coming from the other direction. We stood so close I could feel his breath. His clothing smelled of burnt wood. It was so quiet I could hear his heartbeat.

My palms were dripping with sweat. I was gripping my shotgun so tight I accidentally forced the cocking lever up. The shotgun made a clicking noise in the echoing atmosphere of the night—so loud it could be heard from a mile away. *I was in it now*, I thought to myself. I felt his arm make a slight shift, and before he could complete his motion, I leveled my shotgun pulling, the cocking mechanism home, letting go of one shell. Everyone scattered to the side of the rode. The silence was palpable. My heart was racing one hundred miles an hour as I lay silently in the ditch, trying to slow down my breathing, but nothing helped. I thought for sure there would be more of them and an all-out gun battle would ensue. No one spoke a word. Everyone lay silently in the sand until the next morning. The sun rose slowly that morning as we all merged onto the road to witness what was no surprise from the night before. A young soldier lay all along spread eagle on the road. Half his face and hand were blown off. I thought it ironic I hated America, but I got the first American kill. Everyone thought it was cool that I killed someone. I was bona fide. The first kill of the day, they said. "You're going to get a medal for this one!" one private yelled as they all took souvenirs from the young soldier's body. I stood there staring at the body. I didn't have time to process what happened before I was summoned to the rear of the squad.

One marine broke his leg jumping in the ditch. He was being evacuated back to the ship, so I reluctantly swapped my 12-gauge shotgun with his M16 rifle then returned to my position as point man. Within the hour, we were walking over the ridge into a small village. The war between Israel and the PLO had not yet started, but it appeared that all the buildings in the village were practically burned to the ground. We broke into two squads of nine and entered the village from two different directions. The first squad moved toward the south entrance of the village. My squad headed in from the west.

Since I was still on point, I was the first man into the building. I wasn't worried about the possibility of occupants because the buildings were supposed to be empty. From the looks of the town, no one could possibly exist in such a barren and burnt-out place. The first building holes were blown in the wall, big enough to walk through. I stuck my head through the hole in wall. Without being too temerity, I judiciously made my way up the steps. One of the privates tapped me on the back of my leg, indicating that he heard a noise coming from outside. Being a de facto leader, I sent two marines to check the noise then proceeded up the steps. As I turned to look up the staircase, a grenade was tossed over the balcony, striking me in the face, then rolling on the staircase, and exploding. I fell from the second flight of the stairs, losing my helmet, and the hand guards on my M16 shattered into pieces as I hit the concrete. Unexpectedly, another small explosion went off just big enough to knock me crumbling back to the floor. Before I could get my focus, someone picked me by my flak jacket and began dragging me out of the building and across the street to another building and threw me down a flight of stairs into the basement. *What the fuck*, I thought as I struggled to get to my feet. I was struck in the face with the butt of a rifle. I was struck once more before blood started trickling down my face, blurring my vision. I lay very still on the floor, pretending I was helpless and unconscious.

I reached into my T-shirt and placed my hands on my palm-sized combat knife. I listened for how many people were in the room. One soldier walked over and placed his foot on my head. He raised his machete high in the air. Then suddenly, the wall exploded, giving me time to spin around and shove my knife into his thigh. I twisted the knife into his leg and put out a chunk of flesh. Suddenly, his head disintegrated into small chunks of flesh. He was shot several times in the face. It was Dunbar. He unloaded an entire magazine into the soldier's face. Within minutes, the room was filled with the first squad. Helicopter transporters were called in, and I was evacuated back to the ship. I wasn't hurt. I just had scratches and cuts here and there, but I was glad to be out of that desolate place and back aboard the comforts of the navy ship. Our recon mission was successful. We provided solid evidence that the enemy materiel had been occupying the town for some time.

I sat on the top deck of the ship and read my novels while Dunbar was locked away in the ship's brig. He was given an honorable discharge. I was so disenchanted by the war I hardly noticed rockets fired back and forth across the vast wasteland. In two weeks' time, the islands slowly disappeared as we set sail out to sea, and another group of carriers arrived. We were relieved and rotated back to the States. The ocean was angry once again, slapping its waves harshly against the ship's bulkhead.

I didn't mind the slamming of the waves this time. It seemed to provide a calming effect from the shotgun blast ringing in my subconscious, the rifle butt to the face, the exploding walls, and the falling pieces of facial flesh. I sat on the top deck of the ship, wishing I was somewhere else. I could see my luminary platoon sergeant coming from a distance, assigning guard duty to anyone on the top deck. He walked toward me at an infantry pace, scribing as he walked. He got within six feet, bent over, touched me on the shoulder, and stared me in the face. Then he walked over to another marine assigning him to guard duty. I guess he could see I'd been through enough in the last month, so he was magnanimous and avuncular at a time I needed space and clarity of thought. Although it really didn't matter whether I stood guard duty or not, I would've still stayed on top deck and off to myself, but I was appreciative of his kind gesture. For the next week, I sat in the weld deck of the bottom of the ship. I climbed into the back of one of the deuce-and-a-half trucks, where I could get a good night of uninterrupted sleep, and no one would hear me crying in my sleep. Everyone seemed to be having a good time, drinking beer, eating lobster and steak, celebrating our last day on the ship. I was suffering a guilty conscience of my American sin. I knew that sins pays wages. Even though I was following orders, it did not abdicate me from the responsibility of taking another's life. I secluded myself from others, staying in the back of the truck for the next week. I only went to the top deck three times a day for roll call. Then I would climb back into my truck and think about home.

Slowly, I began to mentally metamorphose from the sound of the shotgun blast torturing my murky subconscious. The sound became denser with each passing day. I made my way up the metal steps, clinging to the hand railing, preventing myself from slamming into the bulkhead because of the violent rocking of the ship. I made my way to the top of the deck, and for the first time in two weeks, birds began landing on the bowel of the ship. I knew we were within eyesight of land, and right before I could complete the thought, a city emerged out of nowhere. I could recognized the coast of San Diego from one hundred miles away. It was the most beautiful thing I'd ever seen, and I was grateful to see the coast once again. Every minute seemed like an hour as the ship slowly docked. We unloaded our trucks and other equipment then convoyed back to Camp Pendleton. The long trip back home was physically draining. We were too tired to hang signs out of the back of the trucks, asking women to show their breasts. Before we even made it back to the base, there were rumors that one marine walked in and caught his wife having sex with three men at the same time. Infidelity was very common around base housing units. It was the closest thing to Peyton Place I'd ever seen.

At last, we were back in the familiar and secured surroundings of our base. We secured our gear and were awarded a seventy-two, meaning we were off for three days. I spent my seventy-two hours relaxing and stretching my feet across the front room table, and for the moment, I forgot about Beirut. I placed my short-lived combat tragedies deep in my subconscious and wouldn't speak of them again for forty years.

Even though Cindy was not home, I couldn't wait to get in the house and allow euphoria to set in. The house was quiet almost to the point of being ghostly. There was no laughter of children, not so much as a mouse squeak, but my neighbors were loud at several notches, letting their children run wild on the playground unsupervised, seemingly only hearing and not seeing them. I sat quietly on the porch, sipping on a beer, free from the thought of amtracs and tanks rolling past my head, or an aircraft spraying me with CS gas, or the dead soldier staring up at the sky on the dark desolate winding road in Lebanon. I was in a moment of euphoria; and all of a sudden, out walked an attractive young Puerto Rican girl seemingly focused on herself, cleaning and grooming her fingers and toenails to perfection, looking as if they were professionally manicured. Her small five-foot frame was athletic and well proportioned. The red tube top she wore could barely contain her 36DD breast. I looked at her like a man in the desert without water, seeing an oasis of fresh spring water for the first time. I knew if I stared long enough, she would become my next mistake; so I got up and went in the house, shut the door, grabbed another beer, and plopped down on the couch for another episode of the *Andy Griffith Show.* My friend Richie came by later that evening to borrow my car and ask if I wanted to go to the nightclub with him. I said, "No, I just want to stay home and relax and listen to the sound of crickets and allow the cool breeze to blow on my face."

The breeze felt so good blowing through the door I walked outside and sat down on front porch. Once again, the breeze on my face was suddenly blocked. I looked up, and there she was, standing two feet from me with a deck of cards in her hands. She asked, "Do you want to play cards? We can play goldfish." I said, "No, I just want to sit here quietly." She was persistent. She asked three times in an insidious way, this time bending over, hanging her huge 36DDs in my face. My eyes went cross as her erect nipples hung less than an inch from my mouth. It was all I could take, so I reluctantly caved into her well-proportioned body and submitted to playing cards with her. There was nothing I could do at that point in time. The blood had already left my head, so I was no longer thinking clearly. I couldn't get up and run in the house because the blood left my feet as well and began to centralize once again in my pelvic region. I was in a temporary trance. She beat me five games straight. I found it hard to focus on anything but her slightly erect nipples protruding through her tube top. She was killing me. I couldn't take it anymore, so I excused myself and limped into the house with a knee-crushing erection. I closed the door, leaving her on the porch to play solitaire by herself.

I must admit that I am weak for the flesh, and I loved wild, passionate, uncontrollable sex; but I was certainly no Lothario. Five minutes later, there was a knock at the door. She was definitely indomitable. There she stood with a bowl of blueberry pie. "Would you like some pie?" she asked. "No, I'm good. I'm just going to watch TV. "Are you sure? It's really good," she said. Because she asked over and over, I began to have visions of smearing blueberry pie all over her huge naked breasts. I submitted to her request once again. I opened the door and walked out on the porch. We ate blueberry pie with a scoop of vanilla ice cream. My imagination began to run even wilder. We talked for about an hour until my erection became so uncontrollable It began ripping through my military boxers. Once again, I excused myself and limped my way inside the house. This time, I closed the door to ensure that no one would bother me. Once again, she was knocking on my door. I pulled the curtain back and peeked out the window. This time, she had nothing to offer, so I let her knock on my door two more times. Before she could knock the third time, I opened the door, grabbed her by her tube top, and pulled her into the house. I stretched her tube top down, releasing the most impressive set of 36DD breasts that I'd seen since 1977. They were so perfect I lost conscious for a couple seconds and stumbled back against the entertainment center, knocking over my boxing trophies and a few pictures. I regained my footing then lifted her in the air, simultaneously pulling off her shorts off with one hand. There she stood in her young naked splendor, skin as smooth as a baby's ass. She mounted on my hips as though she were bronco busting a black stallion. I grinded her for two hours before she fell lifeless from my arms onto the couch. She labored in her breathing before hurrying to get dressed. She grabbed her clothes and stumbled outside onto the porch. Her knees buckle as though she were hit by a car.

She covered her mouth with her panties, embarrassed by what had just happened. She ran into her brother's house half dressed. I didn't even break a sweat. There was no feelings involved for me. I felt nothing. After spending twelve months in Japan and paying $15 for random sex, I became desensitized to the lovemaking process. It became difficult for me to relate sex and being in love. All my sex partners in Japan didn't display emotion because it was their job, not their first choice of employment. It was what their economics required at the time. On the other hand, I had no excuse for my infidelity. I was doing it just to fill the empty void for the moment. It was just something that I did, so I shut the door and continued to drink my beer. By this time ,my beer was warm and undrinkable. It tasted like piss, so I poured it down the sink. Just as I was reaching for another beer, she was knocking on the door again. I didn't even have time for the fifteen-minute refectory. I pushed the door open, thinking it was my friend Richie returning my car. She stepped through the door and said, "Take me." I thought to myself she's really pushing the envelope. This time, I was going to break her ass off something.

I paused for all of two seconds before grabbing her by the waistband of her shorts, pulling her in the house. I was bound to teach her to respect the jungle snake. I pulled her shorts off and lifted her in the air on my shoulders. I shoved my tongue deep in her vaginal cavity for an hour. She went wild, sliding down to my waist. She knew the drill. She wrapped her legs around my waist and settled in for the sexual hammering of her life. I probed deep inside her wound, hitting the G spot. Throwing her head back, she let out a yell as if she were a pig led to the slaughter. She yelled and screamed uncontrollably in Spanish. I did not understand her, but it sounded very sexy. As I shifted into third gear, a wet sticky substance ran profusely down my leg as if someone had poured a sixteen-ounce jar of syrup on us. I held her head gently in my hand and pounded her long and hard as she dug her perfectly manicured fingernails deep into my back, bloodying up my favorite T-shirt. I gave it to her long and hard for three hours; and finally, she went limp, fell from my arms, and curled into a fetal position on the couch. She broke into a thousand goose bumps all over her legs and arms while she lay there, shaking like leaves on a tree. I sat next to her on the couch, drinking my beer as if nothing ever happened. I was ready to go a third time, but she lay there lifeless. I didn't want to hurt her, so I let her rest; and after an hour, she got up looking like she had been in a twenty-hour orgy. Unable to put her panties back on, she pulled her shorts up and limped back home like a horse that threw its shoe. The sexual experience was nothing to me. It was just another proverbial $15 on the table with no emotion required.

I never heard from her again, but unbeknownst to me, her sister-in-law was listening at the door. She could hear the yelling and moaning as I was breaking her young sister-in-law off something proper. The next week after pulverizing my opponent in a boxing match, I was walking down the sidewalk toward my house when the young girl's older brother was coming down the sidewalk from the opposite direction with his wife. His wife was clutching his arm, digging her fingernails into his flesh, preventing him from attacking me.

I wasn't worried because I knew he saw the First Marine Division championship boxing trophy in my hand and realized that he could get the brakes beaten off his dumb ass, so he just walked by, looking angrily at me out of the corner of his eye. Our sexual escapade would never happen again. Soon after, her brother was discharged from the marines within three months of our triple-X one-night stand, so I never heard from her again. Cindy returned home shortly after. By this time, she was more than seven months pregnant with our second child and more than ready to drop this load. I did feel guilty about my sexual promiscuity. I didn't have any real excuses for messing around. I suppose I just did it because I could. Most of the time, I thought I cheated because I got married too early, or it was because I was like my father, or I was just bored, or it was because I wasn't in love when I got married. I was trying to do the honorable thing by marrying her. At the time, I thought the honorable thing was the only way.

Our life became routine: going shopping on the weekends, walking on the beach, or walking around the part of the base called Main Side located near the PX. We took pictures standing in front of the armored tanks, and later that day, we drove from one end of the base to the other, just taking in the sights. One morning I was getting dressed for work. Cindy said, "My water broke. I am having the baby." She said it so calmly I didn't believe her, so I kept getting dressed. She said, "Take care of Michaela. I'm going to the MP gate for an ambulance." I got dressed and hurried Michaela to the babysitter's. By the time I got to the MP gate, she was gone. Miya was born November 1, 1980, in the naval hospital on the Marine Corps base in Camp Pendleton.

She had black eyes with beautiful curly hair. Most people thought she was a Hispanic baby, She was the first in my family to be born in another state and on a military base. Cindy and I were very happy and content with our lifestyle. We attended church one block from our base housing unit every Sunday. Miya was the star of our church. Everyone wanted to hold her. Before I knew it, she was on the other side of the church, being passed around from women to women. I had to go get her from some women I had never seen before. I must say she was an attractive little girl with curly coal black hair and big black eyes.

I believe those were just old family genetics popping up to say they're still around. I didn't think I could make something so beautiful all by myself. After all the excitement of church, I forgot it was Easter Sunday and I was supposed to be sitting at the barracks behind a desk as the duty NCO. I totally rebelled against the idea of standing duty after twelve weeks of being in the desert. I knew I would have to pay the consequences for not showing up to stand my post, but I also knew the gunnery sergeant was wrong for continuously placing me on duty every weekend. After returning home from church, I was informed by one of my friends that the first sergeant was banging on my door. I knew at that moment they were going to try to court-martial me when I would arrive at work the next morning.

I arrived at work anticipating the worst. Before I could get in formation, the first sergeant called me into his office. "Stand at attention," he yelled. Reaching into his desk, he pulled out a short three-foot wooden club and slammed it on his desk. He stared at me as if he wanted to kill me while rolling up his sleeves. "I'm going to kick your ass," he said. "Where the hell were you Sunday?" I stared at him for brief a second and said, "I'm not afraid of you, First Sergeant." He yelled, "Stand at ease." Then he marched out of the room into the captain's office next door. "Report to your captain," he yelled. I came to attention and marched into the captain's office. "Go back out and report in right," the first sergeant said. I did an about face, walked outside, then pounded heavily on the hatch. "Sir, Corporal Rawlings reporting as requested, sir, Captain." "Why didn't you report for duty on Sunday, Corporal Rawlings?" "The gunnery sergeant repeatedly put me on duty every Sunday for the last two months, and all the other NCOs have duty one weekend per month," I said. Captain said, "Well, that's no excuse." I said, "Sir, before we go any further, I would like to request to see the commanding general." "Step outside, Corporal Rawlings." I stood outside for two minutes that felt like an hour after which time I was ordered back into the office. They decided to give me duty one more Sunday before I was discharged. I began packing my house and returned the furniture to base housing in the rental stores. I sold my car for slightly more than I paid for it; therefore, I spent the next six months riding my bike to and from work fourteen miles each way. The road was long and dark. My generator-powered light provided very little reflection, making the ride more difficult, while the wheel of generator rubbed against the back tire, creating energy for the light. I tried to cover the hard bicycle seat with a specially designed seat cover made of rabbit skin but to no avail. My testicles banged against the seat like a pinball machine. By the time I got to work, it was time for morning PT (physical fitness training), including eighty sit-ups, twenty pull-ups, jumping jacks, and a three- to six-mile run.

I ran my last PFT (physical fitness test) without motivation, as if I didn't care. My platoon leader yelled at me as I was just about to walk across the finish line, finishing the three-mile run in twenty-two minutes. "You're not even sweating," he yelled. I just looked at him and walked over to the barracks. I was a short-timer with less than three months left in the corps, and I knew there was nothing he could do to help me or hurt me. Three months later, I had served my four years, and my contract was over. I reported to the Main Side base at Camp Pendleton to receive my final pay and discharge papers. That must've been over fifty of us getting discharged that day. We were so happy we staggered the line and talked loudly about our civilian plans. A sergeant started yelling from the top of the steps, "Shut the fuck up and get in a straight line." The voice was so distinctive I recognized it right off. It was Sergeant Hondo. He had returned to his old job and no longer was a drill instructor. After waiting for forty-five minutes, I stepped in from his window and said, "Sergeant Hondo." He looked up at me with a stern look and said, "Where you mine?" "Yes, sir, Platoon 1059." I couldn't help but feel good. It seemed the beginning and the end came together. I smiled as I went down the steps. Just seeing him again reminded me of what I had achieved.

I was discharged from the United States Marine Corps with an honorable discharge and returned to civilian life, ready to be placed in a job I thought I rightfully earned, but I soon found out that was not the case. I spent the first couple of weeks back in civilian life walking around the old neighborhoods on Delaware Street and Park Avenue, reminiscing about old times. I walked past John's old house on Washington Boulevard and remembered it wasn't long ago that I sat on his steps, begging for candy. I even took an occasional trip to Riverside Park, hoping to catch a glimpse of old friends. I didn't have a car, so I just rode the bus everywhere I traveled, enjoying the nice, quiet ride while touring through familiar places. I even passed Saul Subway, stopped, and peeked in the window. It had only been four years that I was away, but it seemed like so much changed. The only thing that remained the same was my family. They worked the same jobs, living the same life, not traveling, or making any big plans. They just continued to live the same routine day in and day out. All of a sudden, I could see why left Indianapolis.

The routine was stale, and the city seemed slow and less progressive than California. Jobs were very scarce, and I was in for a big surprise when I went looking for one. I thought being in the Marine Corps would give me the advantage. Employers would just love to have a young fresh marine straight out of the military. I couldn't have been more wrong. No one cared that I had been in the military. I was just like everyone else. If you didn't have a skill or a college degree, you didn't have a job. I worked in field artillery for four years and had trouble matching my skills with any civilian employer's qualifications; therefore, civilian life was a big adjustment I had to get used to—unorganized and slow-moving civilian behavior. The other bad news was we didn't prepare for the move back home, so we moved in with Cindy's mother until we could get our own place.

I wasn't overjoyed with the decision, so I hung out at my mother's house most of the time. Miya was too young. Therefore, she stayed at home with her mother while Michaela went with me to go to the park and to play in her grandmother's backyard with her cousins. I hung out in the front with my brothers, drinking beer and talking about old times. Cindy called two hours later, requesting that I bring Michaela home to eat dinner. I didn't think much of it, so back over the bridge, I went to her mother's house. I found it difficult to stay in a strange place not knowing whether I was really welcome, but it seemed Cindy was right at home, cooking dinner and seemingly more alive than she was just a week ago in her own home. Her conversations had more of a bite to them because her mother played with her mind. She tormented Cindy with conversations about my escapades in Japan and how I probably left children in Japan waiting to come to the United States.

I didn't think it was funny at all. As a matter of fact, I believe Cindy was taking her mother seriously and began to show signs of jealous impulse. Anytime I left home, she wanted to go with me. Even a casual stroll a half block down the street to the variety store, she went to come with me. I was beginning to feel smothered and overwhelmed by the entire situation, so I escaped into myself, playing with my kids on the couch and riding them on my back around the room. I looked through the newspaper every day for work but was sadly disappointed by the lack of job opportunities in the capital city. I began to pound the pavement, newspaper tucked under my arm. I wanted to impress employers, so I wore a pair of Stacy Adams and a pinstripe suit I had made while in Japan. I headed to the downtown circle where multiple businesses lined the streets. I when door to door but had little luck finding a job, but the day wasn't a total waste. I bumped into a couple of old flames from my high school days. They saw the wedding ring on my finger but didn't care if I was married and invited me to come by after hours. They even gave me their phone numbers, but I dropped them in the trash when they weren't looking. I didn't need any more drama in my life than I already had. I escaped unscathed from my extramarital affair with the Puerto Rican girl, and I just didn't need the hassle; so I kept pressing forward, trying to find a job. After several days of walking around, I just couldn't get any traction. I wasn't making any ground because most of the jobs had moved to Carmel, Indiana, or out toward Eighty-Six Street. I was destitute. Without a car, securing a job was next to impossible.

I returned home that evening less confident than I was before I left. My wife was big on saving money, but we had to dip into our account. We discussed buying the car Cindy's brother had for sale, a 1976 burgundy Cutlass Supreme with a half-white top and burgundy crushed velvet interior. Her brother kept the car in immaculate condition. The paint was flawless as well as the inside of the vehicle. He wanted $2,000, but I waved $1600 in his face. He didn't even break stride as he ran over, grabbing the cash and tossing me the keys as he walked into a corner to count his newfound wealth. I couldn't wait to take the car for a spin, and to my surprise, Cindy let me take off by myself. I drove to my mother's house, showing off the car to my brothers. My eldest brother, Ray, conned me into buying two old antiquated speakers. He even made an honest attempt to install the speakers but hardly had a clue how to mount them properly in the back of the car. It took three hours, and finally, they were installed. My sister Sherry yelled out the door, "Cindy wants you on the phone. Bring the car back to the house."

I thought to myself, *Now it starts*. I didn't want to look like I was weak and henpecked by my wife, so I hung out for another hour with my brothers. Besides, I hadn't seen them in eighteen months. After downing a couple more beers, I headed back to Cindy's mother's house. I was greeted with low-key aggression as I stepped onto the back porch, Cindy reaching and clawing trying to snatch the keys out of my hand. I shoved the keys deep inside my pocket followed by her hand, probing deep into the pelvic region of my pocket, trying to retrieve the keys. She won that battle. She ran upstairs and hid the keys in a secure place, ensuring that I would not journey out of the house again that night.

I could understand how she felt, but little did she know the more she tried to control me, the more she pushed me away. After spending four years in the marines, I wasn't taking any more orders from anyone else. I didn't like being controlled or understand why her mother felt it necessary to talk about me going back to Japan to be with Asian women. It didn't make sense. I thought it was childish and insensitive and only served the purpose of making Cindy angry. Cindy became more and more of a cling-on. I felt the walls closing in on me. I lay in the bed staring at the ceiling while everyone else slept peacefully. I could feel the walls closing in on me; so I walked downstairs in the middle the night, staring out the front window onto the quiet, peaceful, but unsafe streets of Twenty-Fifth and Central Avenue.

I knew somewhere among all those thousands of buildings, there had to be a job for me. I felt responsible for my children. I wanted them to live in their own house, sleep in their own bedrooms, and eat what they wanted without have to ask permission from their grandmother. I wanted my wife to be the woman of her own home and not feel as though she had to tolerate the behavior of her crazy-ass mother. Occasionally, Cindy showed little respect for her mother, engaging in toe-to-toe arguments, something my mother would never let me get away with, and I would never disrespect my mother in that manner in the first place. For the most part, I thought Cindy was a sweet, loving girl until someone did something not to her liking. I began to grow increasingly tired of staying around the house day in and day out. I didn't have a life, and it was getting old quickly, but Cindy loved the idea of me being around the house day after day. She loved having me within eye distance and all to herself. I went along with it for as long as I could, but I couldn't stand it anymore, so I grabbed the car keys. Off I went cruising around parks, hanging out with buddies that I hadn't seen in years. I played a few games of basketball and drank a couple of beers. Just as I was beginning to feel good about my newfound freedom, Cindy grew impatient of my disappearance. In a fit of rage, she walked over to the park. She concealed herself well behind the big oak trees and waited for the moment I turned my back to run to the other end of basketball court. Then she made her move. She ran to the park bench, grabbing the car keys. She jumped into the car and fled back across the bridge toward her mother's house.

I ignored her for the most part because I knew she wasn't going anywhere out of reach, so I continued to play basketball until everyone decided to end the game for the night. I was somewhat embarrassed as everyone jumped in their cars and headed off while I had to reluctantly walk home to a place I didn't want to be. I stepped into the front. The house was very quiet to the point of being eerie. Normally, her mother was repeatedly listening to renditions of the song "Clean Up Woman." I didn't even smell her cigarette smoke or food cooking in the kitchen. The house was surprisingly quiet. I asked myself, *Where are the kids?* I noticed the keys lying on the fireplace. Before I could reach them, Cindy beat me to the punch. She ran around the chair. I jumped over the back of the couch. Without breaking stride, she very athletically snatched the keys off the mantel in one motion. She stuffed the keys in her pocket, winked at me, gave me a half smile, then pranced her way into the kitchen, summoning me with her finger to the dinner table.

The meal was exiguous: a pair of pig's feet laced with barbecue sauce, macaroni and cheese, and collard greens. I thought this meal should be served on Sunday, considering it was the beginning of the week. I sat at the table and watched Cindy's sister devour her pig feet, bite after bite, ripping the skin away from the bone like a carnivorous prehistoric animal. Cindy prepared a plate of two pig's feet and all the trimmings then proudly slid the food in front of me as though she had prepared a meal fit for a king. I didn't want to be ungrateful, but hell would freeze over before I ate those pig's feet. A knock at the door temporarily distracted Cindy, so she left the room for a split second, giving me time to shove the pig feet's back into the pan. Her younger sister watched as I slid the pig's feet off my plate and into the pan. I bribed her with an extra pig's foot if she didn't tell.

I put my finger to my mouth, signaling her not to tell. I didn't want to hurt Cindy feelings. She was from Mississippi and pig's feet were their traditional type of meal. I had never eaten pig's feet in my life.

As a matter of fact, I had never seen a real pig's foot on anyone's plate before. I only saw pig's feet attached to the pig's body. The macaroni and cheese was filling enough for me, so I retired upstairs, and Cindy followed close behind, slapping me on my butt as I climbed the stairs to our room. We sat on our bed, occupied by nothing but time. We talked and tried to come to a decision about the use of the car.

I felt it was my car because I used my money to purchase a car. Cindy was very pugnacious by nature. She couldn't let go of an argument until she believed she won, and other times, she would have an affable personality. I told her, "I don't care about what you thought. I am going to do what I want." I slipped my pants off and lay back on the bed in my boxers. Cindy casually got up and disappeared into the hallway. I didn't trust her. I knew I had to stay awake even if I had to use my night-vision technique. Several minutes later, she came back into the room wearing a provocative nightgown, totally distracting me from any signs of danger; but I noticed she had one hand behind the her back. She slowly caressed my thighs, and before I knew it, she grabbed my penis. As if her hands were a pair of vice grips with locking channels, she pressed a razor-sharp meat cleaver against my penis.

I didn't care whether she was serious or not. Her wish was my command. At that point, she totally had me by the balls—literally. I couldn't move and barely breathe. She looked at me with vengeful eyes as she grinded her teeth. She leaned forward and whispered in my ear, "I ought to cut your dick off." I jokingly replied, "Then you won't get any either." She pressed the meat cleaver deeper into my flesh and angled down as though to make a final cut. She began to draw blood. Then I let out a high-octave yell that could wake the dead. She released my penis and tossed me a towel while shoving the meat cleaver under the mattress. I thought to myself, *I have agape love for her, but I'm not trying to die for it.*

I got to my feet and hurried downstairs, applying pressure to the wound, trying to stop the bleeding. Cindy came downstairs and place her head on my chest. Laughing to herself, she said, "I'm sorry. You'll be okay, baby." To be honest, her crazy ass turned me on, but she was crazy to the thirteenth degree; and I knew if I didn't get away from her, she would do more physical damage that may not be repairable. I didn't know what to do. I was at a total loss. I didn't want to leave my kids, although I trusted Cindy to raise our girls in the past. But now I was beginning to have serious doubts about her mental state. She definitely appeared to be quick to anger, but she could always suck me back in two minutes after our fight once she's back to being the sweet angel that I met outside of Saul Subway. She knew where to touch me and how to touch me and what to say when she was touching me. Yes, she had my number, and she knew it. I stayed awake most nights, thinking about our marriage and how long I could go on facing knives every time we'd get into a minor argument.

I just didn't know what to do. I was so attached to Michaela. I had not yet had a chance to bond with Miya. But I knew our marriage wouldn't last because Cindy was still mentally wounded by my sexual escapades in Japan. I didn't know what to say or how to say it. Every time we made love, she commented on how much better I was at having sex after I returned from Japan, so I must've been having sex with a lot of women to develop that kind of sexual prowess. I was pleased that she thought I was good in bed, but I was tired of sleeping with one eye open. I was no longer in the marines. There was no reason to conserve my night vision by closing one eye while keeping the other one open. I slept with both hands covering my groin, I even thought about wearing a jockstrap with a protective cup. Sleeping nude with this woman was a thing of the past. I went to bed fully clothed and slept on my stomach with one eye wide open, scanning the area for meat cleavers or flying knives.

Over the next several months, I tried everything to be on my best behavior. I stayed at home, not only at home but in the house, only going on the front porch and occasionally to the variety store visible from the front porch. I wanted our marriage to work, so I was willing to sacrifice myself, but there was one small problem: I needed a job. I couldn't stand being caged up. Depression slowly crept into my murky subconscious. I felt as though I was losing myself for another human being. I felt trapped and couldn't breathe because the walls of un-marital bliss we're closing in. It was the month of August, and I had been out of the military thirty days. My travel had been limited to my mother's house and back home. I couldn't take it anymore, so I took off walking until I walked the boredom out of my system. I didn't know how long I was gone or how far I went. I just kept walking. Finally, I arrived back home three hours later. Cindy was standing in the kitchen with a scarf tied around her head. She stood at the stove, boiling hot water with a box of grits in her hand. She said, "These are for you." I said to myself, *I never had grits before. This might be a nice change.* I sat on the couch, anticipating eating something different for once. Five minutes later, Cindy came around the corner with a pot of boiling grits, and before I knew it, she was drawing back to throw the grits at me. I flipped over out of the way just as the grits splashed on the wall. I tried to get to my feet, but I slipped in the grits and fell back to the floor on one knee. Before I could stand up, she came charging out of the kitchen with a butcher's knife. Something clicked in me as though it was an automatic reaction. I grabbed her knife-wielding hand and flipped her over my back, disarming her of the butcher's knife. I tossed the knife on the floor and made my escape out the back door while her brother held her long enough for me to get in my car and drive off. I truly didn't think she would've hurt me with the knife, but I wasn't going to stay around to find out.

I believe most of the time she was just acting out, putting on a show for her mother or whatever family members she could use as an audience; but unfortunately for her, I grew very tired of being in survival mode all the time. I spent one night at my mother's house, which didn't make any difference in regard to my sleep deprivation. I still stared out the door at 4:00 a.m. My mind raced like the cars in the Indy 500. I couldn't hold a single thought in my head. I worried about everything: work, my children, where I would be 20 years from now, my marriage—mostly about my children. I knew deep inside I couldn't stay away from Cindy no matter how crazy she was. I'd grown to love her, and it deeply saddened me that we were apart. It bothered me more not knowing if we would ever repair our marriage.

I spent the next several months living with my oldest brother some apartments off Thirty-Eighth Street call Grass Moore Apartments. We were living the bachelor's life. He had an occasional girlfriend spend the night, and I had an occasional old flame from my boxing years drop in for the night of sexual ecstasy. I wasn't mentally attached to any of them. My mind was still on my wife, so I shared with all the women before any sex took place that I was married and wasn't going to leave her. I didn't care how they felt or if I hurt their feelings because it was just sex, a cliché, something for the moment and nothing more. I wanted to give my marriage another chance. Cindy would have to prove her anger was under control and she let go of my past sexual escapade in Japan as I let go of her past sexual relationship she had with her old boyfriend who lived across the street from her mother when I was in Japan. She had sex with one person, and I had sex with many, and I believe that's what upset her. After endless months of scouring the newspapers and pounding the pavement, I was hired for the graveyard shift as a security guard at a helicopter engine manufacturing plant. It was definitely the good old boys' club, and I knew in no uncertain terms I wasn't welcome. They we're just filling a quota. Either way, I didn't care. I just wanted to job. I never thought it would be this difficult for veterans to find work. I was under the illusion that veterans had preference.

That fantasy flew out the window along with all the other idiocies that I learned about being a patriot serving in the military and waving the American flag with pride. My military service didn't mean much to employers, and it was beginning to mean even less to me. I spent four years operating million dollars' worth of equipment, firing artillery shells over the head of troops, coordinating fire, and working as a section chief of a twelve-man crew; but none of this could be applied to a civilian occupation. I received $1 million worth of training in the military, but the training was valued at $3.25 an hour in the civilian world. I walked around the plant as though I was standing guard duty on a military post, the meter clock neatly strapped to my shoulder, My clothes were finally pressed, and my corfam shoes were buffed to a high gloss.

Every hour I would cruise through the planet. When one guard returned to the guard booth, the other guards would walk around the planet, punching his clock at selective stations. I hated his job, but I had to support myself and my children. I stopped by every weekend to visit with my kids. Cindy was at her best behavior because she wanted me to return home, but I was still skeptical of her unmanaged and displaced anger, so I visited my kids then went back to my brother's house for a night of running the streets and club hopping. Those nights were beginning to remind me of my old days in Japan. I was free to do what I wanted, and I didn't have to answer anybody as long as I came back to the base sober. All the club hopping we did didn't amount to much. I never picked up a woman in any of the clubs, so I was beginning to lose interest. I started staying around the house more. I worked, I went home, and every weekend I visited my kids and took them to the park. I felt empty inside. I wanted to be with my wife, but I didn't want to argue and fight.

One day, out of nowhere, it started pouring down rain. The rain was so heavy I was forced to pull to the side of the road. After five minutes, the rain began to lighten. I still could only see twenty feet in front of me, so I drove slowly and cautiously, taking my time because I had nothing to do and nowhere to go. I saw someone standing on the bus stop in the pouring rain, wearing white pants, so I pulled over and asked her if she would like a ride. She said, "No, thank you." I said, "Stop playing and get in this car." At that time, lightning struck, cracking like a whip. She folded her umbrella then quickly jumped in the car. She removed her scarf, and she looked attractive, so I wanted to see where she lived. I offered to give her a ride all the way home. In my mind, I thought she lived where every other struggling young adults lived in the Grass Moore Apartments, but she lived on Thirty-Eighth and Emerson, much farther than I could afford to go, so I looked at her then at my gas gage. I had a fourth of a tank of gas, and I didn't want to waste it on someone I had no intimate connection with, but I was overtaken by the size of her perfectly round butt. I wanted to see more, so I sacrificed my last drop of gas so I could sneak a peek.

I slowly crept up to her apartment door, taking my time to make this day last a little bit longer. We sat and talked until the rain stopped. She hopped out of the car and made her way down the long sidewalk toward her apartment door. She waved good-bye, but I didn't move an inch. I was too busy watching her wide forty-inch butt sway from side to side. She looked back over her shoulders to see if I was enjoying the view. I was not only enjoying the view. I was in total amazement, Once again, the blood left my feet and my brain, centralizing in my pelvic region. I got dizzy but was able to refocus before driving off. I knew when and where to pick her up, so I made it a habit to cruise by her job every day in the same place. I was very friendly, make make no mistake about it. I wasn't simply rescuing her from a bus stop. I was trying to take one for the team. We dated four weeks. She wasn't giving me any signals about the direction our relationship was going.

I began to wonder if I was wasting my money and my time on her. She was eating out of the house. She loved McDonald's barbecue rib sandwiches. I bought her three barbecue rib sandwiches on three different days, and still, she didn't even let me smell her panties. I was getting sick of her begging ass. She was getting free meals and free transportation home every day. At this point, our relationship was purely platonic. The onus was on her to make the first move. To my surprise, she invited me into her studio apartment she shared with her brother. The apartment was arranged like any young person's apartment: quite empty, nothing on the walls. A couch in the middle of the room was the only piece of furniture occupying the two-room apartment.

The peephole on the door was jammed with a wood of paper to prevent anyone from looking inside. The apartment was dimly lit as if they were trying to save money on their electric bill. We sat close on the couch and talked for what seemed like hours. I was close enough to her I could smell the absence of perfume on her body. Her lips were chapped and dry, and she squinted her eyes as she bit into the cold barbecue rib sandwich she had left from the day before. She offered me a bite, but I shook my head no as I watched her savor every bite as if she hasn't had a meal in weeks. She let out a belch and wiped the barbecue sauce from her mouth with her sleeve then headed into the bathroom, closing the door behind her. I sat anxiously on the couch, anticipating her next move. The bathroom door was slightly ajar. I could see her reflection in the mirror. First, she took off her blouse, then her pants, intensifying each moment as I watched her like a Peeping Tom. She undressed all the way down to her black satin panties clinging to her beautiful brown skin. I moved to the edge of couch. I wanted so bad to shove the bathroom door open and claim my prize, but I was going to be the gentleman that night and wait patiently for her to give herself to me.

Suddenly, I was summoned to the bathroom. I leaped to the bathroom door as though I was shot out of a cannon. When I pushed the door back, she was lying in the tub naked as a jaybird, body shaped like an hourglass, with skin like Queen Nefertiti. She reached up and grabbed my hand. "Take off your clothes and get in," she said, but I was too shy to comply with what she was asking. The apartment was too small, and there was nowhere to escape and put my clothes on if her brother walked in. "No, I don't feel comfortable, and what if your brother comes home?" I said. She pulled me closer and said, "Don't worry about him. He always comes in late." I still didn't get in the tub, but I did help her dry off, taking my time rubbing the towel all over every inch of her well-proportioned body. My sexual appetite was being fed, I felt her warm breath on my neck. I became so concupiscent my eyes went cross, and I lost conscious for couple seconds. When I came to, there she was standing in front of me disrobed, her beautiful brown skin on display, not a blemish or unsightly mark to be found. Her coal-black hair hanging slightly past her shoulder only served to accentuate her hourglass frame. All of a sudden, I no longer felt the financial loss of three barbecue rib sandwiches. I was about to get paid in full and with dividends. It was my birthday. I believe that was the reason she let me make love to her or, for a better term, break her off.

I didn't love her—at least not yet. We were getting acquainted with each other one sexual episode at a time. I didn't know if I would ever love her. I was still married and had no intention of leaving my children for her or any other woman. As bad as my marriage was, I still thought about Cindy and my two girls all the time. I wasn't a perfect husband, but I wanted to be a perfect dad. After several months of dating , Gina and I moved in together. I don't know what the hell I was thinking or if I was thinking at all. She was so toothsome and voluptuous my hormones ran wild, not allowing me to think, not with common sense anyway.

Gina and I were both way fortunate to have full-time jobs. Our combining incomes didn't even equal $10 an hour. I worked for a security company, and she worked at a dental office, making false teeth. We were doing okay for a while. We went to the movies regularly and out to dinner on several occasions. I got to meet a few of her girlfriends. One girlfriend in particular (Pat) Gina thought I was having an affair with, but there was nothing between us. She was attractive, very well groomed as if she lived at her beauty shop. She had a long slender body with big 36DD breast. I could see why Gina was a little jealous. It was competition, and Gina knew what parts of women l liked. Pat would often come over strutting around the apartment wearing tight blue jeans and her stylish white shirt showing off her figure, knowingly driving me crazy, while she sat on the end of the couch, allowing the sunlight to reflect through her shirt, giving me a view of what she thought I was missing. After six months of living together, I lost my job, and so did Gina; and to make the situation worse, my car transmission stopped working. My car broke down right in front of the transmission shop. I had no choice but to push the car onto the transmission repair lot. The shop wanted $400 to repair the car. I didn't have two nickels to rub together, so I left the car shop and walked six miles home. Gina and I spent the summer searching for jobs. I worked for manpower day labor. She worked various jobs throughout the city, never finding a permanent work. We got bored sitting around the house, so our sex life blossomed. We had sex every day, sometimes twice a day. Our refrigerator was empty, but somehow we seemed to be able to feed ourselves at least once a day. I found myself walking every day looking for work. Sometimes I walked seven to eight miles each day wearing a three-piece suit and Stacy Adams shoes.

Once, I took a bus to apply for busboy job at a popular restaurant on the east side of town. To my surprise, the line of people was stretching around the corner for one busboy position. The word got out that someone already got hired for the position through nepotism. I couldn't believe it. I'd come all this way for nothing. I had no money in my pocket, and it's eighty-five degrees outside. I had to walk home from Fifty-Sixth and Keystone to Thirtieth and Post Road. I was tired of being broke, not having a penny in my pocket. I needed my car out of the shop so I could expand my job search. So I sat outside on my apartment steps, contemplating about my life and where I would get the money from to get my car out of the shop. I went for a walk around the block to clear my head. I couldn't help but notice that one man was working at the gas station by himself, and then it hit me. That's how I could get some money: rob this gas station.

The next day I walked to my brother's house. We sat and talked for a while before he offered me one of his beers. I said, "Sure, I'll have one." I opened the refrigerator door, and to my surprise all the cans were yellow with one big word: *beer.* I took a sip and tasted nothing will barley. I held the can of beer up in the air and stared at it. There were no inscriptions on the beer other than the word *beer,* I tried to drink it, making polite conversations, then asked if I could borrow his gun. He did not ask any questions. He opened the gun chamber to ensure it was loaded, closed the chamber, and handed me the gun. All that day I cased the gas station across the street from the apartment complex. I watched the movement of the men inside. One man went home, and the other stayed to close the shop. *This is it,* I thought to myself, putting my ski mask on my head. I slowly made my way across the street toward the gas station. I opened the chamber of the gun to ensure that it was ready. Suddenly, the chamber fell on the ground, and the bullets scattered all over the sidewalk.

It took me ten minutes to recover the bullets. By that time, I could see clearly that this was the wrong thing to do, so I put the gun away and walked back to my brother's house. I sat out on the balcony and drank one of his generic beers and handed him back his gun. Things were starting to get uneasy around the apartment. Gina and I were spending too much time cooped up in our small apartment we were beginning to slowly drift apart. Sex couldn't make up for the discontent in our relationship. I tried to make our evenings more interesting. I had my daughter come over and spend the night. Cindy did mind Michaela spending the night with me, but she let her come anyway, but this wasn't without reciprocity. She wanted a full report once Michaela got home the next morning. The 6:00 a.m. the phone began to ring. It was Cindy requesting that I bring Michaela home right now. I told her I'd bring her home in two hours when I get up, but she kept calling and calling until I agreed to take her home.

I arrived at Cindy's mother's house at around 7:00 a.m. I knocked on the door then turned the knob. The door opened, and I stepped inside the house. I went up and got in the bed. "Michaela," I said as she ran toward the staircase. She reached the top of the steps, then stopped, and came down midway. She sat down on the steps and stared at me as if she was looking right through me. I waved bye to her and said, "It's okay, baby. Go on up to bed." She got up and made her way up the steps. At that moment, Cindy stepped from behind the door, jumped on my back, and placed a butcher's knife to my throat. "I ought to cut your fucking head off," she said while applying pressure to the knife placed against my throat.

In a split second, I did what was natural for me to do. My mind clicked over, and I flashed back to my hand-to-hand combat training. I grabbed the knife-wielding hand and took one step back, flipping Cindy over my back onto the floor. I tossed the knife on the floor then headed for the door. Before I could reach the car, Cindy began throwing knives and bricks at me from the front porch. I stood there blocking the bricks and knives with my hands. She was out of control, and I didn't know what else to do; so I walked up to her, intending on slapping some sense into her. But as I swung, my hand did not open, and I ended up striking her just below her left eye with my fist.

I felt horrible. I felt so bad I grabbed her, hugged her, and said, "I'm sorry. I didn't mean to do that. I'll let you hit me back." Before the words cleared my mouth, she coldcocked me, cutting my eye in almost the exact same place as hers, but she didn't stop there. She ran to the kitchen, grabbing more knives from the kitchen drawer. This give me time to make my getaway. As I drove off, she ran behind the car, throwing bricks, barely missing my driver's door window as I skidded around the corner. It would be a month before I go to visit my children again. It would have to be in a mutual place, not at her mother's house. I spent most of the summer looking for work or hanging out at the apartment, doing nothing. I was extremely bored. Some days I would walk from Post Road to Twenty-Ninth and Talbott Streets to visit my mother. Then I would walk home later that day. The marines have prepared me very well physically but not so much in the area of employment. The marines didn't provide me with any transferable skills. Everything that I learned in the marines or thought I knew I can't use in the civilian world. I was forced to look for low-income jobs or to go to college, something I wasn't prepared to do.

I was struggling in all areas of my life. I couldn't see any way out or any possibility of improvement. I was stuck. Here I was. I had just served my country for four years, and I couldn't even get a job as a busboy. Gina and I were beginning to really get on each other's nerves. The sex had run its course. She was young and inexperienced and couldn't take me sexually where I needed to go. After having sex five or six times a day, in three- to four-hour sessions for six months straight, we both were bored with it. I began to see another side of her, a very childish side of her that would irritate me to no end. She would do little things to try to pick a fight, but I would just ignore her and watch TV. One day she was picking with me just out of spite. "I never see you get upset," she said. "Get mad. I want to see you get mad." I didn't even remember getting up. Before I knew it, I grabbed one of my Japanese swords off the stand on top of the TV and put it to her throat.

With her feet dangling in the air, I didn't notice I had her at knifepoint until I felt her tears running down my arm. I released her from my grasp. She fell to the floor and immediately started scrambling around, packing her suitcase. She was moving so fast you would've thought she was in boot camp. Her friend Pat came to pick her up and help her carry her bags to the car. I continued to watch TV, hardly noticing she left until later that evening when loneliness set in. For the first time, I was by myself and had time to think about what I was doing with this women and where this relationship was going. I decided to call it quits. I packed my bags and went home to my wife and kids.

I knew repairing our marriage would not be easy, but I had to try. I didn't want my children to grow up without me. I know what it feels like to be without a father, and I made a promise to myself I would not abandon my children like my father did to us. He walked away from us and lived scot-free over the responsibility of providing for us. The child support bureaus were not as established in the sixties and seventies as they are today. The government did not actively seek out and put fathers in jail for not providing support for their children; therefore, my mother was left all alone to figure it out. I harvested hate and grew a distaste in my mouth for my father and swore I would never abandon my children. I could be a better man, but the question remained: was I mature enough to demonstrate the qualities I possessed? Cindy scoured the newspapers until we found the perfect two-bedroom apartment on the west side of town, south of where we both worked full-time.

Cindy found a job as a housekeeper in the Indiana Teachers Association building. I, on the other hand, became a special deputy sheriff, a fancy term for security guard with arrest powers. We were doing okay. We took our savings and purchased a new front room and dinette set and a new bedroom set. We were settling into our new apartment, and I thought everything was going okay until three months later, I received a call from Gina. She was pregnant and want to money for an abortion. Somehow I gathered the money, took it to her apartment; but she packed up lock, stock, and barrel. There wasn't a crumb to be found in the apartment. I didn't know where she was, so I made contact with a few of her girlfriends. After three days of searching, one of her girlfriends finally confessed she moved to South Bend, Indiana. I was infuriated. I drove down the street sixty miles an hour, searching for the first phone booth I came across.

I spotted a phone booth on the Zayres parking lot. I grabbed the phone, frantically dialing her mother's number, and she answered, "What do you want?" She asked, "Why didn't you tell me you were pregnant?" "I didn't know at the time," she said. "Are you coming back to Indianapolis?" I asked. "I thought you were going to get an abortion." She angrily replied, "No, I'm keeping it because I'm tired of you leaving me." Then she hung up the phone. I sat in my car for an hour that day, thinking of what a mess I made of my life. What was Cindy going to think if she found out? I just couldn't take any more of her bipolar episodes, but in this instance, she'd be justified in whatever reaction she chose. I headed to my mother-in-law's house to pick my children then to Cindy's job to pick her up before we headed back to our apartment. That became a routine for the next forty-five days. All of a sudden, Cindy stopped talking. I had not yet revealed to her Gina was pregnant. Even though Cindy and I were separated for one year during that time of the pregnancy, I knew in Cindy's mind that wouldn't matter. It wouldn't matter if I left the planet and got an alien pregnant on the moon. It wouldn't change the situation or how she felt about the situation or how she would react to the situation.

Over the course of three days, our marriage trouble intensified. Cindy started communicating physically rather than verbally. One day I worked the graveyard shift at a trucking yard. After working eight hours, I decided to stop downtown at the donut shop and have myself a cup of coffee and a donut. It was only six in the morning. Very few people were up moving around on the snow-covered streets. I sat quietly in the coffee shop with my back against the wall, seemingly enjoying my favorite pastime. Then I realized I have been there for thirty minutes, so I gathered my things and drove home. I walked in the door. I knew it. She was totally predictable. My luggage and clothing bag lay on the front-room floor. My luggage was sliced into little pieces. My clothes were sprawled all over the floor as if they were kicked around. Ten seconds later, Cindy came out of the room, screaming mad, "Where the hell you've been all morning?" I was too tired to respond. I just slumped on the couch and looked at her in disbelief.

She said, "Get your stuff and get out." I was too tired to argue or fight; so I grabbed my bags, collected my clothes, and headed for the door. Cindy jumped in front of the door, holding on to butcher's knives one in each hand. She said, "You can go, but you can't take the car." I looked at her with a puzzled look on my face. "There's snow and ice everywhere. I know you don't expect me to walk out of here carrying the stuff in my hand walking over ice and snow." I opened the window, which was ground level, and threw my bags and luggage out. Jumping outside the window, I picked my bags up and tried to run to the car. By the time I got there, she had sliced three of the four tires. She looked at me and said, "Now you can go." I knew there were gas stations nearby within two blocks, so I jumped in the car and drove the car in reverse, trying to make it to the gas station before all the air went out the tires.

Before I knew it, Cindy jumped on the hood of the car and started stabbing the windshield with the butcher's knife. I kept driving as if she weren't even there. I exited the apartment complex, hitting ice sliding sideways, onto Thirty-Eighth Street. I turned left, heading toward Lafayette Square Mall. I proceeded toward the gas stations two blocks away, but I wasn't sure if was going make it, so I picked up speed to about forty miles an hour. Cindy rode on the hood, clutching each windshield wiper to maintain her balance as I did a U-turn into the parking lot of a tire repair station. Just as I came to a stop, three of the tires went flat. Cindy stood there, yelling and stabbing wildly at the driver's door window. I sat in the car with my hand placed over the trigger of my 357 Magnum. It was eight o'clock in the morning, and

I thought to myself, *It's too early for this shit.* Cindy stood there in her cotton nightgown with no shoes and a scarf wrapped around her head, clutching a knife, yelling and screaming. She was so angry I didn't even think she knew how cold it was. She must've stood there for at least an hour, making threats, yelling at me to get out of the car. Michaela began walking down the street. I could see her from a distance, and I pointed in her direction. Cindy stopped her rage for the moment to took Michaela back in the house. I sat in the car in disbelief, not even noticing seven hours had passed. At 3:00 p.m., Cindy came back to the car no longer angry. she offered me money for my tires. She said she would not hurt me and it was okay if I slept on the couch. She went back to the apartment, and I sat in the car for thirty more minutes, wondering whether or not I should trust her. I went to my trunk and took out my shoulder gun holster. I shoved my Magnum into the holster under my jacket, leaving my bags in the car. I reluctantly headed back to the apartment for a sleepless night.

I was willing to do anything to be with my children, but she was making it impossible for me to stay. I knew at this point she was bipolar and needed help, but she had a real sweetness about her. It was hard for me to walk away from my marriage, so I stayed the night. I slept on the couch with eyes wide shut. My eyes were closed, but I was very conscious of any movement around the apartment. I felt like a stranger in my own home, not really welcome but just there to support other people and their agendas. The next morning Cindy walked into the room and tossed rolled-up bills onto the couch. "This is for your tires." She laughed to herself and walked off. I picked the money up and looked at it, and it was only $25. I said, "What is this? How am I going to buy three tires with $25?" She looked at me, walking back and forth between the bedroom and kitchen, smiling and laughing to herself. She really didn't believe I would be able to drive the car off. In her mind, she had me beaten, but I had other plans. While sitting in the car earlier that day, I noticed a stack of tires in a bend on the side of the building. I selectively pulled one tire from the massive stack of hundreds of tires.

The tires seemed to be in pretty good shape. I couldn't understand why someone would discard perfectly good tires. These tires had good rubber and deep threads. As I pulled the tires out from the stack, it seemed that one tire was better than the next. It was a gold mine of tires. I stacked three tires beside my car then jacked the car up, carrying the new tire and rolling the flat down the street two blocks in the snow to the Shell gas station. I was charged $5 per tire to mount the tires on the rim. It was perfect. I couldn't believe it. Finally, I was given a break, and something was working in my favor. The snow was so deep I had to walk in the street. I slipped and fell on the wet ground in the ice and slush. I didn't even notice both legs of my pants were soaking wet with snow clinging to the bottom until I was finished replacing the tires. I was overjoyed. I gladly drove down the street. My car wobbled it way to my mother's house. I couldn't tell at the time all the belts were broken in all three tires, but I was able to make it to my mother's house. I sat on the couch, holding everything inside. I tried to mentally process what had just happened and caught my breath.

I still had my work uniform on from the day before, and I had to be at work in three hours. I didn't move. I just sat on the couch, trying to forget the day and get two hours of sleep before going to work. I didn't know what the future was going to be—the future of my marriage and, more importantly, the future of my children. I went to work that night with socks still wet from earlier in the day and stomach growling because I had not eaten since the night before. I arrived at work twenty minutes early so I could compose myself before going in. No matter how hard I tried, I couldn't be the same happy, positive person I always was, so I sat in my car on the parking lot of Popeye's Kitchen until I collected myself, gathering strength from places I never knew I had. I walked in the restaurant, waved at the employees, and positioned myself in the back corner. I hardly watched the patrons enter and leave, smiles plastered on my face carrying bags of pieces of caucus Home so they can sit and devour them infront the TV. I was so tired I was in a daze for ten hours. I wasn't only tired. I was mentally tired. I watched the clock every second tick by slowly. As the night drew in,

I walked outside to my car and discovered that three of my tires were flat. There was a gas station a half a mile away. I tried to drive it, but my car gave out; a half block from the restaurant, the tires were totally flat. I called a tow truck then walked in the snow and slush four miles to my mother's house. My sister Sharon grudgingly opened the door, mumbling something that only made sense to her under her breath. I stomped my feet twice on the porch, shaking the snow off my boots. I sat once again on the couch and let out a sigh of relief, trying not to think about tomorrow because it would surely bring its own problems.

I sat up listening to the house fall asleep. The floorboards squeaked as my sisters settled in for the night. Everyone had somewhere to sleep except for me. I was in the midst of turbulent times in my life. It had been two days since I had eaten. I didn't care. I was focused on buying new tires and reestablishing my life together. There were rumors Gina was back in town, but my life was so out of control I didn't want to add to my problems. I tried to stay as far away from Cindy as possible, but it wasn't long she called my mother complaining about my abandoning her and the kids, and she didn't have a ride to work. I told her what Cindy had done, and I wasn't going to buy new tires again. I made arrangements with Cindy to take her to work and pick her up. I dropped her off every night for a month. The drive began to become taxing. By the time I got back to my mother's house, it was 1:00 a.m. It didn't make sense for me to drive all over the city, and I didn't get home until 1:00 a.m., so we changed our arrangements. I began to sleep in the front room on the floor of the apartment. I got my clothes in the car, only bringing into the house a small travel bag containing underwear, toothbrush, and change of clothes.

Things seemed to have been going well for couple weeks, and Cindy and I managed to sleep in the same bed, even having occasional passionless sexual encounters. I still loved her, but I still slept with eyes wide shut. Mornings came in and went. I could tell over the next couple weeks something was bothering her, but I just couldn't put my finger on it. Anytime I tried to ask her what was wrong, she just walked into the other room, not saying a word. The one thing we agreed on was church, but neither of us was in the mood for being preached to. We needed professional marital counseling, but neither of us made more than minimum wage. I was barely able to pay the rent. Therefore, paying someone for advice about our life wasn't even an afterthought. We just couldn't afford it.

The Exodus

As usual, my days were very predictable. You could set your watch by me. I would get off work, drive by Cindy's job, pick her up, stop by my mother-in-law's house, pick the children up, then drive to the apartment. I was living an uneventful, boring life for a twenty-four-year-old. I was beginning to believe this was my permanent place, and I didn't foresee any changes in the future. We had been living together for over a month. We were rediscovering each other—so I thought. One night I picked Cindy up from work, as usual then back to our apartment. She didn't say a word the entire trip home, although I tried to strike up a conversation. She was nonresponsive and just stared out the window, seemingly preoccupied with something else. Once we arrived at the apartment, I barely had the car in park before she flung the car door open, grabbing Miya by one arm snatching her from the backseat, she walked off leaving the car doo ajar. I took Michaela from the backseat and carried her in the house, closing the passenger door before I went inside.

I could tell she would try for another fight, so I walked Michaela inside the apartment and said good night to Cindy, but she asked me to stay. I stood there for a moment, staring at her. I asked her, "What's wrong with you? Why are you so quiet?" She looked at me teary-eyed and said, "I just had a hard day at work, that's all." Once again, I fell weak for her, and I stayed the night. I took off my gun belt, unloaded my gun, and placed it high on the closet shelf. I didn't feel like arguing. Instead of going to bed right away, I sat on the front-room floor and watched the *Benny Hill Show.* Cindy came in the room several times and interrupted the TV program by turning off the TV. I didn't know at the time she wanted attention. I wasn't educated, and I didn't have a clue what she was doing; so I sat on the floor, watched TV, and ate my cheeseburger until five o'clock in the morning. I heard rustling in the hallway. I looked up. Cindy was in the closet, fumbling around on the shelf near my gun. I said, "What are you doing?" "I'm just getting my Bible." She extended her hand out toward me, showing me her Bible. "See?" she said before going back into the bedroom.

I got up. I walked over to the closet. My gun was still secure in its holster, so I sat back down and finished watching my TV program. I finally decided to call it a night. My stomach was full for the first time in weeks because I wasn't mentally distracted by constant drama. I walked into the room. Cindy was lying very still on her side with a very intense stare. She clutched her Bible in her right hand, occasionally flipping through pages, even ripping out three pages and placing them on the dresser. I lay in the bed beside her fully dressed. I tried to watch her, but I slowly dozed off. I was soon awakened by the sound of pans rattling. I wasn't disturbed. I figured she was just in the kitchen preparing breakfast for the kids, so I slowly began to dose off once more. Unexpectedly, I was awakened by a loud bang. I was so tired I struggled to get my focus. I heard Cindy call my name. I sprang to my feet. I ran into the front room. I looked at her and said, "What are you trying to do? Why is it so smoky in here? Turn the stoves off."

I rushed into the kitchen and turned the knobs. The stove wasn't on. I began choking from the smoke, so I went to the window and tried to open it. I heard Cindy gasp for breath, so I turned around in astonishment, there it was: my 357 Magnum lying on the floor. Cindy gasped for air, arching her back high in the air. I quickly grabbed her, laid her on the floor, and placed pillows under her feet. I knew this much from my first aid training in the military. Then I frantically ran around, beating on the doors, asking for someone to call an ambulance.

My heart was beating a thousand minutes per second. The police and ambulance arrived within minutes as well as the news. I was escorted and told to sit on the apartment's steps while the police detectives conducted gunpowder burns test on my hands and fingers and halfway up my arm with a cotton swab dipped in a clear resolution. Somewhere between all the chaos, I was able to call my mother to come pick up the kids. I was placed in the back of a police car and watched them load Cindy in the back of ambulance and whisk her off to the hospital. I was transported to the downtown police headquarters. I was placed in a small 6x10 room with carpet padding on the wall and a small metal table placed in the center of the room. I was left alone in the room for what seemed like an hour before a young white female detective went in the room with a clipboard and a tape recorder in hand. She asked questions in duplicate, writing on a pad sometimes and other times using a tape recorder. Before I knew it, it was 4:00 p.m. One tall gangly police sergeant walked into the room. He looked at me and said, "Your fingerprints are all over the gun." I squinted my face, looking at him in total disgust. "Of course my fingerprints are all over the gun". "It's my gun" I said. "I carry it to work every day," The detective came back into the room, telling me I was free to go.

I walked out into the lobby, and to my surprise, my entire family was there in full support. For the first time in my life, I saw my entire family in one place just for me. I was still in a daze and overwhelmed by what just happened. It was as if I was standing outside of my body, watching myself go to this horrific ordeal. I was driven from the police station to my mother's house by my brother-in-law and my older brother Karl. Before I could reach the house, my sister received three calls from Cindy's family threatening my life. I didn't bat an eye. I was numb by the process I just went through. I didn't want to speak to anyone or think about anything. I didn't even know if I wanted to continue to live. I was hurt right down to my core. Crippling pain took over my mind and body. I knew I would have to return to the apartment to pack up all my furniture and move out. I knew it would be impossible for me to live in that apartment again. So with the help of my family, I packed up and moved out of the apartment. My mother and I packed up the bedroom. While going through Cindy's clothes, my mother found a suicide letter written by Cindy explaining why she killed herself. I didn't know my mother found the letter until several days later. I tried to read it, but I was still in a lot of pain and had trouble processing the information. We finished cleaning out the apartment and threw everything into a storage bin— out of sight, out of mind.

The next day my mother came with me to make funeral arrangements. We were escorted through a room that seemed to have endless caskets lined in rows of five, stretching to the back of the room. My eyes found a beautiful pink-and-silver casket. I had no clue as to how I was going to pay for the funeral. I gave the funeral director the title to my car without blinking an eye. I didn't know what it cost or how long I would have to pay on it. I wanted her to have it. The next day I took my wife's clothes to the funeral home, but the director said Cindy's mother purchased her a dress. The dress was a loud pink with puffy shoulders and ruffled sleeves. In other words, the dress looked ridiculous, but I was so emotionally distraught I didn't have it in me to challenge her decision. Before the funeral, I gave Cindy's mother rabbit fur coat, a new watch I bought for her for her birthday, and several of her rings. The day of the funeral, I sat to the right side of the casket. My friend Billy said my brother Ronnie asked him to sit with me in his absence, so he sat next to me and provided tremendous moral support.

My grandmother sat in the front row with my sister Marsha. It was reassuring and made me feel better just having her there. As the room began to fill with people, my cousin excused himself, saying that he had to leave to go and open up his studio. I noticed most of the family members were Cindy's relatives. There must have been well over sixty of her relatives in the room. I could hear loud talking coming toward the front of the room. I looked up, and it was Cindy's brother yelling and talking loudly, putting on a show for his friends and family. He turned the corner at the end of the chairs. He made his way toward my grandmother. Within seconds, he was at my grandmother's face, yelling and talking loudly at her. I sprang from my chair, tearing across the room. Before I could reach him, Billy grabbed me and pulled me back down in my chair. I fought and dragged Billy and his three hundred pounds closer to the fight. All of a sudden, the sound of squeaking chairs intensified as Cindy's family rushed toward the front of the funeral parlor, pinning me against the wall. I was still trying to make my way toward Rayford, barely grabbing his jacket. We tussled occasionally, slamming into the casket. The casket began to rock back and forth. I thought for sure Cindy would go out onto the floor.

My friend Eric heard the commotion and ran from the back of the funeral home with his gun high in the air and told everyone, "Get back. You're not going to hurt Mikey today." I didn't have time in that moment to really appreciate what he had done for me, but I know I am forever in his debt. The police swarmed the funeral parlor and forced everyone to leave.

My mother was outraged by the incident. She called all my family and told them what happened. Cindy's family kept calling and threatening my life. I wasn't fazed the least. I was totally focused on putting my wife in the ground and going on with my life. Two days after we destroyed the funeral home, I buried my wife. Everyone in my family that attended the burial was carrying a weapon except for me. My mother and stepfather and brother in-law had pistols in their coat pockets. All my sisters had knives and my older brother had a pump shotgun. Two police officers were assigned to me to ensure another fight would not break out. I stood there surrounded by fifty people, but I felt so alone. The preacher was praying, but I couldn't hear him. I was numb to everything around me. I felt an incredible weight in my heart. It was as if someone had pulled the plug on my life. I knew I had no time to sit and feel sorry for myself. I had to keep moving. Feeling sorry for myself wasn't going to take care of my children or put a roof over our heads. I tried to get back on point and focus, but there seemed to be a quite storm brewing within my personal space. Chaos and order were at odds with each other.

For weeks I sat on the back steps of my mother's house, watching my daughters play with their cousins in the backyard. All my senses were numb. I could see them yelling and screaming. I just couldn't hear them. They were very happy for the time being, temporarily forgetting any thoughts of their mother's death. I waited and waited for them to ask where their mother was and if she was coming home, but the question never came.

Throughout the next several weeks, Eric would come by my mother's house to try to encourage me and elevate my spirits, but I was too far gone to respond. It didn't matter how often someone tried to encourage me or say kind words. My subconscious would not give my mind permission to hear their kind words. Even Sergeant First Class Woods from the ROTC program called and tried to lift my spirits but I was too disconsolate. I was lachrymose from visions of Cindy lying lifeless on the front-room floor, tubes coming out of every extremity. I was on the mental journey of mortification. As penance, I chose to give up sexual relationships. I no longer gallivanted around, looking for easy prey. I accepted it as a form of retribution. My predilection for huge breasts and long brown legs had all but mentally disappeared. I had to travel this road of discontent and despair all by myself. This wasn't a joint venture. I was trying to live a peripatetic life. I had to change because until now every bad decision I made had a female accelerant.

When someone commits suicide, not only does it kill that person, it damages everything in its path. It disrupts life by creating unsuspecting battles of blame and fault between the survivors (Whip Rawlings).

Sergeant Walt thought it best that I go right back to work rather than sit around thinking about my wife's death; therefore, three days later, I was back at work, carrying a new 38 pistol issued to me by my security agency until I could afford to purchase a new gun. Because I carried a firearm, I was placed in some of the most economically depressed areas in Indianapolis. I worked in these arears before, but under my current mental status, I was in no mood to arrest or handcuff anyone. In fact, I didn't even load my gun. There was a time I would have made three arrests in one day, but now I just stood in the food freezer and watch blindly as the local kids stole from the store. I knew

I was not doing anyone any good, so I requested to work twelve-hour shifts on the highway, putting batteries in the yellow blinking lights and directing traffic away from the construction zone. I found myself working in a small town on the outskirts of Indianapolis. I didn't know the town existed until I started working there.

I carried a six-pack of beer on the front seat and a nickel bag of marijuana to help me get the ghost out of my head. It worked for a short while, but once the high was gone, pain rushed into my body like someone had lit a match to my soul. I parked behind the construction barriers and chucked rocks at the cows on the other side of the fence. I got lost in space and time watching the cows eat grass while I smoked my grass. I never liked marijuana. It made my head feel weird and my eyes burn. I got so hungry I left my post and ran to McDonald's every fifteen minutes, but I didn't have a choice. My mind was clogged with thoughts of the morning of March 29, questioning whether I could have done something different that would have prevented this tragedy or if I was predestined to travel this road. As they say in the Marine Corps, I didn't know whether I was shot, fucked, powder burned, or bitten by a snake. I was going down shit creek without a paddle. There were organizations that could have helped me, but I wasn't aware of any of those resources. I was a very private person and told my business to no one. I was also too proud to ask for help. I liked to handle things on my home with as little interference from the public as possible. My greatest fortune was my mother had the foresight to see that I needed space and time to recover, so she stepped in and took charge of my girls, which gave me a chance to catch my breath and regroup.

The Bible Lesson

I moved into a shabby, run-down studio apartment on Thirty-Eighth and Emerson. My two girls lived with my mother, giving me time to collect myself and recuperate. The apartment was small. It couldn't have been more than two hundred square feet in the whole apartment with just a front room and a bathroom. I didn't care because I was never home alone in the apartment for more than an hour at a time if I wasn't sleeping. I worked two jobs to ensure that I was mentally occupied for most of the working hours of the day. I worked two jobs back to back, one job so that I can pay child support and the other job so that I could support myself and my girls. I worked nonstop with a two-hour break between jobs with just enough time to change from one uniform to the other.

Each job required me to be constantly on my feet for twelve hours or more. I walked through the grocery stores on one job, and on my other job, I walked the hallways of a very ritzy apartment complex half asleep and physically wiped out. Cindy was haunting me from within. I couldn't escape thoughts of her in my head. My mind raced constantly, plunging me deeper into depression. I worked six days a week at mostly twelve-hour hour shifts with one day off each week. I spent most of my free time working on my car, ensuring the maintenance was up-to-date. Occasionally, I would see a tall woman walking past my car clutching her Bible to her bosom. Her dress hung slightly past her knees. She gave me a broken smile and never said a word as she went up the steps into her apartment. Sunday after Sunday, she walked past. Trying something different this time, she waved, acknowledging my presence. She smiled at me, and into the apartment building she went, not saying anything.

One day I was repairing a broken center length on the bottom front of my car. In an instant, a shadow was blocking the sun. I stuck my head from under the car to see what had eclipsed the sun. I stared up, and there were two long unshaved legs standing right over my head. I could see right up her knee-high skirt. She was wearing no panties, and her camel toe stuck out like two fists side by side. I politely turned my head to the right, trying not to disrespect her by looking up her dress. I said, "Can I help you?" She said, "When are you coming to church with me?" She stood there clutching her Bible. She was wearing a high-collar silk blouse with hair tied to the top of her head as if she was a secretary. She wasn't overly attractive, but she seemed genuine and religious, but I couldn't get the picture of her large exposed labia majora out of my mind. I didn't feel threatened by her because I was in no mental position to date anyone.

I ignored her and continued to work on my car. She said, "All right," and back up the stairs she went. Every Sunday she would stop by and invite me to come to church with her, and every Sunday I refused. I was still angry at God for allowing Cindy to take herself away from her children, so I denied her based on the fact I worked six days a week and didn't want to spend my only day off in church. After three months of her asking me to attend church, I caved in like a cake in the oven. Sunday school began at 8:00 a.m. I was dead on my feet because I worked the graveyard shift at Morrat Apartments until 7:00 a.m. After four hours of church, I was ready for bed, but she wanted to continue on with the lesson. Once we arrived back at the apartment, she invited me upstairs for more Bible study. I told her I was tired, but she was relentless and insisted I come upstairs. She said, "Come up in fifteen minutes," so I went into my apartment and changed into sweatpants. I grabbed my Bible and a pad of paper then headed upstairs.

I noticed her apartment door was slightly ajar, so I knocked on the door. "Come in and have a sit. I'm in the tub," she said, yelling from the bathroom. I stepped inside and looked to my right. There she was, sitting in the bathtub with the door partially opened just enough for me to see that she was in the tub. I thought nothing of it, so I sat quietly on her couch until she finished bathing. I could hear her drying off and the water draining from the tub. She yelled from the bathroom, "Close your eyes. I'm coming out." She wrapped a small white towel around her body, hanging just an eighth of an inch below her vaginal area. She quickly walked into her closet.

I sat on the couch, thumbing through my Bible, waiting for the Bible lesson to begin. All at once, she emerged from the closet wearing a black see-through gown. She strutted back and forth across the room, purposely stopping in the light reflecting through the window, giving me a clear view of her unshaved vagina and erect nipples. I didn't know what to think. Was she trying to seduce me into sex? Or did she really not know I can see through her gown when she stood by the window in the light? It really didn't matter because I was brain dead and emotionally drained at the moment. I was damaged goods. Sex was the farthest thought from my mind. For the first time in my life, I didn't recognize a sexual opportunity right in my face. I sat there turning the pages of my Bible, waiting for the Bible lesson that never came. Eventually, I headed downstairs, leaving her sexually aroused and wanting. As I reached the staircase, I heard the door slam behind me in sexual frustration. I returned to my apartment disappointed because I didn't receive my Bible lesson. I opened the door to my dark cold apartment and fell facedown on my sofa bed. I was so tired I was asleep before my head firmly touched the pillow. I woke up six hours later. I showered and started to get dressed for work. I sat in the chair next to the window, tying my shoes, and that was the last thing I remembered. I fell asleep sitting up tying my shoes. I was an hour late for work that day. My uniform was neatly pressed, my gun was empty, but my mind was full.

The same voice played over and over in my head like a broken record: "She just checked out . . . she just checked out . . . she just checked out, leaving our two girls." I couldn't get the voices out of my head, so for the next several months, I worked nonstop day and night until I dropped from exhaustion or had no room in my head for thoughts of Cindy. But it didn't work, so I hit the nightclubs in between shifts, trying to find comfort in a bottle of liquor. I had two half pints of Windsor Canada, one in each pocket. That wasn't good enough, so I purchased two cans of beer and mixed beer and wine all night until I couldn't walk. The irony of the whole drinking event was I didn't like alcohol. I couldn't stand the taste of it, but I wasn't drinking for enjoyment. I was drinking to get wasted.

I got so drunk I was carried to the door by a coworker from the grocery store. He pointed me in the direction of my car then shoved me in the direction where I was parked. I slowly walked, slipped, and slid my way to my car, eyes crumbling beneath my feet and the wind cutting through my suit like razor blades. Ice covering the windows and doors prevented me from entering my car very quickly. First, I drunkenly chipped the ice from the key hold and forced the door open, separating the ice from the door hang. I flopped down lifelessly onto the driver's seat and tossed my keys on the floor under the seat. Within seconds, I passed out.

I was awakened four hours later by tapping on my window. Someone was asking if I was okay. In that instant, my fingers began to burn as if they were frostbitten. I frantically began searching for my keys. After several minutes of searching, I located my keys and managed to start the car. My fingers were stinging really bad I couldn't even make a fist, but somehow I did get my car started. I jumped on the highway, heading for home, going five miles per hours the entire way. I barely noticed the other cars blowing their horns and flashing their headlights as I crept down the highway, swaying back and forth, crossing several lines before exiting the highway on Emerson. I knew I couldn't continue this pace. My life was flashing before my eyes. It seemed nothing I tried was working. I worked two security jobs; both jobs required that I carry weapons. I might just be enough money to pay child support and a few of my bills. I could even make payments on the funeral. Cindy lay in Hill Cemetery with an unmarked grave. I couldn't focus on that, for right now, I had to focus on the living. I had to focus on raising my daughters. Everything else was secondary. I needed college, but at this time, it wasn't an option. I wasn't groomed for college as a child, and even if I had been groomed for college, I would have fallen in the process because of my current mental state.

Armed but Not So Dangerous

Before the weekend, I received my new work schedule; and to my surprise, someone assigned me to work at the grocery store two blocks from Cindy's brother's house located in a low-income part of Indianapolis. It was very typical for an armed guard to be placed in dangerous locations. Even though I knew how to communicate with people, this location was a double threat, so I had to be really careful and stay out of harm's way. But I also knew Murphy's law: if something can go wrong, it will go wrong. One day Murphy's law showed up. As usual, I was in my depressed mood, lost in thought, and everyone knew it. They knew I wasn't the same man working in their grocery store two months earlier. I had changed, and they could see it was a dramatic change. I no longer felt compelled to arrest anyone. I hardly paid attention to anyone walking in the store, but one day two men walked into the store and positioned themselves on each side of the door. I automatically knew something was wrong. We stared at each other until the store manager signaled me over. He said, "These two men robbed the store the year before. The men made us all get undressed and lie down on the floor."

After hearing this news, my heart began to beat faster. My palms were sweaty. I knew my gun was not loaded, so I made my way to the back of the store, then slipped behind a two-way mirror in the back of the meat department. I loaded my gun then went out the opposite end of the storage room out of the view of the store mirrors. I watched the two men in the mirrors as I slowly walked back to the front of the store. I left the strap of my gun unfastened and leaned back against the grocery carts with my right hand slung over the trigger. The two men stared at me very intensely. I believe they thought they could punk me and make me back down, but if they only knew what I had just gone through there would've hastily left the store without a hitch. But that wasn't the case, so we stared intensely at each other, barely batting an eye. The stare went on for five more minutes. We were frozen in time in dead silence you could hear a pin hit the floor. The two men began to breathe heavy, looked at each other, then quickly stuck their hands down the inside their coats. At that moment, I fully gripped my gun with my finger resting alongside the trigger guard.

Just as I reclined a little more against the grocery carts, the carts began to roll back causing, me to lose my balance and fall toward the ground. The two men seized the opportunity and began to pull their hands out of their coats at the same time as I was falling back on the grocery carts. I drew my gun from its holster, simultaneously cocking the trigger back as the gun began to level in their direction. The two men threw their hands in the air and yelled, "Okay, man, we're gone" then ran from the store. That incident was a sobering assessment of reality. I knew I could no longer live this way. I had more to be concerned about than myself or just making a living. I was placing my life and my children's future in jeopardy. I felt overwhelmed with life I couldn't see a way out. If I didn't know any better, I would have thought the moon was in my fifth solar house. I felt trapped. Here I was working in a low-income dangerous job with no future prospects, not even health and dental insurance or life insurance. I was making just enough money to survive. This idea of feeling trapped kept me up for nights pacing the floor and staring out the window, wondering about the future of our children.

By this time, Gina was trying to reenter my life. I started out just watching my son while she went to work. Then occasionally, she would bring her favorite meal: cold cuts and chips with a two-ounce bottle of Pepsi to wash it all down. We sat on my sofa bed, ate lunch, and talked about nothing, trying to reestablish a relationship that would never come into fruition. Love was lost because I had an anger brewing inside of me for her that burned hotter than fire. I was told by family members a few weeks after Cindy passed away, Gina was calling her on her job and telling her she was going to make me marry her because he was pregnant by me. It was hard to believe she did all those things. I just couldn't see that in her spirit. I was totally disappointed in her and could barely look at her without my eyes watering from rage and disappointment.

I just didn't believe she would do that, but I was wrong, and I promised myself it would be the last time I would be wrong about a woman's personality. I was to trust no one and feel nothing for anyone. I was just going to go through the motions, leaving broken hearts on a tearless path. There was no time for tears. I had to make a shift in my life, but I didn't know where I was going or how I would get there. I knew I had to do something even if it was drastic. I needed a third income, so I decided to take the exam for the Marine Corps reserves. Then a lightbulb came on in my head, so I returned to active duty in the marines and was promptly sent back to component within a week. Traditionally, marines don't allow single parents with children to serve, but I had an ace in my pocket. May had been after me for some time to marry her, but I wasn't ready at the time, but now I was without a choice. She knew my kids very well, and they appeared to be emotionally attached to her.

I had known May and her family for most my life, so I decided to marry my high school sweetheart. Our first attempt at marriage fell by the wayside. With all the uncertainty around me, I wasn't sure if I could go through with it; therefore, I didn't show up the day we were supposed to go to the Justice of Peace. May was thoroughly pissed off and refused to have sex with me. She said, "I'm saving that for my husband." I just couldn't bring myself to do it. It had only been twelve months since my wife passed away, and I just wasn't ready for another commitment; but every time, I looked at my girls, I got weaker. I knew they needed a female presence in their life, someone I could trust, someone that I'd known for a long time, someone with some measure of integrity. I decided to move forward with the marriage. The next day May wrapped her arm around my arm then escorted me downtown to the Justice of Peace.

She wouldn't let me out of her sight for one second until the vows were read and we exchanged rings. I was still feeling the wrath from my first marriage. I wasn't certain if I could consummate our marriage. May went into the bathroom to get ready, and I sat on the couch, trying to remove the attention from around my eyes. After she finished, I went to the bathroom once she lay on the big orange pillow, waiting for our first night of marital bliss. I stalled in the bathroom, taking a long shower than usual, trying to psych myself up for night of passion and unbridled sex. Little did she know I wasn't in the mood. I was put off by the idea of her being my latest mistake. *What did I just do?* I asked myself over and over, trying to find a moment of clarity about the shackles of love I once again signed up for. I was still bleeding inside from the mortal wounds of my first marriage. I knew I couldn't love her fully at the moment because I couldn't love myself. She lay ready, waiting on a large orange pillow in the center of the room for our first attempt at making a child. I was just a shell of the person in bed I once was. I no longer cared that she had a perfect set of 36DDs that made me crumble to my knees just from the excitement of seeing them. I was still mentally traumatized by the events of my first marriage. I stayed awake that night and stared out the window as May slept quietly on the large orange pillow. I stayed awake watching the night walkers come out while all the working stiffs prepared for a night of rest.

Once a Marine

My head was full of excitement and fear. I had just reenlisted in the Marine Corps, something I never thought I would do again. After my first enlistment, I thought I was surely finished with the corps, with banging my knees up, freezing half to death in thirty-below weather, running up mountains and going on a 24.3-mile forest march with full gear. Reenlisting in the corps was the only choice I had. Four years would give me time to clear my head and collect my thoughts and make an effective plan for my kids and myself. I was truly the only parent now, and I had no time for tears. I had to think five years ahead because my situation was a chess game, not checkers. I had a wife and three kids with one on the way. Every move I made at this point in my life was financially critical. I never thought in my wildest dreams I would be married to someone who didn't want to work or work as a team to secure our financial independence. But that was the reality. She didn't want to work, and it would all be left up to me.

I was passed my prime for taking orders or putting up with anyone's nonsense. The corps was full of people that loved to usurp their authority or play head games such as washing trucks while it's raining, cleaning weapons all day, or performing drills from sunrise to taps. The only good thing about reenlisting was I didn't have to go to boot camp again. If I was aware that I had other options, I would not have reenlisted in the Marine Corps. I was never groomed for college, so the thought of going to college or a trade school never entered my mind. Jobs were hard to find. Most days lent filled my pockets in places money should've been. Trying to support three kids on minimum wage wasn't an easy task. I often found myself shortchanged, just a little money to pay my bills and food. I struggled horribly. I needed a break. I needed to go where I could make a decent income and not worry about where my next meal was coming from. The marines were a tough outfit, and because I was a little older, I was uncertain whether I could keep up with the excruciating fast pace the marines demanded. I requested to be shipped out as soon as possible so that I could get situated before my family arrived.

The first thing I had to do was find us a apartment near my base in Camp Pendleton, which was no easy task. I needed an apartment located less than ten miles from the base entrance, because my camp was another ten miles inside the base. Cindy's spirit followed us right into the military, walking around the new apartment, peeking out of closets at our children, and occasionally scaring May half to death.

This marriage wasn't too bad, I thought. She's not pulling knives out on me, and her moments of anger could be diffused with an evening out to dinner or a small gift. After five months of marriage, I began to open up just a little bit, but I was being sexually deprived, never feeling comfortable enough to express myself sexually freely. We were having sex three times a week, and I was beginning to develop some feelings for her, but my murky subconscious was screaming, "No! Don't trust it." I ignored the voices in my head because I wanted this marriage to work. I was willing to put every part of myself into it even if it meant I had to put my feelings on hold and bend over backward further than I ever had for anyone. I was willing to do it because I wanted to stay married. I started off right away practicing what I preached. I stayed home, I didn't talk to or chase other women, and I spent most my recreation time running five miles a day or watching the cableless TV.

I was with my family seven days a week except for the times I would be deployed to training. We spent the next five months getting to know each other's faults and the things we enjoyed. I enjoyed watching her get out of the tub soaking wet, and she enjoyed when I took her to places and brought her things. I quickly learned she had two deal-breaker faults. The first fault was she didn't know how to cook. I knew it was common for many first-time wives to lack in their ability to cook, so I ignored it and pretended to like whatever she prepared, such as the overcooked pork chops shrinking down to the size of a silver dollar. It was like eating leather without seasoning. Ravioli fresh out of the can was the other main course I suffered through weekly. I didn't even complain about her famous meatloaf, which tasted like cardboard with ketchup poured over it. Her second and greatest fault was she didn't perform oral sex on me. She loved to have it performed on her, but she didn't return the favor. Our sex life was very basic, no experiment in the bedroom, and there was no element of surprise to our lovemaking. She did nothing to make me want her or want to be around her. I knew the exact date, hour, and minute we were going to have sex; and it drove me crazy. I was bored out of my mind. I'm a Sagittarius, and everyone knows Sagittarius are some of the freakiest lovers on the planet. The one thing we hate more than anything else is boring sex.

Within six to seven months of being married, she achieved her ultimate goal: she was pregnant. I must say her skin was as smooth and healthy looking as I had ever seen it. But her insides were turning into something sadistic and evil. She plotted her escape from our marriage day by day, week by week, and month by month, decisively and secretively setting money aside in a separate account unknown to myself. Very often, she complained about not having enough money; but she set around the house watching TV, constantly refusing to work or offer any help with our financial situation. However, I did respect her ability to save money, but she wasn't very overt and inclusive with the money she squirreled away. After having our daughter, she changed her personality like a burnt-out lightbulb. The things she did were no longer hidden. They were up close and in my face. She became cold and withdrawn, not wanting to have sex or sleep in the same bed because she felt I wanted too much sex. She spent every waking hour poisoning my daughter's mind by whispering negative thoughts in her virgin ears.

By the time she was eighteen months old, she wouldn't come within a foot of me. I believe I lost her, never having a chance to bond with her. I was shut out from having any relationship with her. Her mother carried her around the house continuously in her arms, not letting her out of her sight more than a second. I was systematically being removed from my daughter's life with hate and lies. The thirty-six months we spent in Hawaii, she made my life pure hell, not wanting to cook and being unaffectionate. She never tried to communicate what was bothering her. Our sexual life was cut down to one day a week, just on Saturdays, which meant we had a sexless marriage. I did not understand at first, but I quickly learned that controlling sex was her way of having power and having control over something in our marriage. I tried everything to make our marriage work, but she became more distant and harder to please.

After being on the island for eighteen months, my unit was being rotated overseas to Okinawa, Japan, for a six-month deployment. I couldn't help but notice May seemed all too happy that I was going away. I spent most of the day packing my gear. She walked back and forth and passed the room, smelling every time I packed a jacket or a pair of pants. I was truly hoping we could spend four hours making love before I departed for the bus, but she waited until the last thirty minutes before my departure before offering herself up for sex. As boring as our sexual experience was, I couldn't turn it down. I would be without sex for six months, so I obliged her for our usual ten minutes' worth of sex. I tossed my seabag in the back of the car then ran back in the house for one last swallow of Kool-Aid. I couldn't help but notice my half pint of peppermint snaps was three quarters gone. May led a very secretive life when I wasn't around. She drank liquor and smoked cigarettes but never in my presence. She was very good at making me believe she was someone other than who she presented herself to be. We rode quietly to the staging area. I removed my bags from the car and got one last unaffectionate kiss before boarding the bus.

—

I was on my way to Japan once again where sexual pleasure was $15 for fifteen minutes and a five-minute cab ride to town, but I was a different person with different desires and needs. I didn't see the geishas in the same light as I once did. I no longer cared about the banana shows or having women sit on my lap half dressed while I bought them watered-down drinks with the purpose of securing a night in their bed. During my first three months in Japan, I spent most of that time penniless. I wrote letter after letter to May, requesting that she send me enough money to maintain my uniforms, but there was no reply. I had to borrow money from my friends or work their shift as duty NCO for the night. I charged $25 to take their shift while they ran wild on the streets of Japan. Being stationed in Japan without money was like going to Vegas just to watch everyone else gamble and have fun.

There were so many things I wanted to buy for my children and my wife. Not having money left me restricted to the barracks and the base gym. Lucky for me, my roommate rented a television for entertainment, so I stayed in my room and watched movies most of the weekend. I didn't need money for food, but a special treat once in a while would have helped me get through the six months. I was confined to eating mid Rations handed out at the chow hall at 10:00 p.m. Everyone else was going to town shopping and having fun. I watched as the honchos (taxi cabs) pulled away from the curb, heading to BC Street or Gate Two. Okinawa was not unfamiliar to me because I lived on this island in 1980 during my youth as a young lance corporal.

I had experienced the island years before most of the men in my unit had joined the military; however, that didn't stop me from poking my head inside the hotels and catching the sight of a couple of beautiful Asian women. One thing I didn't have to worry about was fornication because I didn't have much money, and the small amount of money I did have I wasn't going to waste on women. Before I knew it, I was boarding a ship on my way to South Korea, a place I thought I would never see again. Orders came down that we were to do a beach assault. It wasn't my first time. I didn't think twice about it, but the other young marines were apprehensive about riding in a landing craft because of the enormous waves. We set out at four in the morning, wearing flak jackets and carrying rifles. I thought it odd that we weren't taking our cannons with us. We rode around aimlessly on the ocean for two hours. Huge waves crashed into the side of the landing craft, nearly drowning us as we held on to the rails. "Abandon ship," yelled the driver.

I thought he had made a mistake. I looked around the boat for holes or damage. The landing craft appeared to be intact. "Over the side—now," he said with a more forceful voice. The sides was too tall for us to climb over. So one man squatted down while the others stepped on his knee and back to jump over the side. I was the first in the water. Heavy ocean waves slammed against me as I fell headfirst into the water, sinking five feet then returning instantly to the surface. It took fifteen minutes to empty the six landing crafts. My first sergeant stood atop a boat, yelling instructions for us to lock arms. The waves were unforgiving. We were being slapped around like a rubber duck in the bathtub. I was one of the strong swimmers, so I was given the task to bring in all the stragglers and connecting them to the rest of the line. The line lasted about ten minutes in an oval. Every time a huge wave took us under water for more than a second, someone would panic and break free off the chain. We spent three hours in the water being slammed by huge waves. I thought for sure I would get hypothermia if we stayed in the water any longer. I was shaking so bad from the ice-cold water my arms almost let loose several times as I rejoined the group after rounding up stragglers. We played in the water until we successfully broke the chain and reformed again and again without breaking the chain because of the massive waves slamming against us. To add insult to injury, it took twice as long to get back in the landing craft as it did to get out. We pulled back into the well of the ship five hours after we left. My eyelids were all but frozen to the top of my head. My ears were red and burning, my fingers were dysfunctional, and I couldn't even unbutton my shirt to get undressed. Everyone shook like branches on a tree hurrying to free ourselves of the below zero clothing. I asked myself the question once again, *What the hell am I doing here?* Although I just had my first taste of freezing Korean ocean waters, Korea was much more pleasant this time. We arrived in the spring. The temperature was around forty degrees much better than my first time in Korea during Jack Frost training. We went straight out to the field. My fingers and ears had yet to thaw out from the freezing ocean water. The countryside was beautiful. There were rice paddies as far as the eye could see.

Captain Head woke us up at four in the morning just for harassment. He made us do jumping jacks, sit-ups and push-ups on the ice-cold rice paddies. He stood on top of a hill polluting the air with his stogie cigar, smiling to himself. We were told to get a quick cold shave before going to chow. Everyone saluted the captain as they walked past, but I knew better. You weren't supposed to salute an officer in the field, so I abided by the rule and walked right past the captain, not even pretending to like or respect him by giving him a salute. The first sergeant reached over to stop me, but the captain said, "Let him go. It's okay." I didn't think anything of that incident for the moment, but it would come back to haunt me a couple of months later.

I show the young marines how to negotiate with the Koreans, trading their MREs for ramen noodles and a soda. Before pulling out, I was told to take my sections and patrol five miles out. I was given coordinates on a map and a compass. I was the highest-ranking member in my section, so I was put in charge of nine men. I put the young men in formation then asked the Korean soldier where the restrooms were. He pointed toward the top of the hill. I sprinted up the hill toward the bathroom. Stretching open the door, I looked around, and there was no toilets. It was just a big open empty room. I closed the door and ran back down the hill. I asked the Korean soldier, "Where is the restroom? That's just an empty building," the soldier said. "Lift up the board on the floor." I ran back up the hill and did as he instructed. There was a bottomless pit of a hole in the floor. The hole was saturated with liquefied feces. *Not again*, I thought to myself. This reminded me of the bathrooms in 1980 during our Jack Frost training. I got fully undressed, went to the head and pinched a loaf, then went on patrol with my men. We patrolled five miles out, checking the area for explosives or North Koreans along the DMZ. We came across hundreds of dirt mounds with three-course meals on plates at the foot of the mounds. We couldn't read the signs but somehow we knew they were graves. Koreans were known for burying the family in the upright sitting position. In the distance, I could see a huge bundle of wood going up the side of the mountain. It would have to be at least stacked twenty feet high and seemed to move on its own. The closer we got, the more we could see that an little old lady was carrying all that wood with amazing strength. We walked through their neighborhoods as occupying forces. I never felt so embarrassed as an American. I knew in my heart the United States would never tolerate an occupying force patrolling their neighborhoods. What we were doing was wrong, and I felt the worse for it.

The young marines were impressed with my map-reading skills and my ability to use a compass. I wish my commanders felt the same way. We returned to Okinawa six weeks later, and I was excited about the possibility of being promoted to sergeant. There was one opening for the rank of sergeant. I wasn't worried. My only competition was a shitbird corporal from cannon number five with a very bad attitude. His uniform was wrinkled, his face was unshaved, and his boots were never polished. I knew when they selected one of us for the promotion, I would win by a landslide. I stood in formation that evening, anticipating to be called forward to have my sergeant stripes pinned on.

The first sergeant called the unit to attention then called Corporal Ving to the front of formation. As he read the promotion order, I couldn't contain myself. I stepped out of the formation and walked away. No one said a thing, not even my captain, as I walked back to the barracks, steam billowing from my ears and total disappointment on my face. I worked so hard the last two years trying to prove I was a good leader, but they gave my stripes to someone that was unworthy of it just to make a point. I didn't care what they did to me at that point.

I was done with the Marine Corps. I had approximately two years left to serve. And if it weren't for my family, I would've got myself put in the brig for disobeying orders. I knew I had to get the captain back for passing me over. I wanted to frag him, but I had no means to carry out the idea, so I forgot about it for now.

All of a sudden, Korea got colder. I was no longer performing extra duties for my troops. I lay back and let the new sergeant assume his position. In my mind, it was sink or swim. I wasn't going to carry him. He would have to do it on his own. I stopped talking to everyone for a while. I had nothing else to say at the moment. I sat in my barracks and read magazines, occasionally staring out the window, watching the honchos lined up below the USO waiting to whisk young marines to town. I envied the young marines' freedom and single status. Most of the young marines admired my married life and how I spent time with my family, going to the beach on weekends and walks around the base at night, but they were looking for the outside in. I was living in the corner of perception reality. Everything they thought they knew about my marriage, they were wrong. There were rumors that one of the sergeants saw May in the NCO club with another man, I wasn't surprised or shaken by the news because I was beginning not to care anymore. I was married to a women that only showed affection when she had a pocket full of dead presidents or when everything was perfect for her. The months passed slowly, and no money came from home. I wrote home continuously, and still, there was no answer. Finally, a small envelope arrived with $180 wrapped in foil. My base salary was $1,700 a month after taxes. My wife was keeping well over $1,600 to herself. We lived in base housing; therefore, our rent was automatically deducted from my pay.

There was no reason for her not to send me money more often. During the last two months of my tour of duty in Japan, I got another letter. I noticed the envelope was stamped with an Indianapolis post mark, showing that the envelope was coming from Indianapolis. My emotions shifted. I could feel the strings of my heart being tugged from Indianapolis. I became very incensed. There was nothing I could do. It was obvious my wife had left me and returned home to Indianapolis. I spent my last months trying not to think of the reason for her exodus. She could have done anything she wanted, but she chose to sit around the house drinking liquor, smoking cigarettes, and complaining about what she didn't have.

The six-month tour of duty had run its course. My unit rotated back to Hawaii just in time for tourist season. As the bus entered the base gate, I noticed wives standing on the sidewalk, waiting for their husbands. I didn't bother to look around for a ride home. I knew my wife wasn't there. I walked six blocks home to an empty house. The grass was overgrown, spiderwebs covered the front pouch, and warning letters from the base housing authority were plastered all over the front and back door. Our new 1987 Mazda 626 was covered with rust and cobwebs because the car and the house went unattended for more than a month. I could see the signs that this marriage was not going to work. She blamed me for everything that went wrong in the marriage, but little did she know it takes two people willing to move forward in the right direction and build on the relationship. My misfortune of burying my first wife just three years earlier left me tenderhearted and sensitive. Just the thought of her death made my throat tighten and my eyes water. I couldn't speak often of her before I had to remove myself from the presence of others. I was emotionally invested in this new marriage, but my emotions were mixed between two women: my first marriage and the women I was currently married to.

I hate failure, and I wasn't going to see my marriage fail. I believed it was all just a misunderstanding and we could work it out. I made several attempts to reach May over the phone but no answer. After one week of calling, she finally answered her phone. I asked her, "What are you doing in Indianapolis? Are you coming back home?" She said, "No, I'm not. I'm staying here." I didn't need to hear any more. I slammed the phone down, ripped the phone cord out of the wall, and tossed the phone on the couch. I couldn't believe her arrogant and unappreciative attitude. She practically begged me to marry her, but now that she had a legitimate child through marriage, she wanted to run off and keep the child all to herself. She had me confused with someone else. I wasn't much for sitting around and crying over spilled milk. Besides, I was sick of her bullshit; so I took a shower, got dressed, and hit the nightclubs. One of my friends, Sergeant Moss, and I headed for Hickam Air Force Base NCO club where marines were not allowed entry unless they were E-5 or above. Moss drove that night. As it turned out, it was fortunate for me.

Once in the club, I scoped the bar with dishonorable intentions in mind. I took my seat in the stands as far away from the crowd as possible. I couldn't help but notice a Philippine woman with long hair stretching down beyond her waistline, sitting by herself. With my drink in one hand, I approached her and asked if I could sit with her. She said that her date was getting her a drink. Several minutes went by, and he still hadn't returned with her drinks. I took a detour by the bar to check out the competition. There he was with two young attractive women. I ran back to the table and pointed at her boyfriend. Ensuring she saw the two well-equipped young girls that he was hoping to replace her with, she moved down by the bar to get a better look, then returned to me, and asked if I could leave with her and show her how to get off the base. I was all too glad to help. I hurried her out of the club to the car so fast she tripped and fell grabbing my crotch on the way down. I was able to catch her before she hit the ground. We disappeared off the base like a phantom in the night before he knew she was gone. We jumped in the car and drove to downtown Honolulu and parked at the tennis court on Waikiki Boulevard. We talked for several minutes, holding idle conversation, until my beer went flat, I offered to drive us to the nearest liquor store, but she said, "There's no need."

She popped the trunk of her car; and I found her trunk to be an argosy of several types of liquor, beer nuts, chips, and ice. I couldn't believe my eyes. She had everything in her trunk that a local bar would have. We sat in front of the tennis courts until three in the morning, drinking mixed drinks and smoking cigarettes, keeping up idle conversations as the liquor and stale smell of cigarettes brought us closer to what we both wanted: unbridled sex and a one-night stand. I had no feelings for her. I didn't love her or cared if I ever saw her again. I didn't even remember her name. I just wanted a quickie. I wasn't trying to fall in love. I didn't want her phone number. I just needed quick relief after six months of abstinence. The one night lasted for three months. Every time I looked up, we were having sex. It didn't matter where or what time of the day. She wanted it all the time. We went to a bar just about every night, never entering the bar, just sitting on the parking lot and drinking our own liquor from the trunk of her car as she chained smoked cigarettes and told me about her future plans. After several minutes of downing drinks, she climbed to the backseat and disrobed. She was always very demonstrative, stretching spread eagle across the seat with one leg on the backseat headrest and the other between the front seat, stroking my side with her foot, provoking me into action. I watched her from my rearview mirror taking deep drags from her cigarette while seductively rubbing her hands between her thighs, inviting me to climb to the back. For the second time in my life, I just wanted to sit and talk, but I thought to myself, *What the hell.* So I disrobed, jumped into the backseat, and rode her hard until the mosquitoes got the best of both of us.

We hung out just about every night, mostly just drinking from the ready-made bar in the truck of her car, talking about future plans, and having unbridled sex. It was a nice break and change of pace from the stalemate marital position I was currently in. I didn't like being unfaithful to my wife, but she was forcing me out to the streets and nightclubs because of her unaffectionate ways and her poor attitude of what she believed a wife's role was supposed to be. I was tired of adjusting myself to fit her attitude. I was tired to coming home to meals that weren't fit for human consumption. I was tired of the sexless nights and sleeping alone. I was just sick and tired of being sick and tired.

For the first time in my life, someone had more stamina than I. It wasn't long before she began to fall in love. After every sexual encounter, she placed $40 in my pocket and told me to go have breakfast. I didn't think much of it the first time it happened, but after each time we had sex, she put $40 in my pocket. I was beginning to take offense to it, so I handed her back the money. She said, "No, you keep it go have breakfast." I said, "Wait a minute. I'm beginning to feel like a fucking prostitute. I don't want your money. You don't have to pay me. I like you anyway." This went on for several weeks, and the idea of taking money for sex was beginning to have a negative mental effect on me. I felt like I was using her, but of course, I knew I was only using her for sex. Money wasn't a part of the deal. The longer we stayed together, the larger the amounts got. Three months into the relationship, I finally got a break. Because of my swimming ability, I was selected to go to the Navy SEAL water survival training in San Diego on the other side of the blue Coronado Bridge. She drove me to the airport that evening. As we stood there waiting for the plane, she noticed two Hollywood celebrities walking past and pointed them out to me. One was my favorite actor in the world, and the other one became famous years later because of his infamous murders.

Before getting on the plane, she shoved a wad of hundred-dollar bills totaling $500 in my pocket. I quickly took the money out of my pocket and put it back in her hand. She became quite upset and shoved the money in my pocket and ran off down the ramp and out to the parking lot. Once I returned from the water survival training, she picked me up from the airport and drove me to a nightclub parking lot. Before the car was in park, she stripped down to her panties and grabbed me by the collar, dragging me into the backseat. She was on fire, but I gave her the right hose to extinguish all her flames of desire.

After three hours of pulsating sex, she pulled out her cigarettes and a wad of $100 bills from her purse. She stuffed the money in my shirt pocket. I said, "What are you doing? Please! Don't give me any more money." She looked at me and said, "Keep it. It's for your birthday." "My birthday is more than six months away." "Well, just keep it anyway. Just keep it for me." I counted the money, and it came to $600. Now I was really beginning to feel like a whore. I tried to turn the money down on several occasions and even asked that she not give it to me anymore, but she was relentless as though she didn't hear a word I said. Every time I saw her, she was pulling off her panties and jumping in the backseat of the car. We were having sex so much I thought my penis was going to go into a coma.

Three months went by, and we were having sex every day three or more hours during each sexual encounter. It was beginning to be more than I could bear—the money, the sex, and the gifts. It was as if she was buying me, and I had no choice in the matter but to be bought. I knew I had to do a disappearing act, so I stopped calling and meeting her. Two weeks went by, and I hadn't heard a thing. All of a sudden, a young corporal came into the office, yelling about a crazy lady at the legal office, telling one of the attorneys Corporal Rawlings robbed her. I jumped my chair like a jack-in-a-box. "I'm Corporal Rawlings," I exclaimed. "Robbery? Who was I supposed to have robbed?" "There's a lady at the legal office right now saying you robbed her," the young marine said. I grabbed my cover (hat) and leapt out like a bolt of lightning down the steps and onto the catwalk. There she was standing in front of my captain's door. I grabbed her by the arm. I asked her, "What the hell are you trying to do?" She looked at me, then striking me on the shoulder with her fist, she said, "You're a shit." She looked at me out of the corner of her eyes. "Come on, let's go," I said as I pulled her into her car, and off we went across the airstrip and down to the beach. She appeared upset, but I knew exactly what she wanted, so I didn't even hesitate or put up a fight. I parked the car in a secluded place, climbed into the backseat, then let her have her way. She jumped up and down on me for several hours, crying and screaming, professing her love for me. I didn't love her—I never loved her. I sat there unaffected by her rants and raves about how much she loved me. All I could do was what I knew how to do: I plowed it in her deep, long, and hard until she relented.

After two hours of pulsating sex, we climbed back into the front seat to discuss what was on her mind. She sat behind the steering wheel of her car and lit her cigarette. Reclining her seat back, she paused for a minute; then turning to me with teary eyes, she said, "Marry me, Mike." Then reaching into her book bag, she pulled out $15,000 cash, still banded together with paper bank straps, looking as though the money came straight from the bank. She placed five stacks of money on my lap. I took a deep breath and thought about the possibilities of a better life. My wife has already left me once, and it wouldn't surprise me if she did it again. I just looked at Luz suggestively as if I might consider taking her offer, talking to myself, *Only if I wasn't married, it would be possible.*

My marriage was in ruins, but I had to give it another chance. I'd known May since the third grade, and besides, she's the mother of my child. I had to see my marriage through to the end. Luz reached across the seat and grabbed my hand. Squeezing it, nervously looking deep into my eyes, she increased her offer to giving me half of $875,000. "Where are you going to get that kind of money?" I said. "Fifteen thousand dollars is one thing, but $875,000 is another." I didn't believe her, of course, so she pulled out a letter from the real estate company located in Los Angeles. The letter stated the airport wanted to purchase her land located right outside of the fence line. The land was large enough occupy fourteen homes. It wasn't even a second thought. I knew she wasn't a young woman. She was fifty-two years old. She would need the money to support herself a lot sooner than I. I was only twenty-eight years old, and I had a full life ahead of me. She was already at the halfway point between life and death. I didn't want to take her money. I didn't even feel comfortable with the $40 she was jamming in my pocket after every sexual encounter.

It reminded me of the time my mother would make me cut my elderly neighbor's grass. They could not afford to pay me because they're on a fixed income, and my mother reminded me not to take their money. But the old man refused to let me cut his grass without giving me something, so he shoved $3 in my pocket once I finished his yard. Although the old man paid me, I still learned the lesson my mother was trying to teach me: help someone who can't pay you back. In other words, it doesn't cost anything to be kind. With this life lesson,

I never used a women or anyone else for money, and I wasn't about to start with using Luz, so I turned down her offer. We parted ways that evening, and I never saw her or heard from her again. I guess she finally got the message that I couldn't be bought. That was a crazy sexual maze I would never forget. All of a sudden, I wasn't mad at May for being such a horrible wife anymore. I missed Luz. I often felt her absence. Most of all, our sex wasn't on a schedule, and it lasted far longer than ten minutes.

I didn't have to pretend I was anything other than myself when I was with her, I didn't have to give her handfuls of money, I didn't have to constantly entertain her, I didn't have to beg her to cook a decent meal or have unplanned sex, and most importantly, I didn't have to explain to her how to treat her man when he's trying his best. Six months had gone by, and I was still living in Hawaii alone. I hung out at the beaches and seemingly had my pick of the foreign tourists, but I decided to let it pass me by because I didn't believe I could endure another crazy romance. May refused to return home, and I refused to let my marriage end, but I wasn't going to kiss her butt or beg her to come back.

Finally, her mother told her she couldn't live with me any longer. She convinced her that she was an adult and married and needed to be with her husband. So she returned seven months after she had departed. She looked horrible. Her face had broken out with acme from constantly eating french fries and potato chips. I could tell by her attitude she didn't want to be here, but she had no choice at this point in her life. As she came out of the terminal, I noticed she had only my youngest daughter with her. I waited at the terminal door and peeked down the hallway. I turned around and hunched my shoulders, asking where my girls were. "I didn't bring them," she said. "Well, that's fucking obvious. Why not?" "I didn't have the money." "I told you to go to the military administrative office on Arlington Road, and they would have issued you free tickets for them." I couldn't believe she had done such an insensitive thing. I was furious. I told her to bring my girls with her when she returned, but she purposely ignored me after

I requested. I needed to see my girls, and I wasn't leaving the island until they had a chance to experience it for themselves. I began to pull out all stops, talking to everyone that had authority. Two weeks later, I flew to Indianapolis and brought my girls to Hawaii. I believe my deceased wife was speaking to me from the grave. I felt compelled to have my girls with me and not five thousand miles across the ocean. Somehow I knew Michaela was struggling with her emotions, and she needed to be around her dad.

I arrived at my mother's house two weeks later on Monday afternoon. I walked in the door. My mother was standing in the kitchen, ironing my girls' clothes, and packing their suitcases. My daughters looked up and saw me, and both came running with arms wide open. I kneeled down on one knee to hug both my girls. I squeezed them tight as if I hadn't seen them in years. Michaela smiled from ear to ear, happy as she could be to see her dad. It made me feel good that I could go get my girls and bring them back to Hawaii with me. I could feel the distance between us, and I had to have them with me at all cost. The plane was so crowded I couldn't get tickets to sit in the same row with my daughters, but someone was kind enough to switch seats with me so that we could all sit together. The five-hour flight was grueling. Miya became very fidgety after two hours in the air, so I let her walk up and down the aisle to stretch her legs. Then eventually, she fell asleep and didn't awake until we landed in Hawaii. This was probably one of the happiest times of my life. I was very glad that I could give my girls this experience. Once we landed, I was surprised that May picked us up at the airport; and for once, she even seemed happy with their arrival. I could blame her for being a horrible wife, but she seemed to be a much better mother than she was a wife. I still didn't trust her fully with my children. She was an emotional wreck herself. Confused about what she wanted to do in life and who she wanted to be. Rather than paying her own way to school, she blamed the Reagan administration for her failures in college, not being able to finish her training in television production because of financial aid cuts. That would become her trademark in our marriage, blaming everyone for everything around her instead of fixing her life. I believe she was internally depressed and wanted me to give her something that I was ill equipped to provide: a sense of purpose.

Often I would find May sitting on the couch at two in the morning, watching TV. I watched her from a distance as she sat quietly, eating from her bowl with a glass of peppermint snaps tucked beside her thigh slightly out of view. I asked, "Why are you sitting out here at two in the morning?" She said, "You cry in your sleep over Cindy," and it drove me crazy. I guess I never got over my wife's passing. I thought about her constantly. I couldn't help it. She was a permanent part of my memory set deep in my murky subconscious. Thoughts of her were automatic. She was forever fermented in my head. I guess May couldn't compete with the thought of another woman hanging out in her house. The thought of their mother's sprit watching over her children scared May partly out of her mind.

Months passed, and I thought I would have forgotten about Luz by now; but every time I sat on the beach and let the ocean water wash up against my feet, thoughts of her came home like truth. I smiled every time I thought about her and her crazy ways. The way she loved me unconditionally and the freedom I felt when I was with her. Those were good memories; but when I left the beach and returned to my house and walked through the door, all those good memories faded away into thin air, returning me to a sobering assessment of reality. I was sick of surviving on an E-4 salary and having a wife that complained about money but never attempted to earn any. I was sick of being depressed and being in a dysfunctional marriage. I was sick of not being able to make love to my wife anytime I wanted to. I was sick of not having a good home-cooked meal and most of all was just sick of being sick and tired. However, I did get some joy out of life. Sergeant Ving got his comeuppance. One of the lance corporals was standing fire watch. He got bored in the middle of the night and decided to take a hit of acid.

The acid had very little effect, so he decided to take another hit. Within seconds of the second hit of acid, the young lance corporal began to flip out. He called the officer of the day, requesting to go to the hospital. The officer of the day asked him what he took. The young marine refused to answer the officer's question. The officer told the young marine, "I'm not going to transport you to the hospital until you tell me what you took and who you got it from." The young lance corporal informed the officer that Sergeant Ving sold him the drugs. The next morning Sergeant was arrested and escorted to the brig. After his trial, he received five years in Leavenworth prison in Kansas City. I wasn't jumping for joy over another man's misery, but I couldn't help but smile when I walked past my captain's door. I gave him the stink eye and a smirk. I said to myself, *How do you like those green eggs and ham, asshole?* I couldn't believe they gave that shitbird my sergeant stripes, but it all worked out in the end.

Before I knew it, we were shipped back to Twentynine Palms Desert for twelve weeks. I couldn't wait to get this trip over with because it would be my last trip to Twentynine Palms. When I returned to the base, I would have at exactly twelve months left in the corps. Once again, we reached the Twentynine Palms base and drove all night into the desert until we were far from the main base. As soon as the trucks stopped, I jumped out the back and dusted a pound of sand off my uniform. Sergeant Tubman called out my name while simultaneously tossing me a round ball. I reached up and caught the ball with my hand. The ball turned out to be a small cactus covered with thorny, pricking needles. I shook my hand violently, trying to get the cactus off my skin. The harder I shook my hand, the more the cactus crawled up my arm. I stopped flinging my arm around long enough to take out my K bar knife and cut the cactus off my arm. I looked at Sergeant Tubman with a look that could kill, but all of a sudden, I had an idea. I began walking around, picking up the small cactus with a pair of wire cutters, placing them in my cover, and storing them under my cot for later that evening.

I waited all night until everyone was asleep. I walked off a hundred meters from the cannon. I fired up a heat tap to heat my cup of mocha. I left my stove burning, making fire watch believe I was one hundred meters away, cooking. To distract the fire watch, I tossed a can in the opposite direction of their position. Like idiots, they followed the noise. Then I crept up the hill to the captain's tent. I stood outside the tent for several minutes to ensure he was asleep. I could hear low-tone snoring coming from inside the tent, so I put on my night-vision goggles and stepped inside the tent quickly as though I was reporting in. I shined my flashlight with the red lens around the room; and bingo, there he was, lying on his side with his back toward the door. It couldn't have been a more perfect situation. I crept over step by step. Using my wire cutters, I sat each cactus from head to toe inside the sleeping bag. Then I crept out of the tent and back to cooking my coffee and cocoa.

I lay on my cot and nibbled on a chocolate bar from my C rations. I stared up into the emptiness of the night, watching the stars race across the sky. I loved the twilight hours. It was my favorite time in the universe. The entire world was dead to me. Everything was standing still. It was as if I were the only survivor after an apocalypse. At 4:00 a.m., I could hear my first sergeant and captain talking in a very low voice; and all of a sudden, the captain burst out of the tent, yelling as he ran out into the barren desert. He clawed and ripped away at his back, trying to remove the cactus that rolled all over his body. He shook vigorously. Two marines tackled him while a third tried to extract the cactus balls with a pair of pliers. I sat quietly in front of my cannon, heating a cup of coffee while I watched the spectacle unfold. I laughed so hard I almost spilled a very good cup of mocha. Fragging him almost made me feel better about not being promoted to sergeant. I was able to move on with my Marine Corps career that I knew would end in a few short months. I was no longer angry at the captain or the Marine Corps for the fact I was done with the idea of serving my country and I no longer wanted to play marine. My new life and the civilian road I was about to face would challenge me emotionally, physically, and financially to the limits of stress I had yet to encounter.

Our time being stationed in Hawaii and my military service had come to an end. I sent my family back to Indianapolis while I looked for work and a place to live in Los Angeles, California. I left the base with $640 to my name and a bus ticket to Los Angeles. I stayed in a run-down hotel in the center of downtown Los Angeles that had a community bathroom I shared with six other families, and roaches the size of my thumb were my only friends.

It was my first time staying in downtown LA, and I wasn't taking any chances, so I hid the remainder of my fortune behind the roach-patrolled mirror in my room and ventured out onto the streets of Los Angeles. The sidewalks were smothered with the dispossessed living in cardboard boxes and panhandling for money. I had little money but felt compelled to share what I had with those less fortunate than me. Little did I know it was faith come calling. I was riding the city bus looking for work but not making much progress, so I decided to walk around the city and take in the sights. At last, I saw a big party at a small park across the street. *This looks like fun*, I thought, so I made my way toward the park. Just as I stepped off the sidewalk, a huge bus came to a screeching halt right in front of me, the doors fling wildly open. "Get on the bus," the bus driver said. I looked at him with a puzzled look. "What?" I said. "Get on the bus!" adamantly he saids this time. "I don't have any more bus money," I said. "That's okay I will take you a few blocks." We traveled about a mile. Along the way, the bus driver explained the reason for picking me up. He said that was a gang members' park where the Southern Mexican gangs hung out. I thought for sure at that moment my guardian angels were truly watching over me. Later that evening, I stayed close to the hotel, not walking more than two blocks in any given direction. I peeked in the windows, and to my surprise, I was able to watch a television sitcom being filmed.

I walked the streets and rode the bus lines for two days, looking for work; everywhere I went, there seemed to be a movie shoot. Extras for the movie were lined up on the street. The motion picture cameras were on high lifts, and other personnel were carrying boom microphone. I thought it was all cool to see a movie made up close and personal, but I had more pressing issues to think about. My money was dwindling fast because of hotel and food expenses.

I had to make a decision because of my shortage of funds and the lack of resources. I was forced to return to my enclave in Indianapolis. The bus ride was two and a half days long, and some of the bus stations were just local bus stops with a sign sticking out of the ground attached to a metal pole in the middle of nowhere. I felt very vulnerable and insecure as I stood there in total darkness for three hours, waiting all alone in some desolate spot for the bus to arrive. The bus trip home cost $180, using up all the money I had left. I didn't even have money for food. I rode the bus for two and a half days with an uneasy feeling settling in my stomach. I was starving. One kind gentleman struck up an idle conversation about the military. I listened as he spoke. I passively nodded my head in agreement while my stomach growled loudly. He stopped talking long enough to reach into his sandwich bag and offered me a vegetarian lettuce and cheese sandwich. Normally, I wouldn't accept food from strangers, but I grabbed the sandwich without hesitation and savored every bite.

I arrived in Indianapolis on Monday evening about 4:00 p.m. It was a much different feeling than living in Hawaii. The air even smelled different. It felt heavier and wet. I took my seabag out of the bottom of the bus storage and walked from the bus station to my mother's house. It was about a three-mile walk. Everything seemed so different and new. A new wave of Hispanics migrated into the area. It made the city polychromatic as well as multicultural. Far cry from when I was a child when the city was primarily occupied by blacks, some whites, with a very small population of Asians. I had never seen the Hispanic persons until 1978 when I entered the Marine Corps. The city had changed drastically. I was so amazed I didn't even notice how far it was from the bus station to my mother's house. It was a strange feeling as I walked down Meridian Street. The street seemed different yet very familiar, and before I knew it, I was turning the corner at Saul Subway. I couldn't help but smile as I looked at the empty parking lot full of memories the younger generation would never know about. I stood on the rendezvous part of the sidewall where I met Cindy for the first time. I paused to consume the essence of her memory and allow my mind to capture the moment that changed my life forever. I was uncertain about a lot of things in my life, but I wasn't uncertain about her menacing presence.

I called May to let her know I was home and wanted to see her. She said, "Where are you at?" "I'm at my mother's house," I replied. She hung up the phone and would not take any more of my calls for two days. Finally, after two days of repeated calls, she answered the phone only to tell me she was leaving me because I didn't find us a place in California. Little did I know my mother was listening to our conversation on the other end of the phone. She looked down at me from the top of the steps and said, "She wants a divorce?" "Yes, Mother, she's leaving me." I sat quietly on the couch in disbelief, trying to wrap my head around another failed marriage. I could hear my mother upstairs talking to someone on the phone. Within minutes, my brother was stepping through the front door. "Come on," he said, "let's go. You're not going to sit here alone tonight." Reluctantly, I got to my feet and followed him to his car.

I sat in the car staring aimlessly out the window as we drove up Thirtieth Street to the west side of town. My brother was talking, but I couldn't hear a word he said. It was as if I were standing outside of my body, watching everything around me. Before I knew it, we arrived at his house. There were three women sitting in the front room, one slightly more homely than the other. They stared across the room at me, whispering back and forth to one another. Neither one of them was my type. They all seemed ghetto fabulous, welfare mothers without a pot to piss in or a window to throw it out of; but none of that mattered to me because I didn't know if I had the emotional strength in me for one more relationship, disappointments, misunderstandings, boring sex, lies, unfaithfulness, and marrying for convenience, not love.

We piled 3-deep into the back seat of his Buick and took a long drive to Anderson, Indiana. My brother brought the first round of drinks, but I was still fuming from the news of my second separation. After several drinks, I began to loosen up. I couldn't help but notice how short the skirt on the woman to my left was and how long and tan her legs looked, or maybe it was just the alcohol. She was the same hood rat at my brother's apartment, but the alcohol was beginning to take effect. I sat back after my third rum and Coke. I watched everyone party on the dance floor, and for a brief second, I sank back into the days when I was in Okinawa, Japan. In that instant, I was able to partially crack a smile. One of the women that drove to Anderson with us was very forward. She came right out with it. "You want to come spend the night?" she asked. I shut my eyes, slightly shaking my head back and forth as if I was saying no; but I opened my eyes, looked at her briefly, and said "Why not?" We got back to my brother's house after a night of clubbing. I really didn't want to go home with this lady, but I had already committed.

So I drove her to her apartment in the heart and soul of the ghetto "brick city." We walked inside her apartment as she drunkenly pulled me by my shirt up through the towering dark staircase, peeling off her clothes before reaching the top of steps. Her butt was as wide as a bookshelf and as flat as a stack of pancakes. She fell on the bed drunk and butt naked, raising her butt in the air, looking back over her shoulder at me. She said, "What are you waiting for?" Plunging over the side of the bed, she threw up on the floor particles of food and liquid, which splattered against the wall and curtains. It was more than I could tolerate. She looked at me and said, "It's okay. Come on." I turned and walked down the steps. I drove around the city all night, eventually parking downtown and walking around the monument circle trying to figure out my life, where I was going to go, and how I was going to get there. I didn't have a clue, and there didn't seem to be any help coming from any family members or anywhere else for that fact.

I was in a lot of pain—the kind of pain that could not be fixed with a stiff drink and a roll in the hay. I was hurt but had no time to focus on secondary issues. I was all my two daughters had. They were depending on me; I couldn't make any excuses or fail in the eyes of my girls. I was suffering two types of pains: the pain of going through a divorce and the painful memory of a deceased wife, which caused me to stray off course from my goals. My lack of education and being a displaced worker made life hard and disappointing. My wife had left me for the second time, and it hurt twice as much. My confidence was shaken, but I couldn't afford to be weak. I had to put things in perspective quickly. After two months of searching for work, all I could get was a job at Domino's Pizza, working as a delivery driver. I was always a hard worker and didn't mind starting at the bottom, but I knew I was better than this. So I continued to work at Domino's Pizza while looking for other work during the morning hours. My stepfather worked as a truck driver for a scrap yard. He told me about a job repairing metal containers. The job paid $4 an hour without health benefits or retirement. I was the most fortunate that my children were healthy. Being fresh out of the Marine Corps, I was still in good physical and mental health. Now I had two jobs: repairing metal containers during the day and delivering pizzas in the evenings. My mother was kind enough to allow my children to stay at her house when they got out of school and until I got off work at 10:00 p.m. from Domino's Pizza. I did this routine for a year, living on the edge and barely making ends meet.

My monthly child support was still a financial issue because the military gave Gina an additional $100 a month raise right before I was released from active duty. The court system didn't care if I had other children to support. They only cared about the one that was on record, so they willfully took out $256 a month from my check. I also sent $200 a month to May in support of my daughter along with supporting my other two girls on two minimal jobs. It was an extremely stressful situation and a difficult task. It would have surely have broken a person with less character. I quit the pizza delivery job several months later and found a job working in security as a loss prevention agent.

My shift began right after I got off work at five o'clock. I went straight to the grocery store and began working as a loss prevention agent from 6:00 p.m. until 11:00 p.m. I stood in the freezer, watching shoppers go about their business, hoping I didn't catch anyone shoplifting. I was tired of working security and putting my life online for $4 an hour while working in the heart and soul of the ghettos of Indianapolis. But I was without choice. I had more money going out than coming in, not because of everyday living expenses such as rent, car payments, or utility bills. It was because I have children, and providing the basic things for my children often put me behind the financial eight ball. I was heading toward thirty years old, and it seemed as if I couldn't catch a break. I was almost afraid to get into another relationship, but the women kept coming from all directions. Two lived less than one block from my front door. The other one lived on the floor below me, and another was across town.

I couldn't get away from it, everyone knew I was single and I was a single parent with have two girls. For some reason, that seemed to attract women. They saw me as a good man, and it appeared they wanted to be a part of my family. But I didn't trust anyone and closed my heart off to any possibility of falling in love. The woman who lived two apartments down was a stripper. She would stop by my apartment twice a week and strip for me in the front room while I sat on my couch and sleep. She became frustrated at the sight of my boredom. She snatched her wig off in disappointment and ran down the steps, cursing my name. I didn't care. I had too many dilemmas staring me in the face. I had to do something, but I didn't know what to do other than go to work and make just enough money to survive, keeping a roof over our heads.

I walked around internally stressed the entire year of 1990. I found comfort at the den of sin a half block down the street from my apartment. Once my children were asleep, I'd slip down to the nightclub, drink boilermakers, mix beer and wine, and try to forget about the sexless nights in my marriage and the unnecessary embittered attitude she often displayed for no reason known to myself. The comfort I found hidden in the wine bottle lasted only as long as the nightclub was open. I knew I had to return home and subliminally watch my deceased wife wander about the apartment, watching over our children. She often stood at the end of the bed, smiling at me, I guess for making the effort, keeping my girls under one roof. She knew it was hard for me to travel this path rather than choosing the predetermine path of least resistance: surrendering my kids to my mother-in-law. Most of the time, I felt like I was not a part of this world but a part of her world because these worlds divided me. I subconsciously carried Cindy with me day in and day out. I felt overwhelmed and couldn't see the forest for the trees.

I must've visited every bar from Piccadilly's to the Office Lounge and all the way out on Eighty-Sixth Street to the Excalibur on Meridian Street. I ran in and out of bars, trying to fill an empty void that couldn't be filled. I became empty inside, leaving a part of my soul on every Barstool. I was so lost mentally I could barely hold a clear thought in my head. I was just going through the motions, barely living day in and day out. I put on a poker face throughout my workday, controlling my feelings while everyone was watching, not displaying what I felt inside to the outside world. I walked around my job welding containers and putting rivets along the scenes of the rails. Most of the time, I didn't even know I was doing it. It was an automatic reaction that I had learned after working with containers for more than a year now. Once the containers were repaired, I loaded them on a twenty-five-foot flatbed truck with a forklift and transported them to the airport where I met a very attractive thin lady. Her only problem was she chain-smoked cigarettes. I found her attractive, but I wasn't inclined to ask her on a date. Years later, I heard she passed away her death was caused by lung cancer.

I was still struggling with my two previous marriages and couldn't possibly seriously get involved in another relationship for the foreseeable future. After work one evening, I thought I needed a little refuge, so I dropped my girls off at their grandmother's house to spend the night. I got dressed and ventured out to a cut-throat nightclub in a very depressed part of town. I sat at the bar, sipping on a Long Island iced tea, trying not to be noticed by anyone. It wasn't long before a tall slender fair-skinned woman sat next to me. After a couple of drinks, she reached over and stroked my thigh. I thought it was a mistake, so I kept drinking my Long Island iced tea. Then she did it again. I looked at her. She raised her hand and rubbed her two fingers together, indicating some type of signal. I didn't have time for such nonsense, so I continued to drink my Long Island iced tea. She reached over once more and stroked my thigh, this time squeezing to make sure that I got the message. Once again, she rubbed her two fingers together. This time, I realized what she wanted: she was offering me sex for crack. I immediately got off the barstool and moved to the end of the bar. She was attractive, but I knew nothing about purchasing crack, and I didn't want to learn. It wasn't long before another very attractive woman sitting in the corner stared at me, smiling while vigorously popping her gum, crossing her legs, displaying her well-proportioned body. She was wearing a miniskirt, with four-inch heels. She had long brown legs with a perfect tan. There wasn't a blemish to be found.

The competition was on. She smiled as she strolled over to the bar where I was sitting. I could tell by her mannerism she was a prostitute, but I really didn't care. This wasn't my first time at the rodeo. It was not long before we were on the road to ill repute. Along the way, I stopped by a gas station for a box of prophylactic. She assured me I would not need to use them, but I thought differently. She pressed me to go to her friend's house where she could picked up some product. I was so naive. I didn't have the foggiest idea of what she was talking about; so I drove over to her friend's house, making idle conversation along way. She tried to pick my brain to see how much money I was carrying. I wasn't falling for this old trick. I just looked at her out of the corner of my eye until we reached our destination. To my surprise, the house was right across the street from my auntie's house on Fortieth and College. I stayed in the car out of fear of being seen by my cousins. I ducked down in my seat, hoping my auntie didn't peek out the window and see me transporting a hooker to a dope house. The girl stepped out of the car, stretching her long brown flawless legs for the sidewalk. She staggered over toward the house and didn't come back for what seemed like an hour, but she had only been gone for fifteen minutes. I should have driven off, but I was paralyzed by my incredible erection and the promise to get laid. So I reluctantly stayed. It wasn't just the sex I longed for. I was lonely for something, but I didn't know what. I wanted to get laid, but more than that, I just wanted someone of the opposite sex I was not related to, to sit and talk to. So I sat in the car while the rain pounded my windshield. I reclined my seat back as for as it could go. I got comfortable and sipped on a bottle of Windsor Canadian that I had jammed between the front seat and the arm rest. As soon as I got comfortable, here she came, staggering across the street, higher than when she left.

Once we were at the hotel, she tossed me a tightly rolled joint. Her purse hanging off her arm, she staggered into the bathroom and slammed the door shut behind her. I took one drag from the marijuana, and within seconds my head began to swim. "What the hell is this?" I yelled. Sticking her head out of the bathroom door, she yelled "A primo." "What the hell is a primo?" I said. "Marijuana laced with cocaine," she said, then closed the door, going about her business. I wiped my eyes, trying to refocus my eyes from the blurriness. I tripped and stumbled over to the bathroom and pushed the door open, and there she sat on the toilet slumped over with a rubber tube tied around her upper arm. A syringe still stuck in her arm hung freely as drool ran from her mouth. "What the hell are you doing?" I said. "Mind your own damn business," she said while trying to close the door. I jammed the door with my foot and snatched her off the toilet with her panties below her knees. Pulling her from the bathroom, I shoved her out the hotel door to the parking lot. "Wait, goddammit," she yelled as I tossed her shoes and purse out behind her in the rain. She was soaking wet within seconds of being outside. She cursed at me and gave me the finger. I said, "We never got the chance" then slammed the door shut.

I watched her from the window as she staggered off down Thirty-Eighth Street, cursing my name, tripping, and stumbling about as she tried to balance herself on her four-inch heels. After slamming the door closed, I slid the locking bar in its proper position, preventing reentry. My head was spinning out of control. I lost balance and fell uncontrollably back on the bed while the drugs slowly took its effect. I finally dozed off. Minutes later, I was awakened by the weight of another person pressing down on my tarsal. I still felt the heaviness of the drugs. As I opened my eyes, I could feel and see my deceased wife on top of me, making love to me. I tried to lift myself up, but she placed her finger across my lips. Barely touching me, she placed one finger across my lips. She forced me to lie back down and close my eyes. I awoke minutes later. There she was, standing in the mirror, combing her hair the way she always did when she was alive. I said to her, "What are you doing here?" She turned and looked at me, not saying a word, and continued to comb her hair.

I fell back asleep. At 7:45 a.m. the next day, the sun pierced brilliantly through the half-closed curtains, hitting me right between the eyes. I sprung to my feet, frantically looking under the bed and in the closet and the bathroom. No traces of her was to be discovered. Was it real? *Is it my imagination?* I asked myself. For the first time since my wife's death, I realized she still loved me and that I had been carrying her all this time in my heart. I was totally touched by the moment, and for the next several months, I just couldn't shake the feeling. I was afraid to go to my apartment alone because I thought she would make another unannounced visit. I was still hurt and unapologetic to any woman I came in contact with. Women would invite me over to their house late at night. When I arrived, they would wear nightgowns and lie across their bed in a very provocative position. I would just look at them unimpressed by their unsuccessful attempt at seducing me, so I would get up and walk out of their house, leaving them wet and wanting. I didn't care what they thought of me. I didn't care if I ever saw them again. I just didn't care. The women didn't care either. They came at me from all directions in the least opportune times, while I was shopping for my kids' clothes or while I was just taking them to the park or the 500 parade. For some reason, women thought it was adorable that I was raising two girls by myself.

For the first time in my life, I was reluctant to have overwhelming amounts of female attention. Some women wouldn't let me off the hook. They invited themselves over, bringing food and wine and wearing skimpy outfits for enticement. I was mentally and emotionally distraught, sending most of the women home horny, angry, and disappointed. It was hard for me to focus on anything other than raising my children. I was living paycheck to paycheck, and no other financial support was within reach. I knew I was missing something in my daughters' lives. I was missing the talks and quality time parents had with their kids. Because I was working so much to keep a roof over our heads, I didn't have the time to sit and go over homework. Like so many other uneducated parents, I was living in survival mode and couldn't see the light at the end of the tunnel.

As confused as I was, I still had two small girls to raise and two other children to provided child support for on a $4 an hour income. Something in my life had to change. I was being beaten down by the courts with the possibility of going to jail for six months hanging over my head if I didn't maintain my child support payments. I couldn't let that happen because my girls would have ended up in the system, and it would have taken me a lifetime to get them back. My income seemed as though it was my main concern, the controlling factor in my life. My income would determine where I could go and what my possibilities were, where we would live, and what chances my children would have in this world. My faith would soon be tested with regard to income and lifestyle. My daughters and I moved into a low-income apartment on Thirty-Eighth Street. The apartments weren't so bad. I was just used to having better. Being a single father, I was making some huge adjustments. I had to comb the girls' hair, pressed their clothes, and cook their breakfast and dinner.

I wasn't a very good cook, but I got better as time went on. During the week, my daughters ate at my mother's house except for the weekends. Occasionally, I would have to work Saturdays. I didn't want to burden my mother, so I trained my daughters not to answer the phone until they heard my voice and never answer the door unless they knew it was their grandmother or me. After six months, we developed a daily routine. My oldest daughter learned how to wash dishes and comb her own hair. I did my best to comb their hair, but I could never seem to get the part right, so my mother would laugh at my efforts and restyle their hair before they got on the school bus. I could feel the presence of their mother around. Her presence was ever so strong when all three of us were together. Being a single father with two daughters, I was often thought of as adorable. Women came out of every nook and cranny for a shot at the title, but I was in no mental position to be anyone's boyfriend. The women were bold and weren't taking no for an answer. At two or three in the morning, they knocked on my door. It was the same girl all the time. At 3:00 a.m., when the clubs closed, she came to my apartment to get sexed up. If I was horny, I would let her in; but most nights, I peeked through the peephole then went back to bed, leaving her standing outside my door, wanting.

Her boyfriend was serving six months or more in the county jail for nonpayment of child support. Therefore, once she left the den of iniquity, she sought sexual relief after a night of partying and drinking. She walked in my door and asked if she could take her clothes off. "I'm not stopping you," I said. She stripped down to her barebones, strutting around my apartment displaying her hairy bush. I sat on the couch unimpressed, watching an episode of *Gunsmoke*. She strutted to the kitchen without shame, displaying her stretch marks and loose skin, indicating that she had spent no time in the gym.

She spread her legs while bending over looking into my refrigerator allowed me to see her fat delicious clitoris. She took out a bottle of vodka and a jug of orange juice and crafted herself a double screwdriver then stood in front of the TV and invited me to lick her clitoris. I said, "Would you mind stepping to the side please?" She was flabbergasted standing there with her hand on her hip, sipping on her drink. "You can stay if you want to, but I'm really not in the mood," I said. She angrily sat on the couch in total nudity, crossing her legs while filing down her fingernails. She bounced her legs up and down, stretching her foot across where I was lying and rubbed my arm with her toe. I slapped her foot down with my hand and said, "Do you mind? I'm trying to watch this program." She exploded with rage and marched into the room. In ten seconds, she was fully dressed. "I ain't never coming back over this motherfucker," she said before slamming the door and making her way down street with my glass. It wasn't until the next morning I realized she stole one of my new pair of blue jeans. This wasn't the first time this happened, and I knew it wouldn't be the last. Different women with different purposes came to my door all hours of the night, but I just wasn't in the market for casual sex.

All types of sexual opportunities presented themselves. There was a very attractive girl one floor below me. It appeared her boyfriend was returning to college, leaving her desolate without a place to stay. Every time she would hear my door open, she would run outside and sit on the front porch as if she was there the whole time. I knew exactly what she's doing, but I didn't have a vacant space in my heart or room in my apartment for another woman. In the apartment building next door, there was another wild-eyed, crazy woman. She was tall and slim with a flat butt and large nipples protruding from her wife-beater T-shirt. She worked full-time in the bail bonds office downtown and worked part-time as a stripper. She loved practicing her art of stripping in front of me, taking off her clothes, displaying every inch of her nondescript body for my entertainment. I found her boring and distasteful, and she couldn't begin to compare to the strippers in Japan or Hawaii. I was spoiled by their shameless pole dancing and banana shows. This stripper could barely get me fired up. I watched her for about fifteen minutes, hoping she would do something that would hold my interest. I grew tired of her and her unperfected art, so I stared out the window at the kids playing kickball in the street.

She became acrimonious at my nonchalant way of ignoring her. She began reaching her climax in the middle of her stripping, moaning and groaning to herself while sucking on her fingers with her naked butt anchored high in the air, displaying every part of her birth canal. I continued to stare at all the children playing in the street. She looked over her shoulder at me with a very distasteful look on her face. I continued to watch the kids play kickball in the street. All of a sudden, she jumped to her feet and walked her tall thin frame toward me and placed her hairy vagina in my face. "Eat me," she said. I put my head back reluctantly, knowing that this was no player's paradise. She was a stripper, and men were running in and out of her like a fast food restaurant. I looked up at her and shook my head no. Then she put her leg up on the arm of the couch then reached down with both hands and spread her vagina's lips with her fingers, displaying her erect labia majora. Still, I said no, pushing her back with one hand. She ran out of the room, diving facedown on her bed, pretending to cry. She said, "Come on, I want you in me." I said, "Just a minute. Let me try something first." I knew she was a stripper, and knowing that strippers had a reputation of sleep with many man, I decided to test her for venereal disease with a home remedy. I searched the refrigerator for a box of baking soda. "Ha-ha," I said, grabbing the baking soda and running into the bedroom. I rolled her over on her back and spread her legs wide open with my hands. I poured baking soda between your legs into her clitoris. She jumped up as though she sat on a porcupine. "It burns. It burns," she said. "What does it mean when it burns?" she said. "It means you're not clean," I said. I said to myself, *Let me get the hell out of here.*

Two weeks later, she was back at my door with medical clearance papers in hand, showing me that she had been treated for VD. I was back on the market. "Come on over," she said. |I want you to hook up my VCR." I reached into the cabinet above the refrigerator and grabbed my three-pack prophylactic then followed her down the sidewalk, noticing how she thrashed her butt purposely back and forth. I followed her into her apartment, and she disappeared into the bedroom, so I followed her to her bedroom door and peeked around the corner. There she was, lying in full nudity. Her long slim body was oiled up just right. I stripped totally naked before I reached the bed. I gave her exactly what she's been working so hard for. She uncontrollably bit and chewed her pillow as I rode her for two hours straight. I had her legs pinned high against the headboard, making her feel every inch. She went into a violent shake. Kicking her legs wildly, she yelled out, "Go in through the back door." I knew exactly what she meant, but I played dumb. I said, "What are you talking about? Your apartment doesn't have a back door." She said, "No, you idiot, I want you to put it in my ass." I was very reluctant to go south of the border; so I withdrew from my sexual experience, cleaned myself up with her overpriced hand towels, then returned to my apartment for an afternoon of war movies and cowboy shows. I wasn't ten minutes into *Bonanza* before there was a knock at my door. It was her wanting to explain why she said what she said about me going into the back door.

I didn't really care to hear any type of explanation, but being the idiot I was, I let her interrupt my episode of Bonanza to explain her reasoning for being so nasty. She stood in front of me once again, hair uncontrollably wild all over her head. She was wearing a very inviting miniskirt with flip-flops. Her cheap Kmart panties barley covered anything, displaying her huge clitoris every time she bent over to look out the window. I grew very tired very fast of her nonsense and asked her to leave so that I could finish my show. She spinned around and through her skirt in the air displaying her buttocks. I rode my eyes at her while pointing toward the door. She walked out and slammed my door, causing several pictures to hit floor. It was just another bad choice I made in my life, and for a while, it seemed as though I wouldn't stop making bad choices when it came to women. Cindy was still deep in my murky subconscious and poking around in my head like a Tasmanian devil on steroids. I couldn't control anything when it came to sex. I was spoiled by the women of Japan with the concept of as much sex as I wanted. No emotion was required, just pay mama-san $15 for fifteen minutes of pleasure. After a year of living that concept, it was very difficult for me to develop any serious feelings about the women I was with. I was emotionally traumatized from three different angles, which meant I was living in chaos and uncertainty. My first thought was to slow it down, don't date anyone, don't look at any more women, focus on my kids. But that concept lasted about as long as my next sexual opportunity.

There was another girl I found slightly attractive and shy. She was married and wanted to get away from her abusive husband. I was angry at the world and the woman who walked out of my life for the second time. I didn't care about anyone else or anything around me other than my children. So I played captain save a hoe and took on the problems of the woman with the abusive husband. I met her in the backyard at her friend's house. She was sitting at a picnic table with my friend's girlfriend. We struck up a casual conversation, but I knew right off I wanted to have sex with her, not a relationship. Before I knew it, I had gotten her hired at my job and was sexing her up in the bathroom.

I made the biggest mistake any man could've ever made. I moved her in with me without thinking clearly. I thought she was a half-decent woman who just needed a decent man. We worked at the same job and spent a lot of time together. When her husband discovered she left him for another man, he was rightfully enraged. I didn't care. I couldn't see beyond what I wanted at the time, her in my bed giving me service when I needed. It was nice having someone there because I was no good at living alone. I guess you can say I suffer from monophobia. I didn't want my daughters to be home by themselves scared out of their minds, thinking someone would break in and do them harm. One day I went to work, leaving China in my apartment asleep in the bed. I went grocery shopping that took about an hour. By the time I got home, China was sitting outside on the front steps, looking as if she was in deep thought. I said, "What's wrong? Why are you sitting outside?" She looked up at me with a strange look on face and said, "Does anyone have the key to your apartment?" "No, just you and me. Why?" "Someone was standing at the foot of your bed, wearing a white dress, smiling at me." I knew exactly who she was referring to. Although I never discussed my deceased wife with her, she described her to a T.

I never told her who the person was. I just said, "Maybe you were having a bad dream." She forgot about that incident for the moment, and her husband seemingly didn't care she abandoned him for another man, so we eventually move into a three-bedroom house a few weeks later. Over the course of two months, her husband became increasingly annoyed at the fact that I was banging his wife and there was nothing he could do to get her to return home. He knew he was wrong for beating her, and she found it hard to return to the same old foolishness now that she had found serenity and peace in her life; however, she still loved him and often visited and lay with him, igniting the fire of deadly passion. She wanted to be with him, but she didn't want the beatings, and she knew no other way of escaping him except to be with another man he was fearful of.

She thought I was such a mark that she could sleep with her husband and with me and I wouldn't know the difference. Little did she know I was helping her get herself together so that she could be on her own. I knew we had gotten together the wrong way and I had to fix it, but I didn't want to leave her desolate, and I didn't want her to return to an abusive husband. So I helped China purchased a car because her husband kept the car they had, leaving her without transportation, which would result in her depending on him to take the kids to and from day care. Unfortunately, China bought a piece of junk. The car was in the shop more times than she was driving it. The first problem was the car was a diesel and there wasn't very many diesel stations in our area. We drove separate cars to work because she needed to pick her kids up from day care and I needed to pick my children up from their grandmother's house. We were doing well. We had two cars and a front room full of new furniture, but I still felt bad about our living situation and the circumstances that would play out in the end. Although I was making $9 an hour, it wasn't enough.

I knew my job wasn't the right job for me. Something was pulling me away from that type of work and thrusted me in the college. I couldn't explain it, so I quit the job and took a full-time job working security at Butler University. I really didn't want to work another security job, but I had to do something to pay my rent, so I accepted the graveyard shift from 11:00 p.m. until 8:00 a.m. I didn't mind working the late shift. I couldn't sleep at night because I was nocturnal, so working the late shift was right up my alley.

Every night at the beginning of my shift, I walked through the college professors' cubicles, shining my flashlight on their walls, displaying their college degrees. One professor had four college degrees on his wall. I was immediately impressed by this and uttered to myself,

I want this. I knew at that moment everything in my life would be directed toward earning a college degree. Earning a college degree would be unparalleled to anything that I've done in my life this far. It would be a huge challenge because I was academically deficient and functionally illiterate. It was an uphill battle that I had to fight. I knew if my children would have any type of future, I would have to lead by example and prove that it could be done.

A lump formed in my throat, and tears formed in my eyes. I knew this was something I had to do. I had no choice in the matter, but first, I had to clean up my life and put my poor decision making behind me before I could begin this journey. Every morning at four o'clock, I cruised the cafeteria and prepared myself a hearty breakfast including cereal and fruit. It was kind of nice having the keys to the entire campus. I could go inside any building at any time and do whatever I wanted. I spent most of my time in the music department, playing the drums at two in the morning in a soundproof room. A lot of the mornings the cleaning crew would arrive at 4:00 a.m. It was part of my job to unlock the doors to the supply rooms. I sat and chat with them as they did their work. Unfortunately for me, one of the cleaning women was slim and cute. She wore a large Angela Davis afro. Her eyes was slightly cocked to the side, but I knew one good night of passion I could knock them straight. I tried to distance myself from her because I knew she would just be another distraction and another mistake. But it couldn't be helped. Every time I turned the corner, there she was, vacuuming under someone's desk. She playfully put the vacuum hose on my jacket, and I thought to myself, *Oh shit, here we go again.*

So I playfully grabbed her, and we wrestled sexually around the office, she pressing her buttocks to my crouch, giving me a nice stiff one. Another maintenance person unknowingly was observing us each morning from a distance. Suddenly, I was called down to the security office. I was informed that someone was filing sexual harassment charges against me. I said, "Who's filing sexual harassment charges against me?" The security lieutenant said, "I can't divulge that information." "Someone's filing sexual harassment charges against me.

I have a right to know who's following the charges." The lieutenant slid the documents in front of me and asked that I sign the write-up. I refused, shoving the paper across the desk back to her. The next morning I saw the slender cleaning lady. We locked eyes for several seconds. I acted very aloof before purposely turning in the opposite direction down the other hallway. I could hear her clogs clucking on the floor, running behind me, yelling my name. "Whip, Whip, Whip, you hear me dammit." I stopped to look at her with total disappointment on my face. "It wasn't me," she explained. "It was the sociopath woman that I work with. She saw us playing and filed the charges. I don't know why she did that. I think she likes you, and she was jealous. That was just her way of getting your attention." "It's cool. Don't worry about it," I said then walked away. "We're still friends, right?" she yelled as I walked away. "We're still friends," I said. Work wasn't the same for me anymore. The wind had just been taken out of my sail. It seemed anytime I had a problem, it had a female accelerant. The rest of my life was okay. It was just when I involved a woman things would get crazy.

During my off hours, I would let China drive my car to work and pick up and drop her children to school until one day she came home with the front windshield of my car smashed out. She jumped out of the car, frantically yelling, "Ross broke the window." I didn't want to hear any explanation, I grabbed my K bar knife and headed toward his house. I parked my car several blocks from where he lived. I lost all perspective of being a civilian and sank deeply back into the night I was on the pitch-black road in Beirut. I reverted back to my military training, unconsciously low crawling through three backyards. I spotted his car, so I lay on the inside of a brick house with knife in hand, wearing my camouflage utilities with camouflage stick painted on my face. I must've lain there for two hours in the rain, waiting for him to come outside. I had discipline that was thrusted into me throughout my ten years in the marines. I could've stayed out there all night; but in a moment's notice, my ancestors spoke to my heart from their grave, "You're wrong, Mikey. Get up and go home." The voices played in my head over and over until it finally broke through.

As I stood to my feet, Alex jumped back, spilling his coffee all over himself. "Where the hell did you come from?" he said, shaking like a leaf. "Man, I wouldn't want to be your enemy."

I silently looked at him, not saying a word. I turned and went back to the house. The next day I dropped my kids off at school and immediately started packing my boxes to move. I ended my adulterous relationship with China. She could not understand why I would just walk out of her life. "Because it is wrong," I said. "The way we got together was wrong. If we don't break this relationship off, someone could get hurt or possibly go to jail. You're not worth the cost of either."

I moved out within two days and stayed with my mother's ex-husband, Tito. I sat on the couch, recounting the stupid decisions I have made and how I really needed to slow my life down and refocus but the women were still relentless. The phone rang, and it was the maintenance woman from the college. I don't know how she found me or how she got my step dad's phone number. She requested that I stop by before I left town. She was point-blank. She came right out with it. She said, "I want to have sex with you. You turn me on. I think you and I could be really good together. I'm a hard worker, I work two jobs, and I will give you both of my checks if you become my man." I was in a depressed state, but I was knocked back on my heels. I sat in the living room chair with broken springs protruding out the back of the chair. I was so astonished by what she said I hardly noticed the spring jamming into my lower lumbar. I took a deep breath and moved the phone away from my mouth to keep her from hearing me as I exhaled. "I don't think so," I said. She began to snuffle as though she was crying, and before the first teardrop fell from her face, I hung the phone up.

I struggled to distinguish the sexual appetite that burned within me. It wasn't something I created. It was innate. I was born with it. One of the rare gifts my father left me, something that most married women would love their man to have, was an unending sexual stamina. I had it, and if used improperly, I could be happily married; but if I abused the privilege of having it, I would become a prisoner of my own sexual fame. Nothing in my life would go according to plan until I fixed this out-of-control promiscuity in the bedroom.

The Final Act

After freeing myself of a bad relationship, my ex-wife returned to Indianapolis. She said she could not pay the rent in California and wanted to get back together. I held a lot of anger toward her, but my two girls loved her and wanted to be with her. My marine reserve unit was packing up to be deployed to Afghanistan. I didn't want to place the burden on my mother to keep my daughters, so I allowed them to return to California with May. The war was over before we had a chance to get ourselves in gear. I was very happy that I didn't have to kill anyone or be killed. I gave my car to my mother, divided my furniture between my sisters, then boarded a bus to Sacramento. I couldn't tell, but at first glance, it didn't seem that May was happy to see me. She started right off complaining, "How are you going to get a job? We don't have a car or telephone." I looked at her of the corner of my eye. I thought for a second, *Damn, this girl has no confidence in me at all,* so I took my newspaper. I went out to the patio so I could focus and plotted the easiest route to the job site located in the paper. The next morning I hit the ground running. I purchased a map of Sacramento so that I could navigate my way around the city. May was sure that I wouldn't find any work, and it really bothered me that she had no faith in me whatsoever.

She repeated herself as I walked out the door. She said, "How are you going to find a job? We don't have a car, and we don't even have a phone." I reassured her that I would find work. I walked every day five miles or more for two weeks until I found a job at a packing company that paid $5 an hour. I was glad to find a job, not just to prove me wrong but to help her increase her confidence in me. I found it very upsetting that she never worked during our entire marriage, but she seemed to have a double standard when it came to me. How could she demand from others what she didn't a expect of herself? She knew I was never an idle person. I worked my whole life and didn't see any reason for not working at this point in my life. My new job was a very basic job. Only a few brain cells were needed to perform the work. This shipping job was boring and sometimes even back breaking. I was no longer the young, twenty-year-old kid carrying one-hundred-pound artillery shells on each shoulder. I was now a thirty-year-old ex-marine in fair to good physical condition.

It was mentally agonizing for me to work at a place that I knew was beneath my intelligence. Something was pulling me toward college. I couldn't explain what it was, but it kept me up at night. I couldn't go to sleep. I didn't know what it was or if it was a combination of the anthrax and BP pills the military gave us before we deployed to Afghanistan. I woke up every night with my T-shirt soaking wet. Bumps broke out across my forehead, and I would have headaches every day for six months. I didn't know what was going on with my body, but I had no time to worry about it because I had to find a way to support my children. I ignored the symptoms while working at that mindless shipping job.

I worked at the shipping job for eight months, walking six miles a day to and from the plant. I couldn't take any more. I knew the job was a dead end, and I was only bringing home $300 after taxes every two weeks. I didn't even spend the money. I gave it directly to May, which seemingly made her more than happy, but it failed to elevate our sexual encounters from one day a week just on the weekends. I couldn't do it anymore. I had subliminal visions of myself working at that job until I was sixty-five years old with the gray hair an aching back and still living in the same ghetto fabulous apartments. I just couldn't waste any more time doing the job that wouldn't have positive long-term financial outcome. I knew I could rise above the situation and do more if the opportunity presented itself, but the fact is if I was going to be given a chance, I was going to have to create the opportunity. There is an old saying: luck is when you're prepared for the opportunity. I believe that concept with all my heart, and it's what I thought would get me through the next phase of my life. I thought long and hard about going to college and what it would mean for my family if I had a degree or some type of certification in training. I decided when I got home that day I was going to talk with May about quitting work in the day and going to school and working at night. To my surprise, she agreed. I cashed my check and gave the entire amount to her to manage. Having money in her pocket somehow made her feel empowered. Somehow she felt in control. However, the day did arrive when I had to quit my job to attend school while waiting to find another job. May became enraged and impatient. The $5 an hour was no longer coming in, and she could feel the empty spaces those dead presidents once filled. During our meals, she would throw my plate down on the table in front of me. Small amounts of food would splash onto my shirt. The plate only had enough food on it to feed a two-year-old child. She became very cold, not speaking and sleeping on the couch once again. She seemed to have forgotten I allowed her to receive the money from my two girls' SSI. She had forgotten I moved from Indianapolis after she begged me to help her. She had forgotten I gave all my furniture away and relocated my life to make this marriage work.

She had forgotten she didn't work for the first four years of our marriage, and I never treated her mean or bad because she did not want to work. None of this meant anything to her. She was living in the moment, and for the time being, she was in the driver's seat and didn't care whether I buckled in with her for life or left and moved on with my life. I was of no use to her. She couldn't get any money from me; therefore, I should leave. I never felt so looked down upon in all my life. She was very cold and unapproachable. The atmosphere was very bad, and the tension was so thick you could cut it with a knife. I chose to leave her apartment, knowing I had nowhere to go and no place to live. But in my head, I believed opportunity was now here. I'd rather live on the streets than live where I felt hated and despised. In hindsight, I wished I had left her in Hawaii for the Filipino woman that offered me all that money and I wouldn't be going through this nonsense with her. She couldn't handle pressure well. Anytime life challenge her, she would crumble and run back to the welfare system or some other form of disability, never standing on her own two feet, surviving off her own efforts. She was weak, and I was glad to be rid of her.

Opportunity Is Now Here

She quit on me for the third and final time. I stayed with her because my children loved her, and I felt they needed a mother figure, but I had to give up too much to be with her. I could not let her break me or make me feel less than a man. I packed my bags and began walking toward the college. Once I got one mile away from the apartment, uncertainty and insecurity began to set in. I felt lost and unsure of what my next move would be.

Once I reached the college, I secured my duffel bag in an empty wall locker and began making my way up Stockton Boulevard toward the welfare office located on Twenty-Eighth and R. My goal was to get a bus ticket from the department of human assistance so I could go back to Indianapolis, but fate had other plans. I arrived at the welfare office just in time for the doors to close until the next morning. I was more than five miles from the college where my clothes were stashed away in a wall locker, so I slept outside the welfare office in the rain, wearing a pair of blue jeans and a T-shirt not providing much protection from the wind and rain. I walked along the side of building, scavenging around for a place to sleep. Every corner, every sidewalk, every nook was saturated with urine. I paced up and down Twenty-Eighth and R. light rail station with my arms tucked inside my T-shirt, freezing cold from the rain and thirty-four-degree weather for twelve hours until the next morning. Cars began to pull up to the building at 4:00 a.m. Someone got out and sat on the steps. Already, there was a line forming, and it was only four o'clock in the morning.

So I walked over and sat on the steps of the welfare office to ensure I was second in line. One knew all the ins and outs of how to get welfare. He told me to apply for welfare benefits and not to apply for a bus ticket back home. I was a very proud person. I didn't want the welfare.

I just needed little help; therefore, I want to ask for a bus pass back to Indianapolis. Once the doors opened at 7:00 a.m., I was the second client through the front door of the welfare office. After completing the paperwork, I was called in for an interview. The interviewer sat behind the desk, looking very smug, occasionally taking a drag from his cigarette. He looked into my paperwork. "What can I help you with?" he said. "I want to get a bus ticket to go back home to Indiana," I replied. "I can't give you a bus pass unless you give me the names of ten people that can guarantee this will not happen again." "I don't know ten people," I replied. Reaching over the desk, he grabbed the stamp, placing a big Denied across the top of the paper. After signing the document, he tore a copy off and handed it to me. It took him less than five minutes before he denied me benefits. I couldn't believe how rude the general assistance (GA) worker was toward me. He acted as if it were personal, and the money was coming out of his pocket. I left their welfare office the same way I arrived: broke and homeless.

My pride wouldn't allow room for begging on the streets. By this time, I had not eaten in twenty-four hours, and my pride was being challenged. I stop by May's house, and she wouldn't even open the front door. She just cracked the patio door and asked, "What do you want?" I told her I had been denied for the bus ticket back to Indianapolis, and I just needed somewhere to stay until I got on my feet. She didn't say a word. She just let the glass door close. I walked away. I didn't know whether to be shocked or be hurt, so I walked over to Florida Mall and sat one of the benches tucked away in the hallways. Once again, I was stunned by the uncaring and unkindness of another human being. She was as cold and calculating as they came. I'd known this woman my entire life, but I'd never seen this side of her. A million thoughts swam loosely in my head. The moments of sorrow were beginning to set in. I was getting ready to feel sorry for myself, but I didn't get a chance. I was asked to leave the mall so that they could lock the doors. I swallowed my pride for a brief second and once again I found myself back at May's doorstep.

Without Challenges, Life Would Be Boring

Everything that I believed in and accomplished at this point in my life was about to be tested. For the first time in my life, I had no answers for tomorrow. I was living minute by minute. My focus had shifted to finding a place to sleep and food to eat. As I departed the welfare office, I headed for the college where my belongings were stored. First, I stopped by my ex-wife's house to see if she would reconsider. Before reaching the apartment, it began to pour down torrential rain. I was soaking wet within minutes. I knocked on the door, and my daughter answered. Her mother had an arrogant look on her face. I went into the apartment and sat by the sliding glass patio door. She sat at the opposite end of the table, eating a greasy pork chop, belching then, tossing the bone on the plate. She pontificated nonstop for forty-five minutes, after which time she reminded me it was time for me to leave.

I asked her if I could spend the night. She replied, "You can sleep on the patio" as she smiled and walked into the kitchen, placing her dish in the sink then pointed toward the patio. By this time, the uncovered patio was soaked with rain, junk, and discarded items that littered the entire area. As I stepped on the patio, she slid the door closed and fastened the lock, sealing any chance of my reentry. I tried to cover myself with loose papers and dirty clothes that littered the patio but to no avail, I was drenched from head to toe. Sitting there and shaking like leaves on a tree, I decided to leave. Before I could leave, the neighbor with the patio directly across from May's patio stuck her head out the door and laughed. I couldn't believe what I was going through. I couldn't believe this was the person I thought was genuine enough to marry. I always thought a wife was supposed to be a help mate, someone I could count on in a time of crisis. I was shaking so frantically from the cold air and rain I could barely hold a clear thought in my head. What did I do so badly to deserve this? My worst crime was I wanted to get a better education so I could take care of my children and provide for my family a secure future. I had known this woman since the third grade. I took her to the ROTC ball dance and to Kings

Island. We were high school sweethearts. I was disappointed in myself because I didn't see it coming. I married her on superficial basis, not for love, and I was now paying the price. I knew I was at a very vulnerable time in my life when I married her, but I didn't expect or have a clue that she would have this nasty attitude. I couldn't believe a person like this existed. Past images of her no longer had any place in my heart. I climbed over the patio and made my way back to the campus. The rain was coming down frightening hard. Large rain droplets were so blinding I could barely see three feet in front of me. I was cold and wet. I felt like I had been walking for miles. My shoes felt like they weighed a ton. They were filled with water, and my bones hurt from the cold and rain. I was about to give up when all of a sudden, I fell to my knees and asked God what it was he wanted me to do with my life. I spoke to God as if he were standing in front of me. I screamed out, "Whatever road you want me to travel, I will travel. Whatever obstacle you place in my way, I will find a way through it, but please tell me what you want me to do with my life." I stood up and walked to the nearest phone booth and dialed my mother's phone number. Before the phone could ring, I hung the phone up. I realized I had to stand on my own two feet. *Be patient and willing to suffer through the transition,* a voice in my head was telling me. I looked up, and that was a bus stop ten feet in front of me. I walked over and discovered the bus stop was closed in on three sides.

I plopped myself down on the bench and thanked God for the shelter from the rain he just provided. My T-shirt and jeans were dripping wet. I hadn't been this cold since my cold-weather training in 1980 in South Korea. I sat there shivering as my mind faded back into the days of my grandmother dragging us to church. It paid off in this time of need. It had given me a voice to speak to God in a way that I would have my prayers answered. All those Easters I spent in church lying across my grandmother's lap as she patted my back while I dozed off through the sound of the preacher's voice. In an instant thunderstruck, I was jolted back into reality into my present situation. I found a safe place to sleep. My first order of business was to find a safe place to sleep. I needed food, and I needed to find a job. Therefore, I combined the two. I began looking for a job that served food. I was beginning to feel good about myself again that night. I sat up most of the night into the morning, not sleeping a wink, making plans for my future one small step at a time. A voice in my head kept telling me, *Be patient and willing to suffer through the transition*, so I developed patience, not caring about material possessions or how much money I had in my pocket. I was beginning to learn to care about the quality of life.

It was a challenge every night getting to the bus stop. The security guard would stop and watch me across the campus. I pretended as though I was going off campus across the street into the apartment complex, but I would just sit on the apartment steps out of the sight of the security guard and wait till he made his rounds before I made my way back over to the bus stop. I saw the security officer's presence as a nuisance, but I began to change my frame of thought. Instead of seeing the security guard as a threat, I saw him as my own private security patrolling and protecting me as I slept. This made me feel good about guard parking right outside of the bus stop booth. Once I was able to process the thought of a security guard in a positive light, I was able to rest a little more easily.

The days were long and cold, and the nights were even longer. By this time, I had not eaten in more than a week. I lived on water, a half-eaten box of saltine crackers, and will power. Negative thoughts would enter my head from time to time, but I reminded myself of the promise I made to God. I really wanted to believe that God was with me, but uncertainty would raise its ugly head and whisper unkind thoughts in my ear. I would listen for a minute or two then move on. It was in the middle of October, during the rainy season. For some strange reason, the rains wouldn't let up. Every night I sat on the bus stop trying to sleep, but my frantic body shaking would wake me up. I prayed more, and with more personal massages to God, I often called his name and asked that he show his power, but misery in the form of rain fell from the sky. I stood outside the entrance of the bus stop and looked up at the sky; my eyes were then directed toward the back of the campus where the gym was located.

I watched the janitor go from building to building, leaving the lights on once he was done working in each building. A force compelled me to walk to the back of the campus. When the janitor finished cleaning the gym, I saw the lights of the building next door turn on, so I walked to the back of the gym; and to my luck, the back of the gym door was open. I made my way through the dark locker room and finding my locker, I removed a T-shirt and a pair of blue jeans, almost tearful with joy that I was in a warm place with a hot shower. I found many bars of soap barely used and a bottle of shampoo half full. I was overjoyed because God has created inside each of us an empty place—a place that only God could fill. Ecclesiastes in the Old Testament says, "God has put eternity in our hearts." This eternity, this empty place God created for himself, I call the glory space. Each one of us chooses how we will fill this *glory space* within our souls. I chose filling my empty space with the promise I made to God. I slept on the locker room bench until the lights came on. Then I would grab my books and head to class. On the way to class, I briefly stopped in the cafeteria and watched as the students sat and filled their faces with donuts, coffee, and freshly cooked bacon and eggs right off the grill. My stomach growled as the aroma from the food provided a great distraction for learning, reminding me of another roadblock I needed to overcome.

Life wasn't fair, but I couldn't focus or waste my energy on side thoughts. I had to focus on the situation at hand, the fact that I had not eaten in days. After class, my job search began. Walking ten miles a day, I barely noticed how far I had walked. I was determined to stay on schedule and feed my face. After wayfaring for miles, I noticed a large sign above the entryway of Long John Silver's restaurant. I never worked in a fast food up to this time in my life, but I did have restaurant experience at Saul Subway. This job was perfect for the moment. Food at last! All I had to do was convince the manager I could do the job. The manager wasted no time. He interviewed me on the spot. The manager offered me a large soda while I completed the application.

One sip on the straw and the cup rattled with ice, trying to fill the empty pockets that were once filled with orange soda. I recalled being so hungry I felt envious of a child eating an ice cream cone at the mall earlier in the day. To my surprise, I was hired on the spot. The smell of the fish and shrimp pierced my nose. I left the restaurant and headed back to the college where I waited patiently two nights before I began work. My first job was to wash dishes and clean the dish room. I was a little put off by the fact that I had to start over in life at thirty years old, but I realized that there was no time for pride, so I checked my pride at the door and scrubbed the walls and floors and washed the pots and pans.

I was only allowed to work two hours my first day, but I was able to tuck two pecan pies in my pockets before going back to the bus stop. Two weeks had passed, and I was moved up to the fry cook job. I could eat as much fish and shrimp as my stomach could hold. I would cook five pieces of fish for Long John Silver's, and I would cook two pieces for myself. I would cook a batch of shrimp for LJS and three shrimp for me. Cooking fish and shrimp required the use of batter, and batter caused a mess. Most of the nights, I went back to the bus stop covered in batter. Many nights heavy rain fell from the sky. I lay in my car and listened to the sound of the raindrops hitting the roof. This was my favorite time of the day, three in the morning. I lay awake staring at the empty streets, watching the lights change from blinking red to solid red.

The rain truly slowed my progress down, making my journey home much longer. I liked working at LJS. Everyone was nice and very helpful. One of the managers was a heavy set black female. I could tell she had a crush on me; she often put me on her work shift and assigned me to close the store with her. One evening she approached me during my lunch break. She talked about sex and the type of intercourse she would like. At this time in my life, I had not had sex in more than two months; but for some reason, I could not find her attractive. She had a huge chin like a Neanderthal's, and she was a little heavier than I liked. I knew she was willing to move her boyfriend out and me in, where

I could find warmth and a place to lay my head, but I would have to service her needs and be under her control. She was a heavy set woman with much to offer, but it was not cold enough outside for me to take on this challenge. I was content for the moment, sleeping outside in my own space where I did not owe anyone anything. After two months had passed, I saved up enough money to treat myself to an occasional bus ride to work or downtown on the weekends.

I had $300 in my pocket that allowed me a chance to revise my living plans. While riding the bus, I noticed there was a car for sale. The sign read $295 down. I jumped off the bus and ran across the street to the car lot. They were all too happy to sell me this broken-down 1975 Oldsmobile Omega. The car was yellow with brown interior. It looked like an egg, but it provided much-needed shelter from the rain. I parked the car next to Kaiser Hospital where I slept every night for next two months. I was lucky to have that roof over my head. I realized God was working in my life. As long as I stayed on the road less traveled, I would receive my rewards that were stored up just for me. It was hard having patience, and sometimes I wanted to break the law for quick money—money that would not serve me in the long run. So I peregrinated to school each morning, back to my car for a change of clothes, then to work. I was reminded often by Mother Nature that I was lucky to have a dry place to sleep. The winter came hard and cold, and the rains followed.

Throw Your Net on the Right Side

The holidays arrived on time, and my place of work closed for three days. I was financially tapped out. I spent all my money buying the car, I didn't have two pennies to rub together, and I was left without food or any way to get food. I spent Thanksgiving Day tarrying around Kaiser Hospital, sitting in the cafeteria and staring at the vending machine, wishing I could afford one of those sandwiches. I meandered in and out the of the cafeteria then finally went outside to sit near the front entrance. I was feeling the holiday blues, missing home and family. I heard a familiar friend calling. It was hunger. My stomach was telling me to get busy and find food, something I had forgotten about in the past two weeks. I watched the security guard patrol around the buildings, wishing I had a job like his job. With no money in my pocket and no family to visit or call, I felt alone and depressed. A voice from within spoke to me and said, *Look on your right side. Throw your net on the right side.* As I turned to my right side, I noticed I was sitting on a wishing well filled with quarters and dimes.

A large smile stretched across my face, something I hadn't been able to produce for a while. I marauded with my hand in the water, removing four quarters then more change, briefly stopping to observe the security officer pass by on his golf cart. I had removed $10 in change from the wishing well. Excited, I ambled around the corner to the 7-Eleven store and purchased two hot dogs with chili, onions, and cheese; a large drink; and, for dessert, a pack of Ho Hos. I ambulated back to my car, with a full stomach and a smile on my face, a meal fit for a king that allowed me to sleep comfortably that night. I returned to the hospital basement, sitting in the cafeteria four hours each night, studying, trying to stay warm, and justifying the reason I was going through this madness. The night passed, and the sun rose again, blasting its way to my windshield, covering my face and slapping me awake as if it was saying, "Get up, you fool. It's time for another day." I sprang to my feet excited as I ran to the college campus three blocks away.

My financial aid was to arrive today giving me psychologically air to breathe. I rushed to the financial aid line that stretched around the building. After an hour of waiting, I walked to the window, I was informed that my check was not there and to check back next week. I continued to go to class, but my heart and mind were not in a learning mode. I sat and watched my classmates participate and interact with other students. Everyone seemed to have a place in life where they belonged. Students often gathered outside the lunch room to play dominos while eating lunch. The aroma of food over powered my sixth sense and forced me to sit at one of the tables. I couldn't eat another saltine cracker. I was thin as a rail but hadn't fully come to realize how thin I was. I knew I didn't want another relationship but women still want to date me although I had nothing but the clothes on my back and a twenty-year-old broken-down yellow egg of a car to offer.

While setting in the cafeteria a small slim African American women stood next to me. It was obvious that she was pregnant. Her personality was so pleasant her breasts was big as two pumpkins sitting side-by-side. I couldn't take my eyes off her. Within the next two days, we became friends. She was damaged goods. Her boyfriend had cheated on her and left her so that he could marry another woman. She was nice and friendly. I thought she had a cute personality, but she was a woman scorned. I knew I would never be able to trust her because both of us had been emotionally hurt, and our pain would serve to destroy whatever friendship we had. I saw her through the delivery of her baby and helped her with small chores around the house. I enjoyed being with her, but she was no longer a one-man woman. She tried to be in an exclusive relationship but never fully trusted that her men would not cheat on her because of her past relationship with her baby's daddy. I thought she was the prettiest black woman I'd ever seen, but I also thought she had loose morals when it came to dating. She wore revealing clothes that didn't leave much for imagination. I couldn't take my eyes off her huge breasts with piercings through each nipple. She was very attractive, but I would never try to marry a woman that dressed so loosely and didn't care what other people thought. Besides, you can't turn a hoe into a housewife. We sat outside at the cafeteria table. She looked around as though she was a security guard. Then she handed me an envelope full of pictures displaying her huge breasts. I have to admit I was thoroughly impressed, and if she wasn't pregnant, I would've offered to break her properly.

Although I had no sexual desire for her, I would be seen walking on the campus with her, but we weren't having sex. We were just friends. Women didn't seem to care what position she held in my life. They often approached me during my first semester of college, offering to go out on dates or to just have sex, but my heart was broken twice over, and seriously dating someone would have been an enormous task for me at that time of my life. I couldn't afford to put gas in my car, but they did not seem to care about my circumstances. They just wanted a man.

This was a gold mine, and I was the nugget. With little effort, I had ability to pick and choose my pleasure. I could sleep over or move in with anyone of my choosing. I rejected all offers. I was not ready to involve myself in a partnership. I was cold and short when I turned down dates; I was straightforward with women. I just wanted sex and nothing else. This was painful but was generally safer and ultimately better for both parties than allowing the cycle of distrust to continue. Stepping out of the cycle helped me learn how to protect and care for myself. I walked around wearing all black from head to toe. I was mourning the death of my wife and the death of my spirit. Detachment from love was difficult but the best solution if you're not ready or unwilling to work though the issues. My need for trust arose from my interdependence with others. I often depended on other people to help me obtain, or at least not to frustrate, the outcomes I valued. As my interests with others intertwined, I also recognized there was an element of risk involved as I encountered situations in which I could not compel the cooperation I'd sought. Therefore, trust could be very valuable in social interactions.

My belief in relationships was nonexistent. One day a tall slim mildly attractive woman walked into my life. She noticed me from across the campus and eventually summoned up enough courage to strike up a casual conversation. She noticed I was smiling for once and asked, "What's the big occasion? Why are you so happy today?" I looked at her and winked. Reaching into my jacket, I pulled out a check for $2,500. "I finally got my financial aid after six months," I said. "Well, you can take me out to dinner." I looked her up and down as I folded the check and stuffed it back into my pocket. "How about six o'clock tonight?" She said okay then strutted off the campus to her car.

Later that evening, we found ourselves sitting at a Chinese restaurant having a cheap $6 meal.

She told me her life story, that she had come from Oakland, California. Trying to escape the violence of the city, she moved to Sacramento for the safety of her children, a moment of peace, and a fresh start. She had two children, a boy and a girl, with different fathers. She made very poor choices of men. Both fathers of her children were serving life prison terms for murder and would never see the light of day outside the gray prison walls again. I learned to read women very well. She seemed to like me a lot, and I knew there would be no problem having sex with her that night, so I sat on the other side of the table with a full erection in anticipation of a night of unbridled sex.

Once back at her house, I walked her to the door. Without asking, she invited me right in. We sat on her couch, and in less than thirty seconds, I had her panties off and her legs high over her head. I was pounding her out of control. She was experiencing months of my abstinence from sex as I pounded and grinded her into a new reality. She squirted juices across the room like a firehose. I was soaked from head to toe. I couldn't believe it. She didn't seem the type to wet so easily. I was totally wrong. Before I could get it in third gear, my pelvic region was drenched with her juices. Little did she know she was receiving the product of my sexual frustrations. As I grinded her throughout the night, she never complained. She just took it. Seven hours later, I walked out of the house, zipping my smoking gun up in my pants. I left her sexually drunk on the couch, unable to move, with her new $60 hairdo lifeless in pieces and scattered all over the front-room floor, mangled up with all the perm sweated out of it. I didn't think I would hear from her again, but the next morning, she saw me walking across the campus. She walked up to me and handed me a book. "You left this book at my house," she said. I looked at her with a puzzled expression on my face. *What the hell are you talking about?* I thought. Then it hit me. She wanted more sex. So I obliged her by pulling her into a dark spot in the drama center. I tossed her on top of the piano and pounded her hard from one side of the room to the other, knocking over furniture in our unbridled lust. There wasn't a wall in the room her back did not touch. I bounced her off every wall and instrument within the one-hundred-square-foot stage.

I was so sexually excited my nine inches swallowed into ten full inches of pure python. I told her to put her ass in the air. I drove it in deep and hard, watching her rip my new $50 jeans into shreds with her teeth. I was just shifting our lovemaking into third gear when I saw a reflection of myself in the mirror leaning against the wall, grinding my teeth and plowing her insides out with every stroke. I wasn't making love. I was just trying to break her off something. I abruptly stopped and stood to my feet. She reached around and grabbed my ass, trying to pull me back down on top of her. "What are you doing? Come on, give me the dick," she said.

I couldn't do it anymore. I didn't like the person I'd become, and I didn't like that image I saw in the mirror. The image in the mirror was very familiar. It was someone I had known all my life, but it wasn't me. It was my father. I had become my father, something I tried my whole life desperately to avoid. I knew I didn't lover her. I was just fucking my frustrations and disappointments of previous relationships out of my system. I wanted to hurt her the way I was hurt, but I'd come to realize I was traveling down the road of least resistance, and I needed a chance to find my way back. She didn't care about my philosophy or which road I was traveling. She liked the way I fucked and was willing to take on the task of loving me back to reality. She was very trusting, allowing me to see her just for sex whenever I wanted it. Our relationship was no holds barred. I could just walk in her house without saying a word and perform my coitus act. I didn't even have to spend the night. I just committed my act of debauchery and went home.

This was the ideal lifestyle for any man. She wasn't too hard on the eyes. Physically, she was attractive. Nice-size 36B breasts, small waist with a huge butt. She never nagged or tried to change me to suit her own image of what she wanted in a man. She could see my potential, and that was enough for her. In adults, the impairment of basic trust is expressed in a basic mistrust.

It characterizes individuals who withdraw into themselves in particular ways when at odds with themselves and with others. She did not want trust issues to arise; therefore, she made sure there were no skeletons in her closet. Trust didn't keep the door to infidelity closed in this case. Unfortunately, for her, the rules of dating might never be definitive, but there were still a few universal dos and don'ts of dating upon which many singles—and experts—could agree. It was a costly mistake on her part to lay her sexual escapades out in the open for me to see, telling me that she had slept with many men before being with me and she even slept with three men at the same time. My imagination when wild thinking of three men climbing on her at the same time, because the truth is a pill that everyone wants but it's a hard pill to swallow. I couldn't imagine myself standing in a historical line of forty or more men that came before me. She tried everything to please me, but I was never going to be led through an emotional maze out into the rainy nights again! I felt sorrow for her as I backed away from the house, watching her crying frantically.

It was a hard lesson she had learned, and I was very doubtful if she would so easily divulge her bedroom secrets ever again. So after our breakup, she was angry and hurt. Life seemed like a joke because she built her life around me. She felt like I did at one time. It's all over, and I'd been there. I thought maybe she would hurt herself, but she never reached that point. I didn't get seriously involved for a while because getting girls was life plucking grass on the ground. It came easy for me, so I would just hit and run. I began dating women that I didn't want to destroy me or get married because I couldn't tough it out and continue what seemed like a stupid, ridiculous game at times (life).

I thought about love as a game, but the game got sick for a little while. Now I was learning about life. It's undeniably unfair and ugly to leave someone in the midst of a relationship. Breaking up with her meant no more warm nights in her bed with a roof over my head, but I did not care. I'd rather sleep in my car and have control over my own life rather than sleep in her bed and depend on her for financial support. For most men, that would have been a hard decision to make, leaving a warm bed and all the sex a body could handle; but for me, self- esteem and self-control were my foremost concerns. Sex was a very important function in my life; sex had always been my weakness. I was strong in spirit but weak in the flesh. My Dionysian exploits were fighting for a while, but their only purpose became breaking hearts of the people. I decided to meander toward the quite life. I prayed and prayed and prayed, but no answers seemed to appear. Just like myself, it was Peter's biggest problem. Jesus told Peter, "Watch and pray, lest you enter into temptation. The spirit indeed is willing but the flesh is weak" (Matt. 26:41). There is nothing wrong with having a body of flesh, but the problem is that our bodies have strong desires that tempt us to sin. "Let no one say when he is tempted, 'I am tempted by God'; for God cannot be tempted by evil, nor does he himself tempt anyone. But each one is tempted when he is drawn away by his own desires and enticed. Then, when desire has conceived, it gives birth to sin; and sin, when it is full-grown, brings forth death" (James 1:13). "Do not love the world or the things in the world. If anyone loves the world, the love of the Father is not in him. For all that is in the world—the lust of the flesh, the lust of the eyes, and the pride of life—is not of the Father but is of the world. And the world is passing away, and the lust of it; but he who does the will of God abides forever" (1 Jn. 2:15–17). Using these passages from the Bible helped me focus on where I wanted to go and how I was going to get there.

I understood that women would always be there, and I needed to grow as a person before I could have a serious relationship. Although breaking up cost me a safe and warm place to lay my head, I became free to develop into who I was to meant to become without any distractions. My entire self derived a vitalizing sense of reality from the awareness that my individual way of mastering my experiences was a successful variant of my identity and was in accord with space-time and my life plan. We observed, for instance, that in our guilt culture, individuals and groups, whenever they perceive that their socioeconomic status is in danger, unconsciously behave as if inner dangers had really called forth the threatening disaster. As a consequence, not only individual regressions to early guilt feelings and atonements take place but also a reactionary return to the content and to the form of historically earlier principles of behavior. I refused to return to my early way of life and thinking, trapping myself in a poverty-stricken lifestyle. While the struggle for autonomy was at its worst, my sense of self-worth was growing because I realized that problems were not the problem; coping was the problem. Coping was the outcome of self-worth, rules of the family systems, and links to the outside world.

Tell me how a person judges his or her self-esteem, and I will tell you how that person operates at work, in love, in sex, in parenting, in every important aspect of existence—and how high he or she is likely to rise. The reputation you have with yourself—your self-esteem—is the single-most important factor for a fulfilling life (Nathaniel Branden).

Challenges Build character

Being homeless help shape my future. I became humble; therefore, I became teachable. I was able to use experiences from the past and convert them to strengths. No matter how bad it seemed, certain things went okay. I gained wisdom and experience. I began to realize that lowering myself to living on the streets had somehow gave me the ability to see other homeless individuals at their level and experience how they lived firsthand. Although I never ventured downtown to Loaves and Fishes where the majority of the homeless population spent their day, I occasionally came across other individuals that were homeless. Another student attending the same college was living in his mother's garage. Somehow he found out that I was homeless. He approached and asked me if I would consider sharing an apartment with him, thereby splitting the rent.

I was reluctant at first, approaching it with curiosity; but I also knew it was time to make small changes in my living arrangements, providing myself with the little things that made life worth living. I agreed, and we found a small studio apartment on the south side of Sacramento. It was ironic that the apartment where I was moving to was across the street from where I parked my car and slept every night; therefore, I only had to move my across the street. This was a very different situation for me. Although I lived in marine barracks with eighty men before, I was a little unsure of my new roommate's behavior and living standards. He appeared to be a nice guy, with thick nerdy, pop-bottle eyeglasses and white hair. It often made me laugh when I looked at him. His eyes would cross when he smiled, and his ears would move forward. He was fast talking and always thinking of the next scam he could pull off. He often spoke of his past criminal record that stretched from Chicago to California.

He was accustomed to living in small spaces and sharing food and coffee; he chained-smoked marijuana like cigarettes, stopping only to get a bite to eat. Calvin was an ex-felon that tested and pushed the law to its legal limits. If there was ever a scam or a way to not pay for what he needed, Calvin was the first to try it. I couldn't go anywhere with him without him calculating a scheme. We ate breakfast at a well-known restaurant in Sacramento, beside the table, and looked up menus. I excused myself and went to the bathroom. When I returned, Calvin was sitting at a different table. I asked him, "Why did you move?" He said, "I got the silverware and salt shakers from both tables." We had a couple of coffee then left the restaurant. I knew from the time on, I would have to be aware Calvin's behavior wherever we went. Calvin did not drive a car because of his secondary vision impairment due to being an albino. He believed that he was the missing link to mankind, but in reality, he was the Piltdown man.

Life has many types of education.
You choose which education you want.

It was new Year's Eve 1992, and Calvin had plans to go out for the evening. I transported him to an outlet store nearby, where he could buy a shirt and tie. I walked with him through the store while he shopped; he held labels on the clothing close to his face, trying to read the label through his bifocal glasses. I always got a kick out of watching him work up scams in his diabolical mind and see the excitement on his face as he moved through the motions. He believed everything he did was for the black cause, but in reality, everything he did was for the advancement of himself. He took the shirt and tie to the counter and paid for them. I was shocked, but little did I know, he was just warming up for the next act. He went back into the store with the receipt, got the same shirt and tie, then took the clothing to the register, and got his money back for both items. He did this two more times for other items at different stores.

I couldn't believe what I was seeing. It was as if I was being reeducated and given a choice between getting what I wanted the easy illegal way or continuing with my education for the next four or five years and maybe get a decent job. I traveled the path of least resistance before, and I wanted to see what result of what I could achieve if I took the road less traveled. I watched Calvin for the next six months, stealing and selling his hot goods. I often came home to our studio apartment crowded with people buying his ill-gotten goods. Once I saw more than ten jackets hanging from the ceiling of our room. I worked all day, frying fish; and he played all day, stealing from department stores. I knew our living arrangement could not last, so I began putting money aside for a new place of my own. I had put some down on a more dependable car, so I thought. The car was a Fiat; the convertible top was ripped to pieces with duct tape, holding it partly together. The dash board was falling out from the stripped screws that once held it in place. Everything else on the car was good except the radio did not work, so I brought a radio from the local auto salvage yard.

I began removing the old radio when a big chunk of hard substance fell from behind the radio. I didn't think anything of it, so I tossed it on the grass. Calvin came outside, picked up the hard item, and asked, "Where did you get this from?" I said, "It fell from behind the radio." Once again, the look of excitement came over his face. We went into the apartment; he pulled out his lighter and placed the flame at the bottom of the hard item. He smiled and said, "This is rock cocaine, and it's worth about $300." We agreed that he would sell the rock cocaine and we would split the money $150 each. I had the money spent in my mind on new shoes and repair items for my car. The next day I could hardly wait to get home from work because money was waiting for me. I walked in the door with a smile on my face. The apartment appeared to be empty, but I could hear faint orgasmic sounds coming from the walk-in closet, as if someone was having sex.

I waited patiently, sitting on my daybed for three minutes until they finished. Calvin emerged from the closet first, walking past me, not saying a word as if I was invisible. He headed for the refrigerator to quench and replenish the draining of his mojo. He drank from his unmarked bottle of orange juice and walked back past me as if I were not in the room. I yelled his name out, scaring him into a defensive stance. I had forgotten for a second that he was half blind and could not make out faces or images. This small misfortune he suffered from would allow me to use it to my advantage in the future. I asked Calvin, "Where is the money?" He explained that he had given the crack to the women in the closet for sex. Soon after that day, he moved her in the apartment, grocery cart and all. She sat all day, waiting for him to come home after a day of criminal activities.

The Beginning and Ending of a Friendship

I knew our friendship would not last. Calvin was traveling down a different road than I. His drug use increased, and his antics were no longer funny, so I moved across town into my own apartment. I was still attending school, but at night, my job had changed. I was now working as a record clerk for a convalescent hospital. My days began at 4:00 a.m. I would walk to the lite rail station, ride the lite rail to watt and man love station, where I would catch the bus to watt and El Camino Ave, lastly catch the next bus to El Camino and Fair Oaks Boulevard one block from my job.

I worked until 3:00 p.m. After work, I walked uphill to the El Camino bus stop where I took the bus to Arden Mall, from Arden Mall to light rail station, from light rail station to downtown Sacramento to Sixty-Fifth Street, to Florin Mall, from the mall to college. Class ended at 9:45 p.m.. I would run to catch the last bus to Florin Mall, then to Twenty-Eighth and R light rail station, then the last rail home by midnight. Once at home, I pressed my clothes, slept for three hours, then began the next day. I did this routine for one year, with no transportation, little money, no phone, and no support system. I spent my weekends visiting my children when I was allowed or I spend my time aimlessly sitting in the mall, watching people live out their lives, wanting what they had: a family, a wife, and a career. While sitting idle in the mall, I noticed a young attractive woman staring at me. She approached, and I recognized her. She was Calvin's niece. She informed me that Calvin was recently released from prison and had nowhere to go. She said he was staying at her grandmother's house, but they were moving beyond the county borders of Calvin's parole limitations. I did not want Calvin to be homeless, so I invited him to live with me. I knew he had issues, but I wanted to help him. He no longer had the drug addict girlfriend but did have a new business he was trying to get off the ground. I always admired entrepreneurs. It did not matter who was at the hem.

During the New Year's Eve night out with Calvin, I met a young lady at the bar. I really didn't want to go to the club tonight. I just wanted to stay home by myself and enjoy the quiet atmosphere, but Calvin was persistent. He wanted me to hold a table while he scoured the nightclub. I sat at the table by myself, sipping on a Long Island iced tea, when I was approached by a tall beautiful woman and auntie. The tall pretty one was wearing a wedding ring. Throughout the night, she would remove the ring then put it back on. She must've done this for five times before finally sticking it in her pocket.

I didn't care. I thought she was attractive, but I wasn't interested. As fate would have it, within a month, I began dating her. She was tall and fair skinned and had a full set of lips. She had long red hair that hung past her shoulder. She seemed really graceful and had a very soft touch. The only thing I didn't agree with was the pancake makeup she wore covering the spots left by her freckles. Somehow she managed to keep a small waist. I didn't know where she put all the food she was eating. She said she loved the way I dressed and it turned her on when I wore a sports coat, dress slacks, and dress shoes. Although I was poor, my clothes were neatly pressed, and my shoes were shined to a high gloss. It took us several weeks before we had our first sexual encounter. I was partially involved in a sexual relationship with someone else. I wasn't particularly attracted to the person. She was just meeting my sexual needs for the moment. On one particular evening, we spent the day together just driving around in her new Ford Escort.

We pulled into my apartment complex around 10:00 p.m. We just sat in the car and talked much about anything. I reached over and placed my hand on her thigh. She looked over at me and said, "If you take your dick out, I'll suck it." Those words barely cleared her mouth before I was slapping her in the face with nine inches of pure python. She went down on me like a scuba diver searching for lost treasure. I could tell it wasn't her first time at the rodeo. She said, "Recline your seat back so I can get to it better." I reclined my seat back so fast I nearly broke the seat as it slammed against the bench seat in the back. She was relentless. Every time she got the chance, she would go down on me two or three times a day. I couldn't believe it. I was being treated like a king for the first time in my life, and if this was how kings lived, I wanted to be a king.

Although she loved performing oral sex on me and she was very attractive, I still didn't feel anything for her, maybe because it was too early in our relationship and the fact that I had been desensitized sexually while in Japan. In my mind, it was just another $15 on the table and fifteen minutes of sex. I no longer cared about sex or how it made me feel. It meant nothing to me. I just didn't want to be alone. Once again, I had a woman who was willing to give me money every time we finished having sex. I didn't know what was going through her head, so I quickly put an end to her trying to buy my love because I didn't want to be a kept man. I told her I didn't feel comfortable taking money from her, and if she did it again, we could no longer be in a relationship. I knew she didn't make much more money than I did, and she had two sons and couldn't afford to give extra money to me. I believed she felt threatened by my education because she often threw her paltry $9 an hour salary in my face. She also received child support from her ex-husband.

After three months of dating, we decided to move in together. I wasn't worried about how much money she made. I was only concerned with how much money I was going to make once I graduated from college. Although none of the members of her family had gone to college and she was a high school dropout as well as her husband, somehow they still obtained a middle-class status, owning two duplexes. Her oldest son dropped out of high school, but her youngest son would observe a different example. He watched meticulously as I sat and studied at night. I didn't mind him sitting so close because he was my video buddy and my informant. I hated video games but loved the information he provided me every time his mother picked him up from his father's house. He provided me with all the details from the time they entered the apartment until the time they arrived at the house. She burned the candle at both ends, often playing both ends against the middle. She was very confused. She loved our sex life but felt a compulsion to return to her husband. I didn't care. Either way, I told her she was free to go, but she couldn't have it both ways. She couldn't see him on the side while trying to maintain a relationship with me. Anytime I made her feel the hurt of losing me, she constantly reminded me she could live in her mother's duplex rent free whenever she wanted. Fortunately for me, she didn't know my little secret. I couldn't be hurt by someone I didn't love.

It seemed like something was missing in her life. She constantly tried to impress me, often telling me how well her family was doing and how much property they owned. After dating for three years, I learned to use selective hearing, only listening to the parts of her conversation that could benefit the both of us. The longer we lived together, the more comfortable she became with wearing sexy nightgowns. It seemed like every night she had on something new and inviting. She even tried to buy me a sexy pair of men's underwear with a banana hanging off the front. I told her, "You got me fucked up. Take this shit back to the store." She laughed and stuck it back in the bag. One thing I came to love about her was she loved performing oral sex on me, and I loved letting her do it. It was 1993, and after living with her for one year, I became accustomed to her way of thinking. As beautiful as she was, I just couldn't tell her that I loved her. In my mind, we never made love. We just fucked. In her mind, we were always making love.

I took her somewhere she had never been, somewhere sexually her character could not sustain her. She was constantly wet and couldn't keep her hands off me. She called me daily from her job. She told me she was thinking about me. She got so excited thinking about me she needed to change her panties. I felt I had to mess with her head as often as I could. She loved performing oral sex on me, and I loved teasing her and making her vagina buzz. By the time I got done teasing her, she could fill a small coffee cup with her secretions. I did not understand how her ex-husband could have gone off and got another woman pregnant while having a sexy, beautiful, sensual woman in his own bed. I didn't know what his problem was, but he was a fool to walk away from a woman who not only enjoyed performing oral sex on her man but was very good at it as well.

We were very compatible in bed. In the bedroom, she'd love to experiment, wearing crazy, sexy lingerie. Because she had a perfect body, I found having continuous sex two to three times a day, several times a day, seven days a week, was very easy and pleasurable. But there was one huge turn-off. She lied at the drop of a hat. I wanted to walk out of the relationship many times, but she always sucked me back in—I mean literally "sucked" me back in. She gave incredible oral sex, and it would have been hard for any man to walk away from that type of professional profaction. I know because it took me five years to leave. Every time I tried to leave, she'd pucker and lick her lips. I would cave in like an abandoned mine and walk back in the house.

We spent a lot of time with her mother and her mother's ancient friends, mostly performing small labor jobs they were too elderly to do. There were so many old people around I thought I was at a convalescent hospital. In 1994 we settled into a three-bedroom house, very clean with all new appliances. Her two sons and my daughter moved in with us. It was a very nice setup, but I knew in the bottom of my heart, it wouldn't last because my heart was not in it. The death of my first wife made it facile for me to walk away from any relationship because I still carried her in my heart. I had huge trust issues, and I came to understand every woman has suicidal tendencies, so I stayed on my toes and kept alert, not allowing any woman to get too close. As great as the oral sex was, it wasn't enough. I had already caught her in several lies, so I shut the door of the of fidelity bank of trust and fed her with a long-handled spoon. I only trusted her as far as I could spit. My security guard job wasn't the greatest in the world. I hated working the graveyard shift, but there was a bonus in for me. I got to stay home all morning and watched my favorite TV shows. Over the course of the next few months, I fell into a daily routine. I popped a bowl of popcorn, grabbed a can of iced tea, and plopped down to watch four episodes of *Andy Griffith.* Just around noontime, I was relaxing, stuffing my face with extra butter and overly salty popcorn. All of a sudden, I began experiencing difficulty in breathing. The glass of iced tea fell from my hand, my chest arched in the air, causing my bowl of popcorn to fall off my chest and onto the floor. As I began to gasp for air, suddenly Cindy came running through the room, wearing a white sheer white gown, flailing as though it was blowing in the wind. I reached out, trying to grab her, but the gown went through my fingers as she disappeared into the walk-in closet. I rolled over out of the bed and frantically crawled into the closet, searching for her while trying to catch my breath. This time I knew it was real. I wasn't mentally induced by drugs or depressed, but I still didn't know what her appearance meant. I thought of her all the time and wondered when would be the next time she would reveal herself to me. Her presence gave me new images of what life and death would be. Now I knew we didn't just lie still in the casket until Christ returned. I knew we were stuck here on earth until resurrection.

Although Cindy's presence was overwhelming, I had to focus on what was before me: my current relationship. I didn't put very much into our relationship. Therefore, I got out of it what I put into it: good sex and occasional trips to the gambling casinos. We traveled between Tahoe and Reno, gambling away our minimum-wage checks for a weekend of excitement. By the time we got back home, we both were dead tired and passed out on our bed at noon. I didn't mind being in the relationship. I could've stuck around for five more years. But the situation in our house was becoming very uncomfortable. I was beginning to catch her lying about the phone bill and why she would come home smelling like a pack of cigarettes. I played video games with her son, probing him for information. I discovered she was going over to her ex-husband's apartment, hanging out until his son got home from school. I knew she had been over to his apartment because he was a chronic chain-smoker. She didn't smoke, making it easy for me to detect when and how long she was over to this apartment and the activities that took place while she was there.

Her son was all too happy to divulge his mother's secret activities as long as I was his video game partner. Every day he came home with new information. The more information he gave me, the more I withdrew from her the best I could; but she made it very hard to turn down sex. She wouldn't even hesitate. She would just reach out and grab my package. Every chance she got, she went down on me, and I wasn't complaining. I knew I had to get a grip and get out of this relationship. My little head was happy, but my big head knew the relationship was going nowhere. She would've been perfect for me at a different time in my life, but right now I was trying to grow. I didn't have time for petty differences or time for a woman with a potential ex-husband.

I had already been through a trianglization of love, and I wasn't about to let history repeat itself. I began sitting on the couch, watching TV, rather than lying on the bed with her. We traveled in two different cars everywhere we went, and I couldn't bring myself to kiss her anymore. Something inside me just turned off. I stopped talking and spending quality time with her at the movies. I would just walk around the park by myself or with Michaela, killing time. Her husband was an ex-army soldier kicked out of the military for alcoholism after fourteen years of serving his country. He moved from Washington to Sacramento and began making demands that his wife return to him. I quickly informed him that if she wanted to leave, she could, but I wasn't going anywhere. She couldn't make up her mind. She ran back and forth to his house, each day coming home smelling like a pack of stealth cigarettes. I told her, "If you want him, you need to go to him. I'm not going to play this game."

I quietly stacked money away each payday, anticipating the worst. In between working and going to school, I searched for a new place to live. My daughter wanted to go to Florin High School, decreasing my choices of apartments to apply for. I tried my best to locate an apartment within that district. It was a total nightmare. There weren't any vacancies anywhere. I rode around for days, looking for a suitable apartment; and finally after a week of driving, I located the perfect location. Within a month, I packed up and moved out. She went back to her husband but not before telling me I ruined her for another man. I didn't know what she meant by that remark at the time. My first thought was I must've hurt her so bad. She didn't want another man or another man couldn't sexually satisfy her. But I soon figured it out.

After months of not seeing or hearing from her, she contacted me out of the blue and asked if she could come see me. She walked into my apartment, wearing thick red lipstick as if she were a prostitute, a long trench coat, and the same old-fashioned 1960s hairstyle she had become so accustomed to wearing. She tried to act as though she rekindled a new relationship with her husband, but I knew it was a farce. I knew she didn't drive all the way across town to provide me with that information. What I did know after five years of being in a relationship with her, was exactly how she wanted to be made love to. She walked in and sat on the couch. I didn't even break stride as I walked over to the couch, opened my bathrobe, and dangled my 9 inches in her face like a banana hanging from a tree. She took a deep breath and turned her head away from my member, then clutched it with one hand, and shook her head no. "No, I can't do this," she said. I didn't care. I stood there hanging it in her face. She began to get aroused, making moaning sounds as I ran my hand circularly, caressing her nipples. Her nipples began making indentations in her blouse. I knew at that moment she wouldn't last much longer before she would take me in her mouth. Within seconds, she grabbed my pulsating member and deep throated me until my knees buckled, sending me into an unforgiving orgasmic ejaculation. My ejaculation was a juggernaut it snapped her head back in a neck-breaking motion. I thought for sure she was dead as she fell to the floor, still clutching my erect member with secretions dripping from her mouth.

She was so overwhelmed she broke down crying at the idea of her unbridled lust for me and her unilateral decision to cheat on her husband, but she couldn't stop. She was in the midst of a concupiscent moment. She kept sucking away with more suctioning than a vacuum cleaner until her lips were like two pieces of baloney flapping in the wind. As good as she was sexually and after five years of being in this relationship, it wasn't enough. I still had no feelings for her. I was still suffering from the tragedy of my first marriage and the discontent and ignominy. My second wife made it extremely difficult for me to say I love you to anyone or sincerely hold or hug another woman.

I knew how to take women to different places sexually, but I had a tough time expressing any feelings beyond my queen-size bed. I didn't care if I was by myself or ever living with another woman again. I was only having sex to fill an empty void. I'd been hurt well beyond repair. My emotional intelligence for relationships and ability to understand and care about women and their feelings had all been destroyed. I looked at life through a tainted set of lenses far different than the average man. My lenses were tainted by death and despicable lies, as well as fake women with sinister plans. I was to trust no one, especially beautiful women. It was very difficult to find a woman that was beautiful and kind. It was an oxymoron, and I doubt I would ever meet such a person in my lifetime.

After we fornicated for about two hours, she left my apartment, crying her way down the steps out to her car. The crotch of her pants was soaking wet from the multiple orgasms. Her hair was slightly out of sorts, and her lips were wiped totally clean of her ruby-red lipstick left behind on the fly part of my favorite pair of white boxers.

Old Habits Die Hard

Calvin was a friend of mine. Although he had criminal, economic, and medical issues he had to overcome, he inadvertently made me laugh. His quirky personality kept me in stitches. It was good to have him around to help me fight depression during times when I overthrew my life, not believing I was where I should be financially. One of his main dysfunctions was he tried taking the predetermined path of least resistance to success in business and education. He often signed up for math classes that were well beyond his mathematical capability. I watched him throw a physics book across the room because he didn't have the foggiest idea how to solve the basic problem in physics. His main concern was walking around campus with physics and geometry books under his arm, believing it would elevate him to some level of intelligence. He wanted success but lacked the discipline or patience to see it through, trying desperately not to take the road less traveled.

Therefore, Calvin relied on what he knew, and the only things he'd ever been successful at had a criminal element attached to it. One day we went to a restaurant for a cup of coffee and talked about our living situation. After ordering my coffee, I went to the restroom. When I returned, Calvin had moved to another table and took the salt and pepper shakers with him. Calvin boasted and bragged about his little salt-and-pepper caper, patting himself on the back while settling down for the evening to a T-bone steak and vegetables smothering his plate, he also stole from the grocery store. Calvin hated the system more than any person I had ever met. He was once a memebr of the

Nation of islam. His ranting and raving got him beaten up and kicked out. He sat daily in his room plotting schemes, smiling from ear to ear as he reclined back on his futon bed in his 10x12 bedroom. Old Calvin was back in action. Only one month out of prison, he had signed most of the residents in the apartment complex up for filing bankruptcy, charging them $230 to complete and file a thirty-day stay, thereby allowing the occupants to stay in their apartment thirty days rent free until the case went to trial. Before the thirty days were up, he would have the occupant file bankruptcy, giving the occupant six months of free rent until the case went to trial. Calvin did not see or care about the future. He lived in the moment, and that was good enough for him.

During Calvin's time in the county jail, he met a female inmate through unconventional methods of communication: by removing the water from the toilet and talking throughout the line that connect the toilets between the man and women side of the jail. He romanced his new Jail girlfriend with toilet poetry and promises of a standard of living she could never have imagine. Calvin was released from jail and found sanction at my apartment, while his new girlfriend was sent to RCCC for a year sentence. Their six months of communicating back and forth through the toilet didn't go to waste. Calvin dropped the M word right through the toilet. She took a deep breath, inhaled the fumes of the toilet, and happily accepted. It was the first time I had ever heard anyone proposing to someone through a toilet, and more shockingly, the other person accepted the proposal. But none of that mattered because Calvin was excited about the possibility of getting married and starting a new life. He didn't stop to think about how well he'd known her and what she looked like. So far, he only heard her voice and never saw her face. She could look like Winnie the Pooh on crack, and he wouldn't even know it until his wedding day. I was excited for him. For some strange reason, I liked Calvin. He had two animals fighting inside of him. Calvin fed the mean animal, leaving the nice animal dormant in the corner, starving for attention. I could see the good in him even though he couldn't see it in himself. And I hope his new bride would see the good in him as well.

I had never seen Calvin so excited about anything. He stayed up all night, pacing the floor, smoking cigarettes, while hastily making plans for his jailbird wife. He sat on his futon, laughing to himself, imagining a night of passion he longed for during his stay in jail. He fantasized about renting a limo and booking a room on the top floor of the Hyatt Regency with champagne flowing from his glass. Calvin was a dreamer. With $630 a month to support himself, he knew that he would have to supplement that income to support himself and his new wife.

Calvin changed his tactics and approaches with new options for paying his rent. He said he would like to pay next month's rent so he could save money to rent a limo and a room at the Hyatt Regency Hotel. I was so happy for him. I could not afford a wedding gift, so I agreed to let him pay the next month. Saturday mornings, Calvin often stood outside in the rain, waiting for rides to go see his girlfriend at RCCC. Most of the time, the ride did not show. After five or six times of not making it to the jail because of no transportation, Calvin turned to me once again, asking me to perform an unpaid favor that would extend into something more down the road. Calvin didn't have money; therefore, he devised a plan to pay me with stolen designer glasses. Every trip I made to the jail, Calvin would steal a pair of glasses and present them to me before we departed for the jail. I gladly accepted his offer, and off we went to the optometrist. He didn't hesitate letting his hands get light. Within five minutes, he returned to the car with two pairs of designer frames. I was pleased, and we headed off to the RCCC jail where his love was waiting. I sat patiently in the car, nibbling on snacks, while Calvin visited his girlfriend. After an hour and a half waiting on the fog-covered parking lot, Calvin emerged, smiling once again from his ear. She must've told him everything he wanted to hear because he was so excited he couldn't wait till the next weekend.

The next time we went to the jail, Calvin had other plans. He wanted me to meet one of the female inmates. I didn't care whether I met her or not. It was better than sitting in the car. During the jail visits, I would sit outside, patiently waiting an hour or more in the car.

Calvin always returned to the car with a big smile on his face. Before returning to the car, Calvin stopped and placed more than $200 on his girlfriend's books. I was upset by this breaking news because he put off paying his rent and he paid me with stolen items rather than in cash. I kept quiet. As I observed his cash transactions over the next two months, he tried to distract me by setting me up with one of the women inmates.

During his next visit, I went inside to meet this mystery woman. The entire facility was watching. Everyone was laughing, even the guards I could see the women inmates jumping up, trying to peek over the eight-foot-high wall that separated the view of the visiting room from the prison yard. The room began to fill as the inmates entered. My date entered the room, and life stopped. She was very slim and tall with a big notch on the right side of her head. Her hair looked as if it had never been groomed. To put it simply, she looked like the bride of Frankenstein. *Oh my god*, I thought. I wanted to break and run, but I remained claim. I knew this would pass, and once I got Calvin outside, I would put my foot in his ass. We stayed for the entire visit, and I honestly felt bad for the young lady. I had been the butt of joke. The strange thing was I wasn't hurt in any way, but the young lady was hurt.

On the way back to the car, Calvin laughed so hard he shed tears then had the nerve to ask if I would go back the next weekend for another visit. I knew there would never be a relationship between that woman and me; therefore, I agreed to visit her again. To the surprise of her fellow inmates, I returned to see her, and she was no longer the butt of joke but my friend. I forgot myself for a minute. There I was once again, playing captain save a hoe. I just couldn't let her go through her own struggle. Instead, I wanted to be her knight in shining armor. So I sat at the metal table. She grasped both my hands and presented me with a scarf she knitted herself. She took the time to wrap the scarf around my neck while gazing deeply into my eyes. Grasping the scarf at both ends, she tried to pull me closer for a kiss; but I reluctantly turned my head, allowing her lips to land on my cheek.

—

I didn't want to embarrass her in front of her girlfriends, but she looked like she had been ridden hard and put away soaking wet. The huge knot protruding from her forehead made me nauseous, but I couldn't leave until visiting had ended. The room was logged down, and there was still twenty minutes left for visitation. She worked hard at trying to get me to place money on her books. She continued to rub my hands, stroking my eagle. She's so much as guaranteed me sex once she got released. Finally, the visit was over; and I hastily made my way to the parking lot, crouching down out of view, trying to catch my breath. I could hear the laughter coming from behind the prison wall. As I stood up and walked to the car, I waved at all the women behind the wall, indicating that it was a perfect visit. I lost contact with her because Calvin's girlfriend was being released within two weeks, and I had no reason to return to the correctional facility.

The next month of February had arrived, and Calvin's rent was due. Once again, he refused to pay me anything, not even half of his rent, saying he had other things to spend his money on like the two new pairs of shoes sitting in boxes on the kitchen counter and the new Kangol hat and trench coat he bragged about costing a couple hundred dollars. He stood there fatuous, counting his money, smiling from ear to ear, throwing his limited success in my face. With more than $1,400 in his hand, he headed back to the streets to collect more money from his misguided and naive clientele.

I was disappointed in him. I thought we were friends, but he had just pushed the envelope and our friendship to the limit. I changed the lock on the door. Then I moved all his belongings out onto the parking lot. Unfortunately, clouds began to form overhead. The weather had changed at a moment's notice. Rain fell from the sky in golf-ball-size drops, saturating all his belongings including his couch, his box of cannabis, and his two new pairs of Stacy Adams. Calvin returned just one hour after his departure. He was enraged to find all his life possessions stacked outside in the rain. It wasn't my intention to ruin his ill-gotten gains, only to train him to think of others before he thinks about himself and to pay his debts.

He screamed, raved, ranted, and made idle threats, yelling at the locked door, kicking the wall, and cursing with broken English or black English vernacular, a language commonly known on the streets as talking shit. Twenty minutes into his yelling and screaming, there was a knock at the door. The knock sounded different than before. It didn't sound like Calvin knocking but the knock of someone having a pity party and a tantrum. The knock was more forceful and with authority. It was the police. They yelled, "Open the door, or I will have to kick it in." They forced me to open the door and gave me the option of letting Calvin move back in the apartment because it was the law. I was at a loss, but one thing was for sure: I wasn't going to allow Calvin back into my house.

He ranted and raved much about nothing. He couldn't contain his prejudice towards the police and began cursing at the police officers, calling them racist white cops. I'm still back quietly leaning against the balcony watching him dig his own grave. His past history and ideals began to come unleash, costing him his freedom. He was handcuffed and placed on the couch. Crying like a baby, he continued to curse at the police while at the same time sealing his own fate. One of the officers looked through Calvin's belongings and found a shoe box full of marijuana, at least one ounce of premium home-grown bud. Calvin admitted that the box of marijuana belonged to him. I looked at him with astonishment. He knew he was still on parole, *why would you say that?* I thought, it was as if he wanted to go back to jail. I began to feel sorry for Calvin. Although he didn't act like it sometimes, he was my friend, and I didn't want to see him go back to jail. I spoke to one of the officers in private and asked him to let Calvin go as long as he didn't return to the apartment.

They explained to Calvin he could go about his way as long as they did not receive any more calls involving him and the apartment complex. Calvin spent the rest of the night pacing back and forth on the catwalk, smoking dope and cursing my name. The next morning Calvin began dragging his couch and clothes down the street to the house of one of his clients, where he would spend the next three nights waiting for his girlfriend to be released from RCCC. Calvin unilaterally did as he promised. He rented a limo and reserved a hotel room at the Hyatt as he had planned several months ago.

Calvin was excited and overly anxious. He couldn't wait to get repaid sexually for the money he placed on her books. Calvin was very proud of himself, arriving at the correctional facility in a long black stretch limousine shined to perfection. He stepped from the limo dressed in his haute couture outfit with flowers in hand, believing she would be enchanted by his panache because he seemed so dashing and romantic. She would automatically embrace him with open arms; instead, she looked in his direction, pretending that she never even met him, then walked the other way.

Calvin yelled to get her attention, then ran over to her, grabbed her by the shoulders, and began escorting her to the limo. She refused to go with him, claiming she was a lesbian and that she was just using him to place money on her books. Calvin's eyes began bugging out of his head. The news was not euphonious to his ear. It was too much for Calvin to handle. He burst into a violent rage, grabbing her by her hair and slinging her to the ground, hitting her in the face repeatedly. Correctional officers ran from the building as though they were storming the beaches of Normandy. They grabbed Calvin and slammed him to the ground, penning him down with their boot on his head, placing him in handcuffs, then placing him in a holding cell for transportation back to the county jail. Calvin's life was in a downward spiral. Everything he worked the last six months for went right out the window. Soon after the accident, Calvin lost himself once again in the crack epidemic, sending him back to prison where he would have some type of structure.

I went on with my life, placing one foot in front of the other, working two minimum jobs, making $4.25 an hour, barely able to pay the rent. Both of my cars were broken down, with no extra money to fix them. I found myself walking to the light rail station and bus stop at four every morning to start my day. It had been eighteen months since my daughters had lived with me, so I moved them back home with no plan of how I was going to support them on minimum wage or how I was going to take them to and from school. Therefore, I had to train them to be independent and self-reliant.

Once I got home from work and school, I pressed their clothes and placed them on the couch. Next I prepared their breakfast, lunch, and dinner and placed them in the refrigerator. I told them not to answer the door and to only answer the phone after they heard my voice on the answering machine. We spent our weekends preparing for the next week. I attempted several times to perm their hair or straighten it with a straightening comb. I was scared out of my mind. I didn't know whether I was going to fail or succeed. My major problem was I was one paycheck from the welfare line or the homeless shelter. I wasn't fortunate like my friends to have jobs with the city, the state, or assembly line at an auto plant, making $15 an hour. I was stuck in a minimum-wage job and couldn't see the light at the end of the tunnel. My children were my responsibility, not the government's. I had to find a way to get through college at an accelerated pace, but my grade school and high school education was so poor I struggled just to get through the basic classes that the average student passed without a hitch.

My daughters meant the world to me. It was hard for me to look at them and not be able to provide basic necessities. Within a year, Miya wanted to move back to Indianapolis. I thought it made sense because all her relatives were living there. I thought it would be a good idea for her to spend time with my family, because being a military brat, she was never in one place long enough to make friends. I felt she would get to know all her cousins who would create a better support network for her than I could create by myself. Michaela stayed with me because she was a daddy's girl from the day she was born.

My daughter and I settled into a two-bedroom apartment on the south side of Sacramento. She was busy attending Florin High School, and I was busy working and going to the local junior college. Michaela was growing fast, and every time I looked up, she had a new list of items she wanted to buy, so I sat her down and gave her some tips on job interviewing. And within two hours, she had her first job interview at Taco Bell. We walked over to the restaurant. I let her go in first. I came in several minutes later and ordered a soda and sat in the corner, pretending as though we're not together. I listened as she answered all the interview questions with intelligence and poise. She was hired on the spot and was asked to begin work within two hours.

I was very pleased because the job was less than a block from the house, which made it easy for me to walk her home from work at night. She worked late into the evening, often not getting off work until eleven at night, so I walked downstairs by the gate and waited to see her turn a corner and get within my view. She was a very hard worker, and within a month's time, she was able to buy everything on her list. We weren't doing too bad. I had two jobs and steady work hours. She worked every day after school. It was too good to be true, and I knew sooner or later, there would be a glitch in our lifestyle. She began to date a thug from the Oak Park Bloods. He was a would-be drug dealer, providing my daughter with marijuana for birthday gifts and leading her down the path of least resistance. Suddenly, she stopped going to school. Since she already missed so many days, they transferred her to an adult education school.

I was hoping she could be more mature and manage herself a little better as I did in school, but she needed more attention and understanding than I was able to give her. The minuscule presence of her mother made it increasingly hard for her to focus in school or at work. I had no choice but to work two jobs. The child support system was unforgiving, they would put you in jail for six at a time if you fell behind on payments. Within six months of being locked up, I could lose everything including my daughter. She would have been placed in foster care, and my apartment would've been rented out to another person.

I had no choice but to stay on top of my child support payments even if that meant not spending much time with my daughter. Occasionally, I tried to take her to a movie, but she would just sit at the far end of the aisles. She was constantly angry with me because

I hated her boyfriend, and I wouldn't allow him to hang around my house. January came around, and she was two months from turning eighteen years old. She got another job at Del Taco and felt as though she was in control and could live on her own. I thought about it for a second, but then I realized she needed to know the true meaning of friends and who in this world she could depend on.

I said okay because I wanted her to know none of her friends would love her unconditionally like her parents. I knew where she wanted to move. I drove by the apartment several times, checking out the living condition of the apartment and the location. I knew I could always pull her back if she got in trouble. I let her go because she had to learn about people and that it was important to have your own place and not living in someone else's. She needed to learn these life lessons before she got too old to correct the mistakes.

She left home, and I didn't see her for two weeks. I drove past the apartment, seeing if I could get sight of her, but she was nowhere to be found. So I drove by her job, and there she was, working at the drive-through window. I sat on the parking lot of the record store next door and watched while she worked the entire shift. I was proud of her and worried about her at the same time that she could be biting off more than she could chew or growing into the responsible young adult I knew she would become.

I kept my eye on her from a distance. I wanted to give her room to grow, but I didn't want her to fall too far, so I did what any father would do. I watched from a distance. Every day after work, I took the scenic route home, driving past her apartment then her job. She seemed to be doing okay, I thought, until one day I drove up to my apartment and there she was, sitting on the steps. "I just came by to say hi," she said. I was holding it in, but I was really glad to see her. She was my firstborn and the only one of my children that I really bonded with from birth. "Can I come in?" she asked, seemingly humbled by her new experience. "Sure," I said, smiling to myself. "Dad, do you mind if I get something to eat?" "No, I don't mind," I said, sitting on the couch, thumbing through my mail.

She began talking frantically about how she was sleeping on the floor in a puddle of water. Her friend's children keep going in her closet, taking her belongings out, and she was forced to babysit six kids after school and couldn't go to work. I said, "You're more than welcome to come back home." "Can my boyfriend come with me?" she said. "No, he can't." "Well then, I'm not coming back home." "The choice is up to you." Two weeks went by, and before I knew it, she was back home, only this time she slept on the daybed and I took the bedroom just for a short period of time to let her know what privilege looked like. I thought one of her problems was she didn't have any family here with her, so I sent for her cousin to come stay with us. They got along great. Her cousin was impressed that she had her own bedroom and thought Michaela was very spoiled.

I was glad Michaela had real family to hang around with. It made me feel a little more at ease, knowing who she was spending her quality time with; but there was one small problem: her cousin smoked crack. She wasn't in the city more than three hours before finding a party in the apartment complex. The twelve months that I had lived there, I never knew anyone selling drugs in the complex. For some reason, my niece was able to find it within minutes of arriving. I tried to direct her toward other activities such as enrolling in artist school, but things would fall apart before she would get a chance to change her life. Eventually, Michaela return to Indianapolis several months later and completed junior college as a respiratory therapist. Miya went to Brown Mackie College and finished with a bachelor's degree in legal studies. I thought about my children a lot—what they would become once they reached adulthood, how would they choose their mate, and whether I was a good example for them.

I knew I couldn't continue on this path of never trusting another woman, but I wasn't ready. My heart was still under lock and key protected by a couple of subliminal pitbulls. Getting laid was no longer the first thing on my agenda; getting through college was. I walked through college in a total daze, hardly noticing all the single women cruising around the campus. I couldn't help but to notice one teacher's particular interest at me. She asked if anyone needed help. Everyone seemed to raise their hand except me, but she found her way over to my desk and took my keyboard from me while I was still typing. She placed her hand on my thigh and demonstrated her typing ability with one hand.

She sat there with her thin athletic frame wearing a tight yellow sweater displaying her huge 38DD breasts. I didn't know what she expected. She had her breasts right in my face. My eyes went cross as I began growing a monstrous erection that went right under her hand lying on my thigh. She paused from typing for a split second and looked me in the eye. "Oh my, well," she said. Her erect nipples protruded through her shirt about a half inch at this time. I licked my lips simultaneously, directing her hand up and down my thigh, rubbing along the nine-inch crescent of my penis. I gave her a half smile and said, "That's what's up." I stood up to pack my backpack, purposely brushing my arm against her erect nipples.

I had become kind of an expert on knowing what the DD cup size was on speculation. I wasn't shaken by what she was doing, but I did understand what she wanted: she was game. But I wasn't going to play even though she gave me all the answers to the test. She wasn't very attractive. She was kind of homely, but if I woke up one night and found her in my bed, I wouldn't push her out. I wanted badly to ride her into the next morning, but I didn't give in to her sexual innuendos, and it cost me two-letter grades. I was tired of women thinking that they could pay me for sex, be it money or a letter grade. I wasn't going to play anymore.

Women were coming at me from all directions; for some reason, they found it appealing that I was raising my daughter. Everywhere I went, I was being propositioned. I couldn't believe how women were acting. They didn't pull any punches. They were sexually harassing me, but I didn't have the heart to rat them out and I wanted to leave the opportunity open for possible emergency sex. I was summoned into a supply room to get a bottle of water for the fountain. Once I got in the room, the woman backed into a corner, positioning herself out of view of the door. She pulled her skirt up, displaying her unshaved vagina.

This type of behavior went on for the entire year I worked at the medical clinic. Another woman walked up to me while I was sitting in my car. She whispered in my ear, "I had a dream I was sucking your dick in the shower." I almost fell for it. I also made her an offer to make her dreams come true, but I let this one pass me by, not indulging her sick little fantasy. I mostly stayed to myself, but the woman knew I was single and up for grabs. I worked for a local clinic in midtown Sacramento. The office was patriarchy. There were only two men in the entire office; one was medical assistant, and I was a medical records clerk. I spent my mornings cruising the hallways, picking up charts and returning the charts to the medical records room for sorting and filing. During my usual routine, I noticed a young slim Caucasian female with beautiful black hair stretching down her back. I asked my friend, "Who's that?" He said, "That's Dr. Pam." I said, "A doctor? She looks like a little kid." She was so young and beautiful, and everyone just loved her. Little did I know she felt the same way about me.

Within the year's time, we locked horns and began dating. It was a whirlwind relationship. Out of the millions of people there were in the universe, we found each other. It was serendipitous that I would find someone like myself in the midst of a chaotic world. I took the relationship slow and let time guide me as it always did; but this time, I led with my heart, not with my throbbing manhood. She was different than any other woman I had been with. She could support herself and wasn't overly emotionally needy. She seemed to have known who she was and what her purpose was in life. Most importantly, she was a vegetarian. she didn't believe in killing and eating the animals. I felt that to be a very kind, unselfish gesture. She didn't smoke or drink, and she was very athletic. We were in a relationship two years before I began to hear the same old voice probing my murky subconscious, *Don't trust her. Don't trust anybody.*

The Test

The years passed quickly, and by this time, I'd been attending the same junior college for four and a half years. I just couldn't go another semester. I was doing all the work, passing all my courses, but I wasn't making much progress in the way of transferring to a state university. I couldn't take it anymore, so I waltzed over to the state university to see a drop-in counselor. To my surprise, I had completed enough units to attend a four-year university. Finally, I thought, I was over the hump and going to a real college. I was excited at the possibility of working closer toward earning my bachelor's degree. My first semester on the campus was pure academic. I had yet to begin my core classes. My second semester I was required to take the writing proficiency exam. I failed the first exam; therefore, I was scheduled to take the writing proficiency class. I was seriously focused on this class, but as always, my focus would get sidetracked by the female accelerant that sat to my right. A tall slender white girl whom could have double for Aaron on the TV series *The Waltons*. She came right up to me and scooted her chair so close to me we were touching.

I thought it odd that someone so young and so beautiful could have interest in a thirty-six-year-old man. She was all over me, grabbing my arms and walking down the middle of the campus as though we're a couple. I pushed her off my arm, giving her a distasteful look. Although she was attractive, I knew she was up to something, so I did the best I could to keep my distance. Everywhere I went, she would pop up. I couldn't even get a sandwich from the cafeteria. She seemed very intelligent, but I had to remember she was in the same class as I for failing her first writing proficiency exam. She had beautiful handwriting and seemed to structure her papers very well. Then the big day came: our second writing proficiency exam. I blasted through the exam in about fifteen minutes. An hour later, I peeked through the door; and there she sat, still struggling with her exam. Her paper was flawless, neat, and well constructed. I must admit I was a little intimidated by her organization skills. The next day, scores were posted outside the classroom door in letters: *F* for *fail* and *P* for *pass*. I reluctantly made my way up to the list. Scrolling down with my finger, I stopped right next to the last for my Social Security number. I couldn't believe my eyes. I passed the exam.

I checked it again to ensure that I wasn't reading it wrong. It was true. I actually passed. I hurried down the hallway, smiling from the ear to ear. As I turned the corner, there she was, popping out of nowhere. "The test scores on the wall!" I yelled with excitement. "Where? Show me," she said. "Find my score for me. I don't want to look at it," she said. I scanned the last four of her Social Security. The *F* next to her last four seemed six inches large. I looked at her with in a nondescript expression and said, "You've failed." She couldn't believe it. "Look again," she said embarrassingly. I put my finger on the *F* then pulled her in closely so that she could see for herself. We returned to our class that afternoon, and I was told by my teacher I no longer had to attend the class, but I could stay in the class if I wanted the letter grade. I agreed to stay in the class and help other students with their writing proficiency. She embarrassingly sat next to me, not saying a word, trying only to focus on what the teacher was saying. After class, I thought she would go about her way, but she followed me to my car and climbed in on the passenger side. *Oh no*, I said to myself, *not another Luz*. To my surprise, she talked about her boyfriend and their recent breakup. He was a student at the campus, and she wanted to make him jealous. That's why she followed me around. I rose every morning and continued to progress toward earning my degree. One Monday morning, I stepped out onto the front porch. The atmosphere seemed very strange and unusual.

I stepped out on my lawn and noticed the roof of my house was covered with more than fifty doves. I found it odd, but nevertheless, I had a strange feeling that something was wrong. I recalled years ago during my childhood, my grandmother once told me that when doves land on your roof, that means someone died in your family. I didn't believe such nonsense. I thought it was just an old wives' tales. I arrived back home around one thirty that afternoon, and before I could pull all the way into the driveway of my house, my wife stepped out on the porch. "I have some bad news," she said with tearful eyes. Before she could speak another word, I said, "My grandmother died." "How did you know that?" she said. "I just know." I went in the house and called my mother, asking about the funeral arrangements. She said my grandmother had died a week ago and she was just buried that morning.

I became so infuriated. I couldn't believe they were so insensitive they didn't even let me know my grandmother passed. No one stopped to think that I wanted to attend the funeral. I loved my grandmother and wanted to pay my respects, but once again, I felt robbed a part of my heritage. I thought about my grandmother every night and how she lay in the cemetery without as much as a marker. So I called the cemetery the next morning and paid for her grave marker over the phone. I didn't even bother to ask my family for assistance because I knew it would be just one big hang-up, and this was my way of laying my grandmother to rest. I purchased a tombstone for my grandmother, and with a little bit of research at the veterans' center, my older brother Rayford and I purchased a tombstone for my grandfather.

I went on to graduate twelve months later with a bachelor's degree in social work. With all the pressures of school and missing my grandmother's funeral, I decided after eight years of being away from Indianapolis it was time for me to go visit my mother. By this time, Pam and I had been together for four years. The news was her father was finally coming to meet me. I drove up to the house in my 1982 Corvette, and there he was, standing on the porch, six feet tall with a head full of gray hair. He made his way out to the car first, looked it over, then introduced himself. I tried to be polite and make him as comfortable as I could. Besides, it only took him for years to meet me. I had yet to have spoken to or met her brother or mother who were definitely opposed to our relationship. Her mother hated my black guts. With even the mention of my name, she would hang up the phone and didn't speak to my wife for a week. She made a black voodoo doll in the image of myself. She spent her leisure time jabbing it with needles then placing it on the mantel to admire her work. Every week she was shifting the needles around the doll in different locations, mostly focusing around my groin area. Her brother is a Hasidic Jew, by choice of religion, but I thought of him as a megalomaniac. He went to the synagogue every week, praying on his knees to a God he had no intention of following. He refused to obey God's command: "Love thy neighbor."

I have a saying: some people go to church,
and church go through some people.

He was one of the people that the gospel passed right through. He wore hate on his sleeve like a badge of honor. It made him feel good, but it was masturbation. It made him feel good, but it produced nothing. I knew he wasn't a typical Jewish person. I lived around Jewish people most my life and always had a welcome and pleasurable experience; but he was mean, selfish, arrogant, and evil. He loathed black people and hated everything that wasn't like himself. He was arrogant and self-centered and didn't know when to shut his mouth. As bumptious as he was, he brow-beat my wife and his wife into getting his way every time. He argued for a living as a prosecuting attorney. I could only feel sorry for any black man that came in front of him for prosecution. He never did any research or try to understand why he's able to live the comfortable life he's living. It's amazing how he forgot that he's a first-generation American in his family, and my family had been here since the 1600s. He forgot Jews are minorities as well, and they're not welcome in neighborhoods just like blacks. But the differences is he could change his name, thereby increasing his opportunities. I didn't understand or care to understand his hatred. He had to be a real sociopath to believe he's better than someone just because of his skin color or social status. I refused to be around someone of such low character and was glad he lived five hundred miles away from him, so I wouldn't have to stare into his twisted face of hate.

—

My daughter Miya was graduating from high school. She was so proud of herself because he was chosen to deliver the closing speech at her graduation. I took out my favorite blue Hugo Boss suit and steamed it perfectly clean. Then I highly buffed my favor pair of black shoes and steam pressed my white dress shirt to a crisp. I sat on the plane thinking about all the years that passed, all the pain and tears that erupted throughout the years, slowing down and even displacing my progress. I thought about the painful memories of my first marriage and the pain my children would experience in their lives. I was so occupied thinking about the last fifteen years of my life before I knew it I was touching down in Indianapolis. I was now making good money, and I could afford the rental car rather than using public transportation to and from the airport.

On the day of graduation, I decided to ride as a passenger in my mother's car so I could enjoy the scenic view of the city. So I climbed into the backseat where there was plenty of room for two more people. At a moment's notice, my ex-wife May climbed into the backseat, practically sitting on my lap. "There is room in the other cars," I said. "That's okay. I will ride with you and your mother." Before anyone could get in the car, May turned to me and whispered in my ear, "Do you want to get back together?" I looked at her with a flabbergasted and confused look on my face. Suddenly, visions of her vilifying me came home like truth. I exploded like a firecracker. It all just came out without any filters. "You must have slipped and bumped your damn head. Hell no, I don't want to get back with you!" I said while climbing out of the car and moving to another vehicle.

I was sorry that her feelings were hurt, but even more importantly, it was something I had to get off my chest that I didn't even know I had tucked away in my murky subconscious. It came out of me, and I had no way of stopping it. As a matter of fact, I didn't even know it was there until she asked the perfect question, pushing the wrong button in me. She sat at the graduation two steps below me, occasionally looking over her shoulder at me with tears in her eyes. I couldn't care less. I was fooled by her crocodile tears twice, and I wasn't going to be a third time. She made a life of lying about me to my daughters. For no reason, she was trying to turn my flesh and blood against me. I did not understand her then, and I wasn't going to try to understand her now. She didn't want me. She wanted something she was too lazy to obtain herself. She wanted my success and what she thought it would do for her financially. Her 36DDs no longer had the power over me they once had. I was growing a distaste in my mouth for her. Every time I saw her, it was like eating black licorice for the first time. It looked inviting, but once you tried it, it left a horrible aftertaste in your mouth.

Anything I ever found attractive in her was now stained with the ugly truth of deception. I realized at that moment I was truly blessed by God. He placed my enemy at my feet and allowed her to see me stand as an upright man, successful and self-made. I had successfully defeated everything she thought about me. While she was practicing hate, I was focused on school and setting an example for my children. I never spoke a negative word about her to my children. I didn't think it was necessary. I knew in time she would unknowingly reveal her true despicable self to them, and that would be her undoing. The best part of all, I no longer felt indebted to her for a debt I didn't owe. I no longer felt the guilt of not being able to be more of a father to our daughter. I no longer saw her as my ex-wife or sexual partner. I learned to see her as another ship passing in the night that I should have never boarded.

I made my way back to Sacramento a week later and secured my first job as a case manager specialist with the Department of Corrections. I stepped onto the prison yard. I was overwhelmed by the sea of black faces smothering the yard. Young men from the age of eighteen all the way to sixty years old, serving life sentences behind a tall gray dim walls. One story more horrible than the other as I sat and listened to their crimes unfolding in front of me. One inmate said he and his friends were shooting a gun from a car window while driving down the highway. It was his turn to suit the gun next. He leaned out of the car window; and before he could aim the gun in the air, the gun went off, striking and killing the man in the car next to him. He received a sentence of life in prison without the possibility of parole.

He has been down sixteen years at this time in his life and is willing to tell the story to anyone that will listen.

There were thousands of stories like this all over the yard—young boys making bad decisions, costing them their freedom forever. Homosexuality ran rampant as if it was the way to be. Young men sat together in the dayroom wrapped in each other's arms, watching TV. It was more than I could stomach, and after a year, I left the Department of Corrections for a job with Sacramento County. The work was easy but boring. I was limited to the type of services I could provide my clients. I wanted to do a lot more in the way of helping my clients than the county would allow. It was a secure job with good pay, but I felt stuck with my hands tied behind my back. I couldn't believe this was what God called me to do. I wanted to help the poor get off welfare and stand on their own two feet, but the county put the kibosh on any extra services I tried to provide, and after five years of working in a cubicle, I decided to return to the prison system. I earned a second bachelor's degree in education and a master's degree in educational leadership, along with a teaching credential and an administrative credential. I returned to the prison this time as a teacher. I was proud of being a teacher and thought I did my job better than most, and so did the European inmates in the prison system. The Department of Corrections where I worked was segregated. Whites only hanged with White's, blacks only hanged with blacks, I Mexicans only Hanged around Mexicans. The whites and Mexicans didn't speak to me on the yard or outside the classroom in fear of breaking the prison racial code. The whites on the prison yard did something that was unheard of: they presented me with a prison achievement award in honor of my excellent service and outstanding track record and diligence in my work. I felt honored to be the only one to be given an award by an opposing hate group. Every inmate in the prison signed an additional piece of paper, indicating they were in agreement with the whites. I felt totally honored as I choked out a few words, thanking them for this award. All two hundred inmates stood up on the yard and applauded in agreement. They didn't notice the time that they had just validated me and what my life struggles had been about. At that moment, I came to realize my life struggles weren't just about myself. They were meant to help other people understand how to survive life challenges and now to get up once they had fallen.

Eleven years have passed, and I still haven't met the other two members of Pam's family. They refused to acknowledge my presence. I was growing ever so tired of their imbecility and their pathological behavior, so I decided to ask her to marry me. After eleven years of being together, it was time to take a dump or get off the pot. My life is turning in another direction. I was entering seminary school.

For the first time in my life, things are looking up. My mistrust of marriage hinged on misogamy; but after eleven years of dating, Pam and I decided to get married and settle into a nice, uneventful marriage—or so we thought. We adjusted quickly without provocation and began making adjustments to our work schedules so that we could spend more quality time together. Not more than a month into our marriage, Pam began complaining of pain in her lower right quadrant. From the way she positioned her hand, I knew it was her appendix. I wasted no time getting her into the hospital. Within a matter of two weeks, she was in the operating room, having surgery.

I waited patiently in the cafeteria, enjoying their eggs, gravy, and biscuit combo. I was so nervous I challenged the cashier, believing she overcharged me for the eggs and gravy. After I stuffed my face and filled my belly, I returned to the cash register and apologized to her for my rude behavior. I knew the surgery was routine; therefore, I had no real concerns, but I had heard of people dying on the operating table for minor surgery. After breakfast, I made my way back upstairs to the waiting room. Just as my foot touched the carpet, the doctor came out with his hand stuck deep in both of his pockets. Callous, he said, "We had to take her back into surgery and put her under anesthesia again because of a blood clot." Then he walked back through the surgery doors, going on about his business. I stood anxiously. I was quite nervous and waited an hour before I went to her room. I sat and held her hand while she slowly came out of her confused state. I began to make myself comfortable, placing a blanket over the chair, moving a table within reach of my feet. I wanted to spend the night in the hospital, but she argumentatively forced to go home and spend time with the cats. I returned early the next morning. I fed her breakfast and read a book while she listened to the beeps of the TPN machine slowly dripping, morphing, into her arm.

Within a month, she was back to her old self, jogging around the park and going on bike rides around Folsom Lake. Three months down the road, our life would take another turn. Pam slowly began to develop a cough followed by complaints of a sore throat and difficulty in swallowing. I tried to convince her to go get checked out, but she refused. The months went on as well as the throat pain. She tried self-medicating with a regimen of sucking on throat lozenges every day and gargling with saltwater. Those methods were short-lived. I finally convinced her to get an X-ray of her throat. To my surprise, the X-ray came back clear, but her throat got worse and worse. Within the next six months, she couldn't even swallow her own spit. I noticed the tone of her skin changed to a yellowish tone, showing that she had signs of jaundice. Then I knew it was time for her to seek more invasive procedures, so we made an appointment at the hospital to have her scoped. We got up at around 6:00 a.m. It normally took me less than five minutes to get out the door, but for some reason, it seemed like time was moving very slow, as if I was moving in slow motion. We arrived at the hospital at nine in the morning. Her employee status helped her get quickly checked in and placed in the presurgery waiting room. The doctor came in and explained the onerous procedure while she anxiously squeezed my hand, preparing for the operation. There was nothing I could do to assuage the thought of the painful operation she was about to experience. I walked with her as they pushed the bed quickly toward the operating room and through the doors. I stood tearfully at the door as they pushed her down the hallway, turning left into the operating room.

I set my watch, marking my time for two hours. I wore out a good pair of shoes as I marched back and forth and up and down the hallways for two hours. A flash of my days in Beirut came back as a familiar pain in my knee developed. An hour and a half later, she was out of surgery and in the recovery room. I waited about forty-five minutes for the anesthesia to wear off. I was not allowed to go into the recovery room. Instead, I was sent downstairs to bring the car around to the front door.

Just as I pulled up, they were pushing her to the curbside in a wheelchair. She tried to smile, but her smell was broken with tears forming in the corner of her eyes. I dared to ask the question. The car ride home was quiet until I took an internal deep breath and said, "What's the diagnosis?' She turned to me with her beautiful, sad, teary green yes and said, "I have stage four squamous cell carcinoma." I didn't know what else to say. I was speechless. They said she had about six months left to live. At that moment, another part of me shut off. I knew the journey she was about to face if she was to defeat this disease, and I knew the journey I had already faced, and the new journey would be twice as painful. I prayed for her day in and day out, repenting of all my sins, considering getting baptized for the second time to ensure my prayers were answered. I prayed for God's mercy, his deliverance of Pam from this deadly cancerous disease. I couldn't imagine what she was immensely going through. She lay in the bed and cried herself to sleep every night until her surgery. On the morning of her surgery, we walked hand in hand into the hospital. She was scared half to death. She sat with feet up on the chair and her arms wrapped around her knees, squeezing my hand until my fingers were numb. Once again, I walked her to the operating room as they wheeled her bed to the door.

This time was more serious than the last. The surgery lasted eight hours exactly. I tried to distract myself by working on brochures and creating marketing materials for my nonprofit business. I watched the clock minute by minute, second by second. Every tick was as loud as a drum beating in my ear. I walk to the doors of the surgery entrance and stared lifelessly down the endless hallway, wondering if she was coming back. Friends from her office came by to see how the surgery was going. I hardly notice they were even there. I was in my own space, my own world, and my head didn't have room for another thought. I envisioned every cut and every stitch. Her parents waited idly by the phone for my call to ensure them that everything was okay, but the call was still seven hours away.

After eight hours of surgery, she emerged in epic pain. "Why did you let me do it? Why did you let me do it?" she said in a stressful voice. I didn't have an answer. All I could do was to summon the nurse to increase her IV drip. She moaned and groaned in pain and agony, and with every moan, I was mentally and emotionally beaten further and further out of reach of ever developing another relationship. I had been through enough emotional strain at this point in my life, and there was no turning back for me. I went home that evening to feed the cats and hadn't realized I walked all the way home, leaving my car in the hospital garage. I didn't have time to be emotionally traumatized; so I fed the cats, washed my face, then walked back to the hospital where I sat in the big chair and watched her sleep throughout the night.

I knew Pam would be okay because she was a very resilient person, but her comeback would prove to be super tough, and I would have to demonstrate that I have the patience to wait hand and foot on her without the help of another person for twelve weeks without a break. There was never a second thought in my mind about my ability take care of my wife and coach her back to good health. The days were long, and the nights were even longer. I lay idle in the bed every night, listening to the rhythm of her breathing and whether she was still breathing at all. I often thought of Cindy doing these dark hours and whether or not I would have to bury another wife. Pam is different. We had been together twice the length of time I had been with Cindy. Our love had a chance to grow and grow deeper by definition of the years. Pam was a fighter. She fought death every waking day. She was up and out of the hospital bed three days after an eight-hour surgery, walking down the hallway in agonizing pain. "I can't let this cancer beat me," she said. While dragging her IV stand down the hallway, she walked lap after lap after lap. She walked until it was too dreadfully painful to take another step. She slowly sat on the bed, slowly reclining back, lying on her side to prevent from lying on the fifty staples closing the wound on her back and to prevent injury from the thirty staples in her chest. She had tubes coming out of every orifice, including places that they invented a hole. It was a horrible sight, and I couldn't even imagine the pain she was going through. She was in so much pain she didn't care about her own vanity, so I cared for her. I closed her robe every few seconds and stood guard at the door while the doctors disrobed her to inspect her swelling around the staples.

Every time she stood up to go to the bathroom, I would pinch the back of her robe together then escort her back to the bed, covering her from head to toe with an electric blanket. I prayed while she was asleep, asking God to relieve her of the pain and let me have it. Every day in the hospital was like watching a new baby learning basic functions, such as how to walk, how to even swallow, and how to hold your own plate or cup. She was so frail and timid I thought for sure I was going to lose her, especially when she left the hospital a week sooner than she should have. Now the ball game was in my court. Everything there was to be done I was to do it, including issuing medication; changing and making the bed; escorting her to the bathroom and shower; preparing her special meals in the morning, lunch, and dinner; changing her bandages; running all the errands; paying all bills; and, most importantly, demonstrating with a positive attitude that I believed she would be okay.

Cindy will always have a deep spot in my heart. She travels daily throughout my subconscious. She never lets me forget her presence. Cindy surrendered to depression before she grew old enough to know how to fight it. I felt caught in the middle of life's full circle. One wife volunteered to die, and the other was suffering beyond repentance. I was totally overwhelmed by the process of today's occurrences and mentally slain daily by an incident that happened more than fifteen years ago.

The next twelve months slowly crept by. Thoughts of reoccurring episodes of cancer were so repetitious it became a common part of my brain and my everyday thoughts for the next twelve months. But Pam didn't have the luxury. Pam appeared as though she was progressing splendidly. She looked healthy, and she returned to jogging two miles once a week around the park. After thirteen months of house cleaning and personal attendance services, I returned to college to earn my teaching credential. Halfway through the credentialing program, Pam became ravenously sick. She started throwing up chunks of flesh and blood into the sink. Temperature ran high. She complained about discomfort around her right collarbone. The pain became so intense we had to request an additional X-ray, which revealed her cancer had metastasized to another part of her body. We sat quietly on the couch, holding hands. I did my best to comfort her, but I didn't know what else to say or do. So I just held her in my arms while she cried on my shoulders. This would have been the perfect time for a weaker man to cry about all his problems, but I knew I had to wait to cry and put up a strong front for Pam because she was going to need all the energy, all the courage, and all the positive emotional strength that I could transfer into her personal space.

We sat on the couch and talked about another twelve sessions of chemotherapy and radiation. She lay quietly in my arms, shaking her head, whispering, "I don't think I can do it again. I don't think I can do any more chemo or radiation." I was witness to how the chemo affected her body the first twelve sessions she had, and I knew another twelve sessions would be more she could bear. Week after we returned to the cancer center, I reluctantly escorted her into the basement for her radiation sessions then upstairs for hours of chemo. I was worn down mentally, dragging my empty body around the house day after day like a horse that throw a shoe. I sat on my bed and listened to the clock hammer away as the hour hand moved closer to another chemo or radiation session. With each passing day, she became weaker and weaker. Each day I begged her to get up and go to her treatments; each day became tougher for me to ask her to do something I wouldn't do myself. People were praying all over the world for Pam, including people in Africa, Australia, Hawaii, Indianapolis, California, India,

Pakistan, and Europe. She was a very well-loved person, and the people's love for her was demonstrated through their powerful prayers.

Pam's dad was also graceful in his efforts to helping his daughter heal. He couldn't help notice the stress and strain I was continuously under, and he knew I needed to get out of the house if just for a few minutes. I shoved $20 in my pocket and went off to breakfast. I sat in the restaurant, sipping on coffee, thanking the Lord for a few minutes of mental peace. I couldn't stay long because my father-in-law wasn't good at handling emergencies, so I placed $3 tip on the table. I stood at the cash register, waiting to pay my bill. Out came the dishwasher with bus tub in hand. She placed the dish tub right on top of the $3. She placed her hand on the bottom of the tub, grasping the money while sliding in the tub off the table. I couldn't help but smile. It was a small reminder to me about the day I bused tables at Saul Subway. Maybe this moment was meant to be. I needed a smile, and unknowingly, she provided smile that I needed—a smile I couldn't conjure up myself for the last two years. Up to this point, I had no reason to smile. I lived the last twenty-five years of my life in survival mode, but I was glad to find comfort in a reason to smile because the little waitress was stealing tips probably for the same reasons as I.

It has been eight years since Pam's last cancer episode. There were some hills and valleys in between that time and deadly scary moments within the last eight years, but she's still here, and I'm still waiting to cry.

Hiding behind the Cross

I thought going to a local church would help refocus and guide my life in the direction God had planned for me. I decided to attend the local church, hoping to come closer to God. Maybe getting closer to God will help heal the ghost that haunts my soul. Once I graduated from college earning my bachelor's degree, I got a good-paying job within the year at the California State prison. And a year later, I was hired by Sacramento County as a human service worker. Before we can start working as a caseworker, we had to complete twelve weeks of training. As fate would have it, I made friends with another coworker who happened to be a pastor of a local church. After spending twelve weeks of training and having lunch together on a routine basis, I decided to visit his church several times before joining. Immediately after joining the church, I was given several dinner invitations by some of the female congregation members. Some women were more adamant than others, walking me to my car, ensuring that I got their phone number and the directions to their house. Every Sunday I was being accosted by one of the

female choir members. She stared very sternly at me from the choir stand. During fellowship, she walked up to me and placed her huge breasts in my face while pretending to give me a legitimate hug.

I became very uncomfortable during fellowship. I couldn't get past the idea of someone trying to solicit sex during church hours, so I stepped outside, and I waited until everyone returned to their seat. One of the female flock of the church followed me outside, pretending she wanted to have a basic conversation. I was keenly aware of her fakeness and her sinister plan from my previous experience with the last church woman who tried to seduce me in 1984. She wanted to let her intentions be known she slapped me on the butt when no one was looking and said, "You be keeping it tight, don't you?" She laughed to herself and walked out to her car. Three months later, the church sponsored its yearly black-and-white ball. I was impressed that they had the ball at an upscale hotel. More than 150 people filled the room. Everyone dressed to impress, wearing tuxedos and their best Sunday suit. Across the room someones hand was waving back-and-forth directing all her energy towards me. *Oh my god*, I thought. The pastor's sister signaled for me to come over. I was very cognizant of her sultry ways. As I approached her, she stretched her arms wide open, displaying her well-proportioned size 38DDs up front and center with a mile worth of cleavage right dab smack in my face.

Normally, my eyes go cross in this situation, and I would have a knee-crushing erection; but this time, for some strange reason, I didn't find her attractive. I didn't know whether it was the fact that her brother could've been her twin or because she was a recovering addict, or it could've been a little bit of both. Either way, we were definitely not going to hook up. I observe women from a distance even if I'm not interested in them. I watch their behaviors and how they respond to the people around him. One day, standing outside the church, she made an inappropriate comment about the height of one of my coworkers, saying she was a midget. That was a huge turn-off for me, and for some reason, I could never see her in a positive light again. So when she pretended she wanted to give a hug at the black-and-white ball, I was reluctant and turned off but hugged her anyway. One hug wasn't good enough. She went for a second hug. This time, she planted one right on my mouth. Her kiss was saturnalia as her tongue roamed wildly in my mouth. I could taste everything she ate for breakfast including the medium rare cooked sausage downed by a glass of orange juice.

She was overt and shameless in her attempt to secure a kiss after which time she was so embarrassed by my nonresponsiveness. She broke down crying and was disconsolate because I didn't respond to her juvenile seduction. I couldn't believe the insincerity that took place within the walls of God's temple. It was worse than Peyton's place. I grew a distaste and a heterodox opinion about church-going people. This was the second time in my life I trusted someone from a small community church. I believed they were grounded in their faith. I felt pressure to leave the church and study the Bible on my own. The women weren't the only problem in the church. The pastor himself expressed parochial views while breaking the seven deadly sins every Sunday when he maliciously forgot about the Bible and began slaying anyone that displayed more success or wealth than himself. During my five years at the church, the pastor and I became very close. We worked in the same office and had lunch together almost every day.

His desk was on the opposite side of the cubicle, giving us plenty of time to talk day in and day out about our religious studies. I was his right-hand man. We went to seminary school together, and he often invited me over to his mother's house for all the holidays. Little did I know he wasn't just being nice. To the point of being Machiavellian, a sense of reciprocity or quid pro quo soon followed his duplicitous behavior. He wanted me to date his sister, but I wasn't feeling it, especially after she tried to jump my bones at the black-and-white ball. I thought she was a nice-enough girl but she wasn't my type, and it really bothered me that he saw this as a requisite for me to become a deacon in his church. They wasted no time in positioning me in places so that I could have quiet time with her. I was quickly maneuvered into every vacant position the church had to offer with little authority but lots of responsibility or positions the deacons would be too lazy to do or take responsibility for. The only job the deacons seemed to love was standing in front of church on Sunday mornings, wearing white gloves, and purporting the appearance of men of importance.

I was finagle into becoming the president of the brotherhood as well as being placed in charge of the library. I organized activities such as painting the church and celebrating the annual men's day. I held weekly meetings for the brotherhood, and that's when I began to notice jealousy from two of the male members. They felt I had the pastor's ear and was in his favor. They thought I was spending too much time with him, and he needed to spend more time with the other men in the church. I could see the jealousy, but I didn't care, so I kept on spending time with the pastor. The deacons did not understand. It couldn't be helped but be around him all day. We worked eight hours a day five days a week in the same office. Our relationship had to grow. It was inevitable. We grew so close I was beginning to see things that I hadn't noticed before. We stood outside on my lunch breaks along the rear door to the department of human services.

I listened while he shared his most intimate secrets. He pointed out women as they passed by. Noticing their long exposed legs, he said, "See that one over there? I would like a woman like that if I were to have an affair." I was flabbergasted. I knew he was just a man, nothing special, just someone who decided to put on a robe and preach the gospel. However, it was an inscrutable light he had just placed himself in. He was an exemplar of what most deacons strived to become. I did place him slightly above the common man, believing he was chosen by God to deliver the gospel in place of himself. His unveiling about the truth of his tainted soul would be the first blow to my spirituality. He pontificated and dissembled about his sexual temptations for another thirty minutes, using up my entire lunch break about what his sexual desires were outside of his marriage.

It was surreal. I didn't know what to believe or how to believe. I no longer knew how much of the sermon he preached he actually believed in. He was preaching a sermon but found it difficult to live the sermon he preached. I understood that he wasn't in Jesus. Not only that, he wasn't even close to being one of the worse disciples. I was beginning to see his sermons and truths as filthy rags. He could no longer lead me because I stopped believing anything that came out of his mouth. The pastor realized I wasn't interested in a sister, and I had known to myself she cried on his shoulder every chance she got about my not paying her any attention. He took all her tears and complaining to heart. He wasted no time in disciplining me from the pulpit one Sunday morning.

He stood probably behind the pulpit, wearing a suit that I had picked for him the prior weekend. He didn't even waste time with the Bible verse. He pounced on me like a cheetah having his first meal of the morning. Leaning over the pool pit and staring in my direction, he said, "The devil can come to church in the Corvette. The devil could wear $300 suits to church. You went to seminary school this year. What are you going to do next year?" The entire congregation laughed. They all knew who he was talking about, and that was what bothered me most. The congregation seemed to concur with everything he said. He was a religious pundit at the moment. Please stop preaching the gospel. He started preaching jealousy and hate. He was indiscriminate in his comments, his voice resonating loud over the microphone verbally trying to destroy every material possession that I owned. He named my accomplishments and my material possessions one by one. I was the only member of the congregation that went to seminary school and the only member that drove a Corvette.

I sat quietly in the pew, not saying a word or cracking a smile. I knew he had just broken at least three of the Ten Commandments, and he didn't stop there. He was breaking commandments that weren't even written. He wore his jealousy and ignorance on his sleeve like a badge of honor. The only purpose it served was to make them feel good, and that he was able to compete with me but on a different stag. He was on a roll. Everyone was clapping and laughing, seemingly enjoying themselves. There was so much laughter I didn't know whether I was at the punch line Comedy club or in church.

I didn't understand how it was possible that everyone was enjoying themselves, and not a word of gospel was being preached. Only hate, enviousness, and coveting were being practiced that Sunday morning. Monday morning I arrived to work an hour early and waited steadfastly in my cubicle until he turned the corner. There he was smiling from ear to ear as though he had just won a Golden Globe Award. I immediately confronted him, but I wasn't as harsh as I had planned. I wanted to show him there's a way to go about doing things, and the way he handled himself in church on Sunday was a poor display or example of what a pastor should be. I let him know that I knew he was talking about me and that I didn't find it funny or entertaining. I thought we were friends, but I guess not.

Someone said the fact that you are not dead is not sufficient proof that you are alive.

I recall my first time patronizing a church in 1964 on Easter Sunday. The church is full of old and aging people, hard wooden benches, and swamp coolers in the windows. As I reflect back on those experiences, I can see myself comfortably following the teachings of my Baptist faith without question and doing my best to obey the rules without protest. As a child, I looked up to my grandmother as an example of a righteous woman without fault in my eyes. I try to meet the moral obligations of being a good person and place my last dime in the offering tray rather than run down to the nearest variety store and purchase two packs of Now and Laters. Forty years later, while in seminary school, I wanted to question the teachings of many so-called ministers, pastors, bishops, or whatever else they wanted to call themselves.

Throughout my studies, I discovered that my prayers were just as powerful as any minister standing behind the pulpit as long as God knows my voice. So the question became why am I giving this man my money? I don't mind contributing to the church and helping to pay electrical bills, heating bills and other church expenses, but I no longer freely empty my pockets into the offering tray for the Sunday morning stickup. I pay my offerings the same way I pay my tips while at a restaurant. If the pastor comes forth with a half-baked and unprepared message or delivers the same old dried-up, unfulfilling sermons from the prior weekend, I deduct it from my offerings. Let's keep it real. We all know that when you pay your 10 percent tithes and offerings, majority of the money goes into the pastor's pocket. Whether you want to believe or don't want to believe, it does not matter. Just look at the obvious truth. Who drives the most expensive car in your church, and who has the biggest home even if a pastor has no other income except the income he receives from a church? It takes out all the guesswork.

I would love to believe that all pastors were leading us to be like Jesus, but most of us can only follow the examples that are placed in front of us; and for some small reason, I don't believe the money grab was the first thing Jesus contemplated. Before moving forward, I like to clarify the difference between the words *belief* and *faith* by comparing and contrasting the two. To a nonspiritual but religious "Christian"—and I use the word *Christian* loosely as a filler word. (I will explain throughout the book what I mean by filler word.) Just believing doesn't cost anything. It's like praying. What do you risk? Belief is used as an empowerment tool at church. If I feel a sense of uncertainty, I pray to strengthen my belief in areas of my life that I have fallen flat on my face. Many ministers, pastors, and bishops use belief in an ambiguous sense to remove money from your pocket and place it in theirs. "Christians," or followers of Jesus, is derived from the word *Christ*; therefore, if we are following Christ, how are we so easily led astray by those who are cloaked of lies and deception? I can't recall anywhere in the Bible where it says Jesus accepted money for prayers and comfort to individuals and stress. However, I do recall Jesus overturning the money changer's table. "He that is greedy of gain troubleth his house; but he that hateth gifts shall live." The Bible says clearly and without ambiguity how God feels about greed. Therefore, why do we continue to believe one man or woman should possess all the riches of the church when Jesus himself would not accept any money or offerings for the service he provided?

Ministers, pastors, and bishops are only men. What's really disappointing is God has shown them a way, but they lead by the temptation of dead presidents and the power that they believe they will gain from the almighty dollar bill. The Bible states, "Yea, they're greedy dogs which can never have enough, and they are shepherds they cannot understand: they all look to their own ways, everyone for his gain from his quarter." The Sunday morning stickup. Throughout all my years of attending church, I never once heard a minister admit to his congregation they have the same access to God as he does. During the days Christ walked the earth, only high priests could enter into the sacred temple. A rope would be tied around the priest's leg, and if he wasn't cleansed of his sins before entering the temple, he would die. Then he was pulled from the temple by the rope tied around his leg. When Jesus died, the veil that once covered the temple tore open, allowing all men to have access to God through prayers.